Dragonfruit

Malia Mattoch McManus

ISBN: 1543232108
ISBN 13: 9781543232103

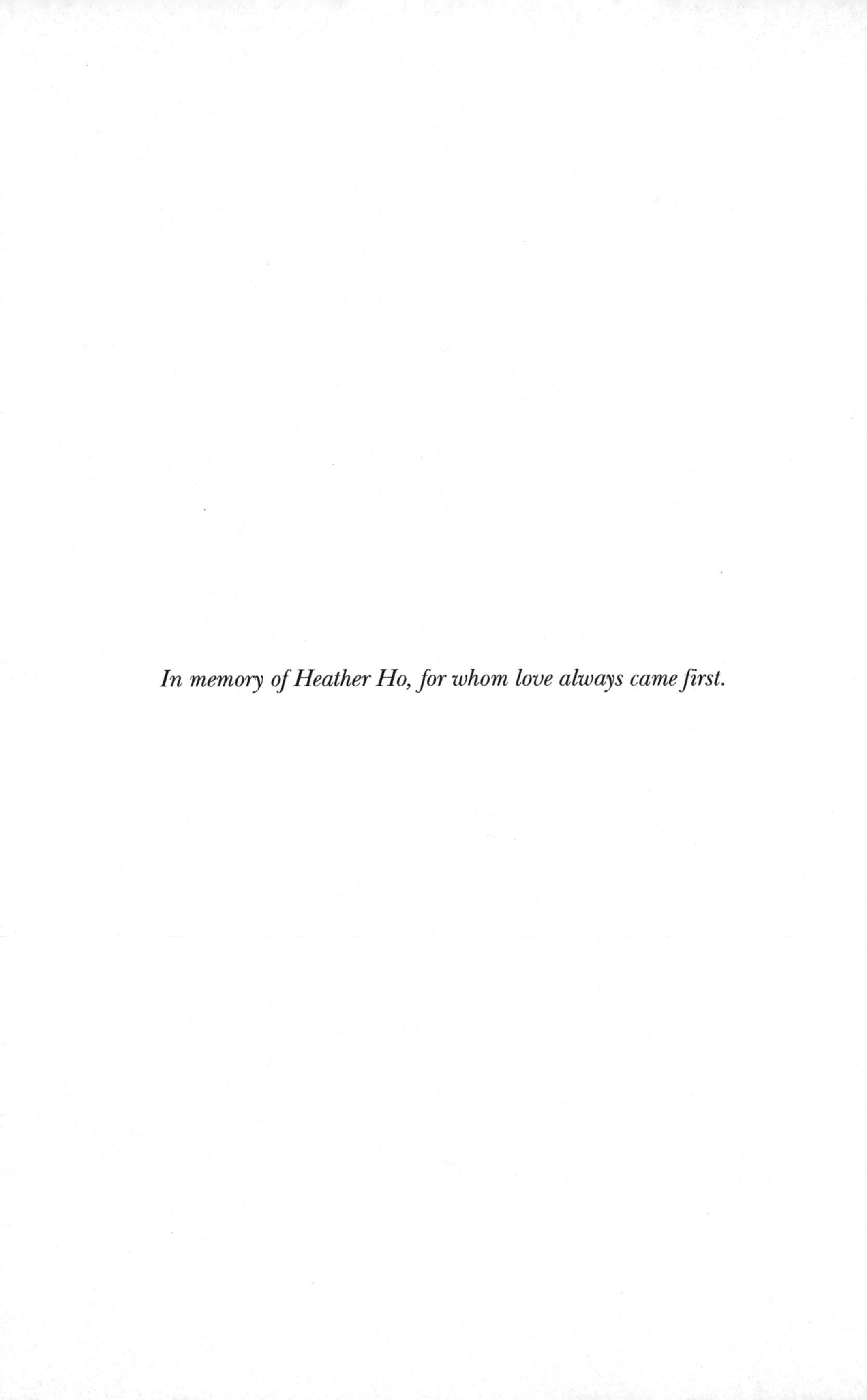

In memory of Heather Ho, for whom love always came first.

The 1887 Constitution of the Kingdom of Hawai'i was a legal document forced upon King Kalākaua by white American anti-monarchists who dubbed themselves, "The Hawaiian League." It divested Kalākaua and the Hawaiian monarchy of nearly all authority and stripped the voting rights of Asians and the majority of Hawaiians. It became known as the Bayonet Constitution.

PROLOGUE

Honolulu
1894

We're traitors, Father and I, though these soldiers have no sense of it. They feign being love-struck as my carriage approaches, their arms outstretched in exaggerated bows. Bored young men made giddy by the sight of an American girl, even one dressed to the neck in black, curls pinned severely back in her mother's whalebone combs. I keep my eyes low, as modest as my missionary grandfather could have hoped. But I watch them in their untested uniforms, amazed they have no hint of what's coming. What I'm actually here to do for the Queen.

Only once was I stopped as Kepa brought the carriage up to Washington Place.

"No flowers today?" a soldier asked. "Sadly not," I said, trying to keep the blanket around my baby daughter's kicking feet. I smiled and pulled her up against my chest, tucking the blanket tightly under her.

My father is funding the impending rebellion against these soldiers, against the government they prop up. He gives me messages written on sheets of newspaper wrapped around ginger or gardenias from our garden, and I deliver these to the Queen's household. Lili'uokalani is now a prisoner in her former Kingdom. We sit in her garden while government troops watch us from Central Union's bell tower. The Queen sings a hymn, tapping the time out on her armrest, waving her fan decorated with ferns. We discuss her tarot cards. We wonder if it will ever be safe for Princess Ka'iulani, her niece, my best childhood friend, to come home. We do not talk about the messages, or the heavy bundle of cash I hid in Clarice's blanket and was sure the soldier would discover as she thrashed unhappily in my arms. Instead, the soldier soothed my daughter with a silly face, fingers pulling at the side of his mouth. He let us pass.

These moments of fear and relief are my connection to Samuel now, my revenge for what Abram did to us, for what he does to my home still. Abram Malveaux is now as feared across O'ahu as he was by me on Moloka'i; he fosters terror wherever he can sow its seeds.

Abram tried to buy my father's plantation when the other planters turned against us; instead my father offloaded his harvest at a loss, sold his plantation and put his money into shipping. His vessels now crisscross the Pacific, and money flows into his home and out toward people and purchases, the details of which are scrawled on the newspapers I take to Washington Place. These soldiers who watch the Queen should turn their binoculars toward the ocean. They should walk the beach at night when Hawaiian men, Kepa among them, offload weapons from one of Father's ships near Waikīkī, burying them in the shoreline until the time comes.

This may end with us in prison at the Reef. Abram is jailing Hawaiians rumored to have spoken in favor of the Queen. He's arresting organists, teachers, innocents. Yet he's never had these men search my newspaper-wrapped flowers, or the blanket of my golden-haired child. His soldiers do not see who I truly am. I am a good American wife. I am a plantation heiress. I am the granddaughter of a Calvinist missionary who came to this pagan land before it was conquered by Christianity, then sugar, then America.

I am the perfect traitor to the privilege of my birth. I am the ideal rebel messenger.

1

Hawai'i
1891

I sit at my father's desk, waiting for the stranger I am to marry. I picture this Abram Malveaux leaving his boarding house on Fort Street with its dusty saloons and shouting drunks. He'll be riding up Nu'uanu Road under the jagged green volcanic mountains of the valley, passing the mossy lava rock walls of one estate after another. Can he guess why he's been called to the grey, turreted home of William Dawson? Why my father would propose this marriage between his only daughter and a man no one knows?

When Malveaux comes up the drive, Father is standing on the lanai. From where I hide at the study window, I can see Father taking the chair facing me, offering no refreshments to his guest. Abram sits opposite, his dark hair my only clue to his appearance. I can't see his face, but I can hear him describe his ambitions on the Moloka'i ranch he manages.

"With time I plan to buy the ranch," he says, his voice carrying over the dull afternoon sound of distant birds. "I aim to turn it into something that will give the island of O'ahu a bit of competition."

His accent is Southern, and he pronounces O'ahu the American way that makes Hawaiians shudder, inserting a heavy "w" after the "O" and drawing out the "u" until the word sounds silly.

"Let's discuss the matter at hand," Father says, cutting him off. His speech is rushed, his voice tightly strung. "In marrying Eliza you will receive more than enough money to buy this ranch of yours now. In exchange, you will be her husband and the father of the child she is expecting, treating both honorably. The child should arrive by November." Father can't look the man in the face; I see him glance down at his watch.

I wait for Abram to say no. I know Father fears he will. But Abram accepts the bargain. Listening to him say yes, a jolt goes through my body, one so fierce that I fear it might cause the baby to leave it.

"On one condition," Abram says. "When your daughter and I have our own children, they will be made the heirs, not this child. This child will receive a set allowance, for I will not make it the heir to my own hard work."

"No," answers Father. "This offer comes at a price. You'll give me your word today that you will raise it as an equal of every child of your union. My papers will reflect this at the time of my death."

In one day's time, Father has thought all of this through, well beyond what I'd managed in weeks of growing certainty that a child was coming. I crumple a handful of my skirt before remembering that I might have to appear before them.

"How will you disguise the fact that the child is born so soon after the marriage?"

"Molokaʻi," says Father, leaning forward and tightening his features. "There are advantages to isolation. I see no reason why anyone in Honolulu must know of the child until several months after its birth. It will be legitimate in the eyes of all and an heir to my fortune, along with any children of your marriage."

Abram turns his face away from Father, and I finally see a bit of him. His nose has a bump, as if it once was broken. His hair is a mass of brown curls. I can't see his eyes.

"If you honor them with respect, our arrangement will make you a very rich man," Father concludes. "This is my offer, and it is yours to accept or decline." He stands, and I take a breath.

"So it is then," says Abram in a surprisingly good-natured voice. He walks to the porch railing, gripping it as if on a ship. "The money will be provided prior to the ceremony?"

Father looks toward town. Then he comes not three inches away from Abram's face and says, "I will give you ten thousand dollars when you leave our home with Eliza."

The figure is shocking, and the guilt of what I've done to him comes to me. I smooth my hair and brush down my skirt, feeling the small bump of my belly as I fluff the fabric out before my waist. But Abram does not ask to meet me; they've already begun to walk down the steps. As their voices grow fainter, I can hear them agree that the wedding will be tomorrow.

"I'll say we know you through distant family," Father says to Abram. "I'll say there was a death at the ranch and you had to return quickly. It's better you leave for Moloka'i quietly."

"When do you want me to meet her?" Abram asks.

"I'll send word this afternoon."

They walk around the bend of the house to the far right of the drive, and I can only catch their long strange shadows in the late day sun. Abram bids father goodbye and turns his horse toward town. I slip upstairs to my room and take out my mother's locket.

"I've just been bartered away," I whisper, kissing her sweet, heart-shaped face and asking, "What would you have done?" My mother's photograph makes her look dated. Only ten years have elapsed, but fashion has passed Lucy Dawson by, and her expression is far more serious than I remember.

"Wouldn't it be better if we were seen together in town before the marriage?" I ask Father. We speak in hushed voices on the lanai, rain falling around us.

"You are already starting to show, Eliza."

The rain's shadows pattern across the walls of the house, where loneliness crawls through rooms filled with my mother's furniture. The grand scale makes the brocaded pieces look shrunken, the rooms empty and severe. Our cook, Mehana, fills the rooms with huge vases filled with cuttings from the garden, giving this house the feel of a natural history museum.

I hear Mehana moving back and forth along the wood floorboards in the kitchen and then out the back door to collect parsley. Her husband, Kepa, our coachman, stands uncovered in the warm rain on the lawn below us, cutting back the banks of heliconia. The rhythm of his machete against their green stalks, the bang of Mehana's pot against the sink when she comes back inside to pour cabbage into the colander, these are the daily sounds of home.

"I'll not risk word of this spreading through town," he continues, clutching his Scotch to his chest. "I should have remarried. A father hasn't the eyes to catch these things."

He looks out at the valley toward Oahu's sun-drenched western plains, where his acres of sugar sizzle. "They'll be setting the fields on fire the next few days," he says in a flat tone.

I picture Father's copper red fields: the bitter black smoke of harvest rendering the juice-rich stalks bare of leaves and ready to cut; the long alleys of shadows his cane cast at dusk, shadows I once loved to hide in. Mother would run along the laborers' paths, parting the cane, calling, "E-li-za!" How much easier it would have been to whisper the secret of this child to her. Mother would have found a better way than marriage to a man willing to be bought.

I count the waterfalls folded into the green fan of the Koʻolau Mountains across the valley. There are eleven, one of them blowing upside down in the winds, falling halfway to earth only to be turned back upon itself toward the sky. Mother said if we managed to climb those impossible mountains and reach that spot, we could disappear into it. After her death, I asked Mehana if my mother was up there, at the falls. I was eight years old.

"Mehana calls that one *waipuhia*," I say, making Father follow my gaze upward. "When the waterfall turns upside down, it's a sign that something is going to happen."

"Your head is in the clouds, Eliza," Father says tersely, clutching his Highland Reserve to his chest. "This is no time to be thinking like a native. Had I forced you to learn the ways of your own people, we might not find ourselves in the catastrophe we do. What will you do if the child does not look European?"

"Our baby will be beautiful," I answer. It will have Ben's eyes. Those grey-green eyes will always be mine to look into.

"*Kau Kau*," Mehana calls out, announcing that dinner is ready.

Father stands, waiting for me. I follow the carved lines of peach blossoms permanently in bloom along the arms of his chair. Mother's father, Captain Hezekiah Knowles, brought it back from a whaling voyage around the Pacific. I remember sitting on Mother's lap in it, running my hands along the wooden carving and putting my mouth against her white neck to ask where it came from.

"China," Mother said, grabbing my little hands and pretending to nibble them. "Where Papa's workers come from."

I trace the swell of a peach. "May I take this chair?" I ask Father. "It reminds me of her."

He looks at me with such grief I think he might allow me to stay. But he only presses a handkerchief to his brow.

"Take the chair," he finally says. "I'll have Mehana wrap it in bedding for you to use over there. I'm afraid you'll find a manager's life on Moloka'i quite bare. You do understand, you're not going there as the owner's wife?"

"I understand entirely," I say, standing to follow him to dinner.

The ranch Abram Malveaux manages is owned by a man who offered me marriage last summer. Since the hour Father learned of this child, he has not let me forget that I declined Richard Irvin's proposal, saying I felt too young to accept. "But you weren't too young for Benjamin Ahsang? Is that what you are telling me?" he'd said, and I met the shame of his stare. I understood he was trying to work through the timeline. Those who lose a loved one are compelled to retrace every step back to the place and moment where fate claimed them.

We take our places at the dining table that could seat twenty, but since Mother passed now only seats two. Mehana sets out a platter of corned beef, breadfruit, and cabbage. At forty-six, Mehana still causes carriages to slow on Nuʻuanu Road. She once showed me a picture of herself twenty years before, bare-breasted in a grass skirt, standing before a studio drawing of Waikīkī, an ukulele in her hand. Her wavy hair was held back on one side with a white hibiscus, in the same style she wears it now. Nothing but the dark spots on her face and the generosity of her hips betray her middle age.

She cups my face. I force myself to smile but turn away in doing so. She knows my every expression. "This rain is making everyone sad," Mehana says, turning back toward the kitchen to eat with her husband, Kepa.

"I thought it was fish today?" Father calls to her, his fork raised above the dish.

"The boy never came with any," Mehana shrugs, her dismissal as fluid as a moment of hula. She looks at me again, her eyes questioning. I try to return her shrug casually, as if William Dawson's moods are the only challenge of the evening. When Mother died giving birth to a stillborn boy, Mehana slept next to me the week of the funeral, the week of no sound in the house, just stillness and the high pale light of Hawaiian winter, pulling me into her arms and patting my back rhythmically until sleep came. There's no reason for Mehana to spend tonight worrying.

There's nothing to be done.

The first thing my father did when he learned of the child was go to Richard Irvin hoping Richard's proposal of marriage might still stand. I waited for the answer on my childhood bed, listening to the sound of Kepa scraping leaves from the gutters outside, reading the same page of a novel again and again and absorbing none of it. I turned to the book's back page and took a pen from my bed stand drawer, scribbling in a reckless hand,

> *Dearest Ka'iulani,*
>
> *I think R will take me still. I do. His pursuit was ardent. Determined.*
>
> *My only sadness is Ben's child never knowing who he is. Richard would not stand my ever seeing Ben again. He will hate him and thank him for making me finally accept.*

Father entered my room without warning, a drink in one hand, the other pressed to his temple. I shut the book around the pen and tucked it under my pillow. I'd just defaced a leather-bound volume with a note that would never be read, one written to a princess who had been my dearest friend but lived in England now, too far away for me to seek her counsel.

"He'll not have you. He said he'd marry you under many circumstances, but not these. I offered him money, but he doesn't need any. I should have insisted before. He's a decent fellow, Eliza..."

I waited for his announcement of what would happen to me next.

"Richard told me of a man who might be willing. His ranch manager down on Moloka'i. No family here. Ambitious. Cash for reputation." Father shook his head. "An orphanage in Boston is by far the safer choice. I can see what relatives we have left there; they can care for you until the birth. We'll say you are in Europe."

I stand, arms crossed. "You know what happens to children thrown into an orphanage. Think of it, Mother's first grandchild tossed away."

We face each other, my father flustered at my obstinacy; my strength when he expects dismay, fear. But through all of his speeches, his threats, I have kept this last secret: my joy in having this baby, this unbreakable tie to Ben. I know it would infuriate Father the most.

"Fine," he snaps, sliding his eyeglasses back into place. "I will find this man Malveaux. But you will be thrown to his whims. Do you understand what I am warning you of, Eliza?"

In truth, I did not. I was waiting for Father to emerge from his wrath and tell me: *Stay. Have the child here. Who cares what other missionary families think? We have enough money to buy the sour looks right off their faces.* I was counting on my father; the man who had grown up on Honolulu's grimmest street with pigs coming uninvited through the gloomy house where his New England parents served up oily stew and speeches for saving souls. The William Dawson who'd been mocked by the cleaner, wealthier missionary children and had never forgiven them for it. The preacher's son who'd married a whaler's daughter when the rest of the missionary kin married their cousins. The man who didn't take me to church, even when his own father, Caleb, lectured us on our wickedness during Sunday visits. The William Dawson who told me, when I was a scared, motherless thing tormented by Caleb's fury, "Books are the true church of the mind. Damnation is for the feeble-minded and the frightened."

I waited and in his face I searched for that man. He looked at a spot past my shoulder and began to speak. "I take some part in what has happened," he said.

I nodded, feeling hope.

"You've been left to find your own path, and I've done little to show you the way of God. I've not spoken enough of the horror and degradation of sin. You've lived in a land where half the populace barely understands the very concept of sin and wrongdoing. Brothers marrying sisters, men sharing wives…"

His voice trailed off, and I knew then that the man before me, speaking in the voice of my missionary grandfather, was far too scared of the scandal of this child to be the father I was raised by.

On my last night at home, I dream I am hiding with Ben along Waikīkī's garden paths. I'm startled awake before dawn by the shower tree rattling my windowpane as if trying to break through. Muffling the noise and my nausea with a pillow, I try to slip back to Ben in my dream, but the tree continues its warning, forcing me into the dark, seasick start of my wedding day. Moonlight strafes the mountain ridge outside my window; in its glow and shadow the trees twist into a line of men carrying torches. Mehana believes Hawaiian chiefs rise from their graves at night to walk in their red and yellow feather capes above the tree tops, drums beating out their passage along the ancient forest path until their torches disappear into the night.

A blue-grey fades up into the sky. The sun is coming. When it sets today, I will be underway on the Moloka'i schooner with a husband I have yet to meet. It is my last morning to watch clouds nap in the crevice of mountains; neither the mountain nor I feel ready to move into the glare of day just yet.

2

"Mehana, may I have a moment with Eliza, please?" Father is standing at the door to my room, dressed in the black suit he usually wears to 'Iolani Palace. I am wearing a dress of blue velvet for the wedding. It is too warm, but the empire waistline is forgiving. My mother's cameo clashes with the blue; Ben's jade brooch would suit it far better. Mehana has packed my trunk and now helps with my curls, which are miserable in the humidity. Father announced after breakfast that I am marrying and leaving today. Mehana asked no questions, a sure sign she's figured it all out. She squeezes my shoulder before she leaves.

Father approaches with a letter box which smells of dried jasmine. I think he means to lecture me, for the box was given to him by Ben's father, Khan Ahsang. It is inlaid with mother-of-pearl and once held a tea Ahsang said sold for more than a 60-year-old bottle of Scotch. That was the sort of gift Ahsang gave my father: a tribute echoing with rebuke. He'd wanted my father to give up liquor and fight the missionary families who were plotting against the King. He wanted him to stand stronger.

Father places the box on the vanity and opens it. It's empty until his hand pushes out the false bottom, hiding bundles of dollars. Next to it, he places my grandfather's Bible. In the months following

Mother's death, I grew overly attached to the Bible's last page, on which Caleb Dawson wrote the names of his Hawaiian parishioners who died in the smallpox epidemic of '54, noting next to each: *Smallpox. Saved.* Mother had explained the disease to me, saying wagons filled with victims had rolled down Honolulu's dirt streets, past empty, stricken houses marked by yellow flags. Her father, the sea captain, had pressed a camphor bag against her face to ward off infection, and during that year she wore it around her neck. After her death, I'd recite my missionary grandfather's list of 31 names, clinging to the dream of death passing over Mother, a camphor bag her magic talisman. "*Moses Kekauiki,*" I'd chant to Kepa as he collected gardenias for Mehana. "*Smallpox. Saved. Kamuela Waihee. Smallpox. Saved. Emma Kapala, Smallpox. Saved.*" Father snatched the leather volume from me. I'd thought then it was because he was angry Mother died. I understand now that he was embarrassed because I was reading Kepa a roll call of his dying race; the names of those disappearing from diseases brought by foreign boats, diseases Hawaiians had never known before we came.

Where had he hidden it for so many years? I open the pages to that list and imagine my own name among the disappeared. *Eliza Dawson Malveaux. Moloka'i. Saved.*

"There may be hard times to come, Eliza," he says, as he sits on the edge of the bed and takes my hand, looking around the room as if he hasn't seen it in years. When I was young he would read to me here; hours of poetry while I watched the shower tree bob up and down outside my window, poetry that I might sleep. Then history and newspaper articles that I might understand the world beyond our tiny freckle cluster of islands. He had been generous in educating me, his only child. Now he wishes he had preached instead.

"Your mother insisted this be your room because of the view," he says. "I thought a child should have something smaller, and this should be for guests. Or perhaps for a boy. They need more space, I think."

“I could stay,” I say. “I wouldn’t care what they said if you didn’t.”

He shakes his head, pretending he hasn’t heard my voice quiver. “You’d be damning yourself and the child.” He gets up.

“Father, I, I’m not sure,” I whisper.

“Of course you’re not sure! For Christ’s sake. All he asked about was money.”

“Give me that money. I could run my own household in Boston—”

“With a bastard grandson for me? No, Eliza. If you want me to, I’ll put you on a steamer to Boston. I will make the arrangements. But the child goes to an orphanage.”

For a second I put myself on Father’s preferred path. The thought of my relatives in a Boston brick home judging me is not nearly as frightening as this strange man whom I have yet to meet. But the handing over of the child. The taking of my baby from my arms. “No,” I whisper.

“Mr. Malveaux will be here at four. I’ll send him upstairs.”

“Here? To my room?” I ask.

“There’s hardly an issue of propriety when it is your wedding day and the door is kept open,” he responds. “I think it better if your first conversation is private. Mehana and Kepa do not know you have not yet met this man.” He goes to the door, turning back to say, “Tomorrow, I will ask members of the club to join me in a toast to the private marriage of my daughter to a man whose family I’ve long admired. I pray he lives up to that lie.”

He closes the door with excessive gentleness.

I lay out my traveling suit, cream and black striped silk with velvet trim, made for the trip to Europe Father had planned for us to visit Ka‘iulani before this happened. Lying down next to it, I tell myself not to think and drift instead into a strange, unsatisfying dream.

I am climbing the shower tree, finding Ben’s gifts tucked into its hollows. I harvest them as I go: shells in my bodice, fuchsia silk tied round my wrist, until I am at the treetop, looking across the valley, down to the ocean. I see ‘Iolani Palace outlined against the Pacific.

I could walk all the way there on the unbroken canopy of Nuuanu's trees stretching before me. But there is a green flash in the sky as the sun falls into its ocean bed, and in my dream I am a solitary night marcher, holding a fiery torch, branches quivering under my feet as I race to the drumbeat of my escape.

A knock jolts me awake, and I sit up with wetness trailing from my mouth. Before I can compose myself, in comes Abram Malveaux.

"You're Eliza Dawson?" he asks.

What other woman would be in this room?

"Soon to be Eliza Malveaux, I understand," I answer him.

He asks permission to sit with an upturned hand toward the chair. I nod; he has large eyes, hair in need of cutting, and he is taller than Benjamin. "I imagine you are relieved," he says, glancing at my stomach.

"I imagine you're excited about buying your ranch," I answer.

He looks at me appraisingly. "I am," he says. "You've been?"

I shake my head. Mehana described Moloka'i while she brushed out my hair earlier. She spoke of an island of sorcery descended from the goddess Pahulu.

"Pahulu practiced the sorcery of dreams, the kind with the most *mana,*" Mehana had said. *Mana* is difficult to find a word for in English. It's like the word power, but a moral, supernatural kind. She'd let the word sit as she twisted my hair into the obedience of a tight knot for my wedding and then bent to kiss the crown of my head with wet eyes. She was begging me to be careful, warning me of the path my father has chosen. The path I have chosen. I'd taken her hand, about to confess all, when my father knocked on the door.

"It is no Honolulu. Americans, whites in general, are very few," Abram says. "Bring whatever you have to amuse yourself." With that he looks at me squarely. "I'll work toward making you happy. I'll build a home for you."

I'm unsure whether I am expected to thank him for this promise. The silence ends when Father comes to the door. "All right then?" Father asks, turning away before I can answer.

No, not all right. I am not ready for this man to take me away.

I walk down the stairs and straight to the minister as if I'm being pushed off a plank.

I feel Father's presence behind me as Abram says his vows buoyantly, as if we truly know each other. My eyes fix on two rows of royal palms outside the living room window. A year ago I walked between them at dusk pretending to be Ben's bride, the trees my cathedral, casting off dark shadows like church walls. "I do," I finally say, my voice coming from somewhere far outside my body. And so Abram and I are married.

It is awkward afterwards. The minister excuses himself rather than stay for supper. Father invites Kepa and Mehana to make a plate and join us. He asks Kepa to say grace, which normally goes unsaid at our table.

"Let us pray. *E pule kākou,*" Kepa says, taking Mehana's hand and then mine.

Kepa urges Father and Abram with his eyes to complete the circle. Abram takes my hand in his, which is warm and rough. But he does not want to lower his eyes. He is staring at Kepa's mouth, where two front teeth are chipped down to jagged white remnants. Kepa knocked them out himself, in the ancient way, to mark the death of his parents. He rarely speaks in front of strangers because of it, but will not miss the chance to praise his Lord.

Kepa stares back until Abram lowers his head. Then, in Hawaiian and English, Kepa invokes deities of his Hawaiian world, and the righteous force in his Christian one. I close my eyes to the beauty of his closing words, "*Ma ka inoa o kāu keiki hiwahiwa ʻo Iesū Kristo, ʻĀmene.*"

"Did I catch a Jesus Christ in that?" Abrams asks as we raise our heads.

"In the name of your precious Son, Jesus Christ. Amen," Kepa repeats, in English, and in a tone he rarely lets himself use. Mehana and I exchange a quick glance; Kepa lived a violent life before he found the Lord. Theft, street fights. He was stabbed once. He knows good. He knows evil. He does not like the man I have married.

"I'd like to get involved with sugar, like you," Abram says to Father.

Mehana refills Kepa's glass and whispers in Hawaiian to him under her breath. He rolls his shirt sleeve up, exposing the zigzag scar which puffs and buckles down the length of his forearm. He'd told me it was from his brother biting him in the womb. That his brother was a shark, the spirit of their family's animal protector, or *'aumakua.* When his mother had born them, she'd released Kepa's twin into the sea, where he lived just beyond the reef.

"It's American plantation owners who'll end up running these islands," Abram adds.

"I doubt the royal family would agree," Father answers without looking up from his plate. He eats his chop as if being timed for a race.

"They'll be gone soon enough," Abram says.

My room looks very lonely with all the books packed. *Bring whatever you have to amuse yourself.* I'm taking every volume given to me by Robert Louis Stevenson. They were already worn when he gave them to me, marked in the margins with his loopy scrawl. Their smell conjures the late afternoon sun at 'Āinahau, Kaiulani's home in Waikīkī. How she and I would listen together as Mr. Stevenson told us fantastical stories after spending his morning writing in his bungalow down the beach at Sans Souci. I pick up her latest letter, wondering if I should take it.

Harrowden Hall
Northamptonshire

Eliza,

It made my heart feel such joy, the picture you gave of Khan Ahsang filling the Palace with hula dancers for the King's ball, all the missionary ladies curdling at the sight of it!

It was good to hear the King seemed his boisterous self. He writes me to be on guard against certain enemies he does not feel free to name in writing. I asked him to speak more plainly, as surely I cannot be on my guard unless I know whom I should fear?

You wanted to know about my lessons. I am taking French, German, music and English, especially grammar and composition. I must close this short letter for they are calling us to prayers.

With much love, Believe me,

Ka'iulani

My condolence letter should have reached her by now. Her letter back will arrive at a house no longer my home. I tuck her letter into a drawer for safekeeping and remove the Bible from my bag, slipping it beneath my bed. A small but satisfying rebellion. I place Mother's locket and a birthday bracelet from Father into the wooden box he's given me and decide Ben's jade dragonfly brooch is a fine match for my traveling suit. I sit on my bed using its small latch to make the pavé diamond wings flutter.

"They're waiting, Eliza," Mehana says from the doorway. "Your father says our goodbyes will happen here, not at the wharf." She helps me close the last bag. "Don't let him see you weak," she says. "Pay him lots of attention to make up for that baby that isn't his."

I nod, letting Mehana put her hand on my belly.

"A little Hawaiian in you now."

So she knows it was Ben. Of course she knows.

"A baby is never a bad thing. Women been having babies at the wrong time forever. In the old days here, there was no wrong time. Whenever the baby came and whoever the father, no bother. Now we're getting complicated. But love is never shame," she says, embracing me.

"I wish my people shared your opinion, Mehana," I say, my voice cracking. Oh, what happiness I would have felt to leave this house wedded to Ben. I think of his bride, dressed in red walking on tiny feet to meet him through a cloud of incense in a courtyard of dragons. The bride Ben's father chose for him, the one who took him thousands of miles away from me. Ben sailed to China before I realized a child was quickening within me, a child who already fills me with crushing tenderness. A child who will get me through this.

Abram walks outside with the bags to wait at the carriage.

"Well, write me with how your voyage goes," Father says. His eyes settle on Ben's brooch, a piece he's never seen. He looks at me with a quick flash of anger, before finally kissing me on the cheek in either forgiveness or dismissal. He turns, walks into his study and closes the door. Mehana begins to cry in the kitchen.

Kepa drives us wordlessly to the harbor as the sun hangs low in the sky, forest birds' ecstatic sunset song filling the silence between us. The sun yields a green flash as it sets into the cloudless ocean horizon, and I remember my dream from this morning. This is all really happening. Kepa unloads Mother's chair as Abram walks toward the pier. I breathe in the old-fashioned coconut smell of Kepa's hair oil as he embraces me quickly, whispering, "The Lord be with you."

We wait a good hour at the harbor before boarding the *Lehua*. Abram keeps a handkerchief pressed to his face; a few yards away is a group of patients bound for Molokai's leper colony, Kalaupapa. None of them will see their homes again, but I swear I will see mine. Once this child has a birth certificate. Once it's legitimate. My father needs only that to bring me back home.

"That's dirty air you're breathing," Abram cautions me. "You'd be wise to cover your face."

No one else at the wharf is doing so, but I follow suit to please him. "I'm afraid we look quite high and mighty doing this," I say through the fabric. There is a great fear of leprosy and no knowledge of how to prevent it. Some think it enters the body through scrapes and blisters; all we know for certain is that it preys on Hawaiians with tragic unfairness. I have little fear for myself because leprosy has left *haoles*, as we whites are called here, almost entirely in peace. "European bloodlines are already weeded by centuries of exposure," my father assured me when Mehana's nephew, Joseph, got it, and I wondered aloud if I would, too.

"Better than looking like a leper," Abram answers. He moves off to check his supplies; the sacks of flour and rice being carried aboard. I find a crate to sit on and watch him move among the rations we will take to Richard Irvin's ranch: tobacco, whisky, rope, nails, a fine new saddle that he carries aboard himself, unwilling to hand it over to the crewmen who offer to help. They take offense and stop loading his things. He carries two large bags of coffee onto the schooner under one arm, still holding the cloth to his face with his other.

I look at the sad cluster of lepers wrapped in blankets, shrouded like biblical times to hide them from the world. The infected have tried for years to hide in the mountains near our home; they are always hunted down and rounded up. I've seen them, prisoners in carts, their noses and fingers eaten away. Almost all are Hawaiian. Smallpox, measles—these diseases killed off whole families in one week. But leprosy likes to take its time. There is no quick death once its cruel grey spots appear.

Mehana's nephew got the sores when he was 18 years old. He dressed in his Sunday best and reported himself to the Ministry of Health. They gave him a day to say his farewells. He came to say goodbye at our back door. Mehana sobbed with Joseph; Father came out of the house and handed the boy an envelope, touching him on his clothed shoulder and patting Mehana on the arm. Kepa took Joseph to the quarantine station. Joseph has been at Kalaupapa for three years already.

The diseased are saying their final goodbyes, some wailing as they're forced apart from their families by two guards. It's not death but new life that marks me, I think, and yet my own father could not bring himself to attend my departure.

"Move aboard!" the guards shout.

Still, I watch as the healthy and sick cling together as the harbor lights flicker on, showing no fear of contagion or aversion to the stench of rotting flesh. Some of the healthy are sailing with their doomed to Kalaupapa to act as caregivers, their *kōkua*. What epic love one must hold for another to do such a thing.

"Get going!" The guards use batons to separate the free from the condemned, prodding the sick onto the inter-island schooner. When the ship's mooring lines are untied, it's not my mouth I cover but my ears. The cries of misery as the dark wooden hull drifts away are unearthly.

"That's the rest of it," Abram says. He's come back down the gangplank with a dusting of flour on his hands. He wipes them in sweeping motions on his shirt sleeves and then helps me up as if we are going to dance a reel down the center of a drawing room. For a man with little money he has learned manners somewhere.

"It's terrible seeing them forced away like that," I say, keeping my handkerchief to my nose to please him. The families of the bereaved are consoling each other quietly now. "Have you seen the colony?" I ask, remembering those first months after Joseph left, how Mehana carried his letters in her apron pocket. I would find her weeping at the kitchen table. Kepa and I would sit with her, serving her coffee heavy with condensed milk until her crying spell subsided.

"The leper colony? I've delivered cattle to the edge of it," he says. "I find it ironic."

"How so?"

"The missionaries taught the natives about heaven just before their sicknesses sent them there. Timed it all perfectly."

"My grandfather was a missionary," I say. "My father's father, Caleb. Though my father would say you're quite right. He far preferred my other grandfather, the whaler."

Both my grandfathers crossed five months' worth of open ocean to live in as wild a place as could be found. But neither had made a trip so daring and desperate as the one I start tonight. "May I ask what your family does? I'm guessing they are not missionaries."

"We had a plantation stolen from us. Since the war there's no future for a white man in Louisiana. A Southerner at least. There was a time when the right families entertained each other, like what I imagine you're used to. We had everything you all have, banana trees, flowers, exotic women. Hawaiian women remind me of octoroons. You know what an octoroon is?"

"A woman who is one-eighth Negro," I answer. "I was told such talk was part of the old way of thinking."

"Yankees think they know which words are nice when they don't know the people involved. Don't you worry. I won't be taking you to the evil South. No family left there for me."

I realize as he speaks that there are no other white passengers bound for our ship, the *Lehua*. Dozens of Japanese laborers now surround us.

"Are those your workers?"

"No, they're headed to Maui. They were unloaded this morning off a ship from Japan." Someone catches his eye and he nods. "They're ready for us to board," he says.

We walk up the plank and onto the deck, and I see my peach blossom chair being moved by a sailor so scarred by the sea I believe he could have crewed on my grandfather's whaler.

Abram presses a few bills into the captain's hand, and he promises to keep an eye on our things, so they "don't disappear in the night." Then he shows us to a narrow room below deck, explaining that it's his, but he understands a lady needs a place to rest. There are two berths, and we each put our things by one.

I can hear the captain commanding his crew to throw off the lines, and the ship is moving before I have even sat down. How will I be forced to fill this night's hours before we reach Moloka'i at dawn?

Without another word, Abram turns down the lamp. I feel my way onto the bed, thankful he makes no move toward me. When must that day come? Tomorrow? A week? After the baby is born? He falls asleep immediately. He is a silent sleeper. I toss in the little bed and get up to stare out the porthole at the retreating streetlights of Honolulu. This was Benjamin Ahsang's view, heading to China. Our ship is following the curve of Waikīkī, scattered gaslights marking its beach houses. I try to pick out the Ahsangs' bungalow, but no light comes from it. When Ben held me there in the dark, the room had sounded as if it were under the sea, waves breaking just outside.

The deck lamps cast light along slivers of water and I look through the waves, imagining forms swimming in the green depths. From just below me comes an explosive sound, and I jump back, expecting a gush of water. There is no splash, but another great heavy exhalation, as if from a giant just off the rail. I realize it is the sound of a whale clearing its blowhole, the sound my whaler grandfather made chasing me around his garden. He would cup his hands around his mouth, suck in his breath and blow like the beasts he'd chased around the Pacific. Hawaiians call breath, *hā*. And that is the sound that comes again: *Haaaaa. Haaaaaa.* I wait, wanting to see the great beast, the magnificent creature whose slaughter brought my mother's family to these shores, but under the new moon, the night's ocean is dark beyond our ship's lights. The whale's breath teases me to look for its shape, but each time I'm sure I spot it, the figure is simply the swell of the channel we cross between islands.

In the hour before dawn, the *Lehua* slams into a wave that nearly throws me from my berth. "You all right?" Abram asks from his side of the cabin.

"Fine. Thank you." There is enough grey light to find the stockings I've taken off under the sheets. I begin tying one end of them to the hand bar above the bed.

"You've been at sea before?" Abram asks as I wrap the other end around my fist.

"No. My mother always wanted us to, but we never made a voyage."

"Your mother has passed?"

"Yes." There is silence I feel obligated to fill. "My grandmother hated the sea. She made the passage out from New Haven on my grandfather's whaler and refused to leave Honolulu ever again. I listened to my grandfather's stories," I say, nodding at the stockings.

"If they were burning whales, you can hardly blame her. The smell is putrid."

"It was a harder journey than this, for certain. My grandmother was pregnant and sick the entire trip."

I realize too late the charged nature of my words. The small pleasure of a normal chat evaporates. In the silence, I think of Grandfather Hezekiah feeding me salty chowders on the viewing platform fronting his Honolulu home. We'd sit together watching the waves race toward us in sets of ten or twelve. "Whaling is a way of life meaner than cat shit," he'd tell me. Not even when I was a girl of six did he apologize for his mouth. He'd left Ireland at fifteen, and his accent made his foul language more entertaining than offensive. "But whaling bought me this white coral house I have here. When we arrived, you could count four dozen natives picking seaweed from the water just there." He pushed his chin out to the shoreline. There were no natives left to count. "And I could spot my crew being collared for drunkenness. I'd 'ave my hat on and be on my way to the Fort 'for anyone had even been sent to fetch me."

I feel my throat tighten thinking of his sandpaper hands, their raised callouses. Hezekiah had survived cannibals in the South Pacific by convincing his captors to let him build them storage boxes from scrap wood. He'd had his eye socket shattered by a fallen mast, but didn't like the feel of a patch so chose to let people stare instead. He outran death in 1871, two years before my birth. His vessel, along with dozens of others, was trapped in Alaska's Bering Strait and crushed in the ice. He was one of twelve hundred whalers, along with a handful of their women and children, who abandoned ship. They escaped on two hundred tiny whaleboats over seventy miles of ocean to find seven ships that had outrun the ice trap and could limp back to Honolulu.

"Only your grandfather went back the next summer to salvage his boat and sail it home to Hawai'i," Mother said. "And you have that blood in you. The missionaries think they're the brave ones for coming out here. But they were only passengers," she'd whisper conspiratorially. "*Our* people were the crew."

I blink back tears, willing myself the strength of my birthright. My grandfather Hezekiah would have had me on a ship to Chile, crewing it himself to get me away from this mess. We would have raised his great-grandchild in a house with a wrought iron balcony and a view of the sea, amongst neighbors who thought us slightly strange. I would have been safe.

An hour passes in dead silence and at last the sea calms.

Abram rises and opens the porthole. I do up my buttons under the rough ship blanket and watch him, with his muscular arms and shoulders, staring outside. "We're toward the west end of the island," he says. "It's dry as stone and just as unforgiving."

I get up to take my first look at this Moloka'i, Mehana's island of sorcery. What I can see is terribly flat and barren. So this is where spirits slip back and forth from other worlds. Where Pahulu's descendent sorcerers turn themselves into trees so poisonous birds drop dead flying over them. In the distance, I see mountains soar like the Ko'olaus back on O'ahu. "Are we going there?" I ask hopefully, pointing to them. "To that side?" I ask.

"That side is east. The north side's the leper camp." Abrams shuts the porthole, "We're headed mid-island."

The boat jumps in the chop. I feel dizzy and turn to go back to my berth, but Abram catches my arm just as I feel the ship put down anchor. "Eliza, it's time for us to go ashore," he says. "They need to turn this boat to Maui."

I brave the stairs up to the deck, Abram helping me to the top. "You'll feel worlds better if you look to land," he says.

I eye a shore which boasts nothing more than a tremendous grove of coconuts and a scattering of huts and shacks. In short order we are in a rowboat stocked with supplies, lowered from the deck by the crew and within moments we are stuck in the mud flats. It is seven o'clock and low tide. I look back to the ship to see if we are making a spectacle of ourselves, but the Japanese laborers have taken no interest in our departure. They've turned their backs to Molokai's shore and are staring at the island of Maui across the water.

Abram shouts toward a group of Hawaiian men on the muddy beach who immediately come out and start to unload our goods. "You'll need to walk this last stretch," he says to me. Then he lifts me up and sets me down. Water seeps into my shoes while he carries sacks of flour to shore. The crewmen push the rowboat off the flats with the help of one of the Moloka'i men.

I lift my right foot only to lose my shoe in the mud. I try to find it in the churning, dirty water by feeling with my right foot; my left is firmly planted in the muck.

"Oh!" I shout, "I'm stuck!"

Abram walks back. He sticks his hand down into the grime and retrieves my boot, placing my hand on his shoulder while he puts my foot back into the shoe. He wipes the mud on the side of his trousers and then turns back for shore. The *Lehua* has pulled up anchor and is pushing off. The captain dons his cap and turns his back to us. I use every bit of restraint I have not to scream *take me with you.*

When I finally set foot on dry land, my traveling suit has a brown sooty ring round the bottom of it, and a sickly sweet scent brings on a rush of queasiness. Abram leaves me to rest on the peach blossom chair, set beneath the terrible smell's source: a hala tree dropping its orange fruit. The fruit will dry into a paintbrush Hawaiians use to decorate their bark fabric, but when it is fresh the smell is foul. Gnats cluster around me, but the men fishing nearby pay me no notice. There are some country cottages in the mesquite trees and a few sheds further down that I assume are for storage.

Abram returns with an old Hawaiian man who beckons me toward a cart pulled by two mules. We set out along a red dirt road heading west.

"Are those sheds for your supplies?" I ask.

"Sheds?" Abrams turns and follows my gaze. "That's their main town of Kaunakakai. Get comfortable; this is a three-hour journey."

We slowly climb up the slope of the island. There is not a soul to be seen, only scattered homes and sweet potato fields that look like graveyards with their rows of neatly arranged rocks. There are old grass houses, donkeys in the open land, and hardly a tree save for a few bare thorny mesquites. After an hour I stop looking for something of interest and stare straight ahead. We are traveling up and away from the ocean, with Maui lying round and womanly across the water. Eventually, the land becomes green and misty. I begin to see little fenced homesteads and Norfolk pines.

"The ride ends rough," Abram calls from the front, and on cue the cart begins to heave and pitch in the corrugated road.

No sign marks the ranch, just a sudden right turn and then pastures and great masses of longhorn cattle. The sight of calves cheers me until I see a group of men trying to ride one of the newborns. The small thing looks terrified, and yet the men clap as one cowhand with a feathered band around his hat digs his heels hard into the calf's sides.

Abram shouts a harsh, "Hey there!" and the men scatter like birds.

We approach a windbreak of pines, beyond which lies a small settlement of low, long wooden structures and flocks of scrappy chickens. The ranch hands and families, Hawaiians all, stop and watch the cart, but offer no welcome.

We come to a halt. Abram hops off the cart. "I've got work to do, and I'd imagine you're exhausted," he says. "You can rest in there." He points to one of the buildings on the other side of a cattle pen. "That's my house. You'll be put off by it now, but with the money, I'll be building something else." He hands me down from the cart, and then he and the old man grab supplies and disappear.

The cabin looks to have been whitewashed at some point, but it wears a layer of red dirt around its base. I make my way over to it and go inside. The same red dirt is scattered across the floor and bed, but the place is not dismal. A chair and desk occupy one corner, and in the opposite corner stands a wood burning stove. A quilt covers the bed, each square a different calico. I lie across the quilt and immediately fall asleep, dreaming that Mehana has come to help me clean the red dirt, but I'm too sleepy to speak. By the time I'm able, she's gone.

3

I wake to the sound of rocks being pelted at the wall behind my head and jump to the window to find a malnourished girl slamming handfuls of dirt at the house.

I throw open the window and say, "*Aloha 'oe*," expecting her to be horrified. The girl looks up, startled, and I realize the punched out belly I took as a sign of poor nutrition is actually a baby. The girl is pregnant, further along than I am. I've seen very young Hawaiian girls with child, but this one can be no more than twelve. I try to hide my shock, but she sees it, turns her face up in contempt and walks away.

"What is your name?" I call after her.

She turns back and pulls up her dress in shyness. "Hina," she says, staring hard at my jade brooch. As quickly as she became shy she now becomes sullen.

Hina is the goddess of the moon, Mehana's favorite. "That's a pretty name," I say.

"I live here," she says.

"We'll have a chance to be neighbors then."

"I live *here*," she repeats.

"Good. I need new friends. Do you like books? I've brought mine from Honolulu." I lift Robert Louis Stevenson's *A Child's Garden of Verses* from my luggage. But when I open the cover and see the author's note scribbled to me I know I cannot take the risk of loaning it. I turn to see her leaning right into the window, watching me, and pass her a leather bound book of English poems. She snatches it from my hands and looks again at the brooch. My child will not be rude, I vow, crossing my arm over my chest, my hand covering the pin. Her eyes are large, tremendous really. She reminds me of someone, though I cannot place who. She holds the book up and opens it, letting the pages fan out. Then she breaks into a run, her hand to her belly as her feet kick up the dust. She catches up to the cowboy with the feather headband I'd seen riding the calf, and from the way she lets him leer at her bust, I suspect he's the man who turned this girl into such a strange version of a child.

By evening Abram still has not appeared. The moon rises in a sky preparing to rain, and I wait long past dark, smelling a meal from the cookhouse across the field, reluctant to venture over unaccompanied. I eat venison jerky from a tin above the stove while it rains.

Several hours past dusk the rain is gone and I walk outside, calling softly for him, embarrassed that others might hear. A few gaslights glow in cabins, and I walk up part of a hill and knock on one of the doors. I can hear voices within. The door opens, and a jumble of what looks to be one extended family is staring at me. Sheets section the house for privacy. The children draw hopscotch patterns on the dirt floor.

"My husband, Abram?" I say.

No one answers or moves. Finally, a middle-aged man says, "We no like know."

I step back and close the door. A layer of mist has settled on the ground. I try to make out the cookhouse, but dinner has surely ended. I hear footsteps down the path. Abram is walking with an arm around someone who parts ways with him wordlessly, and he nearly collides with me as he walks past, saying, "You lost? The cabin is this way."

I catch up with him and ask, "Who was that?"

"It's none of your concern," he answers evenly.

I wait till we've entered the cabin before saying, "You went to Honolulu looking for a wife. Surely it is my concern."

Abram walks to the bed and takes off his boots. "I will not touch a woman filled with another man." He looks at me squarely. "We both have our indiscretions. You have no right to question mine. Your father would tell you the same. I've given you what you need. You have no right to ask for more."

I sit, stunned. Relieved. He gets into bed.

With no other choice, I get into bed beside him. It is not large, and though we turn away from each other, I must push against him to fit. I pretend the strong back I lie against is Ben's. That we are falling asleep together after a long day at sea en route to China. It could have been so. He had wanted it too.

I waited for him in the dark, just beyond the reach of the palace lights and watchful eyes. Parked carriages sat flower-decked and empty beneath the banyan trees. The Royal Band played on the veranda facing into the ballroom, their music reaching the King's guests through open windows. From my hiding place, I watched the musicians' backs move with the motion of their instruments. It was my 17th birthday. I wore my first proper gown: bustled and rust-colored, shoulders exposed. My satin shoes sank into the earth. This, I felt sure, was a good spot. Mehana said every patch of earth has history. Something wonderful had happened here. I felt his hands around my waist, his lips in my hair. We'd been in love for two months, meeting secretly in the forest behind our neighboring homes. My father was helping the King fend off threats to Hawaii's sugar plantations. Benjamin's father, Khan Ahsang, planned a marriage for him in China, a marriage we plotted daily to derail. Ben pressed something cool into my hand. I lifted it toward the palace lights to see a dragonfly of the thinnest, greenest jade.

"It came through Father's shop," he said. When he smiled, his lips pulled slightly more to one side. That crookedness was the charm of his face but the jaw was its pride.

"Your father would object. It's too precious, Benjamin," I whispered, tracing the scar on his cheekbone.

"My father knows," he said.

I looked into his face. The Chinese blood of his father and English-Hawaiian blood of his mother mixed to form a creature fairer than either.

"I spoke to him tonight about combining our families' fortunes. He said he might consider our match."

I made sure every musicians' back was still turned before throwing my arms around him. He smelled of lime and dust from his father's store.

"Will you speak to my father tonight?" I asked. "He leaves with the King on Monday—"

"It's good he'll be in California for a bit. Your father's been telling people you'll marry Richard Irvin. This buys us time." Ben put his finger to the hollow of my throat just under my choker and traced the line of my sternum. He pinned the brooch inside the bodice, hidden.

"I love that you're negotiating for me," I said, pressing his hand to my breast, looking straight into his eyes, surprising myself. He leaned down to kiss me, his hand staying where I had placed it. Applause crackled within the Palace as the band started a waltz.

"We should go back," Benjamin whispered into my hair.

I left him to take a separate entrance, walking dazed through the Palace, my eyes following the strands of maile and jasmine lei strung from chandelier to chandelier. Father stood engulfed in cigar smoke and the rare attention of other plantation men. Ben's sisters, Clara and Emilie, lounged against the foot of the palace's koa wood staircase, their dark hair glimmering red under the electric lights, their Paris gowns made of turquoise and marigold silk, jade ornaments heavy around their necks. Every year at this ball, they brought the King gifts from their father. Once it was a tiger cub that outgrew the Palace within months and was sent back to China. Another year they brought Mandarin acrobats who so pleased the King that they never returned home. Earlier that night, Ben's sisters had entered the ballroom with a line of robed servants holding hundreds of orchids imported from Siam, each bloom a different shape or color. I watched the lacquered baskets being placed at the foot of the King, knowing a single purple freckled cymbidium was missing from his gift, blooming at my bedside.

I was not jealous of Ben's sisters that night, though the spot they held as court darlings had once been mine. When the King's niece Ka'iulani lived here, I was her favorite. I knew nearly every room in this palace as if it were my home. That was before the other missionaries convinced the King that Ka'iulani needed to be sent away.

"Eliza, you've almost missed the entertainment," Emilie said, swirling her sandalwood fan. The green silk lining of her open cuffs matched the shade of her jade.

"Watch the stairs," Clara whispered, squeezing my hand.

In Clara Ahsang's rounded eyes and soft, out-turned lips I saw echoes of her Hawaiian great-grandmother, Chiefess Ahina. I never could find the Hawaiian in Emilie; she shared Ben's high cheekbones, though her eyes narrowed in a way his did not.

The pounding feet of a dozen bare-chested native dancers drummed down the staircase. We followed them to the ballroom, where they dropped to their knees before the King, whose soft curls and huge brown eyes gave him the look of an inquisitive child surprised by middle age. He nodded, and the dancers sprang up again.

"Your Highness, my final gift to you before your voyage," called out Khan Ahsang. His rich, low voice silenced us all. He was a man who had no need to shout.

He bowed to King Kalākaua and touched the back of his neck. Not twenty years before, when he was an indentured worker on my father's plantation, he wore a long queue of hair in a true Chinaman's style. His hair was silver now, but as full as a young man's, his eyes set so wide apart his detractors mocked them as the source of his fortune, saying they allowed him to see from both sides of his face. Khan Ahsang had worked less than a year on Father's plantation before spinning mysterious savings into a chain of commerce and property running from one end of O'ahu to the other. His influence with the King annoyed every plantation man in the room.

Ahsang put his hand on Ben's shoulder. "My son and I brought these men from all over your Kingdom to wish you a safe voyage and to thank you for the tireless work you do to keep Hawai'i independent."

My royalist father clapped with both hands raised above his head. Other white planters—Andrew Blackwell and Lorrance Clarke—looked skyward. These men from missionary families wanted the King powerless and felt no need to conceal their wishes. Three years earlier they had forced a new constitution on the King, stripping away the voting rights of every Asian and every Hawaiian lacking property or wealth to ensure their own electoral control of the legislature. Hawaiians called it the Bayonet Constitution, because these men threatened the King with force to make him accept it. Father was incensed: "I simply don't see how you can take away a man's vote in his own damn land!"

"I don't think vulgar language and politics should mix," Lorrance Clarke had said as we sat on lawn mats listening to the Royal Band play the Star Spangled Banner during a July 4th celebration at the Hawaiian Hotel. "How many Hawaiians or Chinese will cast a vote for our sort, William?" he added.

"Do something of worth and you may be surprised," Father said.

My father was the gap in their armor; he was at school with the men behind the Bayonet Constitution. They'd mocked him and liked to flick his glasses from his face. They made a joke of my grandfather's sermons, his emptying congregation, his home surrounded by shacks when the rest of the missionaries lived in the cool green valley of Nu'uanu. The King was a nobleman's son then, not expected to take the throne. He was a student at the missionary-run school as well. He never took up words with the others, but at the end of each day, he walked beside my father, his massive body a dark, silent partition between the tormentors and the lonely boy my father was then. Now my father repays his loyalty: if the King needs funds or a friendly white face to show outsiders, my father is forever his man.

The dancers started the hula, their malo cloth coverings exposing thighs and hips. Whalebone and hog teeth hung at their necks and ankles. Their movements made the American ladies hide their eyes behind their fans dramatically. Missionaries like my grandfather had banned the hula; King Kalākaua brought it back to his court.

When the hula was done, Kalākaua was the first to rise, the loudest to cheer for the performance. "Your cordiality tonight is evidence that I may rely upon the best to sustain my efforts in upholding the independence of my kingdom and the welfare of my people. Imua!"

Imua. Go forward. Move with strength, he said, his arm raised in a fist as the knot of plantation men tightened in front of him.

I wake to an empty cabin. A mosquito darts around impatiently. I wash at the basin and find Abram has left coffee and two boiled eggs on a plate covered with cloth atop the stove. I eat them at the window. The mist has cleared, and in the distance I can see men moving cattle upslope, miles away.

I force myself to go to the cookhouse. It is long and narrow, with crude wooden benches and tables. Some children gather and stare, reaching out to touch my skin or the fabric of my skirt before darting back to their parents, who keep their eyes averted. The children watch while I consume a sweet roll. Their clothes are castoffs from their elders, tied with string or bits of cloth. They ask me to play tic-tac-toe in the dirt outside and I comply. I write my name at their bidding. To my surprise, they know their letters, thanks to a missionary school a mile away.

That afternoon I am so very alone. I sit under the shadow of a kiawe tree with Robert Louis Stevenson's verses and let myself drift along the current of his words.

He'd arrived at 'Āinahau in his strange billowy striped trousers and a jacket of worn brown velveteen. His hair was long, his mustache eccentrically curved. He made a bow to each of us, and then with a jester's flair he threw himself on the ground in a mock collapse that made us laugh. Ka'iulani and I stretched out on the grass looking up through the banyan's canopy, asking him for one story, then another.

"A storyteller must hear other tales," Stevenson said. "I want a yarn from one of you." Ka'iulani told him the legend of Pele, goddess of fire, who punished a man she loved because he loved another. "Pele turned the man into the naupaka plant up in the mountains with only half a flower, then she turned his love into the plant with the other half flower but down by the sea. We can take you to see the lonely naupaka right here on the beach in Waikīkī."

"Forever separated from its match. I will put those heartbroken half flowers in a story somewhere," he told us. "And they will be famous the world over."

I've attracted a crowd of ranch children. I look at the circle of dusty, desperate things waiting for me to speak. I read Stevenson to them instead:

> *When I was sick and lay a-bed,*
> *I had two pillows at my head,*
> *And all my toys beside me lay,*
> *To keep me happy all the day.*

"How many *haoles* like you live on O'ahu?" a child interrupts, grown impatient. They want descriptions of Honolulu and the great ships that bring news and goods from the world.

I shrug, "Far too many to count."

There are gasps, and not happy ones.

"How many rooms you get in your house in Honolulu?"

"Quite a few."

"How many?"

"Four," I say, though it is actually six.

"For how many people?"

"Four." I add Kepa and Mehana to the count, though they do not live in the house or those rooms: there is a burst of sound as the children absorb this.

Some older boys who work with the cattle are sitting a bit away from us, and I've noticed that Hina is partly hidden by a corner of the cookhouse. With the wind in her hair, she looks like Ka'iulani to me. I close my eyes, yet when I look again the resemblance is still there. Hina's face has those same smooth features. "*Let's go to the sea,*" I say to Ka'iulani in my mind's eye, our feet moving quickly over scorching sandy paths cutting from 'Āinahau to the beach, trying to squeeze together into small shady spots to cool our soles. How good the ocean would feel right now, away from this red dirt.

"I can tell you a legend," says a little boy whose hair looks like it was chopped with a knife, shaking me back into the present.

"Tell me," I plead.

"My story," he says, standing for his audience, raising his voice to a fullness well above what his height warrants, "is from when the first King Kamehameha came for conquer Moloka'i."

He pauses to build suspense. This is clearly a child used to telling stories around a campfire.

"The great warrior Kamehameha brought his army to Kaunakakai. He brought so many men with him, our beaches groaned under their weight. Our *kahuna* heard the sound, and so they prayed. They called on all our islands' powers for protect our men. But the god Kū was with Kamehameha, and his men killed thousands of ours. They threw the bodies in the surf, and so many sharks came for feed, the water boiled."

Here his audience makes disgusted sounds, but they are enjoying the horror with a sweetness possible only in children.

"The sharks tore the bodies so hard, the heads and arms were thrown up above the water. And they washed ashore and stayed there, rotting in the sun."

"Fine job, Ikaika," interrupts a woman who has materialized behind us.

Ikaika returns to sit in the dust with no regrets on his face. Some of the children reach out to touch his leg as he passes, and he smiles.

"You speak well," continues the woman, an older lady with silver hair and a red handkerchief tied at her neck. "But maybe it's time for a story that won't give us nightmares. There are happier stories about our past. Who can tell me how Moloka'i was made?"

"By me," says Hina, chewing on a piece of dried meat. Then she pulls her dress up to her stomach, exposing shoddy bloomers and making kissing noises.

"That's right, by a goddess with your name. Hina was the wife of Wākea, and it was she who conceived Moloka'i, our beautiful island. *'O Moloka'i a Hina he keiki moku.*"

This story does not go over nearly as well as decapitated heads rolling in the surf of Kaunakakai, and before the newcomer can continue, the boys dash off to skip rocks, and Hina vanishes behind a wall. "I'm Keala," the woman says, waving a fly from her face.

"Do you have any books for talking German?" Ikaika asks me; he's lingered behind. "I like go to Germany someday."

"Why Germany?"

"Our old doctor was from there."

"I'll see if my father can get me such a thing," I say, and Ikaika darts off.

"He's Hina's brother," says Keala. My face betrays the impression Hina has made. Keala adds, "Hina's not a bad child. She's just . . . confused."

I nod. "She is not fond of newcomers. I suppose no one here would be."

"People are glad you're here."

"Oh, I don't know about that. Why would they be glad?"

"Because they hope you'll help. This has become a rough place. *Haole* men are a lot better when *haole* women are around."

"There are so few *haoles* here," I say, hoping to distract the conversation from myself.

"Or Hawaiians," she says. "*Pau. Kānaka make.*"

Done, Hawaiians are dead. "It is the same on O'ahu," I say softly and see that she is surprised I understood her Hawaiian.

"But on Moloka'i, no cheap laborers have arrived to replace the dying. Perhaps you'd like to help me? I tend to the cowboys' scrapes. We have a doctor, Dr. Webster down at Kalaupapa, but that is a steep trek below the ranch, so his visits here—"

"Oh, but I have no training."

"No training needed. I use simple ointments and we do our best. Just… keep the workers' troubles to yourself. They're terrified of losing their jobs."

Though there is no one in sight, Keala speaks in a whisper. "I'm sure you understand."

Dear Father,

I'm settling in. It is what would be expected.

Would you mind sending a note to Mr. Paty at his store to see if he might order something on Germany? Something appropriate for a child of nine or ten years?

Perhaps Mehana might also be able to send a few more of my house dresses—the ones I used for helping in the garden. It is harder than expected to keep things clean and I have no angel like her here to help me.

I can think of nothing more to add for now. I miss my home. I hope you miss me.

In the weeks that follow I apply the missionary belief that busy hands stave off misery. I tend cuts with Keala, read to children in the afternoons. I rarely see Abram; he spends his nights somewhere, but not with me. I have seen him with the sister of the cowboy with the feather band, and I suspect Abram spends his nights with her. She is my age, I would guess, and has the Polynesian looks which haole men lose their minds for: tranquil round eyes and hair tumbling so thickly down her back I doubt four white women together could equal its volume. I suppress my smile of thanks so as not to startle her.

The baby has started to move, and this gives me the daily strength to make my way through the next four months, when my child will be born and, by virtue of Abram, legitimate. Then Father will bring me back to Honolulu. He will.

Dear Ka'iulani,

I think I should write you stories, and when we are home again I will give you them to keep. Father made me promise to write no one but him. He is so terrified of what I will reveal under the influence of loneliness. He says this is all a secret that is not mine to tell. In a fashion his order is a relief. I could not stand to write you lies.

But you will know reading this that I thought of you all the while.

When you are Queen, we can visit this place together and open the doors to every sad little cabin. We'll tell them it's safe to come out. They need not stay here any longer.

The camp becomes friendlier to me as my bump pushes out. In the cookhouse workers wave me over to their tables to eat with them. When there's a joke in pidgin I laugh at the right moment, or toss in a word myself, which astounds them.

"How you know for talk li' dat?" they ask.

"My Auntie Mehana," I answer, inwardly thanking Kepa and Mehana.

I ask about their children and where their families are from, and slowly I learn bits and pieces about my new neighbors. I discover that Ikaika and Hina's parents left a year or two earlier for O'ahu, because of "trouble" no one has yet explained. They ask nothing about my growing belly, and I offer no explanations. I arrange my days so that I see little of my husband. Abram shows me some kindnesses. When my clothes become too tight, he gives me two pairs of his trousers. I wear them with one of his belts tied loosely under my belly and the cuffs rolled up four times. His nights continue elsewhere, leading me to believe I will survive this untouched.

"Those urchins like you better than they'll ever take to me," Abram says, finding me as I leave my charges one afternoon. "It's good to keep them busy. They'll steal if the temptation's there."

I keep my expression neutral. I left my sandalwood fan on the ground after one lesson, not realizing I had until I later found it on my bed with a leaf that had the word "Eliza" inscribed on it by little fingernails.

"Anyhow," says Abram, clearing his throat, "we're taking some of the herd to Kalaupapa; they'll be beef for the lepers. It's a short distance to the lookout—then we drive them down the path. I thought you might join us, enjoy the change in scenery. That is if it's all right in your state?"

"I'd like that. Not on a horse, but could I walk behind? Perhaps bring Ikaika and we could carry something for you?"

"That's fine. There'll be water bottles to take. I'll wake you at sunrise."

K,

When you read these someday, you will probably be so worried at what I endured. But it is tolerable. I prohibit myself from complaining. I miss taking hot baths in tubs that do not contain bugs floating in scum. I miss carriage rides to bookstores. And how I miss the ocean!

On my worst days, I let myself imagine what living in Boston would be like. Clean baths and butter sauces. Thick, expensive clothes. Would distant cousins be kind or condemning? Knowing that one would reach into the bassinet to give the carriage man an infant for the orphanage reminds me to be thankful to eat my sour poi and scraps of meat. I remember how you love your three-day-old poi, and Mehana will be proud I have become accustomed to it. We will wonder at all this someday, you and I. The travels we survived. Tomorrow I will look down on Kalaupapa and think of the poor souls condemned there forever. Truly, I must be thankful I have what I do.

Abram opens the cabin door at dawn.

"Eliza, ten minutes. I'll make the coffee."

He works at the sink as I dress quickly behind the door. He puts a hot tin cup in my hands and without another word walks out of the cabin. I feel thankful, even a bit happy. Ikaika waits outside with two cowboys. They are speaking sternly to him; he cries out, "I like ride a horse like the men."

"No," snaps Abram. His voice is so harsh that Ikaika looks as if he might cry. The cowboys look to the ground.

"When you're bigger, Ikaika," I say. "You're the only boy going this morning so you need to be helpful." I pick water bottles off the ground and hand him one, Abram and the cowboys mount their horses, the cattle get moving and we're off. We follow on foot, and as it gets lighter, Ikaika and I discuss which cloud looks like what. "All those clouds pretty much look like trains, Miss Eliza," he finally admits.

"When have you seen a train?"

"Never. But the German man, Dr. Eger, he drew one, and that's what I'm going to make. A train for Moloka'i."

A train for a place with no people. We've already passed a clearing with what looks like the remnants of an old village—stone walls in the telltale square shape of a Hawaiian *hale* done the old way with lava rock and what would have been a grass structure before the sicknesses came and the forest was cleared of its sandalwood.

"Ikaika, I'm certain your train would be lovely, but are there enough people here to need a train?"

"Cows need trains, too. Then we don't have to spend all day moving them. We'd put the cows on the train and wave, goodbye! A-lo-ha!"

This he shouts, twirling and dropping his water bottle onto the grass. Abram looks back at us. I pick the bottle up and hurry Ikaika along. We begin to walk through forest. The cows are bellowing. The ironwood trees give off a Christmas smell, and the eucalyptus branches rub against each other in the wind, making a lovely, caressing sound. I think of lying with Benjamin, our limbs entwined with sheets. The memory kicks the happiness right out of me. I stop and feel the roundness of my belly, reminding myself that Benjamin is always with me.

The men are looking down a cliff. When we catch up Abram takes the bottles and offers me a sip of water before the cowboys drink. "Have a cocktail with the view," he says, spreading his arm across a marvelous vista of ocean and a flat plain of sunburned land, as if he created it.

I look at the rows of homes, trees, and churches. The leper colony looks like a happy hamlet. Mehana's nephew, Joseph, is somewhere down there. It occurs to me: how strange that Mehana didn't ask me to bring something for him. But then again, how would she have known my new home was near the colony, that it shared a doctor who travels back and forth. Or was it just too hard to say his name?

Abram's cows have gone stone silent, and I wonder what has spooked them. Abram nods toward a switchback trail cut into the cliff side. "We should start. It takes us two hours to get down. At the bottom, we'll be paid for the cattle. Then we'll climb back up."

I nod and Ikaika and I sit down on grass still dewy from the mist of the previous night. We watch the men descend. Ikaika reaches up to my cheek and pushes my face gently. He wants me to turn my head so that I can see how the cliffs continue as far as the eye can see along the coast, their ridge lines falling straight into the ocean.

I've discovered many of the camp's children have never touched the sea, Ikaika among them. Only a generation ago, he would have been in a canoe at birth. Hawaiians speak of the ocean as Americans speak of freedom, yet these children have never known either. Their fates seem already decided: following their parents in service of Abram—and by extension my former suitor, Richard Irvin. I hear his name occasionally. "Mr. Irvin bought us these ones for Christmas," Ikaika tells me, showing me his collection of pencils, rabbited with teeth marks. I add 'box of pencils' to my list of things to ask my father for. I look for reasons to write again though he has not yet answered.

"Would that make a very fine picture?" Ikaika asks, clearly having heard a haole person say that same thing.

"Yes. It's stunning," I say. And it is true. It is something I've never seen back home.

He beams at me, so pleased I like his island—and then we hear frantic shouts from the men below. We jump to our feet and are astonished to see the cattle jumping from the switchback trail and falling a horrific mile-and-a-half to the ground, their legs spread forward as if trying to jump the moon.

"Oh my God!" I shout, turning Ikaika away from the sight. But he twists back to watch, fascinated. One of the cows explodes into a pink cloud upon landing.

Abram screams at the hands in Hawaiian that I didn't know he knew, and some English so foul I hope they can't understand. Then another animal explodes, and still one more. Nausea overwhelms me and I gag, my shoulders thrown forward: the cows, the lepers, the ranch. It's too much.

"We go ma'am, we go!" says Ikaika. "We gonna get lickins here."

We start to run until I remember I should not, for the baby's sake.

"Ikaika, I need to slow down. Abram will have his hands full, I promise. He won't punish you." But the boy is right. Abram won't get paid now. That meat won't be usable.

"I guess it nevah matter to the cows though, huh?" Ikaika asks. "They got to kill themselves. No one slaughtered them. They outsmarted one *haole luna*!"

Haole luna. White master.

He beams until he remembers himself. Then we walk in silence. We pass the shivering ironwoods again, but now I hear nothing Christian or caressing in their sound. It is the sound of hair twisting upon itself in the wind, it is a dead man's foot causing the tree to quiver and sigh.

"Do you feel the scariness?" Ikaika asks, slipping his hand again into mine. He cannot be more than eight, but his hands are calloused from milking the cows. "The night marcher sound is in the trees, Miss Eliza."

I feel it. I feel the great chiefs of his people's past walking above us, the beat of their drums. *"If you hear them, your only hope of escape from death is to hide yourself low upon the ground,"* Mehana warned me when I was a child. I thought she told the story to make me stay in my bed and stop crossing the darkened lawn to sleep in her cottage. On nights with mist or high winds, she left the front and back door of her home open to let the spirits pass with no hindrance. "*We've built these things in their paths,*" she would say in a scolding tone.

"I'm scared," says Ikaika. "I no like die."

"*They march to welcome new warriors to their ranks,*" Mehana taught me. "*To reclaim rightful territory, to search for an entrance into the next world.*" I think of the land we stand on, which is Richard Irvin's, but a hundred years ago was a large village. I think of the cows, leaping, searching for an exit and entrance. I banish the images of pink explosions and turn to Ikaika with the same assurance Mehana gave me at his age.

"You are safe from them, Ikaika. You have a respectful heart. No night marcher would take you because you are not boastful."

He looks up and melts me with the warmth of his trust. "And you're certainly safer than I am, you probably have an ancestor among the marchers to protect you," I add.

"I'd tell him, count you too," he says, taking a handful of my skirt to lead me out of the trees, toward a clearing. "Do you see it? The boat?" Ikaika asks.

Even though I know they still are far down the switchback, I check behind us, thinking of Abram coming our way, angry at me for wandering off. I scan the uneven, red dirt around us, searching even the branches of trees at the clearing's edge. Ikaika laughs, delighted. He takes me a few steps forward, to where the ground drops off into a huge pit carved into the ground like the hull of a ship.

"I heard of these from my grandfather," I say, amazed. "I've never seen one." The pit floor is covered in shrub, dating back to the days when Hawaiian chiefs ordered natives to abandon their taro and sweet potatoes to harvest sandalwood for China. Famine and misery followed, driving men to pull up any sandalwood saplings they could find in the hope that their children would not be forced to cut and carry the spiced wood into the ship-like pits that had been dug into the mountain so that one might know when a full cargo was reached.

This abandoned hull stood as the only proof that sandalwood had ever grown here.

"Do you know how old it is?" I ask.

"Older than me," he says.

I laugh, which feels good after watching the cows die. Then I gasp and hold my stomach. "My baby kicked hard. It must want to be your friend," I say, pointing to the spot on my belly.

Ikaika rubs his hand on his pants and then puts his small palm, fingers up, on my stomach. "Maybe he likes my voice because it's a boy voice, and that's what he is."

"Maybe," I say, giving his hair a ruffle. So this is what it will be like to be a mother, I think, as my baby kicks again.

"Is that one?" Ikaika asks.

"Yes, that was a big kick."

Ikaika picks the bottles up and looks at me, nervous again. "You know Mister Abram get one haole boss too. And Mr. Irvin, he gonna give Mr. Abram lickins now. Mr. Abram gonna be all mad at us."

"Oh, Richard's not a mean man. He understands things happen. Animals get spooked."

Ikaika is stunned. "You *know* Mr. Irvin?" he asks, as if it were Saint Nick we spoke of.

"Yes. Yes, I know him."

I barely notice Richard Irvin until he is standing over me in the banquet room. I'd spent most of the palace dinner in silence, watching Ben and Father bent over plovers on toast and fried oysters further down the table. My dinner companion was the Brazilian envoy, but he'd tossed up his hands in despair when we were seated, unable to hear above the crowd.

"You look like your mother, with your hair put up that way," Richard says, pulling up a seat between the envoy and me. Richard's skin is so fair he frightens Mehana. "No blood or breath in that one," she grumbles. But I find Richard striking. His dark red hair and blue eyes are unusual in Hawai'i;

far more so than the blend of the Ahsang family. We have family history: both of our grandfathers came from New England around the tip of South America on the same ship. His grandfather headed up a church on the other side of the island from mine and, like our family, the Irvins moved from the harvesting of souls to the planting of sugar. Our lands are still irrigated by water his father sells to mine. His is the one missionary family on O'ahu my father can abide, because Richard's father hadn't been in Honolulu tormenting him.

"You're too kind," I answer, but I'd thought the same when Mehana fixed my hair. I've grown into my mother's face, with the same blonde curls and skin that goes olive in the sun. "Your whaling grandfather's swarthy roots," my father likes to say.

"And you're seventeen now," Irvin says, as his eyes appraise my bodice. Then he turns away, reddening as he struggles between propriety and desire. Ben's eyes always lock on my face. His desire is cool, liquid. I am the one left gasping, blushing.

I declined Richard's proposal one month ago, saying I was too young. Now I say nothing.

"Well, thank goodness your father's going to San Francisco," Richard says, filling the awkward silence. "It's the first encouraging sign we've seen in months, the King taking a plantation man to work on this sugar issue. If he can't solve the McKinley Tariff, we'll be forced to push Kalākaua out and get these islands brought into the U.S. before we all go broke."

The King sits at a neighboring table in deep discussion with Ahsang, no doubt discussing the fact that Hawaiian sugar is hemorrhaging money. Years ago, under pressure from planters, he gave the States use of Pearl Harbor in exchange for importing Hawaiian sugar as if it were an American product. We planters made our fortunes from the arrangement. Now Congress has changed the law and put in this McKinley Tariff which favors Louisiana sugar. The tariff makes our sugar too expensive, and every planter in the room is blaming the King for it. Every planter but Ahsang and my father.

"Richard. It's not civil to speak of the King in such a way. We're in his palace."

"His palace. How much did the good barbarian king squander on this European fantasy?" Richard whispers, his eyes running over the etched glass windows, the polished wood floors reflecting the gold braid uniform of the military officers walking past us. "Each member of this family outdoes the last in folly and ineptitude."

I give him a face, and he sighs and holds up his hand in apology. "I forget myself. You no doubt miss the lovely Ka'iulani. She is an exception to my uncharitable characterization of their family."

"It's been more than a year," I say. "They said it would only be one year."

Ka'iulani was sent to England for a future queen's education at the urging of Lorrance Clarke. In less fraught times I doubt the King would have made her go. These days, he must court the missionaries' approval in all matters to try to keep the throne safe for Ka'iulani to inherit one day, after his surviving and childless sister, Lili'uokalani, reigns as Queen. If she gets the chance to reign; Lili'uokalani is a Godly woman, but she lacks her brother's charisma. The King has a charm which serves as his talisman against his detractors. He inspires devotion in a way Lili'uokalani does not, at least not yet.

Ka'iulani asked the King to give me a Hawaiian name when I was eight or nine years old.

"Kūpa'a," he said, taking a feather lei from around his neck and putting it around mine. "Like your father."

Kūpa'a—loyal. I would forever defend this King.

"You certainly can't say this palace he's built is backwards. He's installed electricity before the White House managed it," I say to Richard, knowing this will irk him.

"Please. He plays at empty pomp and pageantry, at progress," Richard answers, bunching his lips to one side. "These royals are costing us good sugar money and separating us from the States. America can do ten times the job this lot does."

It is odd to hear him so impressed with the States. Like me, he's never been there.

"In matters of the King you are ever your father's daughter," he adds gently. "Your opinions will evolve, Eliza. I can assure you they will."

"I'll let you argue that with my father, Richard." I glance at Ben. He has turned his chair to face Father. Their duck sits untouched. "Would you fetch the steward?" I ask. "I'm parched."

Richard puts his glass down with such pleased determination I feel guilty. I put my hand to the V of my bodice, checking that Benjamin's brooch is still there. There are eyes on me. I feel them and take my hand from my gown to raise my napkin to my lips. Once Richard leaves the room I walk quickly toward my father, and stares follow. They watch a motherless girl they thought was a good child until she turned down a fine proposal.

Benjamin stands at my arrival, his chair scraping the floor. I take the seat he's offered. His hand glances off my shoulder as he helps me push my chair in place, then he nods to us before going to his father, who is seated next to the King.

"I saw Richard Irvin paying attention to you," my father says as I take a sip of Ben's port. "It's time to accept his proposal, my dear girl. He is a very decent sort. Between the two of you, you'll have nearly half the island's sugar and then you can really tell these old grumps what's what."

"I'm not sure you quite understand where Richard stands," I say in a low voice, glancing over at Ben. "He gave me an earful of annexation talk." But Ben thinks like you do, I add silently. Is my marrying the son of a Chinese tycoon so different from you marrying a whaler's daughter?

"Oh, Richard is young and influenced by all the chatter at the club. His family wants nothing to do with politics, believe me. He can be steered straight. Let's accept before I go to California. Let's have the matter settled."

"I would like very much to decide my future when you return," I answer, touching mother's pearl choker. "I fear Mother had a daintier neck than mine. This is starting to hurt."

He removes his glasses and pinches the bridge of his nose. "She used to complain about that too." His eyes start to droop under the effect of too much wine. I watch his head begin to fall into slumber, wishing I could put the secret of my love for Ben in his mind as he dreams, and that he could wake, wondering how he's never seen it before.

Ikaika has a lingering sore. Keala and I bring the cloth and medicines Abram purchases for the camp to the cookhouse once a week and treat the workers before the dinner hour. I never touch their wounds directly, using boiled rags to wash their skin and then to apply the alcohol and ointment.

"That's not a good sore," Keala says ominously.

I feel a flash of annoyance at her words the way my father would if he were standing here and loved Ikaika as I do. "Hawaiians have a terrible way of giving in far too gracefully to fate," he barked when I repeated Mehana's tales of natives going to find a cave to die in when they saw death approaching in the way the ocean moved, clouds caught in odd formations. It was a surrender to nature which offended the Yankee spirit in us. We preferred to fight it. Deny it. Ignore it. "Ikaika's out sliding in the dirt every day," I say. "When would it have time to heal?"

I bandage the sore again.

"The other boys will tease me if I wear this," Ikaika protests.

"Do it for me. Just for the next day or two, until the doctor comes for his visit," I tell him, kissing the top of his head. "The *kauka* will have something to fix it," I say for my own sake, as Ikaika is jumping in his seat waiting to be released, unworried by his scrape.

Keala looks away. She loves this boy too.

Dr. Webster arrives that Monday, an hour or so past dawn. I open my cabin door to find the entire camp assembled silently in the cattle pen between my home and the cookhouse. The men huddle in one group, the women in the other. The doctor sits with his back to me, leaning forward to peer into the mouth of Keala's husband, Charlie.

"Your teeth are good, Charlie. How is that cough you had last time?" the doctor asks. His voice is a surprise – foreign, with an accent that sounds English, yet I'm quite sure isn't.

"No bother," Charlie answers. He looks nervous and unhappy. Abram is watching the examination from a few steps away, listening.

"If it comes back as badly as before, you need to let me know. It can lead to something very serious, understood?"

Charlie nods unconvincingly, and the doctor lets him go. In his place comes Keala, who lets the doctor examine her mouth, the skin on her arms. "Perfect health," Dr. Webster says, patting Keala on the hand.

"See if there isn't lice," says Abram. "Her hair is coarse. I don't want another outbreak."

The doctor stiffens and leans forward to peer at Keala's scalp, shaking his head. He has ruddy blond coloring and a lanky build. His freckled arms are covered with fine light hair. I guess his age to be near thirty.

"Anything troubling you?" he asks Keala quietly. She shakes her head stubbornly and looks up at him for permission to leave. It goes on like this, the doctor alternating between the groups, calling first a man, then a woman for examination. Nearly everyone has been seen when Ikaika comes in the yard, kicking a rag ball with Hina following close behind. The doctor is in the midst of looking over another patient when he straightens and takes a long look at Hina. He finishes quickly and calls Hina over. "How are you feeling, Hina?"

"Okay," she says quietly, casting her eyes down and chewing a bit of her hair, her hand resting pertly on the dome of her belly.

"Have you been eating well?"

"I don't know," she answers.

"You need to make sure you get enough nourishment. It will help in your development as well as the child's. Let me take a look at you." The doctor feels her stomach softly through the grey fabric of her dress. It looks like an adult's dress that was once white, then dyed to cover its stains. I catch the doctor taking a quick look at her pelvis, and imagine he's wondering whether she can survive a child's birth.

"That will do it for this visit," says Abram. He breathes a little whistle out his lips, challenging Webster to contradict him.

"Would you mind having a look at Ikaika?" I call from inside the cabin's shade. Dr. Webster turns at the sound of my voice, and appears shocked to see a white woman at the camp.

He asks Abram, "Shall I examine the young lady as well?"

"No need," says Abram. "That's my wife, in from Honolulu. She hasn't been here long enough to worry about getting ill."

"Ikaika has a sore I was hoping you might attend to," I clarify.

"Of course." Dr. Webster glances at my swollen shape and calls for Ikaika, who is kicking his ball against the side of the cookhouse. He picks the ball up and comes running, sliding onto the bench his sister just left as if it were a game. The doctor looks in his mouth and asks him to pull his sleeves up. He opens the bandage and takes out a metal instrument to pat the skin of Ikaika's arm in quick light movements.

"Some sort of cyst I believe. It would be easier to treat out of this sun," he says.

"Do that. I've had enough for today," says Abram, leaving us all. Hina trots behind him to the hitching post under a group of kiawe trees where he's left his horse. I watch them speak for a few minutes, worried she's telling him about Ikaika's sore. He'd throw him out, I think. But Abram has no patience for her and gets straight on his horse.

"Mrs. Malveaux, I'll need your assistance. Do you have a sewing kit in there?" Dr. Webster asks, indicating my cabin. "I'd rather this was done somewhere out of view."

"Come with us, Ikaika," I say, my arm around his small shoulders.

"Is this gonna hurt bad?" he asks, holding onto his arm protectively.

"Hopefully it will hurt a bit," says the doctor.

We enter my cabin. The doctor places his medical kit on my side table, settling Ikaika onto the edge of the bed. "Are you experiencing any unpleasantness?" he asks, looking at my belly.

"None. Just a little out of breath here and there. Some nausea."

"That's certainly normal, nothing of concern. Bring that needle if you don't mind," he says. I take a sewing needle from the kit and use a bit of soap at the sink to clean it. Ikaika jabs at the different quilt squares, saying the colors of each out loud, using food names like "sweet potato" for purple and "haupia pudding" for white as he works his way around.

"Look away, Ikaika," says the doctor. Ikaika immediately looks straight at the needle.

I sit next to him and take his other hand. "Look at me and think about your train," I say.

The doctor takes the moment to poke the needle into the sore. Ikaika registers nothing. Dr. Webster pulls the needle out in a way that scoops a bit of skin with it. He turns back and shakes his head behind Ikaika.

Not this little man of mine, I plead with my eyes.

Dr. Webster takes a fresh bandage from his box and wraps Ikaika's sore carefully.

"Ikaika, you can go now," he says.

Ikaika is out the door before the doctor has scraped the bit of skin into an empty canister.

"I fear the worst," says Dr. Webster, keeping his voice low. "I will examine the sample at Kalaupapa, but I'm already quite sure." He closes up his bag, looking at me with sympathy. "I am very sorry. You seem extremely fond of him. The only comfort I can give you is that soon you will have your own child to worry about."

"Yes," I say, "though that will be of no comfort to Ikaika."

The doctor sends word by messenger the next day that it is indeed leprosy. I wait to tell Ikaika, letting him enjoy the children's story hour and staying long afterwards to answer his every question. In the evening he sits next to me at the cookhouse and eats a chicken leg with relish, licking his fingers and accepting my portion too.

The next morning, I find him by himself, milking the cows in the barn. The others are done, but Ikaika is younger and slower and happy to be alone with his own thoughts.

"This one couldn't jump that trail if she wanted," he says. "She's so heavy with her milk she couldn't even ride the train if I built it."

I sit next to him and touch his unblemished hand. "Maʻi Pākē, Ikaika," I say quietly. The Chinese sickness.

He bows his head and shows no reaction at all. He starts his milking again. "That's why the doctor poked me?"

I nod. "Yes."

"There's nothing to do when it's that, huh?"

"No. The doctor will come tomorrow to take you down the path, to make sure you get to the camp at Kalaupapa safely."

He looks up, terrified, and I'm sure he's thinking of the cows jumping the trail, for I cannot help picturing them either. "I will walk with you to the head of the switchback. I will get you a German book from Oʻahu, and any others you like. I will send them down with the doctor on his next visit." I reach out for him and hold him tucked under my arm. He moves to lay his head on my lap. I stroke his hair, not touching his bad arm for the sake of the baby, but unable to deny him some comfort.

"I can swim in the ocean down there," Ikaika says.

Don't cry, I tell myself.

He rises. "I want to go play outside now."

"Yes, you get some air today. I'll take the milk to the creamery."

"Okay. You gonna come with me tomorrow?"

"Yes," I answer, brushing the top of his head and picking up the bucket to leave him. I turn after a bit and see him walking away with his hands in his pockets, hunched over like the grown man he will likely never become.

"Oh, Jesus," Abram says, pacing in my cabin. His footsteps are better placed than mine, avoiding the creaks in the floor. It reminds me this was once his home. "I'm getting that doctor up here every month, every week if I have to. I won't let the filth spread. Which one is Ikaika?"

"The one who carried the water the day we went to the trail," I say, avoiding the mention of the jumping cows.

"Oh great, that goddamn mess I had to explain to Irvin." Then he squints as if trying to remember who was with us, so I say, "Hina's brother."

Abram squares up to his full height. "Don't use that tone," he says. "I've asked you to stay out of my business."

"Your business?"

He jerks his head back, then rubs his eyes like he's just woken up. "My apologies. I thought you were trying to throw Hina in my face."

"Hina?"

"Yes." He says this solemnly. Like he's being honorable about it.

"She's twelve!"

"She's thirteen. And I wasn't the first. Not that it's your affair, but she's far better treated now than she had been. I don't hit her, or any woman. And I'll take care of the child, unlike whoever left you."

My face burns. He looks repentant.

"Hina's my mistress. You're my wife. I assumed you'd figured that out by now. It seems to be working out all around." Abram turns his gaze toward the window and exhales heavily. His thoughts seem to have returned to Ikaika, to a possible outbreak here. As if what he has just told me is a side note.

His mistress. His little girl mistress. That is what Hina had tried to warn me of the very first day.

I live here, she'd told me. I live *here.*

K,

I am thinking of signs tonight. Clues the world gives us which we ignore until the evidence is overwhelming, and then we rage at the unfairness of being surprised.

Did they tell you, K, that the red 'aweoweo fish returned the day the King left? Floating like pools of blood in the harbor as your people begged your uncle not to sail to California. He assured them it was a trip for his health, a rest from all the strains of ruling. But they had not seen the fish since that week your mother took sick so suddenly, and they pleaded with your uncle to heed the sign of royal death in the water around the ship. They wailed while the band kept playing until my father and the King boarded. He looked so well that day, your uncle, in his jolly straw hat, his white suit. It will pain you to read this one day, I fear. But it is much on my mind tonight.

Mehana says the elderly no longer know when it is time to find a place to die. That the fish will stop bothering to come in warning because they go unheeded. Progress has overwhelmed the senses. I am part of that oblivious progress. I am a fool, and so very angry tonight.

This boy I love, he will be going away as you did. There is no husband to share my thoughts with. I need my child to be born, to fill my head with other thoughts than these. I need to have a bit of Ben so that I might remember what that felt like. I thought the signs for a life with Ben were auspicious, I truly did.

I always believed I saw signs as Mehana does, but I only used what she taught when it suited me; a romantic addition to my world when it served my desire. Had I used her lessons not as a pleasantry but a discipline, would I have seen what I should have? I think so. Yes, I would have.

I woke the morning after the King's ball wanting an excuse to see Ben. Carrying stalks of white ginger from the river bank, I hurried down Father's drive onto the dirt path of Nu'uanu Road. A carriage passed, spinning out a cloud of dust. I covered my eyes and mouth, stopping to cough between the stone lions guarding the Ahsangs' gate. In the hazy afternoon, bees hovered like small storms over water lily pots lining the Ahsangs' drive. The star fruit on their trees looked bruised and spoiled from the sun.

Beyond the garden stands the mansion Father said was bought with opium money, an oversized dollhouse, edged entirely in white lattice. Bell-shaped stephanotis drag themselves up narrow trellises to a second story balcony where Ben's sisters sit every Sunday to be admired by neighbors in passing carriages. The Ahsang family follows the Catholicism Ben's mother Hannah adopted. They attend Mass Saturday evenings, leaving the girls free to wear vivid silks and wave their fans at the pale procession of missionary families heading to Sunday service. The girls' rooms take up the entire flowering floor. The vines continue toward the top of the house, stopping just short of the window that is Ben's.

To the left is the old coach house Ben's mother converted into her own apartments. Hannah is a recluse; she follows a regimen of bed rest to avoid mental strain. Her daughters fight this fate with tonics prescribed by Western doctors. They ingest these prior to their own strictly enforced daily naps. At night they take a foul-smelling herbal mixture their Chinese doctor prescribes.

Across the well-shaded courtyard sits a third building, formerly Hannah's tea salon and now Ben's billiard room. Outside, along the river is a circle of green ceramic stools where the sisters are watching Ben shoot a traveling palm with fronds nine feet wide. Behind them, servants are setting up for the King's visit tonight, the eve of his departure to San Francisco with my father.

"Eliza!" Clara calls out, waving, her face tender with goodwill for me.

I hold the flowers up like a torch.

"Ah, white ginger. The most ethereal of flowers," says Emilie.

"Eliza, you've brought me good luck. I'm sure to hit my mark now," Ben says as he walks toward his target, stops, and fires. Sap spurts from the tree. Emilie claps, but Clara recoils. I feel an odd undercurrent of worry for her without knowing why, as if I've hidden something for safe keeping but now

cannot remember where. Ben touches the small of my back walking toward Clara, and my worry dissolves. We will be husband and wife in this house by the King's ball next year. I will be presenting the gifts with his sisters, though I will stand behind them and always let them go first.

"Oh, Clara," Ben says, "It doesn't hurt the palm, you darling thing." He crosses the lawn and gives her a swift kiss on the cheek, which makes her look even more unsure.

"Benjamin, you're getting very sentimental," reproves Emilie. "Are you love-struck?"

"How could I be? I'm always stuck in Father's office," Ben says, looking down while he breaks apart the rifle; I feel the heat in my face.

"It's already our rest time," Clara says, nodding toward a servant who has emerged from the house with two glasses of tonic. I kiss the girls goodbye and walk toward the river that joins the back of our two properties, wanting to avoid the dust of the road.

The riverbank is solid and mosquito-free in the day's heat. It is as if the forest is conspiring to bring me swiftly home with no need to pull a shoe from mud or stop to slap an insect from my arm. I am nearly there when he steps out of the forest. He swings me in his arms. "Come and see what my father's bought for the King," he says, pulling me back.

"Your sisters will think it odd—"

"My sisters are asleep." He walks me back into their greenhouse, past rows of hanging orchids that reach out to touch my skirt. In the corner is a spectacular plant, seven feet tall with a head of thick twisted vines falling downward, like decorated hair.

"Dragonfruit," he says, breaking a fruit from the vine. On it blooms a flower, white and glorious. Extravagantly pure and spiked like a star.

The fruit feels like a large river rock; its skin is red as a pomegranate with flat green fins. Benjamin cuts into it carefully. Bright pink and flecked with black, the fruit is so glossy with magenta juice it looks bloody, the flesh on the metal knife he holds toward my lips is as translucent as stained glass.

I take the slice before I hear him say, "It stains."

The fruit's taste is not as glorious as its appearance; it is watery where a mango is silken. Ben touches his handkerchief to my lips and turns my palm upwards, rubbing my pink fingertips. He kisses me deeply, opening my mouth, his hand in my hair. When he stops, my body is slack against his. He embraces me, whispering, "I'll have them set a table near your house so you can hear the King sing tonight. You love his voice."

He kisses me once more before letting me turn away down the row of orchids, their blossoms now whiskered faces looking at me with identical scowls of judgment.

When the King sings that evening, I stand at my bedroom window and watch through the branches of the shower tree that stands between our home and Ahsang's. In summer its canopy blooms pink as the inside of a ripe guava. Since August, when the tree shed its color, I've found gifts and notes from Ben in its hollow: a silk purse filled with foreign coins, a shell the size of my fist which he dove for deep on the reef.

Ben sits to one side of the King, his father on the other. The King sings a love song in Hawaiian, veering between sad and sweet, a champagne glass in his raised hand. When the song ends, servants approach with platters of raw cubed fish and seaweed salads, whole steamed fish and roasted prawns. The King and Ahsang are both fifty, but Kalākaua wears the girth of a man of pleasure while Ahsang is as lean as if he still harvested cane. The King lights his cigar from the lantern. The men throw their arms around each other as the King sings something raucous. Servants relight lamps with long tapers and carry away empty champagne bottles.

The next morning fishermen find rare swarms of 'aweoweo along Oahu's south shore. The King's sister, Princess Likelike, mother to my Ka'iulani, died the last time they were spotted in such numbers. She made a feverish prediction on her death bed: her daughter would leave Hawai'i for a long time, would never marry, and would never wear the crown. Servants passed the grim account from house to house. Mehana repeated the prediction in ours.

"It was her fever speaking, not some ancient power of clairvoyance. Ridiculous, absolutely all of it," said my father

But within two years Ka'iulani was sent away to England. She looked so bereft waving to us from high on the ship's bridge, even as boys fully dressed in their Sunday best jumped into the water, diving for coins thrown by the crowds as her ship cast off. The King had stood up in his open carriage, calling out farewells in Hawaiian over the bellow of the ship's horn.

My beloved grandfather, Hezekiah, had just passed. The two losses compounded each other, and I was unhinged as I watched her go, unable to stop sobbing. The King tipped his hat as his carriage passed ours. He slapped the side of his twice for the driver to stop, a jaunty sovereign with his lit cigar and bowler hat. "William, bring your Eliza to the Palace for a root beer. We can have a port and talk about these jackals circling me to give away Pearl Harbor. I wish I were the one sailing away today." He'd pretended not to see my ruined face and dress smeared with dirt where I'd wiped my tears after leaning against a lamppost. "Our little bird left today so she can grow into a Queen, Eliza," the King told me, his eyes cast sideways. "It is a hard thing, to see the world as it truly is, my dear."

By morning word has spread, and the whole camp is outside Hina and Ikaika's cabin offering comfort. Hina clutches Ikaika to her. I can barely look at them, or be seen looking at them. Everyone in the camp knows I married a man capable of this child's pregnancy. Their coldness when I first arrived. My being the last to understand. Abram is nowhere to be found today.

The cowboys hold their hats to their chests and speak low simple words to the boy. The doctor has arrived for Ikaika's last journey outside the perimeters of the leper settlement.

"You know, Ikaika, there are many other children at the settlement," says Webster. "Some of the boys are your age, and they will enjoy having you as a new friend. They like to play games and have races. Do you think you'll like that?"

Ikaika nods, keeping his head down.

"I want to go with you," I say.

"You're fine on foot?" Dr. Webster asks.

I nod, and the three of us begin walking as quickly as possible. When we pass through the trees he'd been so frightened of, Ikaika does not try to take my hand but instead holds on to my sleeve. Can this little boy so quickly understand the protocol of the disease? I put my arm around his shoulders as we approach the top of the cliff.

At the lookout, I tuck some of Father's money into his pocket and point to the horses below. "You buy one of those. But have someone teach you how to ride properly. Promise?"

"Yes. Will you be nice to Hina?" he asks.

His question shames me. "Yes, I promise," I say. I do not want to think of Hina. I want to think just of him. I want to shore him up for what will come. "And I expect you'll be a great man, Ikaika. One day you'll build your train and it will crisscross this cliff." Here my voice catches in the lie, and he puts his head against my round stomach. The baby gives a swift kick at his touch, but Ikaika does not acknowledge it.

"I have to go," he says, and with a lift of his hand he turns and begins down the path on his own.

"I'll teach the boy to ride if no one else claims the role," Dr. Webster says kindly. "And try not to become overwrought, Mrs. Malveaux." He peers down at me, worried, and looking up at him, I realize how much I've missed having a protector. "I'll make sure Ikaika does as well as can be expected. But you need to remember that you have your own child to prepare for. Strong emotions in pregnancy are not ideal."

"Dr. Webster..."

I want to ask him if he knows about my husband and Hina. I want to ask him what I should do. I want him to let Ikaika stay somewhere hidden if I offer some money. Instead, I say, "Should he need anything, you'll tell me?"

He nods, and then he too starts down the switchback trail. I watch until they are out of sight, and then I run unevenly through the woods, blocking out the tumble of emotions, Ikaika's love for me, Hina's hate. I refuse to hear the voices of the trees, to think of anything but going back to lock myself up alone.

I reach my cabin, close the shutters and lie on the bed, trying to picture Ikaika with a clean bed and better food than he had here. In my head the children he plays with are not yet bloated with the disease, suffering only a few sores under their white clothes. Then I put Ikaika under Kaiulani's banyan tree at ʻĀinahau. Robert Louis Stevenson promises he will write down Ikaika's stories. Kaʻiulani will give Ikaika his train. We eat a meal together, feet tucked under the low lūʻau table, a woven lauhala mat for Ikaika to nap on in the tree's shade.

K,

The boy I told you of, he was like a little brother for me. I seem to always find my missing sibling, my missing mother. Do you do that in England?

When you left, there was this same chasm in my heart I feel tonight. I filled it then with the girls next door, and that step led to another, and then another, and now I am here. If I'd never crossed the riverbank, never started making the Ahsang home my own, where would I be sleeping tonight? In a country house visiting you? On a plantation, married to Richard? Perhaps. Who knows? But not here. Not Molokaʻi.

We eat a Christmas Eve supper of poi, fish, and breadfruit and then decorate a Norfolk Pine Kepa has placed in the foyer. I sort through the ornaments my grandfather brought back from every port, giving the Chilean straw figures to Mehana to hang. Kepa turns the pounded tin stars over in his hands, studying how they were fashioned. We attend midnight service at Kaumakapili Church.

How Father would hate the long service, the fervor of the prayer. The minister speaks in Hawaiian, his voice so beautiful. I wonder if Father would ever let me marry Ben in this church.

On Christmas Day, after Mehana and Kepa leave to visit her family in Kuliouou, I walk up the Ahsang drive past trees dotted with winter tangerines. A servant appears, bowing his head; he takes my gifts for Ben's sisters and shows me into Khan Ahsang's study, a room I've never seen before. Ahsang stands up; his desk the size of a dining table, empty except for two stacked accounting books, an abacus, and an inkwell. This is more than the holiday visit I anticipated. "The children are with their mother," he says, motioning for me to sit.

I nod, trying to imagine the four of them in one room together. Clara is called for daily by her mother. But Ben keeps his visits to once a week or so, uncomfortable with his mother's silent rejection of outside life, and Emilie is almost never invited to her mother's quarters. "The two of them are either too alike or too different," Ben tells me.

My eyes look past Khan Ahsang to a painted scene of a Chinese village in fall, a path traveling past a well to a tiny group of houses, then up to a mountain stream carrying autumn leaves. Ahsang holds his hand up, and a cook appears with a tea service and preserved plums.

"How is your father's trip progressing?"

"He is enthused in his letters from California," I answer.

"We could use men of his viewpoint in the legislature."

My father will never be allowed by Blackwell and Clarke to sit in the legislature. Ahsang knows that. "I do not know if he would be at ease there," I answer. "He doesn't even go to his plantation much. Too many memories of my mother. We used to go out with her for the harvest and stay in the manager's house."

"A long drive for a child."

"I loved it," I say, remembering the celery green fields, their stalks swaying in the trade winds like children with their arms slung around each other's shoulders. Father broke off a stalk of cane with his boot, peeling a length of it for me with his pocketknife. I chewed each fibrous bite down to the last drop of sugar water. My mother let me feed the cane tops to the horses.

"He came once with your mother when I worked there," Ahsang says, "before you were born. Your mother brought us tangerines for Chinese New Year. A thoughtful gift of good luck for us. I was the only one who spoke English, so I asked her, 'How did you know to bring us these?' The other workers were frightened I was asking a question of the owner's wife. But she was friendly. She told me that her father had gone to Hong Kong to bring back furnishings. That he admired Chinese things."

"We still have those pieces." I play out this image of Lucy Dawson, my mother, handing Khan Ahsang a tangerine. It has been years since I've had a new picture of my mother to paint in my mind. I try to cast Ahsang as one of the sun-beaten field workers, red dust caught in their clothes and hair, fingernails blackened. I can't imagine it. Ahsang passes a bowl of plum candies to me. "How is it you already knew English?" I ask.

"My father was a merchant in Macao. We grew up speaking Cantonese, Mandarin, Portuguese, English. Hawaiian is my fifth language, and the one I find the most beautiful."

I nod, eating a plum and looking again at the painting, envisioning Ahsang in the village, though he would have been in a city, with tiled roofs and crooked alleys like those I've seen in books.

"My son speaks of your good mind," says Ahsang. "Had I known I would have hired a Hawaiian woman like your Mehana instead of an English governess. My girls need more than a dowry for a good match. They need to develop agreeable minds."

Ahsang has started displaying the girls for marriage. He'd invited me for a brief Saturday morning visit to his store on Mauna Kea Street to prove to suitors that his daughters had a friend of missionary lineage. In my sand-colored skirt and white smocked blouse, I drew little interest from the harried shoppers who stopped to watch Clara and Emilie in their multi-hued silks gliding past packed shelves of dried fruit, tonics, baskets, and teas. The sisters posed with their father for a newspaper photographer along the display case in the back showing bolts of silk, carved ivory horns, lacquered ware, gold and silver jewelry. They lifted their skirts over dusty stairs to pay a courtesy visit to Ahsang's money men who count out thousands daily at abacus on their desks. Money collected in rent from shops, warehouses, houses, and fields. Ahsang's properties stretch from Mauna Kea Street across Nu'uanu valley, over the Pali of the Ko'olau Mountains to windward O'ahu where farmers tend watermelon and pigs on the land Ahsang leases them, carting the fruit and carcasses back over the mountain pass to sell at his store. That Saturday Emilie had lingered over the bundled rolls of cash wistfully. She would be a good heir to the business; her love of money has a sense of purity to it. But it is marriage her father wants for her, not the life he's fashioned for Ben.

And some of his world is not meant for a lady. When it was legal, opium was sold in the back of the store, with Ahsang paying for the one license to sell it. Since its ban, opium is smuggled into the Kingdom in granite blocks that serve as ballast for the sailing vessels, and my father says those blocks are split behind Ahsang's store. He says that after the opium is extracted, it disappears into Honolulu's myriad illicit dens and that Ahsang sells the granite blocks to pave Honolulu sidewalks. I doubt Ben's sisters know this chapter of their family history. Then again, the missionary granddaughters I sit across from at baptisms have no clue that some of their fathers are rumored to be reselling opium confiscated at the Harbor back to merchants in California. We are all pleasantly deluded on this island. Otherwise, it does not work to live so closely amongst each other.

"What advice could you share regarding my daughters?" Ahsang asks, a trick of his Ben has warned me of. He asks people advice to learn their thoughts. Flattered to be asked, people forget themselves.

"Your daughters…" I pause. His girls lack Kaiulani's mental vigor. Clara asked me what all the fuss was about "this McKinley person." I started trying to explain the disastrous tariff, but she just burst into giggles and embraced me. "You are surely the picture of your father!" she'd said, dismissing the topic though her gowns are paid for in sugar. And Ben joked that if you asked Emilie about the Bayonet Constitution, she'd grow excited thinking it was a new ship coming to port.

"Your daughters are a great source of adventure," I say, my mouth puckering from the fermented plum.

"Adventure? I can't even get them to go to Maui," he scoffs, with a snap of the wrist to dismiss my praise. My father boasts to all who will listen that I can finish a good book in a single sitting. Ahsang cannot tolerate even the smallest

compliment to his own children. "He's Catholic, but he still believes jealous gods will take us if they hear us praised," Ben confided. "Fate will snatch what he covets."

I think of how I can explain what his daughters are to me. That they are like foreign travel. They dare me to drink murky teas, to climb their father's lychee tree and eat its milky white fruit seated in branches, dropping the red, lizard-skin peels to the ground as if we were creatures of the jungle. They pull me out of my books and Father's politics into their world.

Clara is like the puff of sweet rice cake she sends home with me for Mehana: soft, and so easily torn that I wonder how a man as worldly as Ahsang could have allowed her to become so vulnerable. Emilie is vibrant, urging us to climb a higher branch, play round after round of Mahjong, cross the room to meet an American officer. When I told her my father was hopeful about his mission with the King, she looked at me dryly and said, "I want a husband who can take me to the Palace, whoever happens to be in it." Then she handed me a new pair of yellow shoes sewn with tiny violets, urging me to take them for myself. "All this white and brown you wear. You're invisible, Eliza. Draw a man's eyes to your feet and he'll think about you when you've left his side."

"My girls are very different from what a Chinese father could imagine in my own land," Khan Ahsang interrupts my thoughts. "They don't follow their correct path, like Ben does. My father had no such worries. He only had a son. Has Benjamin told you anything about him?"

I shake my head, wondering why he is taking the time to tell me this.

"He was a kind man, a kinder man than I am, certainly. He was also an opium merchant. One night a group of men dressed as policemen came to our home demanding a shipment they said had not been declared to the authorities. What they really wanted was a large amount of cash my father's partner had tipped them off to. My father had hidden the cash in the top floor bedroom and told them he would surrender it. They stayed downstairs ransacking our home. My father jumped from the third story with the money and was very injured. He crawled to a neighbor for help, paying the man to hide him and find me. By the time this neighbor located me my father was dying. He told me to leave Macao on a ship that evening, one full of laborers set for Hawai'i. We called Hawai'i Tan Heung Shan. *Sandalwood Mountains. He said I could*

harvest sugar; I had no other way of escape. So in a fashion, your father saved my life, as it was his plantation fetching us that night. Though I suspect that was not what he had in mind," Ahsang laughs. "I used half my father's money to buy myself out of my three-year contract with your father. I gave your father's luna the cash myself."

I stumble for what to say next. "Is it safe for you in Macao now?"

"Those men disappeared, but there will always be others like them. Macao became a Portuguese colony three years ago, and I don't like doing business under others' orders. I do business in Guangzhou, which is close. China is a dangerous place. There are bandits and warlords, plagues and uprisings. I balance my ambition for Benjamin with my concern for his safety. Benjamin will be safe as long as I live, but then? Your father probably feels the same."

"I think he believes once I'm married he won't have to worry."

"Yes and no. Your wealth can attract the wrong sort of husband. I know Benjamin's feelings for you are very strong. And I don't blame my son. You carry yourself with the same grace your mother did."

"Thank you," I say, feeling myself taken to the point Ahsang clearly planned.

"I want to speak of this because what my son wants is complicated, and I've come too far to gamble what I've earned for him. So much depends on things that are changing as we speak. If the King gets the agreement for Congress to treat our sugar like an American product, I will speak to your father about a joining of our two families and properties. If the King does not, the American planters here will make Hawai'i a part of the United States by force. They will succeed. It will be the end for me and my son here. We have already lost the vote; we might keep land, but our future would be China."

"Are you asking if I am willing to follow Ben to China? I am."

"No, surely not. If I decide we must go, I will tell him to leave you. And if I do, I need you to understand why I have."

We both drink tea. Is he testing me? He holds his hand out to the teapot, offering me more. I shake my head.

"When I fled Macao aboard your father's ship, I left a wife I loved. She was my first wife, my kit fat *wife. They were not taking women. Even if they were, her feet were bound, and it was not a voyage for a woman who could not walk. It broke my heart."*

Ashang's eyes drift away as he tells me this. I know from Ben that his father still visits his kit fat *wife once a year. She has born him four children.*

"The choice none of us can afford is indiscretion, Eliza. It will ruin the prospects for both you and my daughters. And even if the King gets the agreement, your father may decline our offer."

"I think my father will agree to a marriage," I say, hoping Ahsang hasn't heard the talk of Richard Irvin.

Ahsang laughs. "Then his opinion of me must have changed. When I worked for your father he paid German and Portuguese workers more than the Chinese. They made five dollars a month. We made three, but we cut more cane. So much more. I came to the luna the first day, wanting to buy out my contract. He wouldn't let me for six full months, and every day was fourteen hours of misery. That visit of your family's, it was the first time I'd seen your father. I came to him, right in front of the luna, telling him I had the money to pay my debt in full. The workers waited to see me beaten. But your father told the luna, 'If he has the funds, there's no use keeping him here. He'll kill you in your sleep if you force him to stay.' Today I don't pay my Japanese laborers much more myself, and I know enough now to understand your father was quite decent. But I don't think he has ever imagined you marrying my son."

You don't understand my father, I think. He has never looked down at you. He is jealous of you. "I tell you, there isn't a haole man in this Kingdom who wouldn't like to see just one thing he touches fail," my father said the afternoon his luna convinced him to adopt Ahsang's latest innovation, using sugarcane pith as fuel instead of imported coal, boosting profits wildly. When the missionary legislature passed a law banning business ledgers from being written in Cantonese, Father was livid. "The Chinese are half the reason we have the wealth we do!"

"Your wealth is very respected by my father," I say simply. "And your friendship with the King is what would be most prized in my marriage to your son."

Ahsang looks away to hide that he is pleased. "I support my son's desire for you if it makes him more successful. My son comes first. My daughters second. My business third."

"I appreciate your honesty, sir. But I am not exactly encouraged."

"You should be very encouraged," Ahsang counters. "A week ago I saw only one course for Benjamin. I'm now considering another. But only if your father and the King come home with the agreement they seek. Hawai'i has to stay in the King's hands."

We hear his daughters in the hall. Ahsang brings a celadon green shawl out from a drawer. It is exquisitely embroidered, tied with Christmas ribbon and a card in Clara's handwriting that says "Eliza."

Ben's father stands. "In all endeavors, Eliza, count half on friendship and half on money."

4

The butter house is a simple shed next to the barn where the Holsteins are milked. Working at the creamery with Keala is one of my little pleasures at this camp. It is quiet like a chapel, with sunshine pouring through the wood slats. We put out the pans of milk for the cream to set, and then return the next morning to skim. I help at the churn, knowing it's done when I hear the butter clumping on the sides. I slather what I've made that morning on every inch of what I eat that night.

Today we work in silence and are startled when Keala's husband, Charlie, comes in and trips over a chair, knocking a pan over. After he has apologized and left the creamery, Keala confides that her husband is, for the most part, blind.

"The doctor doesn't know?" I ask, surprised.

"The doctor doesn't *tell*," answers Keala. "Nothing can be done for it. Most days he gets through just fine and not a soul notices, but it worsens by the month. It began after our daughter left us. She married a man who helped drive your husband's cattle. They delivered to ships that transported to O'ahu. Some cattle went missing; some of the hands had been stealing. Your husband brought charges against every man. They were all sent to prison on O'ahu. Their women and children following to be near them."

“What an awful story,” I say. Benjamin once told me he’d seen Hawaiian women selling themselves near the prison. “You didn’t want to move to O‘ahu, too?” I ask. “To be near her?”

“Charlie and I don’t want to be that old Hawaiian couple in Honolulu, drinking our whisky from tin cups with no land to live on,” she says, tossing her hands up in the air. “I wouldn’t even know where to find my daughter now. She is lost. Along with Hina and Ikaika’s mother. She followed their father and look at those poor children now. One a leper at Kalaupapa and the other…”

I look down at the table.

When August arrives the heat starts to dig in. Abram rounds up the cattle slated for sale on O‘ahu. The drive starts at dawn. Every man at camp is needed to take the Longhorns down and now the camp is only women and children.

We make a breakfast of pancakes with guavas that the children collect. I listen to stories told in Hawaiian, and after breakfast each woman grabs bits of mending. I am hemming Abram’s pants to fit me. Hina crouches near Keala to watch her handiwork. She starts picking up pinches of dirt and eating them.

“How are you feeling?” a woman asks.

She closes her eyes and grimaces and then opens them to look straight at me with her hand on the great moon of her belly, and I brace myself for what she will say. With the other women Hina speaks Hawaiian. With me, she chooses the roughest of pidgin English. When others on the ranch use it, it sounds playful. “Try for go,” they tell me when they invite me to a game of Portuguese horseshoes. Hina’s pidgin is an assault, a way of telling me how much she hates me being here.

“We should all go to the ocean sometime,” I say, hoping to buffer her blow.

"Ikaika by da ocean now," Hina says. She starts to cry. It's unexpected, and the women start fussing around her. "I like Ikaika come back," she sobs. "I like him be with me."

I sit outside this cluster of grief, hesitant to speak further. "I wish I could bring him back, Hina," I say at last. "But they would take him from us again, no matter what. And you and your baby might get the *ma'i Pākē*, too. Ikaika would not want that."

Hina crosses her arms around her belly. "He told me you was good to him. He told me you was nice."

Her beauty reasserts itself in her grief, and I see the lovely wisp of Ka'iulani again. My K, just after her mother died. I'd stayed with her for days. The two of us reading silently, side by side, because talking hurt too much. She'd been Hina's age exactly then. Comfort Hina, I tell myself. Be kind.

"Hina, would you like to work with us making the butter? It's a good thing to have your hands full when you're sad." I hear echoes of missionary zeal in my voice, but I have nothing else to offer her.

She comes that afternoon as I pour milk out into the pans. "We gon make ice cream?" she asks. "I nevah had dat. Mr. Abram wen told me was da best." She licks her lips all the way round, slowly, unmistakably lustfully. I turn away.

"I haven't the ice to manage that now," I tell her over my shoulder. "But perhaps I could arrange it. I was once at a birthday party where they had an ice cream cart, so that the guests could choose whichever flavors they liked. Strawberry. Chocolate."

Kaiulani's birthday lū'au. The King chanted fifteen generations of his niece's genealogy before hundreds of guests sitting at low tables on lauhala mats under the open sky at 'Āinahau. Father had beamed at me, beside himself at the sight of his daughter sitting beside Princess Ka'iulani under the kāhili feathers being waved by two Hawaiian women to mark her royal status.

"One day," the King said, his eyes filled with tears, "after my sisters have passed, this child will have my throne." He put his hands to the side of K's face. "She is the sole heir and blessing this generation has produced. The only hope that our line will continue." The King took the green maile lei from his shoulders and put it over Kaiulani's small frame. We all rose to applaud our King.

"You was real rich, yeah?" Hina asks. "That's why Mr. Abram marry you and nevah marry me. Plus you haole."

My heart goes still. I move the pans of milk and cover them with the same pieces of cloth I used and washed out the day before. "You're too young to marry, Hina," I say, taking excessive care in tucking each bit of cloth round the pan corners.

"I like be *hāpai*," says Hina. "I like Mr. Abram plenty!" She jumps up in her enthusiasm and knocks the table, sending the cream splashing up against the cloth. She flinches, expecting my temper, but I simply blot it with my apron and this seems to embolden her. "I like get married to one haole," she says quietly. "I like have someplace bettah for live."

I think of what my life was like at Hina's age. Riding in a tortoiseshell carriage with Kaiulani's father, Andrew Cleghorn, from St. Andrew's Cathedral to 'Iolani Palace. The King allowing us one sip each of his champagne as he taught us cards around the koa table he kept his state papers on. Days listening to Robert Louis Stevenson recite poetry softly in his Scottish brogue under the banyan. And here is Hina, barefoot in a dirty shed, pregnant and dreaming that the master who uses her for his own pleasure might love her.

"I like marry Mr. Abram if you was nice and told him he could," she says in a low voice. "Den I could be boss lady here, and I let you be da big boss lady over me."

Many a haole man has taken a Hawaiian woman as a wife, but Hina has neither the land nor the cunning to hold Abram's ambition. I know Abram will never marry her, even after I am long gone and forgotten from this place. "After we have the babies, I'll see what I can do," I placate her. "Abram will be happy because you have his baby. We can talk to him then, all right?"

How she glows when I tell her this. She does a little dance in her threadbare *mu'u mu'u*, the loose gown Mehana wears in rainbow colors, but Hina's is stained a muddled grey. When she stops, there is a thick sheen of sweat on her face, which in the slanted light of the afternoon makes her look as if she has been glazed in sugar icing.

There's a letter from Father. I slip the shoes off my swelling feet and lie across the bed to read his words. The paper is finer than anything I've touched for months. I can imagine him in his study, the atlas askew on the desk. I picture myself back there at this exact time next year, a baby napping over Mehana's shoulder.

Dearest Eliza,

I hope this letter finds you in good health. I have received your requests and am arranging a shipment to the ranch that should ensure you of comfortable yet appropriate attire as well as reading materials for the many souls you seem to have adopted. I am not surprised. You have always found it in you to see the good in all.

There has been fine weather here. I hope Moloka'i has enjoyed the same.

Last weekend I traveled out to the Stedmans' estate in Waimanalo to speak to the Queen on several pressing matters. Major parties in town, men you yourself have grown up with and sat next to at royal celebrations, are now moving swiftly and conclusively against the monarchy. It is only a matter of time before the family is overturned. I spoke to her of such, but I fear she does not truly understand the level of deceit and rebellion that surround her in the highest circles.

During my visit I enjoyed a marvelous view clear across the channel to Moloka'i. I thought to myself, is Eliza in that patch of green? If so, I imagined you acclimating yourself to your new surroundings and making the best of it for, Eliza, it has become increasingly clear to me it was a necessary step. There was some speculation here as to the suddenness of events. Those same troublemakers, Blackwell, Clarke, how they love to needle me with their innuendo. But Irvin has kept his vow of silence, and it has calmed down. I am assured by him that all is in order. I let it be known at the gathering that you and Abram have told me I'm to be a grandfather and that I am thrilled, so that people might become used to the idea.

You should know that I saw Emilie over the weekend at the Hutchinsons. She has informed me that Clara has gone to Rome to pursue religious studies.

I feel a burst of improbable joy at this. Clara in Rome. What a clever girl.

Emilie also informed me Benjamin is expecting a child with his wife. I hope this news does not bring you too much heartache. Eliza, nothing could have been done.

The letter continues with news of Honolulu, but I understand none of it. I had imagined Ben's marriage might be like mine. A business arrangement. A shipping container within which he sat trapped, missing me in the cage that contained him. But Ben's wife was a real wife. She expected his child while I wiped red dirt from my face in this miserable place where my only joys have been a doomed boy and butter.

Grey clouds transform the afternoon to evening. I walk without shoes into what becomes the heaviest downpour I've ever seen. Weeks' worth of heat bursts into water, and I begin to sob. I feel the suction of mud on my bare feet, the violent pelting of rain on my face and hair. Water pastes the clothing to my body, but I do not care. I lost my modesty with Ben, and the appearance of it is only a sham now. I remember the sound of surf at the bungalow, the smell of a chocolate orchid trapped in the room. For an insane moment I think of going to the top of the path that leads to the leper camp and jumping. I hold my arms around my belly and wonder if I'm going mad to fantasize such a vision. "Walk back inside," I tell myself.

I'm almost to the cabin when the men return from the cattle drive.

And there is Hina, chasing after Abram. He does not get off of his horse to walk with her, does not even acknowledge her. She is a loyal dog, loving her master no matter what he does to her, and I cannot claim to be any wiser.

K,

I have decided if it is a girl, I will name her Lucy, for my mother. A boy will be Samuel, with Ikaika as his middle name. I am hoping the Hawaiian meaning of strength will be given to this baby. He may need it.

I wonder if you've heard I'm married, heard I'm pregnant. If you've written me. I know Father will not forward your letters, not take the risk I will answer them truthfully.

I'll need to tell you one day about what I did. Do you follow every rule in England? I suspect you do. Your role in life requires greater discipline than I've shown. I wonder if you will be ashamed of me. You would never have done it, I know. I never would have thought I could either.

We met on Nu'uanu Road, his horses pacing and eager. It was a full moon.

"They're happy not to be tethered to a carriage tonight," Ben said, kissing me in the middle of the deserted street. We hadn't seen each other for a week.

"It felt like your father was never going to let us see each other again," I said as he boosted me into the saddle.

"He likes to remind me he controls things. That's a Chinese father for you. Are haole fathers any different?"

"Probably not with their sons. I haven't had a letter from California since Christmas."

"Nothing about the agreement?" Ben casts his eyes away as he puts my boot into the stirrup. "My father will take us back to Macao if the King doesn't solve this."

"Your father is a plantation owner, he'll be running things, just like the others. There'd be no need to go," I say.

"Eliza, there won't be room at the table for my father if they're in charge. He's right about that."

"But couldn't you stay? The planters don't think of you as Chinese."

"But I am," he says, kissing my hand, "half, anyway. Don't look so glum. They'll get the agreement. Who can deny the King?"

The smell of mountains changed to ocean salt as we rode down the valley onto King Street. We picked up our pace at the sight of two dozen riders in front of the coral wall of the Palace. The men, Honolulu dandies who liked to race through midnight streets, tipped their hats to me, registering that I'd come with Ben. A few Hawaiian girls were with them, their hair flowing down their backs, loose, flowered dresses pooling around their thighs, legs bare against their horses.

"My sisters are on Maui, so I've been charged with escorting their lovely friend, Eliza," Ben said. One of the girls leaned over to feel the ruffle on the sleeve of my silver-grey silk dress. "Nohea,*" she said. Beautiful. They take in every detail of me.*

I was relieved when the girls gave their horses swift starts with their heels. Ben and I watched them race off, then continued down King Street until we'd cleared the tram tracks. We cantered past coal storage buildings and closed shops before turning up Fort Street past the town's old mansions. My grandfather Hezekiah's house stood there, sad in its state of disrepair under the hands of an absent California owner. Paint peeled around the viewing platform Grandfather and I had loved so well, the platform where my father had first seen my mother staring out at the sea.

I lingered. "That platform," I said, raising my hand. My crop raked over the horse's mane, accidentally snapping one of its ears. The horse jerked and bolted, and we careened away, my spooked horse running off the road onto a rough trail cut up toward the empty volcanic crater of Punchbowl. Snarls of lantana caught my dress, shredding the skirt. I began slipping from the saddle, one foot caught through a stirrup. I'm going to be dragged, I realized.

"Hold on!" I heard Ben yelling.

"I can't!" I screamed, the mane slipping out of my fingers as his horse caught up to mine, and he reached out, pulling me back up and into the saddle. Ben had my reins and as he made low hushing sounds, the fight went right out of my horse. Everything slowed and then came to a halt. He dismounted and brought me down. I leaned against him, shaking.

"Eliza, my God." He had both arms around me, motionless.

"I don't want to go back so all those people can stare at me," I said, like a little girl. I was shaking. "And I don't want to go home. Take me to the bungalow. Please."

"I'd say that was playing with fire," Ben said, his voice unsteady.

"We can ride back home when it's still dark and no one will know. Please, Ben." I put my hand to the side of his cheek. He kissed the palm of my hand through my riding glove. We set off together. Honolulu's dusty clapboard storefronts, lumber yards, and coal sheds gradually became Waikīkī's rice paddies and groves of monkey pod trees rattling in the wind. The few remaining grass shacks built in the ancient style looked furry in the moonlight.

We reached the Ahsangs' bungalow just past midnight. I waited inside while Benjamin tied up the horses. Even shuttered, the bungalow was lovely. Massive carved day beds draped in green and cream silks encircled an old opium table topped with celadon pots full of star-shaped orchids that smelled of chocolate. Khan Ahsang purchased the land from the King, intending to make it the family's home. But Hannah hated the heat of Waikīkī, and

Ahsang had instead built this simple beach bungalow, leaving it in the care of his son.

I dropped my gloves on the table and pressed my ear to the louvered doors to listen to the sea. It was here that I first fell in love with Benjamin. Day after day, I sat with his sisters beneath the breadfruit tree watching Ben paddle his koa surfboard through the surf. I studied him as he tilted his body under the waves. When Clara and Emilie took their midday naps, I waited for our aged Chinese chaperone to nod off and then slipped back out. Under the sound of pounding waves I too drifted off, waking with Benjamin standing over me, the tree's shadows falling across my skin like the pattern of a quilt.

He grabbed a blanket from the bed and led me outside. The beach was electrified: the sand a rumpled blanket of reflected light and palm shadows, its ocean a hundred miles of melted silver foil. We sat underneath the thatched outrigger shack.

"I remember last summer watching you surf, and wondering what it would be like to be far out in the water like that," I said. "Once we're grown, ladies are never really allowed to swim. I can't remember the last time I was in the ocean. Probably with Ka'iulani before she was sent off to England."

That feeling of ocean, Ka'iulani and I sinking down together, pressing our palms together under the water and kicking up only when the governess's shouts became frantic. I remembered floating in the sea as the feeling of a full and peaceful heart.

"There's no one here now. Can you swim in whatever you have under this?" Benjamin said, lifting a corner of my shredded skirt off the blanket. "I won't peek before you're safely in the water."

I looked down the empty beach. A light flickered in the Bryans' bungalow far away. "You don't think anyone can see?"

"I could have you back inside the house before anyone even came close." He helped me stand and raised the blanket between us to let me change. "My sisters don't care for the ocean," he said through the fabric. "When we're married, we can go night swimming for excitement rather than you giving me the scare of my life galloping around Punchbowl."

"I never claimed I was a perfect rider," I said, fiddling to undo the hooks and eyes down the back of my dress.

"What were you were pointing to? Before the horse bolted?"

"My grandfather's house. Where my father first saw my mother. She'd sit watching for her father's ship. My father worked in a lumberyard nearby, and he walked past every day, waiting for her to notice him."

"Your father in a lumberyard?"

"For years. He wanted to buy land. It took him a year alone to get the Captain's blessing for my mother's hand. He spent a lot of time walking past that platform." I looked at the tiny lilies of the valley embroidered onto the bodice of my petticoat. "I think I'll keep the rest on," I said.

Ben wrapped the blanket around me, picking me up and carrying me to the ocean. He unraveled the sheet by walking a circle around me until I was free and standing in the night. He looked at me in my petticoat, the moonlight so bright I felt I was glowing. He tossed the blanket on the sand and tilted his head back as if needing air. "If our children ride by our houses, side by side, one day," he said. "They won't be very impressed by how far I went to find you."

I put my ear against his heart. "They'll know how far it was."

"I could have lost you tonight," Ben said in a pained voice. I felt the vibrations of it through his chest. I kissed his neck, his scar. His hands held my wrists. "I'm breaking my own rules," he said. I felt fearless, pulling him down onto the blanket, on top of me, and the momentum changed.

His movements quickened, his fingers undid the buttons of my skirt, and I panicked. This was not allowed; the scandal was too much. I felt my words and emotions stall. I shivered, and he covered me with his whole body, pressing down on me, and in a burst there is a brief pain and then something else: the weight of him, the smell of sea salt and leather, the feeling of how much he wanted me: his chest against mine, with skin so smooth, so golden colored.

"Are you alright?" he asked, holding me to his chest, after. He held me protectively, almost possessively. He was quiet. Too quiet.

"Do you think poorly of what we've done?" I asked, feeling tears coming quickly.

"No," he answered, his hand squeezing mine. "I'm just thinking about how much depends on things that are out of our control."

"I think they're in our control now," I said, willing it to be true. "Don't worry," I teased, kissing his shoulder, "It's too late for any man but you."

"You're certainly more your mother's whaling stock than a Dawson," he said, looping a section of my hair around his finger and swirling it, wonder in his eyes. "There's no missionary in you."

"Oh, there's some," I said. If Father knew where I was, what I had done. He was sitting with the King in California, thinking his daughter was about to be tied to Richard Irvin, to a family like ours. That was impossible now. Perhaps that's what I'd wanted. "Let's really go swimming."

He picked me up and dropped me playfully into the sea, knowing I wouldn't protest on a beach lined with bungalows. I let myself drift in the water, weightless, hair floating around my face. My whole body lifted and opened. His hands reached me underwater to pull me up. I blotted the salt water from my eyes and pushed the hair from my face. Clouds covered the moon, and the sea darkened around us. I looked at the sky and traced the constellation Scorpio. Mehana called it Māui's fishhook for the handsome demi-god who pulled these islands up from the sea, his instrument embedded forever in the sky. I unclasped my hands to point.

"Look," Ben said, his lips brushing my neck. "Phosphorescence."

All around us, blue-green flakes drifted like a peacock's gown.

5

Hina's labor begins late afternoon in the creamery.

"I hurt," she says, sitting down on a bench and clutching her sides dramatically. I roll my eyes and Keala asks, "Would you like to go outside, Hina? Have you had enough work today?" We are used to her claiming headaches when she's tired of being indoors.

"I like sit here," she says, sweat dribbling down her face. The creamery is filled with so much light and dust that the air looks smoky. We've already thrown out one batch of cream because a layer of rust-colored particles settled on the pan the minute we placed it on the table. I watch Hina sweat, thinking she might, in fact, be feverish when her mouth opens wide as if to yawn, and she lets out a scream.

Keala and I each take an arm and lead her out of the creamery and across the grass toward my cabin, which is closest. Hina screams again and drops to the ground, refusing to rise no matter how many times we promise her the comfort of a bed. Finally, we manage to drag her to my room. "I no like be here. Your stupid house," she mutters, thrashing on the mattress.

"Stay here with her. I have medicine," Keala says, darting out the door as I stand frozen, unsure what to do next. I put a hand on her arm to comfort her.

"Stay away from me!" she screams, and I move to the window while she moans and writhes.

Keala returns with a bowl in hand and goes quickly over to the sink. "Take this cloth and put it to her forehead, give her some comfort," she says reprovingly. I do as she says; Keala joins us with terrible looking brown water that she strains through a piece of coconut bark.

"You need to drink this, Hina," she says soothingly. "It's going to help you," she promises, lifting it to her lips. Hina makes as if to spit it out, but Keala's expression stops her.

"Mahalo," says Hina obediently, thankful for someone to mother her. I watch as Hina lets Keala stroke her head and whisper to her. I offer my hand too, and there's peace between us.

"You'll feel better now," Keala says. "There's sap from the hau tree in there. It helps the baby come. And Hina, hau is a special tree to you. The goddess Hina—her sister changed into a hau tree."

Hina's eyes are drooping; she stares numbly at Keala, who continues speaking in a calming tone. "Haumea is the goddess who watches over childbirth, so she's in this room watching over you, and in this water you drink." Keala gives her another swallow. "You remember which tree hau is, Hina?" she asks.

Hina shakes her head.

"It's the one with the yellow flowers in the morning, orange in the afternoon, and red at night. It's like our lives. Remember Auntie told that story?"

Hina nods.

"And it's such a sacred tree, the chiefs had to give permission to cut it. And here you are drinking it because today is the day for you and your child."

Hina gasps in pain, and Keala gives her more.

"There are lehua blossoms crushed in here. And there's a story about those for you, too. Once the goddess Hina took the form of an ʻōhiʻa tree to watch over a child. Hina is a protector of women and babies."

Whatever truths lie in Keala's words, they do the trick. Other than a low groan, Hina works through the rest of her labor bravely, silently. It falls dark, and I begin lighting the lamps, thankful to move away from the bed when the metallic odor of blood becomes strong.

The temperature has dropped, and a draft comes up between the floorboards. Keala and I wrap ourselves in every blanket I own, but Hina throws off any covering we put on her. She can't stand the feel of her clothes and asks Keala to strip her. She lies naked, sweating and squeezing Keala's hand. There is a knock on the door, and I answer to find Abram, still covered in dirt from the fields.

"She's close," I say, refusing to look at him. I look instead at the moon, low and orange, encircled with a red ring. Hina lets out a great moan.

"Should I get Dr. Webster?" he asks. His Southern accent sounds stronger, rougher, as if a mask has slipped.

"Keala is managing nicely. It's up to you," I reply.

He shuffles his feet. "Right. I'll see to the animals. They're going into fits themselves, knocking against their pens. It's the moon making them all crazy, I suppose."

It is grotesque to watch a child birth a child. I watch with my fist to my mouth as the baby's head crowns, wondering how Hina can stand it. But with just one final groan, she bears a little boy.

"Give me him! Give me, give me!" she cries, not letting Keala clean him before she has him in her arms. She looks down on him, beaming. "He look plenty haole," she says.

"But good Hawaiian hair," says Keala, running her fingers through the child's wet curls.

There is a knock and in comes Abram, his face registering distaste at the stagnant, bloody smell of the room. He walks to the bed and picks the child up, taking him to the window and unwrapping the old towel to inspect his son. Keala gathers herself quickly and leaves my cabin for her own. I prepare to follow her and let this strange new family be alone.

"See she gets something, some money," he says to me as I reach the door.

"He's a lovely boy, Abram."

"He'll do fine," he answers. "We can adopt him as our own."

I want to slap him for saying this as if I knew about it. Hina, who lies with matted hair on the bed, abandoned, looks at me with such hate. "He's got a mother," I answer loudly, for her benefit.

"Fair enough," he says, lifting his free hand up as if all he wants is for everyone to be happy.

I decide against intruding on Keala and Charlie, and with no place else to go, I return to the creamery. I light a lamp to clean up the chaotic scene we left behind. A pan of cream that was knocked over is now curdled and sour on the ground. Using the blanket still around my shoulders as a cover and lying on surplus bags of rice stored in a corner I fall asleep.

Abram rides around on his horse the next day, holding the tiny boy and calling out for others to admire the baby, more genial than he's ever been. He announces he will build a bigger schoolhouse in his son's honor, so that all the children of the ranch can attend the missionary school together in the mornings, rather than being split into groups as they are now. And the children can work the afternoons if their parents want the wage. This is greeted with disbelief and thanks.

He makes the workers laugh by moving the baby's arms and using a high voice to pretend the infant is speaking. Afterwards he surprises the ranch by bringing in squid, fish, and even slipper lobster from three or four fishermen whom he allows to camp out for the night. Everyone is served beer, and most get drunk. Abram asks the cowhands to sing around the fire and slaps his thighs along with the tunes. He introduces the baby all around, saying he's named his child Lee.

Abram exudes such joy I actually ask, “Named for your father? Or General Lee?”

“The name is for the man who stepped in to be my father,” Abram says. Never in these months have I heard a word about his past.

“My father told my mother she had *slave* blood.”

When he says slave, he pulls the word out as far as it will go, to make a joke of it. Now I can imagine a bit of something other than European about his face. It gives it whatever handsomeness I thought it had before I knew him better.

“He headed north and didn’t take us with him.” Abram looks off into the dark and says nothing more. He’s holding Lee in one arm like a puppy. Someone’s started a new tune.

“And this man, Lee?” I ask over the music and the shouting.

“I just told you,” he snaps. It feels like a slap.

“You have to watch out for his neck,” I say.

Abram looks apologetic and cradles the baby into him.

“Keala wouldn’t take any money,” I say. “You might give Charlie a day or two off. They’ve got some family they could visit.”

“Why should I do that?”

“Because she made all the difference. Hina was screaming like the end was coming, and Keala mixed up a special tonic and it went very easily after that,” I shout, unsure if he can hear over the singing.

“So she does some voodoo, and I’m supposed to lose one of my best hands?”

“It’s up to you, Abram.” I make to walk away.

“Fine.” He dramatically deflates as he says this, as if in defeat. Is he playing with me? Or is this some stage of his drinking? “Tell Keala they can visit their family. And I want you to adopt Lee. If I’m going to support your child, you can support mine.”

“Abram, that would kill Hina—”

“It’s her people who are always doing this *hānai* thing.”

I'm surprised he knows the term. *Hānai*, giving one's child without termination of the parents' rights. Mehana had been hānai'd to a childless aunt. "Hānai is when the parents have many children and someone they love is childless," I say. The King's sister, Lili'uokalani, had been hānai'd to a higher ranking chief's family because it was an honor. "Or if it is a chief's family, and so it's an honor—"

"Well, see. You'd be the chief in this equation."

I hold my tongue. This is not the hour to convince Abram what he proposes is a cruel theft. Lee begins to cry, turning his head in search of food. "Let me take him back. He's hungry," I say.

"When she's done nursing, that would be the right time," says Abram, giving me Lee. "I'll have the house finished then, this ranch will be paid for and all mine, and its heir will live there with you," he sweeps his hand over my belly, "and whatever else comes of this. My boy'll grow up with a mother who has an education and can turn him into a gentleman, fit for a landowner. Hina can still play with him. She can start going to school. She needs it. How can she not understand that? Natives never understand things, no matter how often you explain. They're a bit short of the whole package."

You certainly find something in them appealing, I think.

Abram turns back to the music. I carry Lee to my cabin, my own baby making slow, languorous movements from one side of my body to the other. I feel hiccups against the right side of my belly. Abram is a fraud; I doubt his family ever had a plantation, or a glamorous history. His gentleman's accent drops when he's angry—or drunk—into something with a much rougher story behind it.

Hina is still in my cabin. I will be sleeping with her tonight. Keala had Charlie fetch a cot from the storage shed after finding me asleep on the creamery floor.

She does not look well. Her coloring is greenish and pale. "You gonna take dis baby?" she demands, her eyes burning.

"No, Hina." I say, putting Lee to her breast. He begins to nurse, and Hina cries. I stroke her hair but she moves her head and keeps her eyes on the wall, so I stop.

"He jus' like da baby now, not me," says Hina, her face softening, and there it is again – my Ka'iulani in this vulnerable small face.

For a moment I stand in two places at once: in the red dirt of a Moloka'i cabin, and with the Princess as we watched her mother taken away by catafalque to lie in state at the Palace. I watch Hina cry.

"You nevah care. You so greedy. You take my house. Ikaika. You gonna take dis baby."

"I don't want your baby," I reassure her. "All I want is sleep," I say. But I do not sleep that night. I spend it rocking and changing Hina's baby, an uneasy truce filling the cabin.

K,

The girl who looks a bit like you here had her baby today. It is all very complicated. I'm tempted to write you a proper letter and mail it to seek your advice. But somehow over time it has become so difficult to write what I would like to say in person. It feels as if I'm trying to talk to you underwater. Time is the liquid around our words, delaying and warping their meaning.

I wrote you condolences when your uncle died, but not the truth of it. I couldn't find how to tell you that his death was the end of a dream for me. It was the beginning of my path here. When we learned he had died, the newspapers said that the torch that burns at midday has been quenched. That is as

> *truthful a phrase as I can think of to describe what Hawai'i felt like the day his ship sailed back to us.*

The day was bright and windless, the ocean flat. It felt odd to walk the beach without the sound of waves. Only a group of children scampering ahead of us provided sounds of life.

"Eliza, do you think your father will bring back anything lovely from San Francisco?" Emilie asked me.

"Only four more days until I can tell you," I said, my eyes turned from Ben's. We were still a secret to his sisters. Ben was afraid that if we told them then the whole city would know too. "Your father will be angry that I didn't come to him, tell him first. He's nearly home, Eliza."

It was true; the city was gearing up for the King's return. The dates of his journey home had been printed in the paper.

"It will be good to have the King back," said Emilie. "It's been—"

"The King! The King!" we heard the children ahead of us scream. "Ka mō'ī! Ka mō'ī!" they repeated in Hawaiian.

Clara looked at Ben in confusion. "Did they hear us mention the King?"

"They've probably just been told he's expected," Emilie suggested, fanning herself. The smell of sandalwood settled over me as I turned toward the bungalow to follow the children's eyes back to Diamond Head. I saw what had made the children scream: the King's ship rounding, its American and Hawaiian flags flying low.

"It's the Charleston,*" Ben said slowly.*

"With its flags at half-mast," I said to him.

"Why scare everyone?" asked Emilie, irritated. "It makes you think the King is dead."

"It may well be..." I wasn't able to say it.

Clara began to cry. "Would they lower the flags for anyone else?"

"I don't know," said Ben, looking numb. "We should get to the harbor."

We hailed a carriage; our driver was a small man who seemed to shrink as Emilie's commands sharpened. "Get through the crowds. Keep going," she snapped. The roads became impossible to pass once we entered town. Word had spread of the lowered flags.

"It will be easier to walk from here," Ben declared at the Palace. He led us down King Street, navigating the uneven wooden planks that passed for sidewalks on some stretches. Shopkeepers at every corner pulled down bunting and banners that said, "Aloha Ka Mō'ī" and "Welcome the King" as they rushed to close their stores.

At the harbor I reached out to touch the victory arch, its gilt, black, and red stripes built in the hopes the King would announce he had struck a deal for his kingdom and over-turned the McKinley Act. I watched people praying, embracing, and I added my own prayer. Please let them have reached an agreement before he died so Ben will stay.

The most desperate of Honolulu poured down the street at this point. Men from the pig farms up the valley with no shirts or shoes. Like night marchers they moved with their eyes straight ahead, unconcerned with the earthly foibles of the living. I listened to them mumbling in disbelief, "Our King is dead."

"Bring a hearse," Ahsang shouted as we arrived at the harbor. "Take that down," he commanded a stunned palace guard, pointing to a banner stretched between two light poles at the water's edge. "Have the others go through the streets and make sure all of the banners are down. If this report is false, we can raise them again."

"It's not false," Emilie said, clutching her father's arm. "We were at the bungalow when the ship came around Diamond—"

"Stop! I've heard enough," Ahsang said. I'd never seen him angry before. "You wouldn't know what to look for," he told his daughter.

Emilie walked away toward the water, fanning her face. I'd moved to go toward her when Ben, under cover of the crowd, squeezed my waist in warning. He was right. She would always associate me with her moment of embarrassment. My father, lacking a son, always told me how smart I was. How clever. But mine was only book smarts. Emilie possessed more of her father's worldly sharpness than anyone here, but Ahsang wanted that in Ben, not her. He wanted Emilie to cry quietly at her brother's side as Clara did. Instead she stood tearless, purposely bored looking. Emilie would have made a formidable man, but she was becoming an angry woman.

"It's true, Father," Ben said so kindly I couldn't blame his father for wanting to hear the news from him. "The ship's appearance left no doubt."

Ahsang allowed himself just one moment. He closed his eyes, accepting the end of the King, his protector in what had been the Kingdom of the Sandalwood Mountains. Then, with the rest of us, he watched as the ship came into view. In the crowd's silence, I could hear chickens and dogs from homes blocks away. The half-mast flags became clear, then in what seemed mere seconds it was close enough that I could see my father next to the ship's admiral on the longboat behind the casket. Great screams and moans rose up. Young men left and returned with hardwood scraps to set alight. Kalākaua's royal house used the torch burning at midday as their royal symbol. At the sight of the sacred emblem the crowd fell silent again.

When Father came ashore he embraced me, but it was Ahsang he spoke to.

"Happened nine days ago. He'd been so tired; tremendous pain in his back. We'd decided to come home, sent word, and then...he fell in and out of consciousness. We kept him comfortable at the Palace Hotel, and called in every doctor they recommended. By two that morning he was gone. The San Francisco papers reported it the same day."

"The red fish," I said to my father. 'Aweoweo foretell a royal death. There was no other explanation.

"The doctors said it was Bright's disease," Father explained, wearily. "The fervor he lived his days and nights with, the constant battling all around him. It was too much. He burnt the candle at both ends."

"The agreement?" asked Ahsang. The Charleston*'s band began a dirge.*

"None," answered my father, removing his hat as American Bluejackets from the Charleston *placed the casket, silver-trimmed and covered in black crepe, on the hearse. The procession moved toward the Palace and guns began to boom. I felt every shot in my chest.*

When the gunshots ended, everyone started to move toward the Palace. It was time to console the King's grieving widow, bow to the new Queen, his sister, Lili'uokalani. Yet my father stood still, his eyes avoiding the others.

"Are we not going, Father?" I asked, my voice breaking. I need you to be there, I thought. I need something to change so Ahsang will stay.

Ahsang looked at my father, and when Father said nothing, he moved away, saying, "Benjamin, come." I kept my eyes on the ground, ashamed.

"Let us know if you need anything," Ben said, shaking my father's hand and tipping his hat to me.

"Thank you," Father answered. "I can't take any more grief today. I've lived it, and I will pay my respects tomorrow. I need to steady myself."

He needs a drink, I thought. Clara and Emilie embraced me before joining their father to follow the hearse. Ben shot me a quick look of concern as he left.

"I didn't bring the carriage. And not even the barouche drivers are working today," I said, tears streaming down my face. Father handed me his handkerchief as we started the first steps of the slow walk up Nu'uanu Avenue.

"The Princess already knows she's now the heir to the throne," Father said. "They've got the transatlantic cable to London, so she knew by the next day," continued Father. "Poor Hawai'i, to learn by a half-flown flag. The Princess sent a cable asking for a wreath to be put on the casket. The wreath faded at sea, but I saved her note to give to the Queen."

I read my K's printed message, Aloha me ka paumake. *My love is with the one who is done with dying.*

"He was so terribly sad at the end," Father said as he stared at a group of white men crowding together on a sidewalk to read something in a newspaper. "As if he knew the end was coming. For everything."

"You'd think he birthed the baby," Keala says the following morning in the butter house. She looks at me and asks, "What do you think he's going to do when your time comes?"

I continue to pour the cream out, knowing I am caught. Keala is asking what everyone at the camp must wonder. "My baby will not please him so well, Keala."

"Doesn't matter what he likes," she answers. "Riding around on his horse with that baby, so high and proud. Buying everyone off with your money. It's *your* money, isn't it?"

I nod, and she shakes her head.

"He's taken up with another *wahine* down the road again," she says bitterly. "Hina's done, all *pau* for him. That rice he kept in here? The bags you slept on? The ones he told people they could not touch or they would get fired? He loaded it up last night and took it down there to that girl's brother, Lopaki."

Lopaki is the cowhand I saw the day I arrived at camp, riding the poor calf. The one I thought was the father of Hina's child. His sister seems docile. He, less so. I cross to the other side of the cook house to avoid his boastful voice. But it is a relief to me that Abram has his sister, even if it is Hina's heartbreak. Let it be anyone but me.

Hina is lying in the dirt to nurse Lee while I teach the children mathematics. I look up from my little circle to see the baby left in the dirt while Hina scampers around the cookhouse. Lee cries, but Hina continues to run in circles until I scoop him up into my arms.

Hina runs back, yelling, "Leave Lee alone. How you like if I took your baby, huh?"

The children look up at me, wide-eyed, as she grabs him, then they turn to watch Hina shoot off, not slowing her pace even as Lee shrieks, his tiny, soft head slipping from her shoulder and bouncing rhythmically against her arm.

6

My labor starts in the late afternoon like Hina's, but lasts much longer. I cannot keep Keala's potion down. In my delirium I ask for Mother, then for Ben. Lapsing in and out of consciousness, I imagine him waiting outside my bedroom door. *Thank God Abram is staying away,* I think.

"Eliza, you need to help me," I hear Keala say through my fog. "You need to wake up and pay attention. Push for me. Push harder than that."

Night comes and goes, and once morning breaks I feel the surging, violent pains. I do not scream, but make my body bear down on the child and let it leave.

"The head is here! I see a beautiful little head!" Keala shouts in encouragement. "Keep going, Eliza!" The baby slips out; Keala's face goes very still.

"What's wrong?" I plead. "Tell me, what's wrong?"

Keala doesn't answer. "Oh God," I cry, seeing her unwrapping the cord from around its neck, seeing my blue-colored baby. Keala smacks it on the bottom and still nothing. She brings the tiny frame up to her mouth and breathes into it and spanks again. There is the tiniest whine and then a choking sound, and ever so slowly color comes into my child.

"He's good. He's good," Keala says, the blood of him still on her lips as she takes a rag and begins rubbing him dry.

Keala hands him over, and I wake from all the pain of the last year. He has the ambient beauty of Ben, recast in a lighter face. His fair hair is like mine, with Ben's green eyes and Khan Ahsang's wide-set bones. He is clearly Ben's son, yet he holds the secret of his parentage well. Father will be pleased.

"Abram knows I've had the baby?" I ask Keala.

"I don't know. He went down to Kaunakakai when it started, Charlie said."

"That was thoughtful." The baby has Abram's last name; it's all he needs. I write my father an hour later while Keala holds Samuel.

Dearest Father,

Your grandson was born this morning. Of course, to his mother's eyes, he is exquisite. He is green-eyed with red-gold hair. I am pleased by the idea that he will carry on your line. I've named him Samuel; the woman who delivered him has given him his Hawaiian name, Kamuela. And his middle name is Ikaika after a boy I admire here. Please share that with Mehana, would you? And please send more sweets with your next letter that I might give them to the young boy I speak of. I ask that I be allowed to bring Samuel to O'ahu. I leave the details of this arrangement to you, but I am very eager to come home now that he is born and secure. I will write more to you of him when I have recovered, but please know we are well and eager to finally come home.

With love,

Eliza and Samuel

K,

With my son in my arms I feel thankful for Father's mercy, thankful for Moloka'i, thankful even for Abram. All of them allowed me to keep this child. I can feel the sweetness of my love for Ben again. There is no bitterness. It is the miracle they tell us it will be.

Hina comes to meet Samuel and tells me it's her birthday. "I'm fourteen. Today," she says, in a way that says no one else remembered. I feel generous in my joy.

"Bring me the box in that drawer," I tell her. Her eyes flash and she rushes the box to my side. I open it to retrieve a charm bracelet, a pretty little piece with gold covered shells and coins. "My father gave this to me on my 14th birthday. I'd like you to have it."

"I want dat," she says, pointing to the dragonfly brooch.

"Oh, no. That is something Samuel will have one day," I say. I draw her attention to the baby. "I named him Samuel Ikaika. For your brother." I wrote to Ikaika of his namesake, sending him the last of the candies by way of a Kalaupapa guard passing through camp on his way to the trail head.

"Nobody ask if I like call my baby Ikaika," she says. "Mr. Abram just tell me, '*His name is Lee.*'"

"I don't see why his middle name couldn't also be Ikaika," I say. "Perhaps you could ask Mr. Abram's permission and blessing when he's in a pleasant mood?"

"So the problem was not race. Why *didn't* you wed the father?" Abram asks the next night, appearing in my cabin.

I draw my son into my chest. "You told me your affairs are none of my business, Abram. I ask the same courtesy of you."

"Ah, but your affairs are my business. This marriage is my business," he says, tossing a woven blanket on the foot of the bed. "I thought you might need this."

It is badly worn, but I do. The bedding Mehana wrapped Mother's chair in was ruined during Samuel's birth. "Thank you."

I motion to the peach blossom chair. He barely glances at the baby, saying, "You bought a last name for your son. I have a right to know what threats there will be to your money. My money. Will someone present himself to claim this child?"

"He does not know. Nor do I plan to tell him. Why are you asking now?"

"Because there is always a good chance a woman or a baby won't make it through, but you both have, and now, this is where we are. I'm not to be taken advantage of, Eliza," he says fiercely. "You adopt Lee as your own and make him equal."

"Abram, Hina would—"

"Hina has no say," he cuts me off. He stands and walks toward the door, saying, "And don't suggest Hawaiian names for my child. I've got better things in mind for him."

K,

This man I married, he is so gentle with his son, cooing and singing softly in his little ears. I'd hoped children were the secret to his moods. But he seems angry at me that my Samuel is here. And alive.

Samuel can move his hands now, and I kiss every finger one by one, thinking that I no longer need to be married or for

Father to forget what I have done. I only need Samuel to live. I need us to go home.

I receive Father's response four days later; his handwriting seems careless in its crooked tilt and there are ink stains on the page.

I am very happy you and the baby are safe. The day will one day come. It will not be immediate. You understand why I'm sure. Patience, patience, my dear. We border on success but must not outrun it. I shall meet my grandson at a respectable time.

There is news here. Clara is taking the veil and staying permanently in Rome. It seems a waste of a beautiful young woman to me, but then I have never been one to understand such devotion.

Emilie is engaged to Richard Irvin. It is a fine match for both, so attracting fanfare in the newspaper columns. They have set the date for summer.

K,

Clara is never coming back home. Emilie and Richard, they make sense, I must concede. Richard would never have married me even after a divorce, knowing what he does now. Nor did I want him to. When I go home, it will likely be to the life of a spinster with my child, but I do not care. I have no need for another marriage after this one.

Father wants me here longer. That is the bitterest of news for me, and I cannot seem to get myself to leave this cabin. Keala, who is my guardian angel as Mehana was, brings me food and tells me the baby needs fresh air. I still feel the joy of his birth, but tears come too when I let myself believe the waiting will never end. Do you feel that in England? Do you long for ʻĀinahau, your peacocks calling you at dusk? You must.

But this will end, for both of us. All things end, do they not?

The King was freshly buried. His sister sat on the throne. Liliʻuokalani was the smartest and most stubborn of the royal family: A Christian, unbending woman. Father spent his days oblivious to my broken heart and to the intensity of the insurgence growing outside of our royalist household.

Richard Irvin visited, bringing a group of angry plantation owners. "Do you know this Queen is talking about a new constitution? Abandoning everything we've worked to put in place?" Irvin asked Father. "Surely that must irk you?"

They sat facing each other on our lanai, with the others standing around them, as if in a corral. Contained as he was in their circle, Father wasn't budging.

"As our Queen, she has the right to do so," he said, biting into his ham sandwich. "Need I remind you the previous one was forced on the royal family by the point of a bayonet?"

"You are in favor of a new constitution giving the vote to every Hawaiian, whether they own property or not? And Orientals as well? We'll be completely outnumbered."

"You all are terribly determined to save these Hawaiians from self-governance," Father said, impatient, his hands gripping the cup of coffee Mehana brought him as soon as the men pulled up, unannounced. He'd been at his Scotch every morning since the King's death.

I passed the sandwiches Mehana had hastily made, and Irvin flashed me a look before continuing. "She ignores our concerns. Treats us as if we haven't been here for a century ourselves."

"We'll make faster progress on a sugar treaty if we work with the Queen, don't you see?" Father countered.

But looking at the men's faces I could see what Father couldn't: They no longer wanted a treaty—they wanted a coup.

"Princess Ka'iulani will return home to rule, and when she does, I won't look her in the face knowing I was one of those who ganged up on her aunt," Father told them. "Her aunt is our Queen, pure and simple."

"She's not my Queen," Irvin answered, waving away the sandwich. "We're from a great nation that has no patience for crowned fools. We do not want a picturesque government. We want one under which we can make money."

He looked through the window toward the kitchen after he said this, He'd taken me aside when he arrived and asked that Mehana not serve the group. I cleared his unused plate without looking at him and went to Father's study. I drew an imaginary line on the atlas between Hawai'i and Macao. The Asian vote. Perhaps the Queen could change Ahsang's mind.

The door opened, and I expected to see my father. "Eliza, you must talk some sense into him," said Richard. "He's going to lose your plantation for you. Sugar is played as a team, and he won't be on it. He could lose his place for cane on the ships—"

"Or you may have to come back here to ask his help after your overthrow fails. All of you. If you're not down in the Reef already, sitting in prison."

"That's really not a very nice thing to say," Irvin said, collapsing into a leather chair and spinning Father's globe, frowning.

"Don't worry, I'll bring you rations," I said. "But don't tell Father I fed failed rebels."

"Eliza, you forget how dark this place was without us. These people were performing human sacrifices before we brought Christianity to them. There was incest at the highest levels of their society. Brothers and sisters," he shook his head in disgust. I looked away. It was a scandalous topic; Mehana once

whispered to me that one of Hawaii's kings had killed himself because he wanted his sister as a wife in the old way, to keep royal bloodlines pure. The missionaries did not allow it and he drank himself to death. I knew the stories, but never had I heard a man speak of them before.

But Richard was enthused. He leaned forward, and as if doing me a great honor whispered, "Hawai'i is ripe for American rule, and we are going to deliver it. We call ourselves the Annexation club. Very small, very secret."

"That's for the best, as you are plotting treason," I whispered back. Irvin and his kind were exactly what Ahsang feared. This is why he wanted to take Ben away.

"Oh, come. Wouldn't you like to be married to a future president of the Republic of Hawai'i? Eliza Irvin, first lady?" He walked over to me, tucking an errant curl behind my ear and letting his fingertips linger on my neck. I jumped away. It was the spot Ben touched.

"I'm sorry. I'm so sorry, Eliza," Irvin said. "I forget how young you still are."

He looked so ashamed. I felt tenderly toward him again, recalling him as a boy after his little brother, Morris, died. They'd been playing hide-and-seek when Morris disappeared. Every plantation worker searched the fields: they'd found the body inside a vat of boiling sugar pulp. Morris had climbed on the ledge trying to win the game. Richard spent the next year looking down: down at the floor of our home when his family came for a visit, down at our shoes at dance lessons, down at the roots of trees at 'Āinahau for Kaiulani's lū'au.

"I am not what you think, Richard. I cannot be your wife." I kept my eyes on Macao, my hands smoothing out the open pages of the atlas. "I'm like my father. I can not be a part of this. You will no doubt find another more suitable."

"I sense your refusal has little to do with the Princess, or politics. I must have done something in our long acquaintance to have offended. You have my apologies." He looked straight through me as he said this. His skin was flushed, searing into his red hair. "They all told me. Blackwell, Clarke. They told me to woo the Ahsang girl instead. Emilie? Heaps of money and she acts

more American than you do. She looks and, more importantly, behaves like one of us." He slaps his hand hard on the back of a chair. "She won't throw politics in my face."

I am stunned. "Why Emilie rather than sweet Clara? Emilie doesn't look at all Hawaiian. Is that it?" I ask.

"Who has taught you to speak so?" he asked incredulously. "And here I told them all I loved you," Richard lets his body fall forward over the chair. "That I didn't care if your father was a drunk. Did you know my father wouldn't let anyone get in a cross word about yours, all these years? We are like cousins, you and I. But here you are, insulting me, deserting me. Deserting your country. For what?" He walked to the door, then turned back. "For whom, Eliza? There's got to be someone."

I almost told him, to help him understand. But he was so angry, he would have walked out and told everyone to punish us both. After he left the study, I heard him bidding stiff goodbyes to my father along with the rest of them. They were washing their hands of us.

"Why do they bother?" Father bristled when I rejoined him. He'd retrieved the Scotch bottle he'd hidden behind a potted palm and gave a heavy pour of it into his coffee. "They never listen to my advice. You certainly had Richard pegged correctly."

"They think you are foolish not to side with them, Father," I said. "Perhaps it's time to seek out allies, outside their circle—"

"What do I care about allies? I've got my lands, more money than you or I need. That's the difference between me and that lot. I have one daughter. I have no need for this trouble. They have sons, or plan to, and want them to run the whole damned place."

So he made no alliance with Ahsang, who posted notice in the newspaper that he was shipping out to China with Ben. He was leaving his daughters in Hawai'i with their lost mother and their impressive dowries. I watched through my shower tree as Emilie and Clara were led through Ben and Khan Ahsang's goodbye banquet. Clara remained passive, but Emilie surprised me. She began to sob openly, in front of all the Chinese merchants. Khan Ahsang gave clipped orders in Cantonese, and suddenly fireworks began and the girls disappeared.

I watched as flames crawled like a clawed, fork-tongued animal up the hanging banner of red explosives, the smell of gunpowder in my nightgown, my sheets. I went to bed tasting the burnt remnants in the air, wishing Ben would climb into my window like the smoke. He'd left a note in the hollow of the tree, asking me to meet him at the bungalow the next day. Something will happen that will change everything, I told myself in the hours I could not sleep. It is not the end of us.

The next morning, Kepa drove me to town. I told him I wanted to buy a new book. I walked down King Street to the Palace and took the two-cent mule tram to reach the Ahsang bungalow in Waikīkī, hiding behind the car's canvas storm curtains with my straw hat angled low, should any passing carriage hold an acquaintance of my father's. In taro patches, I watched young boys scramble up palm trees to fetch coconuts, catching silver coins tossed by a small crowd of American visitors.

I was the final passenger when the tram stopped at the lily ponds marking the end of the line and the beginning of Khan Ahsang's property. I waited at the bungalow in the dark, leaving the blinds down. Ben arrived, embracing me. We sat together on the edge of the daybed. A squall passed overhead, the rain making the room smell like a hot iron. I reached to unbutton his shirt, but he caught my hand. "Eliza, I can't," he said. "It was wrong of me. I'm so sorry."

My cheeks stung. "Why did you ask me here?"

"I wanted to tell you," his voice was choked. "I have tried everything. I begged to take you with me, as my wife. But he won't have it. He says I must make a match there, for him. That our future depends on it. If there was any way of marrying you without losing everything for my father, you would be my wife. I promise you that."

I took his hand, ready to make my case. "Your father chose to marry someone here. How can he force you not to?"

"He married my mother because we needed land here. He left behind the woman he loved. Now we need protection in China, and I need to make the match for him. I can't dishonor him, Eliza. I can't."

"Why can't one of your sisters make an alliance?" I asked.

"If you could see the way Chinese men view my sisters... they're not the brides desired in Macao," he said, lying down, holding my hand against his chest. "They haven't learned to be deferential. Perhaps Clara can be when it suits her—but Clara would never survive China. She is so vulnerable. Will you look after her? I will look for news of you in her letters."

I understood his meaning: I couldn't write to him. He wouldn't write to me. I started to cry. He sat up and pulled me into him. "I'm sorry, I'm so sorry," he said. "This would never have happened if the King hadn't died." I felt the wetness on his face. I'd never seen him cry.

"Please," I implored, "let's run away." He lifted my face upwards.

"We'd be ruined, Eliza. I have no money of my own, nor do you. I won't drag you into a life of desperation. And to do that to my father would be impossible." His voice broke.

"Someday perhaps we will be able to do this," he said, sounding angry. "If there's ever a way to come home to you honorably, I'll take it." He held me to him for a long, silent time. The hum of crickets started, along with the clicking sounds of little lizards in the fall of night. He took me home in his Phaeton carriage, racing through town, down King Street past the coral wall of the Palace. We played the end out dangerously, driving together through town, our families, unaware, waiting for us side by side in Nu'uanu.

He stopped the carriage just past Father's gates, helping me out and walking me to a clump of wild bamboo that hid us in our own valley. It had rained, and water splashed off the bamboo onto my face. He wiped the water from my cheek and kissed my forehead, putting both hands on my arms, holding them to my sides, his hands shaking. "You'll doubt I loved you some day," he said into my hair. "You'll hear I've married, and you'll hate me as a cad. Your father will pick someone else for you, too. And it will crush me when I hear of it. Always know, Eliza, it was you I wanted." He let me go then. There were tears on his face, but he turned and was gone.

The despair was unearthly. With both hands gripping the bamboo, I cried for not being what he needed, for the lies I told my father and Mehana and the need to pretend that I was all right. That night I held my pillow, imagining it was him and dreaming shamefully vivid dreams, waking in the middle of the night to walk to the shower tree. I knew I would be disappointed, but put my hand inside anyway. There was a gift, so smooth to the touch, wood that had been sanded down again and again, so that the grain of it became as velvety as the downy head of a babe. My fingers played over its surface, delaying the final delight of seeing what I knew it to be. The tension of the moment, the mystery and pleasure, they were as close as I would ever come to having the bungalow again.

I leaned against the tree, my arm raised above my head into the hollow, my forehead pressed against the trunk as I listened improbably for footsteps from his house, footsteps that would end with his hands on my shoulders telling me he couldn't do it, he couldn't go.

I brought his gift down. A sandalwood fan, tied in a remnant of fuchsia silk, the sort of fan I had coveted, but never told him I wanted. I wondered when he'd caught me eyeing one as it flapped through the plump air of a summer recital, cutting the sort of heat that made me feel I might let out a loud gulping breath and have every eye turn on me. It was the sound I would make two months later when I heard that he had married.

"Hello, Mrs. Malveaux?" comes a voice outside my cabin door. "It's Dr. Webster. Have I come at a bad time?"

"Just a moment!" I throw a shawl around myself, clutching it to me as I swoop down to pick up the cups and hide them in the sink. The bed is unmade, and I am still in my nightclothes.

"Come in," I say, opening the door to misty weather.

"Good morning," Dr. Webster says, removing his hat and smiling at Samuel. "Well, hello handsome thing. This is my first time seeing you." He leans in to kiss Samuel's foot in a charming way. "The foot's the safest place to kiss," he explains.

"If you say so, I believe it." I lead him into the back room and put the kettle on the stove. "How was the trip up?"

"A bit slippery, but the rains have left everything green." He sets his medical bag on the bed. "It's the kind of winter I thought I'd left behind by coming here. All wet and grey."

"Are you English?" I ask, already knowing I'm wrong.

"Australian." He says this with a swagger I hadn't seen in him before, and I feel myself blush despite every bit of me trying to stop it. Suddenly having him alone in my cabin feels scandalous.

"My father's a country doctor outside Melbourne," Webster says, pretending not to see how flustered I've become. He takes Samuel from my arms. "Now let's take a look at this little one."

I can hardly hide my pride as Webster puts Samuel carefully on the quilt and examines the length of him. The kettle whistles, and I make the last of the peppermint tea sent over by Father.

"Ahh, what a treat," says Webster, watching me put his cup on the side table. "He's a well-formed child, Mrs. Malveaux. There's no doubt there." He tickles my baby's feet, sending Samuel into a lopsided smile; my son clasps his hands together as the doctor checks his eyes. He makes little kicks as the doctor listens to his heart.

"There's a slight rattle in his breathing. Have you noticed it?" Webster asks, wrapping my son expertly in the shawl and making my heart swell. Samuel widens his eyes and makes a singing sound. Webster lifts him with one hand under his neck and bounces him a bit.

"He coughs at night," I admit, setting my cup down, taking Samuel. "It gets so cold here. And there was a scare at his birth—he didn't breathe right away." That could be a reason to give Father, a reason from a doctor. "Would you say it is advisable that I take him to Honolulu?" I ask, my voice betraying my desire to leave.

He raises an eyebrow. "It's not anything urgent, just something to watch. He hasn't got a fever. And there's no sign of any trauma from the delivery." He washes his hands at the faucet while I give Samuel my pinky to suck. "Are you happy living here, Eliza?"

He hasn't used my Christian name before. His question is put quietly with his back still turned, an invitation to confide in him. "Yes, it's fine." I say cautiously, unsure how much I can trust anyone, though his manners are lovely. "I feel despair about Ikaika."

"Ikaika has adjusted as well as one might," Webster says, leaning back on the sink board. "He enjoyed an immediate boost in status thanks to all the sweets and toys you sent to him, and he was quite wise in how he parceled them out to the other boys."

The doctor sits on the peach blossom chair, wiping his spectacles against his shirt, which itself could use a wash. He looks as if he's been up most the night, too. But there's a confident physicality to his large frame, a vibrancy to his company. I want him to stay, at least for a bit.

"Ikaika's lesions have not started," he says, laying his glasses on his lap and pressing the inner corners of his eyes with his fingers. My father makes the same motion. "He bought his horse with the money you gave him and rides along the sea."

I carry Samuel across the room to get a box of dates rolled in coconut, chocolate-covered apricots, and candied almonds. Father sent them with the vile letter, a small luxury I've allotted myself when I wake in the middle of the night and cannot chase Ben or his wife from my head.

Webster smiles when he sees them. "My mother always had these at Christmas for us," he says. We eat a handful each while Samuel lies on the bed kicking at imaginary figures in the air above him.

"I wish I could visit Ikaika," I say. "Were it not for my son…"

"No, of course. You could not do such a thing, and I might say I should not allow it regardless," Webster says. "Your gifts help. The letters help. He came to me with such pride when he read you'd given his name to your child. And of course he knows he has a nephew, too."

"You found Lee in good health as well, I hope?" I say, uncomfortable.

"A big fat jolly boy," says Webster. "Looking more like his father, I think." He stops, obviously realizing he's made a gaffe. He smiles over it. "Well, I should be getting back."

I can think of nothing to do but look down at Samuel. He's fallen asleep. The doctor puts on his hat and is nearly out the door before turning on his heel. "I nearly forgot. There is another who knows you in the settlement."

"Joseph," I say, naming Mehana's nephew.

"No. A young woman. She's newly arrived. Of mixed race. From the look of her clothes and the sound of her, I'd say she's of a very good family. She says she lived just by you, and that you were great friends. It's a Germanic name, a "k" name..."

Clara. It can't be. Clara is in Rome. "Clara?"

"Yes, that's her name."

"Has she come over as a *kōkua?* A helper?" I ask, stunned.

"No, sadly she is most assuredly a patient. It's difficult for her to adjust to losing her looks so violently. It's hardest for attractive ones; they're used to people being drawn to their faces, and to feel them repelled is a bitter pill. The wisest ones get past it, and Clara has begun to do that. She's concerned with the welfare of others and volunteers to help me, which I appreciate. She rolls bandages and takes soiled linens to the laundry area, that sort of thing."

I struggle for something to say. "Please give her my best. Tell her I am so sorry." I go to the desk and pull out a few bills I've kept in an envelope for Ikaika. Webster puts them into his coat and shows me an envelope addressed to Ikaika in Keala's hand.

"It is from Hina," he says. "The boy is so literate while his sister can't write at all."

"She's not attending school. She's been...kept here," I say, feeling humiliated and at a loss to explain further.

"Shall I give some of the money to Clara as well?" he asks.

"She won't need money. But I want to send something down to her," I say, relieved. I look around my little dwelling. We've finished off the last of Father's delicacies. I pick up my Sunday hat, wondering what use a striped, flowered hat could be in such a desperate place.

"Ah, that is a fine gift, Eliza," the doctor says kindly. "The women at the settlement love their Sunday hats. Church is the biggest event of the week. And a good hat becomes something to save their pride a bit."

I put the hat in its box. "Clara will recognize it," I say. "I'd wear it at St. Andrew's Cathedral for baptisms. Clara and her sister thought my dresses were too plain. But this hat, they loved this hat."

Dr. Webster leans against the door. I sense he wants more of my story, that he misses such trivial bits of normal life. As do I.

I pick up Samuel, who is stirring, and shift my weight back and forth. "After the services you would hear gossip about the poor breeding of the Ahsang girls, daring to wear violet on a Sunday morning, but later, the same woman who complained would add violet ribbons or a magenta sash to her eyelet morning dress. The colors were infectious."

"An ironic word under the circumstances," says Webster.

It takes me a moment to understand his meaning. "Sorry," I say, suddenly feeling terribly sad. I breathe in Samuel's powdery smell.

Webster reaches out and touches my baby's fine hair. "Send me word if his breathing worsens."

I open the door for him. He walks down the dirt path, a few scraggly chickens crisscrossing in front of him.

"Clara," I say, kissing Samuel's crown, "your aunt. Your poor, sweet aunt."

There was this day at the bungalow, K. If you'd still been in Hawai'i, you would have been with us. It was before anything

started with Ben, but the feeling was already there. We walked the beach behind Emilie and Clara. They were scraping the sand with their parasols, looking for shells. They never wanted to swim the way you and I did. They dressed to be seen for their beach strolls. Wide-brimmed hats, jade. I had to convince them to go barefoot, that their embroidered slippers would be ruined.

When Hawaiian children gathered to touch the silk of their dresses, Emilie moved away toward tourists wanting to photograph her. Clara let the children run their fingers along the silk trim of her sleeve, the hem of her skirt dark with ocean water. It was before she'd started to wear wraps and gloves. I suppose before the grey spots of leprosy started to appear, and she'd known she was doomed.

"Your sisters' beauty is much admired," I'd told Ben as we kept our distance behind them. A strand of hair slipped from my hat and flew across my eyes. I reached to get it, but Ben got there first. He tucked it back for me, keeping his hand on the nape of my neck for a second, and then turning to look at his sisters with such calm that I doubted he'd meant to make me blush. "That and their dowries may save me from having to take care of them when I'm combing grey hair," he'd laughed. Then he'd seen the color in my face, and his eyes turned so tender. Now there will be no dowry, no wedding, no children for Clara. I imagine Ben opening the letter, his grief. To sit in a foreign land and read two words: Clara. Leprosy.

I lay curled around a pillow on my bed. A week had passed since Ben left to be married in China. Heartbreak had unleashed a strange, unending flu upon

my body. Clara surprised me by calling out from below my window. She wore a high-necked dress despite the heat; I thought she looked like a missionary wife first landing off a New England ship. I put my book down unhappily to meet her. I had no wish for visitors today.

"Eliza? The ball at Claus Spreckels' last night. You didn't go?"

I understand that her question asks something more of me. Through the thin white gauze of her wrap I see a white scar on her hand, like a burn.

"Emilie went," Clara says. "She showed me her dance card this morning. Filled with Richard Irvin."

"Clara," I say, not entirely kindly. "I declined him."

"She thinks," Clara looks unsure, "Richard told her he thinks there is someone else? For you."

"There is not," I say. It's true now. I wished I had K to confide in. It was impossible with Clara.

She pulls her shawl tighter. "Emilie says that the Queen no longer deserves our loyalty. That the whole family is corrupt. Imagine, a Hawaiian saying that of their own ali'i?" She pitches her chin up, like Kepa does when he is offended. "She never visits Mother. Will you come, Eliza? And visit Mother with me, please?"

I could think of nothing worse. Hannah Ahsang frightened me. She was descended from the Chiefess Ahina, famous for climbing into the hot lava pit of Kīlauea volcano. She did this to prove that the kapu—ban—against the goddess Pele no longer existed for those who accepted Christianity. I simply wanted to stay in my room and lose myself in a book set on the English moors and feel good and sorry for myself. But Ben had asked me to take care of Clara, and I supposed this is what he meant.

We found Hannah Ahsang sitting on the little lanai Khan Ahsang built for her on the river, her hair pulled severely back, missionary style, her bare feet spread wide across the wooden floor like matching fans, reminders of a childhood spent wild and shoeless. Ahsang's first wife could not walk on her tiny bound feet; his second had used hers to surf and dance hula.

The last time I saw Ben's mother, she looked like the athlete she'd been in her youth, when she'd surfed daily with her grandmother, Ahina, who—until the final year of her life—paddled out without covering her bosom, daring the missionaries to arrest her, which they dared not. Hula, nudity, and adultery had been banned by then, but Ahina followed no missionary laws, and kept a string of young lovers a quarter of her age. Her volcano performance on behalf of Christianity had earned her unlimited freedom from missionaries like my grandfather.

But Ahina's granddaughter had now rounded into the shape of an elder. Hannah looked startled to see me. She took Clara's hand and began to sing beautifully in Hawaiian. Her song asked, where have you disappeared to? Come back and stay with me. Then she turned to me. "Ben left. His father took him. Like the other."

Had Ben told his mother of me? I wondered. Which other was she speaking of? Hannah turned to Clara. "Did you see him in the forest today?"

"No. No pueo today," Clara answered.

Pueo meant owl. There was a round-headed pueo living in the forest behind our homes. I'd sometimes startled it; Ben was better at spotting its yellow eyes following us from a branch.

"Tell her," Hannah said, pointing to me.

"The owl is our 'aumakua and protector," said Clara, keeping her eyes on her mother.

"When Kamehameha landed on O'ahu for the battle, my great-grandfather Kala was at his side," Hannah said. I could tell she told this story to herself, to Clara, daily. "They landed at the coconut groves of Waikīkī and marched across the plains to Nu'uanu where Oahu's army waited. They pushed them to the cliffs of the Pali…"

She'd lost her train of thought and looked crushed not to find it again. She turned to Clara.

"Hundreds were pushed to their deaths in the battle," Clara continued. "Kala pursued a warrior who ran into a mountain cloud to hide. Kala ran after him, but an owl hit him hard in the face, knocking him to the ground. When he stood, the cloud had cleared and he saw that in another step he would have fallen off the cliff. That pueo saved his life."

Why had Ben never told me of this? All the time we'd spent together in the forest, my head on his chest as we listened to the owl sound out, "tchak, tchak,

tchak." I'd told him Kepa's 'aumakua was the shark. Why did he not say the owl was his?

"What a miracle," I said to Hannah, and she was pleased.

"When my grandmother died, I ran away twice to the Pali, to that spot of the battle to pray for strength," Hannah said. "Twice they sent constables to take me back to the guardian they'd assigned me against my will. Albert Penwell. He wanted to marry me. He wanted my land. The third time, I ran away to Khan Ahsang. He'd been kind to me in his store. I came to his home and I never left. I was sixteen."

I knew from Father that town gossips had read with delight her guardian's legal notice:

> *HANNAH KINA'U MERRYWEATHER: HAVING ELOPED OR BEEN ENTICED AWAY FROM MY GUARDIANSHIP I FORBID ALL PERSONS HARBORING HER UNDER PENALTY OF LAW.*

The notice ran every day for a week, by which time Hannah and Ahsang were married, beyond the reach of Albert Penwell.

"I did not care that he had a kit fat wife," said Hannah. "Ahsang wanted me to have only his children. So I had only him. I gave him Benjamin, then Emilie. Then you, Clara. You were born while he was in Macao, with her. When he came back he told me if my next child was a boy, he would be sent to Macao. That she wanted another son, and was too old to have one. He told me he needed more sons in China, but only one son in little Hawai'i. He said this was hānai."

Hannah spit the word. I looked at Clara, worried. Her mother was agitated.

"My next baby was a little boy. Perfectly formed, but only enough breath in him to live an hour in my arms. He's buried beyond the river bank. The pueo watches over him."

Now I understand why Ben never told me this, and why Hannah sits on her lanai day in and day out, watching the river.

"I told Khan Ahsang my boy died from the heartbreak of knowing he would leave Hawai'i forever. Hānai is by agreement, never force. I told him he killed our son."

7

K,

We are in the midst of a drought. The men pick up sheep carcasses in the pasture and burn them in the empty pen right in front of my cabin. The fires turn the sheep into singed prehistoric rocks. They turn the air grey and putrid for days, making my throat and chest hurt when I wake. Even the cows brought back to the pen at night sound raspy as they breathe in the smoky air.

I listen to Samuel's chest, the wheeze in his lungs. They've already taken the cows upslope and built the morning's fire, the wind blowing the stench of it right to my cabin.

"Could you burn them further from my house?" I ask Lopaki. He wears the feather-banded cowboy hat I remember from the day I arrived at the ranch.

"Mr. Abram say burn 'em here," he answers.

He doesn't look me in the eye, doesn't try to get a wave from Samuel as other cowboys do. I wonder if he thinks I'm competition for his sister. She can have Abram to her heart's desire; I only want to get myself and Samuel out of here. I listen to Samuel's chest, the wheeze in his lungs. There are a dozen better places to burn these carcasses. *You will be very happy when I disappear,* I think, livid that he will not move the stupid fire. *May your sister inherit Hina's wrath.*

Hina and I largely avoid one another now; Lee still dips his head down to catch my eye and smile at me from below Hina's harsh stare. I wish my son could have a playmate in the boy without the mother.

"Please, the smell is awful," I tell Abram when he finally shows himself. "Are you trying to smoke me out of my house?" I ask, trying to sound amused rather than angry.

"Move to my new house, and you'll have clean air."

"I'm happy in my cabin, Abram," I say, expecting his temper. He has been asking me to move to the new house for some time now.

"Well, you won't move to the house, I won't move the fires," he says with an affable smile. "But I'll take you to Kaunakakai if you want. I've got crates to gather from town." I wonder why he's giving me this now. I've asked for weeks to go down to buy oats for my growing baby. We agree to go the next morning.

Samuel is content in the clean air, resting his head on my shoulder and watching the scenery change into kiawe trees and dry scrub. I watch the fields roll by, remembering that first day on this island when I'd thought they looked like graveyards. Now they just look like sweet potatoes.

Abram leans in close. "I have been a gentleman and allowed you to repair from the birth."

You have been busy with Lopaki's sister, I think. *And I am so grateful.*

"When the time is right, I intend to give you a child who deserves my name," he says, as if he's doing me a great favor. "I am going to be a force in these islands, and you're going to feel lucky I gave you my name."

I stare straight ahead. Abram is a buffoon, a braggart. He doesn't really want me. He likes young girls who don't recognize him for the fraud he is. His gentleman's accent drops the minute he's angry into something with a much rougher story behind it. He's just another kind of carpetbagger, and my knowledge of that withers his manliness.

"You are a good father to Lee," I say. It's the only kind thing I can think of to placate him. And it is true. He takes Lee everywhere with him. Lee is treated with the reverence of an heir by the workers, and credited by them for the better food and treatment they are getting now. The second room for the schoolhouse was put up over one week's time, as he promised. Abram is becoming respectable. People think that he's changed; that he's decent.

"Papers came from Honolulu today," he says, giving a small kick to a saddle bag on the floor of the cart. Now I understand why he took me on this trip. His face is set and hard. "Hina can't raise him right. I want a man who can go back to the South and do himself proud."

"He is Hawaiian. If you want to raise a Southerner, that's a different child than this one."

"This is the one I care about," he shouts. He begins to speak again, more softly. "Before I had him, I'd have told you I'd have others. Put my best dreams in them, the white ones. But his color goes away when I hold him. I want everything for this boy, Eliza. My father, when he left, he gave his land to the next set of brats he had. Left me with nothing. I won't do that. I won't give Lee second best, or leave him with a mother who doesn't tie up her top and can't speak properly."

"Hina can learn English. I could teach her. Lord, I'd teach her to dance a waltz, or play whist and bow if you wanted me too."

Abram actually smiles when I say this. But emboldened, I then overreach and make a terrible mistake. "No one can teach a mother to love a child the way Hina loves Lee," I say. "I could never love him as she does. Samuel would always be first in my heart."

He stops the carriage and says, "Well, fuck you, Eliza!"

I raise a hand over my head to absorb a blow that does not come.

"I get anchored with another man's slut, and you cannot love my child? I have rights to you I haven't taken. Watch how you tempt me to set you right. Right now, if need be."

I hold Samuel tight to me. He has burst into tears. Abram tries to put his hand on Samuel's back as if to comfort him. Samuel crawls away as high up onto me as he can, taking great handfuls of my hair.

"I won't make you be my wife, so long as you be Lee's mother. Is that a deal you can understand?" he asks, dropping the reins to pick up the bag of papers. We are in the middle of nowhere, with only the island of Maui staring up at me across the shadowed ocean as a witness.

I feel sick as I sign the papers he thrusts at me, stroking Samuel's head to soothe him. Samuel begins making little twilling noises to comfort himself, which sound like the rolling R's I'd failed to make in French lessons.

Abram holds the papers up above his head to check my signature, as if it could be counterfeit. "See? That's all you needed to do. Fair is fair. Furniture's coming for the house. I'll settle you all in then."

Father, bring me home. I'm frightened. He's made me adopt his son with threats. You must come or send someone for me to get me out and keep me safe until the divorce.

I give my letter for Father to Keala, to keep safe until the next time her husband, Charlie, is sent to town and then I hold my breath for the next several days, waiting for Hina's fury, but she is nowhere to be found, while Abram becomes almost kind to me for a day or two.

But our fragile agreement frays when he hears me telling the camp's children about our late king, Kalākaua.

"Why are you filling their heads with silly talk?" he asks. "Kalākaua was the bastard son of a Negro carriage boy. Everyone on Hotel Street knows that."

"That's the stupidest lie, Abram. I know the family very well. He was my King."

"He was my King," Abram says, imitating my voice. "I just love these natives! I have so much damn money I don't have to earn a dime."

I stand still, waiting for him to leave.

"Some of us actually have to work for a living, Eliza. Some of us aren't pals with the royalty, which is fine. They won't be royalty for long."

Hina seeks me out in a patch of long grass apart from the camp while Samuel naps on his blanket, arms thrown over his head and lips moving in sucking motions as he nurses in his dreams. Behind us is Abram's new house. He made promises to build more homes, but so far he's only built his own. It already looks like an unhappy place. Hina runs one hand along its fresh whitewash while holding Lee tucked in her other arm.

"Mr. Abram said Lee get his own room," she tells me. "You such a liar," she shouts. The anger and rage is awful to hear. "You sign and you gonna *take* him! Abram wen tell me today." She rocks Lee too hard and starts to sob. "He say I gotta wean him. I get one week."

"Hina, he's forcing this on me." I can't look at her. I've taken her child to protect myself. Samuel stretches and frowns. I pick him up.

"You think you so much bettah than me," Hina hisses. "You some haole lady who think you Hawaiian, but you nevah gonna be nobody to us."

Samuel starts crying, and I can't trust Hina with my plan to leave. I just watch her stagger away in silence.

Abram begins to brand the calves, and so the fires begin again. The cattle sound their terror of the hot iron, kicking up enough red dirt to give my floor a fresh coating. Samuel's breathing labors with the smoke.

I let him touch the smooth, cold surface of Ben's brooch. "Jade," I say to him. "Green," I say. I let him hold the weight of it in his hand. He begins to chew it and fights as I take it back. He has gotten so strong.

I look out my window where Abram stands in the pen with Lopaki, ten feet away from my cabin, separating calves from their mothers and then castrating the young males with a pocket-knife. The steer kick and make short, choking sounds. It sounds as if hell has opened up at my front door.

I escape to the bathhouse. Samuel's sturdy body squirms against mine. "Shhh, shhhh, shhhh, shhh," I whisper to him.

Samuel's skin becomes slick to the touch with fever. At daybreak, I carry him to the cookhouse and find Keala having a bread roll and coffee with Charlie.

"Keala," I say and she turns to take in my son's sweating little form. "It's gone on now for six hours at least."

Keala feels his cheek. "Charlie, get us the ti leaves. The ones behind the milk shed."

Charlie stuffs a roll whole in his mouth, stands up, and puts his hat on. I see him put his hand out to feel the doorframe as he leaves. "It's all fuzzy for him, but when he wants to find me at night, he has no trouble," Keala once boasted.

"Take the baby back," Keala says now. "I'll grab what I have to help." She leaves her coffee to walk back to their home, which has a roof that slopes heavily off to one side. Plants grow from the corrugated tin for Keala's home remedies. It is a shack, but their home is for just the two of them, a rare luxury on the ranch.

Keala returns, lifting her hand to show me the heart-shaped leaves she clutches. She waves them in the air as if they can chase sickness away.

I lay Samuel out on the bed and undress him. His skin is flushed, and there is a rash on his chest and back. Keala bites into one of the leaves and chews it, spitting the green paste into her hand and rubbing it inside Samuel's mouth.

"You know *'awa*?" she whispers to Samuel in a calming tone. "It helps relax you, puts you to sleep. Feverish children need to sleep, it's important." She puts more in his mouth; his face crinkles at the taste.

A knock at the door makes Samuel scream. I bend low to kiss his forehead, trying to soothe him as Keala opens the door to Charlie. He hands her the ti leaves along with some envelopes. Despite Charlie's failing eyes, he does well as postmaster. Keala reads the names, and he orders the envelopes accordingly, never making a mistake in delivery.

Keala closes the door and returns, tossing the letters on the bedspread and carrying the ti leaves to the basin. "Here, we'll soak these and get them on him," she says. She dunks the long green leaves in a bucket of water she draws beneath the faucet. She carries them dripping to the bed, drops of water turning the red dust on the floor into watercolor.

"Eh, *ku'uipo*," she coos to Samuel. "This is going to make you feel better." She drapes the length of the leaf on his bare little chest, and then rips up another glossy ti into pieces to paste onto his forehead and legs. He stops fussing and looks startled as the leaves stick to him.

"Nature's washcloth," she says.

"Oh," I exhale. "I don't know how to thank you and Charlie."

Keala looks up. "You need a real husband, someone who can help you," she says gently. "Eliza, you're the nicest, saddest haole I know. There's so much grief in you," Keala takes my hand as she says this, mothering me as Mehana would have. "You have nobody to talk to at night. Nobody knows why you're here."

"I had to come, for him." I point to Samuel with my eyes. Keala runs her hand over his matted wisps of hair. I sit next to him and stroke his head. His eyes go heavy under my touch and he grabs my fingers in his fist.

"Does Abram know the father?" Keala asks.

I shake my head no.

"*Keiki o pueo*," she says.

"Owl child?" The yellow eyes of the Nuʻuanu owl come back to me. *Tchak, tchak, tchak.*

"It means a child whose father is not known."

"I've never heard that before," I say, thinking of the beautiful man I had once. His other child is born by now. Ben is no longer real to me. I recreate our story, giving it different scenes and imagined conversations, spinning my own book out of it to get me through lonely nights. But then day breaks, and Samuel cries out for me. As long as I have him, all of this is all right. Everything is survivable.

"I'll let you rest," Keala says. She grabs an envelope. "This one is for you."

I jump up from the bed to take the envelope from her. "Thank you, Keala. So much."

She waves a little goodbye to Samuel, but his eyes are glazed and he does not smile back. The door closes softly. I rip it open.

Eliza,

I thought you would want to know that Benjamin Ahsang has a daughter. Things here are dire. The Queen has been betrayed a hundred times over.

He goes on about the Queen and the planters in a rambling fashion and I wonder how many glasses of Scotch were consumed before the letter's writing. There's no word of my escape or Samuel. Is he so caught up in his pride and drink that he doesn't care how frightened I've become?

I drop the letter on the floor, where it drinks up the wet red dirt like blood.

It is time to stop waiting to be saved. I am utterly alone.

8

K,

I've been up all night trying to figure out how I can be my own salvation. I need to get to Kaunakakai to get onto a boat. I could ask the doctor, Webster, to sneak me out, but even if he agrees, he has no cart. It's three hours by cart. How long would it take to walk with a child strapped to my back? Far longer than it would take to be discovered. I could bribe the fishermen to take Samuel and me down the next time they come, but mullet is a rarity to be rationed here. The fishermen must travel six hours' round trip to make the trade. Who knows when they will arrive next? And if they did take us to Kaunakakai, where would I hide until a boat comes? Abram would find us. The missionary school is useless. They are fiendishly devoted to Abram these days. All night I went round and round, always ending up in the same place. Trapped.

"He loves your hair, doesn't he?" Webster asks, looking at us from the sink while he dries his hands. Samuel has grabbed a piece and is winding it around his fist.

"Keala tells me I shouldn't let him, but it's too sweet a game to stop," I concede. I crave my child's touch the way I used to wait through the day for his father's. I love the minutes Samuel tries to fight off slumber when I walk him back and forth, bouncing lightly over the cabin floor. He lays his head on my shoulder and reaches both hands round my neck to play with my hair. When I feel his tugging stop, I know he's down for the night.

"Let's have a look then." Webster moves closer and slips the stethoscope up the back of Samuel's smock. He places a hand on my arm while listening to Samuel's chest. "The treatments you're using seem to be warding off the worst of it. I'm happy to say you have no use for me today."

"As long as I am here, I will always have a need of you," I answer. I take Samuel and bounce him a bit, though there is no need to.

"Do you plan to leave us?" he asks after a moment's pause.

I meet his eyes; I set Samuel on the bed.

"Are you all right, Eliza?" Webster asks, putting his hand to my forehead. "You're a little warm. Are you perhaps with child?"

I laugh out loud. "No."

"You're sure?"

"Most assuredly." I sit on the bed. If ever there is a time to ask for help, this is it. I start to gather the phrases I've worked out: Abram is a danger to my baby, I need aid in finding the next boat back home, someone willing to take me down to the beach. But I feel unhinged and frozen. Might he go to Abram because he thinks I'm plotting to steal his son? "I think it's my nerves," I say, losing courage. "Is there perhaps something you can give me?"

"Your nerves?" He sits down next to me. His gaze is too direct. It feels as if we are a couple, alone in our room together. If I were not so worried I would be enjoying this moment of pretending I was married to a man such as this.

"I'm very agitated," I say. "I… haven't slept."

He opens his bag and lifts a few bottles before finding one that he gives to me with obvious reluctance. I've seen this tonic's label.

A bottle always sat on a side table at the bungalow; Ben's sisters took a spoonful before their daily nap. I serve myself a spoonful at the sink and shudder at the taste. "May I keep the bottle until your next visit?" I ask. I want him to come back. "I'd love to be able to rest."

"Well, Samuel seems very ready to teach you how." He points to Samuel lying snug and settled on the bed. "I'll leave you two. I have Hina and Lee to visit."

"When will you be back?"

"I will try to come back next week."

After I've shut the door, I take a second spoonful and lie down beside Samuel. "Do you want a story to go to sleep?" I ask, pressing my pinky softly on the center of his lips. He reaches out to touch me in the same spot. I smile and whisper Stevenson's *Counterpane* to him. "*When I was sick and lay a-bed. I had two pillows at my head. And all my toys beside me lay. To keep me happy all the day. And sometimes for an hour or so. I watched my leaden soldiers go. With different uniforms and drills. Among the bed-clothes, through the hills.*"

His eyelids droop. My smile turns to tears.

"*And sometimes sent my ships in fleets. All up and down among the sheets; Or brought my trees and houses out. And planted cities all about. I was the giant great and still. That sits upon the pillow-hill. And sees before him, dale and plain, the pleasant land of counterpane.*"

I close my eyes, and I am stretched out next to Benjamin on a day the forest clearing blooms purple with impatiens. "Is it true we walk on sidewalks crafted by the flower drug?" I whisper to him, tucking my head onto his shoulder.

"That is your father talking," Ben says.

"Would you rather I didn't ask—"

"No, it's better than rumors. My father had the King's license to sell opium when it was legal. When it wasn't, he stopped. American merchants bring it in now. One drowned in the harbor last year. Fell out of the landing boat with too much gold belted on him."

"Mehana told me. She said he drowned in his own greed."

Ben brushed my lips with his fingertips. "You realize that some of the women you see at garden parties are addicts, don't you? *Haole* women enjoy opium more than Chinese women."

"That's *your* father talking. I don't know any ladies addicted to opium."

"They are. Father makes almost as much money now selling the legal form as he did the drug. There's opium in Cherry Pectorals and Sarsaparilla tonics."

I scoff. "Those are medicines for coughs and," my voice lowers, "feminine things."

"It's opium served with high grain liquor. Why do you think my father moved my mother out of the house? The servants give her a glass of tonic in the morning, then at lunch and again at night. The only way to make her smile is to serve her from the bottom of that green bottle, where the strongest medicine lies."

I lace my fingers through Ben's as wind ruffles through the trees. I shiver next to Samuel, feeling my mind descend into the beginning of sleep and a dream of both of them, Samuel and Ben together. It ends with a knock. I rise unevenly, hopeful it's Dr. Webster again, but it's Keala's husband, Charlie.

"Letter," he declares, walking into my cabin quickly without being asked. I feel so groggy that for a moment I forget that he plays the role of postmaster for the camp. He slides past the window to stand against a solid wall. Then he hands me my letter. It is addressed in a hand I do not recognize. Immediately I hope it is Ben, writing through a third party. My eyes dart to the bottom, and I recognize the name of my father's solicitor, Jeffrey Jensen. I tear open the envelope. He has sent the paper work confirming Lee as my heir. How could Father have him do this after I've written about the nature of the adoption? How can he not be concerned?

Charlie says, "Keala wen for take medicine to da mission school. Somebody sick."

I nod my head, having no idea why he is telling me this.

"Mr. Abram," he whispers, "he say I gotta give your letters to him first. If I no like dat, me and Keala lose our house," he says sorrowfully. "When Samuel was born, that one went without him looking." Charlie stops. "And Lopaki said… is baby boy awake?" he asks, pointing to Samuel.

I glance at my son; he is sleeping, turning on to his side, his cheeks flushed. "He's fine," I say. My thoughts are racing, blurred by the tonic. Father has no idea what's happened? "He's just dreaming. Now please, tell me what Lopaki said."

He looks down at the floor. "I no like get in trouble."

"You won't, I promise! Now please."

"Abram told Lopaki you think you going home some day, but you nevah will."

I cup my hands before my face.

"Please, Eliza, I came 'cause Keala's gone right now—"

"Charlie, you've done me a great favor telling me. I will never say a word."

When he leaves I sit near Samuel and touch his head to calm myself. *Webster might still be with Hina and Lee,* I think. *Please don't let him be on the path down to Kalaupapa already, not due back for another week.* I heave myself up clumsily, knocking over a glass and stepping on a shard. I pull the glass from my foot, lace my boots, and after putting a pillow on each side of Samuel, run to catch Webster.

The yard is empty. I run to Hina's bunkhouse, but no one opens the locked door. I find her in the cookhouse with Lee. She's nursing him, there is no weaning at work, thank God. She covers a book she's been looking at with a burlap sack laying on the table.

"Hina, have you seen the doctor?"

"I no need tell you nothing," she says. She takes Lee from her breast as if to leave. I stop her by placing a hand gently on the baby. "Hina, I need his help."

"Samuel sick *again?*" Lee is grabbing at her breast and she smiles at him.

"Where did Webster go?" I hear myself drag out each word. I regret taking that second spoon of tonic.

"Down da path," she says, placing Lee's mouth back to her breast and measuring me with her eyes. She looks at me with a detached heart. As if all the love I've known from Mehana, Keala, and Ka'iulani has been soured in Hina.

"Hina, can you nurse Lee in my cabin and keep an eye on Samuel? He's sleeping. Please? I'll be straight back. If you do, I'll give you that sandalwood fan you like. Please?"

"Fine. I get da fan." She closes the book in front of her, and I realize it's the book of verses I gave her the afternoon I arrived. She shoots me a hateful look as she puts it in the bag to carry. She seems happier when we enter the cabin, especially after I toss the fan onto the table. Samuel makes clicking sounds in his sleep. I kiss him and walk backwards out of the cabin, watching Hina begin to nurse Lee in the peach blossom chair.

I tear down the path, my foot throbbing. "Dr. Webster!" I shout into the ironwood grove. The trees are bobbing, forward and back. They answer my call with a question. *Where do you go? Where do you go?* they ask as they lean toward me, then away. Mehana's sorceress Pahalu has finally done her work on me and I am inside a dream. "Dr. Webster, please!"

"Eliza?" I hear back.

I feel so overcome, I start laughing in relief.

"What's happened?" he asks, when he finds me. "What have you done to your foot?"

I look down and see blood soaked through the boot's canvas.

"I think there's glass in there," I say, still laughing.

With one arm around my waist, he helps me to the ground. He removes my boot, touches the wounded spot. I wince as he takes out his tweezers. "Now what on earth did you run all the way here with glass in your foot to tell me?"

I breathe in the scent of pine needles. "I need to leave. It's a matter of my safety. Samuel's safety. I can think of no other way to get myself back home than to take a ship from Kalaupapa. If I go to Kaunakakai Abram will find me and stop me. Please help us."

He does not answer. He takes the glass from the cut, holding the piece up. The trees move behind him hypnotically back and forth, back and forth. I feel strange; aside from the tonic and my foot it's the absence of Samuel, of not having him in my arms, hanging from my neck, pulling my hair.

"Eliza, you need to tell me more," Webster says hesitantly. "I have considered it for some time but… I am at a loss as to the truth between you and Abram. I hesitate to interfere in the private affairs of another man-"

"It is not a true marriage. I loved another, and Samuel is his." I cross my arms tightly around myself. I feel so powerless, giving this secret away. What will this man do with it?

"By law you're his wife, and Samuel is his son."

"Abram has prevented me from asking my father for help, he is intercepting my letters. He wants me to be alone and desperate." I cannot read his expression. His silence tells me he is reluctant to get involved. "I fear him. Is there a boat—"

"Tomorrow night." He rubs a spot of dirt from my cheek. "The Honolulu boat comes to Kalaupapa tomorrow night. I can get you on it."

"I will get down there tonight. I must get Samuel away from here—"

"Better you act as if all is normal until tomorrow. If he realizes you are missing he might come down to look for you. I can secure the patients' silence, but there's nowhere to hide in Kalaupapa—you'll see that soon yourself. I will meet you at the top of the cliffs and walk you both down the switchback trail at sunset tomorrow. I'll help you go home, Eliza."

I tiptoe to kiss him on the cheek just as he turns to leave, and he turns back with a bold, serious look. Then he takes me in his arms, lifts me slightly off the ground and kisses me with no hesitation, no apology. It is so different from Ben. Webster's height makes me feel tiny, desired and pursued, even at this most horrible moment of worry. Samuel.

"I truly must go," I say shyly, overwhelmed. "Samuel will be waking."

"Goodbye until tomorrow then."

"Sunset," I confirm. The thought that there is finally an end to this purgatory makes me want to kiss him again. Mist rises as I start toward my cabin. I glance back, rubbing my hands to warm myself, and see that Webster is staring after me, smiling broadly. I grin back at him. What a strange day! Then I walk to camp as quickly as my injured foot allows, listening to the whispering of the ironwoods, the sound Ikaika hates. It's getting late and the grasshoppers start making a carpet of noise along my path. They sound happy for me. I smell something warm and woodsy in the air. A grey cloud of smoke curls dreamily upwards from beyond the trees that hide the camp. *I'm going home.*

"*'A'ole! 'A'ole!*" I hear Keala screaming as I leave the path: their cabin is burning. Oh, God, Abram found out that Charlie told me and burned their cabin. Smoke spreads wide across the sky. I start to run, panic rising. I come around the cookhouse. It is my own cabin. Flames have split the house apart, bursting from the top. The camp gathers in the orange circle of light. Dogs keen and paw at the ground, running in frenzied circles. The workers' faces are slack; some weep. I push through the crowd with an ugly wordless cry, my fists clenched. Hands come at me, holding me back from the flames. I fall to the ground. "Where's Samuel?"

Keala's hands are on me now. "Charlie tried to save him!" she sobs. Through a dozen sooty legs I see Charlie panting on the other side of the circle.

Abram towers above us, holding a bucket. Water or sweat soaks the whole of his shirt and the top of his trousers. His hair is wet, stuck to his skull, and he looks exhausted. He staggers down to the ground and puts his head to his knees.

"Samuel is with Hina!" I correct her. "I left him with her! Where is she?" I scream.

The taste of the smoke makes me gag. I vomit as Keala tries too late to hold my hair away from my face.

"She's in the cookhouse, Eliza," Abram says. "Scared out of her mind."

"My baby's still in there?" I ask, disbelieving. I picture him, curling up into the burnt rock I saw the sheep become. A baby cast in stone. I become sick again. They carry me to Abram's new house, put me on a new bed as I choke and cough. I hear people coming in and out, talking in the corner. Keala rubs a paste onto my teeth as I shake my head violently back and forth. Charlie murmurs to Keala, and she hushes him. "My baby," I whimper.

Abram gives me a tin cup of warm whisky, and I gulp it down. "Why did this happen?" I wail. "Why? Why?"

"Shhh," Keala says. "Shhh."

I wake with Keala by my side. She's brought *'awa*, and I take it. The room is painted a glossy white, untouched by dirt and not yet furnished. There is only the bed and a side table. The windows are wrong: too high, like a jail.

"Come Eliza, you need to bathe."

I let Keala lead me to the basin in the next room. It is fancy, worlds away from the worn nickel tub I have used since my arrival. There are pink and aqua tiles behind it and a round mirror, identical to the one in my father's guest washroom. Abram has copied my home.

Keala hums sadly as she strips me of the skirt, stiff with vomit. It sounds like the hymns my grandfather, Caleb, sang, old missionary songs I thought I had forgotten. I lie under the water, my body extended and floating in unwanted luxury. The camp uses one cramped bathhouse, separated into one room for women and another for men. Samuel always clutches onto me there, unconvinced of his safety until we're settled into the water. I begin to choke.

Keala runs the cloth along the inside of my arms, which hurt. I remember hands holding me back from the flames. "What happened here?" she asks, looking at my foot.

I turn to the wall as the tears roll into the bathwater. None of it matters now. Keala helps lift me up and dries me in a worn clean cloth she's brought. She dresses me in an old brown mu'u mu'u. I hang onto her like an invalid while she pulls the dress down, then let her help me to bed. But when she tries to feed me rice, I pull away. Samuel, the smoke clogging his throat, his chest heaving with the effort to breathe. I cannot stomach any food.

"There is no greater pain," Keala says. "I lost three. Measles, pox, measles again."

She comes again, the next day or night. I am not sure. She puts down the rice bowl and brings out a roll. I turn away from it.

"You will have other children. It will not change how much you grieve, or stop you from loving the next." Keala goes into the washroom and comes back holding the soiled dress. "You just call when you want me. Just shout out the door."

"Do you think he was scared?" I ask, my voice cracking. "He thought I deserted him. I wasn't there. He died scared and alone."

Keala begins to cry too, holding me. I ask for 'awa again.

"No, no more, Eliza." Keala blots my face with a damp towel. "You need to eat."

"Just a little piece to sleep—"

"I watch you sleep all day. No more 'awa." She shakes her head back and forth. "Everyone wants to give you condolences," she says, changing the subject. "I told them, stay away right now. Give her time."

"Did Hina ask?"

"No."

A thought has been rolling about in my sluggish mind, "Keala, you don't think Abram would have set the fire to harm Samuel? Or Hina?"

Keala looks at me with pity. "It was an accident, Eliza. The workers burned some rubbish and a spark hit your house. Hina panicked. She's so young. She went for help. Abram tried to save Samuel. The men all saw it; he couldn't reach him. Charlie went in, and he… he couldn't find him. All the smoke."

"It was my fault," I cry. If I'd just moved into this house as he wanted, protected my baby instead of myself. So afraid Abram would touch me.

"It wasn't your fault. It wasn't." She cups my face with both hands. "That house was old and dried up. Could have been any of us."

I move my head slowly, like I understand.

When I sleep I dream I'm at home in Nu'uanu, standing at the pink-tiled basin. *"Father?" I call. "This is the same basin they had in Moloka'i."*

No answer. I walk into the salon. It is such a beautiful day. I'd forgotten the green and shadows of Nu'uanu. "Father?" I call again.

"I'm here," he calls back from the coat closet.

"What are you doing in there?" I laugh.

The closet is always a bit of a joke, designed by someone in New England who assumed everyone needs a coat closet. I open it. There hangs the rust-colored gown, the one I wore to the Palace the night Benjamin gave me the pin. It has been too long since I've felt silk and beading.

I hear a noise and move the gown aside to see if Father is hiding behind it. There's Samuel, his skin flushed rose, his fists raised. I bend down to pick him up, but he starts nibbling on the bottom of my gown, taking bites from the silk hem.

"I'm hungry," he says. "No one feeds me since the fire." His voice is a grown man's, like Ahsang's. I run to the pantry and take down the biscuits. I come back to feed him, but the door is swollen and stuck. I grow panicked, but finally it gives. I crouch down with the food. But he is gone, the gown pooled on the floor in his place.

Samuel! Samuel! "SAMUEL!"

"Eliza!" I open my eyes, my dream carrying over into the late daylight. Abram's bedroom is cast in the blacks and whites of bright light and shadow.

"It's all right," he says, one hand on the bedpost and the other shaking my arm.

"I dreamt Samuel was hungry. Stuck alone in a closet."

"Don't go conjuring up ghosts in my house!"

I gasp and burst into tears.

"I'm sorry, I'm sorry," he says. "I just can't … I don't want to be haunted in my own four walls."

"I would be so happy if Samuel would haunt me, so happy…" my voice trails off.

"I didn't mean that. Here, Keala says you need to eat."

I smell the fried chicken he's brought. It smells rancid. I think of Samuel cooking like meat. Burning alive.

"I'm going to be ill. Please take it away."

He puts the plate on the table, and that smell lingers.

"Take it *away*, Abram! Please, it smells terrible!"

He walks to the window and throws the chicken out. "I opened the window," he says. "This room was stagnant. The camp smells of the fire. That's what you're smelling. Do you want me to close it?"

"Yes."

He pulls the window shut. Even he has to stretch up on his toes to reach it.

"Why did they start a fire so close to my house?" I accuse. "Why did they start it up wind?"

"They're young," he says, wiping the back of his neck with a handkerchief. "Lord knows we tried," he says. "Charlie nearly died going in there." He sits on the edge of the bed and looks at my arms. "You'll shrivel up if you don't eat," he says. "It's not good, Eliza."

I'm amazed he can be so concerned with food after what has happened.

"Hina's put out you're in here," he adds.

"Why would you say that now?" The world has gone mad.

"Because one good thing has come of this sadness," he says. "My wife finally moved into our home."

Samuel's death has made me the sort of woman Abram likes. Damaged. The tears begin again. He blots them with his handkerchief, which smells clean. Who washes his things? Not Hina. His girl down the road?

"I am very sorry Hina got in our way, Eliza. It was foolish of me to start your life here that way. I am a father and I know what it is to love your child," he says carefully. "I am trying to be helpful. How can I help?" He actually looks like a father who understands.

"Is there anything, anything at all for me to bury?"

"The heat was so strong. The place is still sparking up. I'll go through tomorrow to find you something. I understand. I would need the same."

I look out the window: it is sunset. I am supposed to be meeting Dr. Webster at the top of the path with Samuel right now. Escape. Now I don't care if I die here or at home. A lifetime of no Samuel and no Ben stretches out in front of me. My only tie to him is gone. "We'll find him for you. We could put up a cross and marker—"

"Yes," I say.

He lies down beside me and puts an arm under my head, turning me toward his chest. "I went in to save him. Charlie said he thought you both were in there."

Was I kissing Webster while my child was dying?

"Flames were all around the house, but I went in, calling out your names. The smoke was so thick, I couldn't see or breathe, and the beams started coming down. I got out and said neither of you were in there, and everyone cheered. Then Charlie shouts that Hina told him Samuel is inside. That it went up so quick and she tried but she couldn't lift Samuel and carry Lee too. She's still small. She thought there was time to get help. Charlie rushed in and stayed inside for so long I thought he was dead. The cabin was about to come apart. Finally he came out, shouting the baby's not there—"

"What if Hina got him out? Maybe she's afraid she'll get in trouble—"

"I've asked her. He was in there," Abram says, decisively, dismissing my hope. "The smoke was so thick; Charlie and I couldn't find him because he wasn't crying. It was too late."

He lets me cry, and then he begins kissing the top of my head. He cradles me under him, and I am dead inside. My mind is with Samuel in a burning room, his eyes wide with wonder. When did his curiosity turn to fear? How long did he cry out before he understood no one was coming to help? I'm in that burning room. It's clear now, Samuel was on the bed looking around the fiery room with his mouth agape, trying to find me. He fell off and that's why they couldn't see him.

Abram moves on top of me, making me his wife.

I see Samuel. He wouldn't have understood fire, but he would have felt heat. He could feel fear. Hina let my son burn alive while she saved her own.

"...I know all about these things." Abram is lying beside me, talking. "You'll have a little baby to love again—"

"Please let me rest, Abram," I interrupt. "I'm not well."

"Fair enough." He rises and dresses with no modesty, clearly proud of his body. I curl up on my side, feeling ill. I am relieved when I hear him close the door.

9

"Look who came to say hello? See if his momma's doing better?" Abram says, putting Lee in my arms. "Don't cry. You'll scare him," he adds.

Lee's been washed. His curls smell of talc. It isn't Hina's way. Abram had him prepared for me. But it works. Clutching Lee, I have my first sleep in days without a nightmare.

Keala brings food early in the evening. I woke next to Lee, thinking he was Samuel. I'd jumped up from the bed. Keala has the smell of the cookhouse on her and tries to hand me a purplish lump of taro wrapped in a handkerchief. "It's boiled. I didn't think you'd like the venison."

I grimace, refusing to take it.

"You need to stop this, Eliza. It doesn't help you or anyone else. I've brought a bottle for Lee. Hina and Abram have gone off in a cart down the road. I don't know where."

She guides me toward the bed. Lee sleeps curled around the pillow I'd put at his side. I slide my pinky into his fist. He is very sweet. "Abram left him with me," I say.

"I know. Did you want him to?"

"It helps for now."

"Do you want me to stay tonight?" Keala asks.

"I can't bear talking to anyone, Keala," I say. "Not even you." Keala takes my hand in both of hers. She says a prayer quietly in Hawaiian. "I pray that you have company in your heart tonight. That you will be watched over."

"Thank you." I feel a gap between the two of us. I know Keala feels it too. I can't imagine being close to anyone ever again.

"I'll check on you in the morning, unless you call." Keala lets herself out with one last look back.

I take Lee in my arms and give him the bottle. I listen to small animals pleading their needs in the darkness, the moaning softness of empty fields. I belong in the company of the vulnerable. *TCHAK. TCHAK TCHAK.* There is a pueo calling from the grove of eucalyptus behind Abram's house. Benjamin told me the dead spend their first hundred days as flying creatures. "A humble moth could be someone entering death," he'd said. We'd met at the riverbank and heard something in the forest. It was likely a wild boar, but he launched into stories of ghosts and spirits. "If a moth or dragonfly flies outside your window, it might be your dead relative visiting. So be sure to say nice things about them."

"Who doesn't say nice things about the recently deceased?" I'd asked.

"My mother," he answered. "She can be fierce."

"A dragonfly can come haunt me all it likes," I'd told him, feeling very cavalier. "In fact, you can give me a moth made of jade, if you like. There's nothing frightening about insects."

"They're not haunting, they're visiting. It's not like a haole ghost, more like a friend hovering between this world and the next."

Tonight, I am not cavalier, listening to the owl. I cling to Lee as he slips back to his dreams. TCHAK TCHAK. TCHAK. Is

Samuel watching this house, waiting for me to emerge and take him home?

The door to my room creaks open. I hear a man's heavy steps on the floorboards. *Abram again.* I keep my eyes closed as he walks in the darkness from the doorway to my bed.

"Eliza, it's me."

Webster? I am astonished to see him, his lanky shadow not a foot away from the bed. "Why are you here?"

"I'm getting you on a boat tonight."

"There's no one to save now, Webster."

"I know." He crouches beside the bed so the outline of his face is nearly level with mine. He starts for a second at the sight of the baby, then he recognizes Lee, which seems to displease him entirely. "I am so sorry, Eliza. I wish I had gotten you out sooner," he says. "This is our chance. There's a boat arriving that wasn't scheduled. It's been diverted to take a rich man home."

There's nothing to run for now. "I can hardly bring myself to rise from this bed. I can't manage the path."

"I'm going to help you, Eliza. You're going to let me."

His voice is so gentle, but there's no gentleness left in me. I snap back, "I don't care. I don't want to be alive." I take my arms from Lee and roll to face the other way.

"Come." Webster lifts me to the floor, holding me up with his strength. "Come with me."

I look over at Lee's curls, his little fists. He's legally mine. I could take this child home with me. I lean over to kiss his forehead, his skin that smells of baby, but not quite Samuel. I look up at Webster. "I could give him such a better life."

He shakes his head. "It's theft," he says, his hand cupping my cheek. I nod. Everything spins as I stand. My empty stomach groans. Webster catches me and looks in dismay toward my feet where the hem of Keala's mu'u mu'u pools on the floor.

"We'll have to rip off a foot of fabric before we try the path," he says. "Where are your shoes?"

"My boots? I think they're in the washroom, over there." I point and he walks slowly down the hall, his hand scraping against the wall to find the washroom door.

He returns with them, kneeling down to put them on.

"They were behind the tub. Looks like they've been cleaned," Webster says. He tears a foot off the edge of the mu'u mu'u. It hangs lower in back than front.

"Can we survive the path at night?"

"Yes. I've done it before. When there's an emergency there's no other choice, and I know it well."

"I can't leave Lee here alone," I say. "It's dangerous. I should bring him to Keala."

Webster moves around in the dark until he's returned with a small crate filled with the hammers that had finished this house. "He'll cry as soon as he wakes, Eliza. Probably too soon. They'll find us when he does. Taking him to someone, it surely would give us away. He'll be safe in this until they find him." Webster takes out the hammers and uses the blanket I'd tucked around Lee only the hour before to line the crate. With a doctor's finesse he transfers the sleeping baby to the crate and pulls the pillow slip off the bed to lay over him. "Come," Webster tells me.

I take a last look at this little boy. *Please have a good life,* I think. I bend down to press a finger to his lips then follow Webster down the hall as floorboards moan beneath him. I walk weightless, steadying myself with one arm stretched out to the wall, as if I have lost my balance. "He was supposed to bring me bones today," I say.

"Come," Webster says. He takes my hand in the dark and walks me to the front door. "I've been watching for an hour outside. Abram's left with Hina. I saw Keala go back in her house. There's no time to say goodbye."

I'm glad. Goodbye would require emotions I can not muster.

We step outside into a full moon. "It's bright as a picnic day," he says in frustration. A dog begins to bark. Webster pulls us into a run with my left arm slung over his shoulders. Pheasants scatter out of our way, and I laugh joylessly at their bobbing run.

"Eliza, try harder." Webster's arm is around my waist as we head into the night.

I stumble over and over. I see the moon's harsh belly. Webster pushes me forward into the tall grass just beyond the ghost trees. They are shaking powerfully; so loud we would not understand one another if we spoke in a normal voice. Webster starts immediately down the path. I stand still: the moon has caught the rim of the land and lights Kalaupapa for perfect viewing. It's impossibly far. The trees breathe behind me. *Shhh, shhh, shhh, shhh, shhh,* they tell me. *Close your eyes and dream a little dream.* "I can't do it, I won't make it," I shout to him below.

"Eliza," he says tensely, turning back. "We will. We'll be fine in this moonlight." An animal runs across the path, a mongoose, and we flinch as if we've been caught. "Down the path now." He takes my hand. "There you go. Easy now. Just small steps."

I look out at the colony below thinking of the patients sitting by their lanterns writing letters and reading Bibles.

"Come Eliza. Do as I say. I promise to get you home."

Why do they bother? How much more elegant would it be to put down their psalms and their needlepoint, walk out to the water's edge and let themselves cheat misery? "When I first came, I saw a whole line of cattle jump to their death right here," I say. "Do you remember when that happened? They chose their death—"

"Let's talk about it down there," he says, looking nervously behind me. "You can tell me everything once we're down."

I walk to the very edge of the cliff's trail and let the exhilaration of the end leap through me. His arm is on me in a second. I let him pull me back, not because I want to see Father or live through another day, but because it's too much work to fight him.

The path smells of wet mountain, earthy and mineral. I slip and stumble on every root as we make our way down. He tries carrying me but stumbles under my weight when we hit a loose rock. Then a shower of stones rains down on us. I taste blood, but I don't cry out.

"Goats," he says, after casting his eyes about until he is satisfied the cause was hooves rather than feet. From somewhere in the darkness there's a seabird's cry.

It takes hours. Hairpin turns and slippery moss slow us until it seems we are making an eternal descent. The path levels out at last, and I can hear the sound of surf pelting the shore. Grey waves destroy themselves against boulders. I smell cheap liquor and realize it's guava, fermented on the ground around us as we step off the trail and onto the peninsula.

"We've done it," says Webster, sounding exhausted. "I have a horse for you, Eliza." There are three finely saddled horses waiting, and a boy standing beside them. "It's a bit of a ride to the settlement from here."

"Eh, Dr. Webster, you there?" comes a child's voice.

"Yes, Ikaika."

"Ikaika?" I whisper.

He comes toward me, his figure taller and stronger. Small pustules dot his skin. I stand before him, humbled. "Oh, Ikaika," I say, embracing him, smelling carbolic soap and rot at once. I'd felt like a thief holding Lee, even as he calmed me. It feels so true to hold Ikaika.

"Miss Eliza," he stiffens. "You better not."

"I do not care." I hold on to him, but he remains rigid with discomfort so I step back.

"You're bleeding," he says. "Dr. Webster, her face is all cut up."

"When did that happen?" Webster asks. "When the rocks fell?"

I shrug and laugh. They both look at me in a way that tells me I am mad.

"Let's get you on this horse," says Webster, seating me on an old mare. "It's an easy ride. Only a few miles."

"Do you still like trains, Ikaika?" I ask.

"I don't need one so much now."

He swings into the saddle, kicks his horse's flank and rides out ahead of us. His shoulders are becoming less childlike. I think of what Samuel could have been at his age.

"He came to me with the news of what happened to Samuel," says Webster, "He'd heard it from those who know the sentinels. He was so distraught. He loves you dearly, Eliza."

"I should take him back with me tonight on the boat. I could keep him at my father's house unknown. Care for him. Please?" Ikaika I could *hānai*. It would be as Mehana understood it. I would raise him as my own, without theft, with no aim or purpose other than love. I would go home with a child.

"Eliza. The captain will never board Ikaika. The disease is marked upon his face."

"I could pay him. I have money," I say, realizing that this is no longer true. There is no money. It all burned in the cabin. I have no money.

"I know Eliza, I know," he squeezes my shoulder. "But they will never board him, and the harbormaster will not release him off any boat. It will be hard enough to get you on. Let's focus on that."

We ride in silence to the settlement. It is a quiet place of pleasant homes that are far better than the cabins of the camp, with orderly gardens of surprising hopefulness. There are lime and tangerine trees. *What measure of optimism, or selflessness, must a patient here possess to plant a tree that will take years to bear fruit?*

Most of the houses are dark, but a few are lit, and I can hear singing, even laughter, within. On some of the patios, couples with disfigured faces watch us pass through. The sound of the ocean is everywhere, and as the patients stare I think of them living under the sea, their bodies covered with lichen and barnacles, their lives calmed by their slow liquid surroundings.

The doctor greets each patient by name; he rides up to each patio and says, "If any should ask if you've seen a haole woman coming through tonight, you have not." They nod. Agreed.

"The ship will come in around midnight," he whispers to me. "I'm keeping you in Clara's cottage until then. You'll be safest with Clara."

Clara. My breath catches in my throat, "Is there somewhere else I could go?"

"I thought you'd be happy to see a friend from home?"

"Not like this," I say, thinking of my torn dress and bloody face, of my unstable state.

"Eliza," he says gently, firmly. "Clara has no face left." He pauses. "She waited quite a while before coming here. I imagine her money protected her. When I asked if I could bring you to her she was excited until she considered her own appearance. I assured her you would be too bereaved to notice."

"Of course," I say, ashamed, urging my horse forward.

The sandy road takes us farther out, and begins to run tightly to the sea. Now the homes are not so much like cottages as remote and lonely lighthouses, for here the sea roars. We come to a dimly lit cottage with a young blooming stephanotis plant climbing its porch. *Clara brought a cutting from home,* I think. Webster dismounts and ties his horse to a post in front of an old wood fence. "Miss Ahsang," he calls.

It feels so strange to hear that name said outside my own mind.

The door opens. Clara is wearing the hat I sent to her, and she's brought it down entirely over her face. She wears a pink gingham dress with a sash that would suit an afternoon stroll through her father's gardens with a suitor. She extends her white-gloved hand from the shadows. "Eliza," she says in a gravelly voice.

I realize the disease has also ravaged her vocal chords. I take her gloved hand gently, feeling where fingers are missing. "Clara," I say, unsure where to look.

"We find each other in situations much reduced. I am so sorry for your tragedy."

Her tender speech, her ruined voice, they open the lines of my grief. I cry the first tears I've shown the doctor, and he puts first one arm around me and then the other. His heart beats out the seconds. I feel I should raise my head and part us. But we stay like that, the doctor holding me, Clara frozen in the shadows, her patience endless.

The parlor is tidy. There is a strong, sickly sweet odor mixed with the smell of the paraffin lamp that lights the room. I breathe in and out of my mouth. Clara stays hidden near the door.

"It bled profusely because it's above your mouth. There's no need for stitches," Webster tells me. He wipes the dried blood so tenderly, I feel shy having Clara present.

"I must tend to a patient now. I'll fetch you as soon as the boat is sighted, Eliza," Webster promises. I follow him outside and feel a surge of panic as he tightens the stirrups of his horse.

"Eliza, come and have a rest," Clara says from the doorway.

I imagine turning around to find her whole again. "Do you hate it here, Clara?" I ask, keeping my back to her.

"I did when I first came. But the sicker I got, the better I felt being here, where I am normal and no one is afraid of me. The only time it still hurts is when I'm with someone who does not have this disease, and I feel how much I repel them."

I turn and look squarely into Clara's face, which pleads for compassion. Most of her nose is gone, a small flattened knob of flesh in its place. Lesions pull the skin below her eyes. There is such sincerity in those eyes. "We are just the same, Clara," I say. "I am finished now, too."

Clara shakes her head. "If I had the chance to take a boat home tonight and wake up healthy in Honolulu, I'd burst with joy. The only things left to me are legs to walk and a tongue to speak. Just look at me. Even with this tragedy, you are so much luckier than the rest of us."

"Had you been a mother, you would not think so," I say, my voice catching. I feel anger toward her, telling me I am lucky when I'd rather be dead.

"No, I will never be a mother," Clara says simply. "Did you know mine came with me? She may not understand who you are."

"Your mother is here?"

Clara nods. "She knew I had the spots. For months she knew. She wouldn't let me turn myself in. And then Richard recognized it."

"Richard Irvin turned you in?" I am shocked.

"No. But Emilie told me I was endangering everyone. Her, the servants. And she was right. Why should I be exempt from the law? Money should not make me the exception. My hands became claws. It was time. Mother wouldn't let me go unless she could come." Clara shrugged, as if it were natural.

My father couldn't come to see me off at the harbor. He had gone weeks without word of me and not been concerned. But Hannah, a stubborn, half-crazy woman, had come to the direst corner of earth for her daughter.

"She has kept me in good company," Clara said. "I have not been lonely. And her life is just as it was at home. Even without the opium syrup, she dreams. Dr. Webster told me he thought us strong enough to live without it."

I can nearly taste the syrup. I want to ask if she has any in her home. The craving I feel for its sweet escape is dangerously close to what drives my father to his Scotch. "I would like to see your mother," I force myself to say.

"Oh, thank you, Eliza. Thank you." Clara leads me inside her cottage, opens the bedroom door. "Mother. It's a friend from home," she calls.

I walk into the little room. Two beds are pushed against the wall. There is a crucifix over each bed, and two chests. Hannah sits barefoot, her chair facing the corner. Her hair is loose and white down her back. She turns to me. "I know you," she says.

"Yes," I say gently. I sit on the edge of the bed facing her.

"May I offer you some tea, Eliza?" Clara asks. "You needn't worry, Benjamin sent some fresh cups for me after I complained to him of the cheap sailors' mugs I was drinking from. So you will have a clean one."

"Thank you." I say, looking at Hannah's white hair, wishing I could find a room like this to hide myself in forever. Clara leaves us for the tea. Hannah looks at me for a long time. "You lost the boy," she says, reaching for my hands. "Clara told me."

I nod, tears starting again. How can there be any left?

"I lost three," Hannah says, nodding. "My baby boy, then Ben, then Emilie. I'll die without seeing them again. Clara will leave me next, when he takes her." Hannah looks at the cross on the wall. "Choose a place where you can die in peace and quiet, as I have. That is what you must do," she tells me.

I think of the opium syrup, of drinking it until I no longer have to worry that I will wake.

"And make sure there is a little bell with your lost boy. That he can ring it if he is not really dead. To be buried like that is the worst fate one can imagine, and it happens."

I pull my hands back the same time I hear a scream. I run out through the back to the little cookhouse just steps away from the cottage. The leather of Clara's glove is on fire. "Clara!"

I plunge her hand into a rain barrel.

The smell is enough to make me retch.

"Oh, don't worry. I didn't get burned badly. It doesn't hurt at all; I was only afraid for my house," she says, pulling her hand out of the water as if nothing's happened and returning to the stove to crumple newspaper like a toddler by mashing it between the two stubs of her hands. She throws the paper atop the stove's flame and then reaches up to the shelf above to take down the tea tin.

"Here, let me at least measure it out," I say, spooning it into the strainer, shaking off Hannah's words.

"Do you remember when you would come visit us with your white ginger, and stay to have tea?" Clara asks happily, seemingly unaware my hands are trembling badly.

"Yes, of course."

"Those were lovely days. And I will always be grateful for your kindness to me here. I have worn your hat every day," she says, raising her eyes to the brim of it. "And the soap! It is so hard to get nice soap here. Always the stench of carbolic. The jasmine ones you sent are such a luxury for us, Mother and me."

"They were small things, Clara."

"No, no they weren't. They may be small elsewhere, but not here. Now I wish to return the kindness to you," she says. "I have fine clothes I've never worn which I can send you home in. Come and see while this steeps. They are beautiful."

I follow her back into the bedroom. Hannah watches with pride as Clara lowers herself to her knees and, with surprising strength, lifts the heavily carved lid of a chest to release the smell of cedar and reveal a collection of gowns with pearl buttons sewn on damask and contrasting shades of silk.

"Who made these?" I ask, holding up a deep violet silk with gold embroidered birds; its coolness soothes me.

"Benjamin sent them. I have no need for them here."

"How thoughtful of him to have them made for you. He would want you to keep them," I say. How different my life would have been as Ben's wife. I would have dressed in gowns like these for an evening out, with Samuel watching me from his bassinet. Samuel would be alive.

"Oh no, they weren't made for me," says Clara. "His wife wore them last year and now feels they're out of date. From the look of it she wore them only once."

"Oh." The silk feels slick as I fold the dress over my arm. "The tea will be ready," I say somberly.

"Mother. We're leaving for the parlor. Do you want tea?"

"No. I want sleep," she says looking at me, a clear dismissal.

"Goodbye, Mrs. Ahsang," I say, knowing it will be the last I ever see of her.

"I'll be out in a second, Eliza," Clara says. "I'm just going to settle her."

I go to drink our tea in the sitting room, where I recognize a bureau from the Ahsangs' study. Its dark walnut top is inlaid with triangles of a lighter wood, like a chessboard.

"I remember this, right under the window," I say to Clara when she joins me.

"Yes. Ben's wife had new things done for the house and Ben was kind enough to send the old pieces I wanted."

"He was in Honolulu?"

"Well, yes. Benjamin and his wife have returned to Hawai'i. It's safer for the children than China at the moment. Something about bandits. They're expecting another child. The last was a girl. So of course they hope."

I am surprised at the intensity with which such news can still hurt.

"I got the piano, too, but I've lost the ability to play," says Clara, sitting in an overstuffed chair from the Nu'uanu parlor. "I sent it to the girls' home here."

She picks up a sandalwood fan and waves it mightily, though the night is far from warm. It is a device to mask the smell of her rotting flesh. My fan burned in the fire. Or did Hina save it and not my son?

"Do you remember that picture, Eliza?" Clara points to a family portrait done ten years before, sitting on the side table. Clara stands in the center, beaming with her brother and sister on either side. The girls are dressed in white. Ben wears a dark suit. He stands by his father, who looks out over a high stiff collar, challenging the world. Hannah Ahsang sulks into the camera. Behind them is the painted screen of Waikīkī.

"Yes." My eyes linger on Ben. "How is the rest of your family?"

"Father writes me once a month. He never asks about the disease, but he sends me packages of curios I give away to the children here. He knows Mother is with me as my *kōkua*."

"It seems you are more her helper, Clara."

"In the day to day, yes. But if it weren't for her, I might have thrown myself into the sea by now. She is my *kōkua.*"

"Then she's a true parent to you," I say, and Clara nods.

In the orange glow of the lamp, it looks as if her face is burning, the lesions moving like scalding skin as she speaks. I think of Samuel's skin on fire and suppress a gag for Clara's sake.

"I was afraid she might catch sick, but she only grows more sturdy in that room. Perhaps it's all that haole blood she never wanted to own up to, protecting her." Clara chuckles and in the moment, I see the friend I knew so well, before her illness. Before her sadness. Before mine.

"I worry what will become of her when I die," Clara says. "Emilie wrote me often in the beginning, but I haven't had a letter from her in some time. She came when Mother and I left on the schooner for Kalaupapa. She wore a veiled riding hat though it was night. She gave us letters stuffed with ridiculous amounts of cash. Boxes and boxes of medicines packed for us, Chinese herbs and bottles of tonic. But when the other families started wailing she couldn't bear it and left. Mother and I stood there, watching people howl with grief. We didn't have anyone howling for us. I mean, you can't blame her for not endangering herself. She has quite a life to look forward to. Her husband, Richard will be president after the Queen is gone."

"Does she say that?"

"Yes. She is very sure of it." Clara answers. "Benjamin writes me. He writes the best letters, full of amusing stories of bad behavior at receptions. His wife is very social."

"I'm sure she is."

"Eliza, you seem displeased by the mention of Ben. And Mei Ling," Clara says.

"Mei Ling? Is that her name?"

"Yes," says Clara, taking a long sip of her tea and watching me intently.

"I once thought I might be his wife, Clara."

"I wondered about that," she says slowly. "You were not yourself when he left."

"I wanted to tell you. After he left. I so needed someone to open my heart to."

"And I wanted to tell you of my sickness, but I couldn't." Clara keeps still, waiting for what I will say next. I am exhausted and spent by holding up the weight of this lie for so long. I have absolutely nothing to lose by telling the truth. Not anymore.

"I was with child, Ben's child, when I left O'ahu to come here. It was his absence that forced me into the marriage I now flee. My child who died was his. Samuel was Ben's son. Samuel was your nephew."

Clara gasps, putting down her tea and raising her gloved hands. "Did he know?" Her hands fall from her face to reveal wet eyes.

"No." If Samuel were next to me, telling the truth would have been liberating. Without him, it feels terribly small. "It doesn't matter now. Ben can't help anymore. It hurts that he has other children, but Samuel is gone. When I am home I will stay far from your brother and his wife. Please do not write him the truth."

There's a knock at the door; we stay in our chairs, not ready to end the confession.

"Eliza," says Webster through the door, "the ship's been spotted."

Clara rises and looks at me, asking permission to invite the doctor in. I nod.

"We should start to get you ready. Perhaps you'd like to wash up quickly?" he asks gently. I'm still in the torn mu'u mu'u.

"I have towels and a basin in the water closet," says Clara. "There's a travel bag under the bed I won't be needing again. Put the dresses in there."

I obey but put only one of the dresses in the bag. It is violet and will remind me of Clara and her days of bright silks. I dip the towel straight into the pitcher to wipe my face and hands and then my feet.

It takes all the water to get the dirt off, and some remains. I put on one of Mei Ling's cast-off gowns: an opulent black silk with a silver sash. It is not appropriate for a boat trip, but I have no other clothing. Webster chats with Clara in the parlor, detailing the acceleration of her symptoms.

"Those are all normal, Miss Ahsang. I wish I had a better solution, but I haven't."

"I know," she says lifting her eyes as I enter the room.

"Much better. We should say our goodbyes," Webster says, rising from the chair and nodding at Clara before stepping outside to give us a moment alone.

"I'm in shock about what you told me tonight, Eliza. I wish you what I hope will one day be a peaceful life," Clara says, her eyes welling up again. "I imagine this is the last time I will see someone from my youth, ever."

I put a hand gently on her shoulder to bid her farewell, but Clara curls up in pain. I take my hand away. "There is a young boy here. Ikaika. I don't know if you know each other?"

Clara shakes her head quickly.

"I met him at the ranch and love him very much. Will you look out for him? He's as close as I have to Samuel now. Will you do this for me?"

"I would like that," Clara rasps, one gloved hand held up in parting as she turns away, overcome.

"Come, Eliza," Webster whispers. "There's nothing more here for you to do."

"We're incredibly lucky this ship is coming," he says as we walk toward the landing. He looks tired and smells of disinfectant. "I've told you it's not a regular stop. There's a visitor here who claims to be in acute distress. He is being rescued due to his money and connections. I think his true illness is fatigue with the sick; he thought they would entertain him better."

"An official?" I ask, picking the silk skirts up, draping them over my arm. I am having a hard time keeping pace with him.

"No, a writer from England. We get a few, now and then, though they're ones I haven't heard of. They've read Robert Louis Stevenson's letters describing his visit here. We seem to be a part of the Hawai'i tour for them."

"I met him in Honolulu. Stevenson, I mean."

"Did you? He is well remembered here. Pleasant man. Played with the children and seemed genuinely moved, unlike this cad we've got here now. He's been whining since he arrived. I am glad to see him leave. Ikaika can do a good impression of him."

"Where is Ikaika?"

"He went to put the horses in for the night. He's coming to see you off."

A group of patients is gathered under the landing torches. I try not to be frightened by the look of them, reminding myself that under their masks are other Claras and Ikaikas, but in the torchlight they almost look sinister.

"Do you ever become accustomed to it?" I ask Webster softly. "The horror of the disease?"

"After years here I still—I hate to concede this, but I still am ill after some of the examinations. Whatever force of nature dreamed up this disease made it the cruelest concoction possible. Somehow many still find fulfillment in the lives left them here."

The lives left them. It seems impossible I'll find a life in front of me. I look for the ship, but see nothing. "Where is it?" I ask.

"I don't know. It seems to have disappeared." Webster steps to the water's edge, puzzled. "Aloha *Kauka*!" a patient calls. Webster waves. "Where's the ship?" he asks.

"Was there, but now no light. Maybe gone already?" says the patient.

The doctor looks at me as we both calculate what that will mean to our plans. It will give Abram ample time to find me. I feel queasy.

"There's nothing we can do but wait here," Webster says, squeezing my wrist softly.

I watch the ocean and think about this island that has taken so much from me. Was Samuel's death fated from the moment Ben left Hawai'i, or was it the moment I stepped onto this island? Sprays of water reach us, and we move back. I'm so terribly tired. I sit down and lay my head on the traveling bag.

Like a miracle, at half past one, the boat's light comes back into sight.

"Ikaika's here to see you off," says Webster, waking me in time to see the disliked writer emerge from the shadows.

"I brought you this," Ikaika says, holding out a multiplication table decorated with flowers, cows and a woman with yellow hair. She looks sad, but he's given her a nicer waist and head of hair than I deserve. He would do well with the ladies with such flattery.

"I shall keep it always," I say, folding the paper into my bag. I'd never considered having to say goodbye to him twice.

"Is Hina's son good, Miss Eliza?" he asks, catching the edge of my skirt's hem to run his hand along the silk of the dress. He crumples a handful in his fist, not letting go. I picture Abram standing over Lee in the crate, my escape discovered. Abram's rage.

"He is kind and calm, very much like you," I say. "Ikaika, I have a friend from my childhood here. Miss Clara. She's lonely. I'm going to send her packages. May I send you things in her packages? So you have a reason to go see that she's doing well? Would you do that for me?"

"I can do that," Ikaika says.

"Come, Ikaika. It's time to load Miss Eliza and the writer in the boat and row them both out," says Webster. "Come, Mr. Wilson," he calls out irritably.

The writer follows us meekly down the landing. The doctor steps in first, helping me in the boat and then offering his hand again to the writer. Ikaika watches us, looking lost. Behind him the group of patients stands perfectly still, a collection of crumbling statues. I notice a young woman holding a little boy's hand, both their faces marked with the sores.

"I like come out to the boat, too," says Ikaika.

"Jump in then," says Webster. Ikaika scampers into the boat unaided, and the writer moves like a crab to get away from him. Ikaika purposely moves to sit right next to the writer, and our audience of patients bursts into laughter. At first it is heartening, but soon their laughter turns mean, with calls of 'good riddance' to the writer.

"Now, now," says Webster to the crowd, though I can tell he is not angry. He begins to row us away.

The patients are shouting out their goodbyes, and in them I hear my name. I turn back to shore and recognize the man calling to me: Joseph, Mehana's nephew. I've utterly forgotten him tonight. His body would be powerful if he was a healthy man. His face is swollen, but he is unmistakably Joseph; we saw each other often growing up. He lived along the fishing ponds of Kuliouou, far enough east of Nu'uanu that every time he came to our house he'd jumped up a size. He'd bring puakenikeni lei for Mehana and me. We'd sit on the grass singing together as Kepa played the ukulele. Mehana wore his golden lei through dinnertime, even as it became bruised, its sugarcane scent all gone.

"Give Mehana my love," Joseph shouts to me. I nod. He makes the sign of the cross and turns to make his way back through the crowd. I do not trust that this truly happened, or if my mind is playing tricks, for I feel as if I have seen a ghost.

"Did you see that man saying goodbye to me?" I ask Webster.

"They all were saying goodbye to you, Eliza. Ikaika speaks of you often. Hold on to the side; the water is rough."

It seems an eternity before we make it a mile off shore to wait for the ship, the lights of which blink in and out of view.

"I wonder if she is the ship after all," worries the writer.

"It is," says Ikaika. "Look, it's coming now." He points out the approaching light, and Webster begins moving toward it. Finally, the ship is before us, and a crewman throws down a line. Ikaika moves to grab it. "Don't touch that," shouts the crewman. "You'll get us all sick." Webster takes the line himself. The writer boards quickly without a word.

I turn first to Ikaika, putting my hand over his heart. "I will send you my love in every package."

"Goodbye, Miss Eliza," he says. "I'll write you."

"Please board, young lady," comes the captain's voice from above.

"Yes, let's get you aboard," says Webster. "You'll need this," he adds quietly, handing me money for the passage.

"Thank you for rescuing me," I say, flustered and embarrassed to accept his money. "If you are ever in Honolulu—"

"Now, Miss!" shouts the captain.

I grab on to the rope ladder, the bottom of my skirts making a wet *thud* as they hit the water. Once I've reached the top, a crewman scurries down to get my travel bag from Webster and returns, pulling the ladder up after him.

"Thank you!" I call.

Ikaika waves in huge circles. Webster raises an oar. The waves are knocking the little boat as Webster turns it around, Ikaika flipping back to watch me so he can keep waving.

"I am being prayed to death. PRAYED. TO. DEATH," I hear a woman scream. I turn to see a young woman of mixed race tied to a railing. She focuses on me as I shuffle to the far side of the ship. "YOU. I KNOW WHO YOU ARE! YOU KILLED MY FAMILY!"

"Take her below to the cargo," orders the captain in a bored tone. I look at him thankfully. His skin is so pillaged by the sun that even in the dark it's painful to look at. "I don't care if she chokes on her vomit," he adds.

"If she's drunk," says the writer as he joins me, "I wish she'd share a bit."

"Her? She murdered her husband. I'm transporting her to the police in Honolulu. I am not a prison warden, and I am not a chaplain," says the captain. "I am simply sent out to pasture in this amateur corner of the Pacific."

I move away from them both, having no desire to be caught in a night of conversation. The woman continues ranting in the hull. I put my head into my skirts and pray for sleep.

I wake at dawn to the shape of Diamond Head. Ahsang's bungalow hides in the faint light behind newly planted monkey pod trees. I wonder if Ben brings his wife there and then force myself to stop thinking about them as we approach the harbor. I can see the tip of Father's roof in Nuʻuanu. The woman below is screaming.

That could be me, I think.

Were it not for Webster, that *would* be me.

I watch the harbor. Something is amiss. None of the usual crowd loiters on the wharf to see what is coming in, no smell of roasted meats wafts from the Chinese shops, no echoes of carriages travel between the wooden buildings. Rather than the merging streams of sailors and ladies, salesmen and servants, I observe only a scattering of souls, one of whom is a hostile-looking American Marine with two native Hawaiian police officers.

"Where is everyone?" I ask a boat hand untying a rope. He straightens to scan the wharf and then shrugs his shoulders and drops the rope to the ground. "Some kind of outbreak again?" he offers, leaving me to wonder on my own.

The captain sets down the walking plank. "Everyone stay back until the criminal is removed," he shouts. The police board the ship, then bring the woman up from the hold. She is trying to bite their arms. I watch her being gagged and put into the back of the police carriage.

"Are you continuing over to Maui, Madam?" asks the captain with a good hint of sarcasm. He rolls his eyes around the deck. The other passengers have disembarked. An older gentleman is greeting the writer, who seems not to know him.

"I'll be on my way," I say, picking up Clara's traveling case.

I walk off the ship onto Fort Street. On a normal morning there would be half a dozen hacks for hire, their drivers jockeying for my dollar. Not a single building looks open.

"Eliza? My goodness, I didn't realize you were back."

I turn around at the sound of my name. There stands Mr. Jensen, my father's lawyer, his eyes opened wide like a circus master, admiring Mei Ling's dress. "Moloka'i has agreed with you," he says.

"I've just arrived." I put a hand on my stomach to calm my breathing. "Where is everyone?"

"Have you not heard the news? They're dethroning the Queen."

"What?"

"The planters are pushing it through as we speak. They had a few hundred American Marines come ashore from a warship yesterday, marching right where we stand. They came through the city before nightfall and are quartered near the Palace." He waves his arm at the unopened windows of the dozens of offices on the street. He looks around. "Where is your father?"

"He…wasn't expecting me."

"Well, I'll take you up—you won't be finding a hack today. It's quite lucky for you I needed to get some papers out of my office. Didn't want to risk some nutter trying to burn the town down. Who knows what will happen? These will be strange times."

Jensen picks up my bag, and we head down the block toward Ahsang's grocery. "I thought it better to leave the horse where people could keep an eye out, at Ahsang's. Looked as if they were gathering papers too. We're on the edge of anarchy I believe."

Jensen loads my bag in the foot well of his buggy. I smooth my hair down, wondering if Ben is upstairs. But Jensen's buggy is the only one on the street.

Jensen speaks of the comings and goings of people whom I can barely remember the whole way up Nu'uanu road. Homes are shuttered, and even on such a warm, bright day no one is on their balconies. It is a day of neither work nor play.

We pass a grove of barren ginger. The season is wrong for it. "Why isn't anyone home?" I interrupt Jensen.

"Meeting in parlors and out in the country. Meeting and scheming."

"Will you scheme with Father?" I ask. He must be repulsed by what is transpiring.

"As much as I can. Your father has little interest in business these days. He's disheartened, I suppose you could say. Perhaps it will be better now that you're here. And now that he's a grandfather. When will we meet your boy? Or boys? You've adopted another? We received the paperwork from your husband's attorney, and I tried to have your father agree to look into it a bit but he seemed utterly unbothered by it all so I assume you are pleased to have a brother to your own son?"

"My son will follow me," I say, unable to think of anything else and feeling sick. We pull up the drive. The garden has grown wild. Vines cocoon around the shower tree. Weeds stand a foot high. A bank of heliconia has grown unchallenged under the parlor windows, its untended leaves reaching up to shroud the first floor from view.

"What's happened?' I ask, as we head to the door and my skirt catches on the sharp stalks of a plant I do not recognize.

"Your father tells Kepa he wants the forest to reclaim the lawn," Jensen says, following me up the stairs to the patio. "William?" he calls through the front door, which is ajar.

Father sits in the parlor, his eyes glazed. "Hello," he says meekly, as if caught. He does not seem to notice me.

"I found your beautiful girl at the wharf, a happy surprise," Jensen says.

Father's eyes find me. He mumbles to himself, annoyed.

"Father," I say, approaching him. The smell of liquor on him is strong and foul.

"Perhaps Eliza should have a rest from her trip, and the two of you can catch yourselves up later, eh, William?"

Father grimaces, and then his face goes slack.

"Yes, I'll go upstairs and maybe you'll sleep as well? Then we'll have dinner together," I say flatly. Father nods forward, mouth agape. He falls asleep. Even if my letters had reached him, he could not have saved me. I'd been doomed by the bottle from the start.

"It's been like this, getting worse every month. I think he was very lonely without you," says Jensen under his breath, drawing the curtains though there's no need. The parlor could be underwater it holds so many cold filtered shadows. The garden blocks every window. The light it does allow in comes through broad wet leaves. The room feels as green and wet as moss.

"Well, that was his choice," I answer, walking away from Father without bothering to lay a blanket over him. "Thank you for your kindness. I'm going to lie down."

Jensen gives me a short bow and steps double time down the patio to his buggy.

I lean against the bannister and take it all in: the curve of the stairs, the cut flowers in good crystal vases placed on furniture around Father's crippled figure. It seems luxurious and achingly empty. The back door swings open, and Mehana's heavy footsteps follow. She puts a blanket over Father. I see her feel my presence; she turns and gasps.

"Eliza!" She hugs my whole body to hers. "What's happened?" she pulls back and asks.

"I lost Samuel." It sounds so odd, almost false when I say it.

"How?" she asks.

"Fire."

"Oh, *ku'uipo*." She rocks me back and forth.

I hold myself stiffly. "I can't yet, Mehana. I can't talk," I say, stifling a cry, making an ugly sound instead. She guides me to the kitchen and lowers me by the shoulders into a chair. She puts tea and bread and jellies in front of me. I tear the bread to bits. She presses a napkin into my hand and pulls her chair closer. "What's happened to him?" I ask, blotting my nose and nodding toward the parlor.

"His Scotch." She pulls her chair closer. "He's barely hung on while you've been gone. Sometimes he goes to his club and doesn't start till the night. But on the days he's home, it's like this. He doesn't know what happened?"

I shake my head no.

"Tell him when he's sober. Otherwise, he won't understand." Mehana stands and peels fruit, arranging the slices on the plate like stained glass. I eat, my first food since Samuel.

"Did Benjamin ever know?"

"No." I swirl my tea wildly in the cup, trying to make it reach the brim but not spill.

Mehana stops me. "They left for China a few days ago, when the demonstrations started," she says. I feel a heady mixture of relief and sadness.

"Are you going to tell him if he returns? You should, Eliza."

"He's married."

"I think he told Mei Ling there was something with you. She was asking the servants. If I figured it out, they might have too."

"I escaped the ranch through Kalaupapa," I say. "I saw Joseph. For just a moment as the ship left."

She sucks in her breath. "How did he look?" she asks, her hand on my knee.

I cannot bring myself to tell her. "It was so quick, I can't be sure it was real. I was in such a state. He said to give you his love."

"It was real then," Mehana says. "Whether it was his body or his spirit you saw."

I nod. I'm back in Mehana's world: if Joseph was physically at that dock, or if he was in a narrow bed dreaming of home and his dream came to find me—it is the same level of fact.

"I saw Clara, too. She is not in Rome. She has the sickness."

"She didn't say goodbye to anyone," she says. "Poor thing."

"Her mother is with her." For the first time since fleeing the camp, I think of Keala. She brought Samuel into this world, and her husband, Charlie, fought to keep him in it. I left them without a word. "As a *kōkua*."

Mehana nods. "Emilie's telling everyone her mother is on a grand tour. Like anybody gonna believe that." Mehana turns serious. "You needed a *kōkua*. I failed you."

"No. Father did, but never you."

I cross my arms on the table and rest my head in them. I am so tired.

I wake to the sounds of guns firing. It's well into the night. A group of riders charges by the house shouting something unintelligible. By the time I reach the window they have passed. I walk quickly down the hall, my black dress dragging on the floor. I open Father's door slowly, but his room is empty. I find him stretched out on the divan.

"Father." I shake his shoulder. He groans.

Again I hear riders, and this time I make it to a window in time to see the blur of torches. They are shouting to one another as they pass. Then I hear a horse coming up the drive and feel a surge of fear. "Father!" I call from the window. "Wake up, something's happened."

I watch a man rein in his horse and look up into our windows. It's Jensen, thank God. "What's happening?" I ask as I open the front door.

"Is your father functional?" Jensen looks feverish, sweat beading along his brow.

"I don't—"

Jensen walks to Father's side and claps loudly two inches above his face. "The Kingdom is finished, William! Finished!" he bellows, as if on stage.

Father opens his eyes like a man woken from the dead. He says in an utterly sober, enraged voice, “What are you going on about? What’s all the shouting for?” He sits up. “Eliza? What on earth? Is your husband with you? I did not tell you to come home!”

“Samuel died. So I came home.”

The two men stare at me. “A fire,” I say. Father’s hands shake and Jensen draws back. “I’m so terribly sorry,” he says, all his bravado and excitement deflating. He walks quickly across the room to leave.

“Why have you come at this time in the night?” Father asks him.

“The Kingdom is over,” Jensen says, pausing at the door with his hat in his hand.

“Over?” says Father, mockingly. “I don’t care which of these preachers’ sons has gone and declared himself ruler. It’s not finished until the Queen says it is.”

“Oh, but she has,” Jensen answers. “The United States Minister has recognized the new government. The Queen has surrendered for fear of bloodshed. Martial law has been declared.”

10

Grief descends on me. I stay in bed, watching the sheerest of clouds move low across the valley, past waterfalls and the smoke of neighbors' chimneys. Nu'uanu becomes a misty Chinese mountain scene. Mehana brings meals of lima beans and chicken. When those sit untouched, she offers thick pieces of toast smeared with butter and guava jam. She removes those, uneaten, and returns in the evening with slices of star fruit.

"Kepa went next door to get these," she says. "He worries about you."

I eat them, tears streaming down my face, the salt and sweet stinging my mouth. I think of Clara in Kalaupapa as I eat the fruit from her trees.

"I think you scared your father straight," Mehana tells me. "He's sitting out on the lanai with his coffee. Hasn't had a drink all day. Could you come down?"

I shake my head. "I'm staying here."

"They have dresses like this on Moloka'i?" Mehana asks, brushing the cloth of my dress still laid across my desk chair.

"It's Mei Ling's," I say, too tired to explain when she looks at me as if I am insane.

"It's raining hard today," Father says. He walks to the window and watches the water flooding the lawn. "Look, six, no, seven waterfalls. Your upside down one is there as well," he says. With his back still turned he begins to speak. "Eliza, what you've been through is more than can be imagined. But there's nothing that can change it now."

I say nothing.

Father comes closer, holding papers. He pats my knee awkwardly through the sheets. "I need to get a message to the Queen. You can visit her on the pretext of Ka'iulani, whereas I cannot."

"Send Kepa with it," I say. A burst of rainwater falls like a dumped bucket from the gutter. I think of workers throwing buckets of water on my burning cabin.

"They will search Hawaiians. If Kepa is caught with my message he'll never see the outside of the Reef again."

"But you're perfectly willing to put me at risk." I look at him through my tangled hair. "Again."

"Eliza, the worst men in this kingdom have sent delegates to Washington to ask for admission to the United States. They've banned the Queen's lawyers from booking passage on the ships leaving for Washington. She's been cut off from most of her funds. She has to pay for an entire ship to get her lawyers to Washington to plead her case. She needs us. Look what they made her sign. Look."

I read the paper he thrusts at me:

> I, Lili'uokalani, by the Grace of God and under the Constitution of the Hawaiian Kingdom, Queen, do hereby solemnly protest against any and all acts done against myself and the Constitutional Government of the Hawaiian Kingdom by certain persons claiming to have established a Provisional Government of and for this Kingdom.
>
> That I yield to the superior force of the United States of America whose Minister Plenipotentiary, His

> Excellency John L. Stevens, has caused the United States troops to be landed at Honolulu and declaring he would support such provisional government.
>
> Now to avoid collision of armed forces and perhaps loss of life, I do, under this protest and impelled by such forces, yield my authority until such time as the Government of the United States shall, upon the facts being presented to it, undo the action of its representative and reinstate me in the authority which I claim as the Constitutional Sovereign of the Hawaiian Islands.

"They will never do anything to a young white woman. A bereaved mother. You'll be safe. And you were right about Richard Irvin: he's leading the charge in this. But everything can still turn in the Queen's favor. We owe this to her. Our sugar is in no small part due to her brother."

I put the paper on my bedside table. "Tell me, Father, did you not think it strange you weren't getting letters from me?" I look straight at him. "Did you not think you should—at the very *least*—send someone to inquire into my welfare?"

"I assumed your life was busy. I suppose I took it as a good sign—"

"I was begging you for help!"

His shoulders flinch.

"Your *drinking*—"

"Yes. You're right," he says. The rain casts a strange dripping pattern down the walls and over Father's figure. He takes off his glasses. "There were long patches when you were gone, that I was not… thinking at all. Patches I barely remember. But now I will have to remember this. Every day of my life." He presses his forehead against the window. "I never liked drink before your mother died. Today I'm done with it. And I will tell Jensen to seek a divorce for you. I will pay what that man demands for the adopted child, Lee. You are no longer obliged to Mr. Malveaux."

"Do you want me to say thank you?" I ask this ghost of my father standing before me. This man will disappear into the shadows with his afternoon drink, I'm sure of it.

He sighs, deeply. "The Queen needs every friend she has at this moment."

I wonder if the Queen knows I'm barely able to dress myself. With leprosy, death's approach is obvious; with grief, the face stays unmarked as the heart fades to nothing.

"I don't know if there is anything to be done," I say.

"The planters did this without the U.S. President's permission. American troops were brought ashore by John Stevens, a minister who did not seek his government's approval. *That* could cost them their victory in Washington. President Cleveland is a good man. We must have faith, Eliza. If you don't want to do this for me, do it for her."

He puts letters at my bedside table. Without even looking I know whose hand they are written in.

Sundown,
Hesketh Park,
Southport

E,

I am told you have married! It pains me that I must learn the news so belatedly, and offer my congratulations in such a poor manner. How I would have loved to have thrown a grand lūʻau for you at ʻĀinahau. How my uncle would have wanted to toast you, sing for you.

Our letters crossed about the King. The tears come now as I write about my Papa Mōʻī. The Queen suspects your own quiet marriage was done out of respect to our mourning, and it touches us so. Perhaps your sensitivity to our feelings has prevented you from writing me of it, but please do not hold back. Please, tell me everything.

I have left Harrowdan Hall for good. Please use the address above.

With love and joyful congratulations,

K

May, 1891

7 Cambridge Road
Brighton

Oh, Eliza, I have been so sad about everything they tell me of home. I fear Auntie will not be able to hold on, though her letters do not show the concern others in our circle seem to feel. I am unsure who to believe. Will you write me the truth? I trust your voice implicitly.

I was sad not to hear back from you since my last letter. My father inquired for an address on Moloka'i for me, but was told by your father that the ranch was much too remote to reach by mail. I received a letter from your father assuring me of your friendship, but it will not suffice.

My education has been moved to Brighton, and I am happy here. They say I have a good soprano voice. I will be visiting the Jersey islands, which I hope will remind me a bit of home. Perhaps by the time I am truly home you will have a child I can fawn over and be an auntie to. There must be something to return home to other than intrigues.

Your K

July 1891

E,

I will not put an address on this letter, for it is the same as it was last I wrote. Your father continues to assure mine that it is simply impossible to get post out from where you are. But I suspect your sympathies may have changed with the new husband you have taken. Father says he is aligned with Richard Irvin, and Richard has gone firmly to Clarke's side. I cannot remember a single birthday party without Richard. But then again, it was Clarke who pushed for me to be sent here. They used familiarity as a brilliant ruse.

Have you also had a change of heart, Eliza? Please just tell me if so.

I will accept if you have gone to the other side. It seems everyone has.

K

Kepa keeps the carriage top up. The roads run thick with mud and puddles, sending our wheels bouncing violently over spots where the paving dirt has washed away. Kepa turns the carriage short of the Palace, and I remember I will not be visiting the Queen there: the planters occupy it now. The Queen has found refuge at Washington Place, her private home a stone's throw up Beretania Street.

Two of the Queen's guards stand at the gates, young men relaxed in their roles. They feed Kepa's horse fruit from their lunch box. I am let inside without hesitation, just as Father predicted.

"Eliza Dawson," I state quietly to the maid at the door. I can hear the Queen playing the piano in a side room, a song of her own composition, *Aloha 'Oe*, Farewell to Thee. The music stops as I'm brought into the room.

"Your Majesty." I curtsy, my head down low as Father taught me.

"Eliza." She closes the piano cover. Queen Lili'uokalani looks infinitely older than when last I saw her: hair greyer, figure stouter. She was never classically lovely, but was always very much Hawaiian *ali'i*. Today she wears a black silk *holokū*. The dress's train pools at her feet. "We are matched, you and I," she says.

I wear the black mourning dress I wore for her brother's wake. The fabric falls loose around my wasted frame.

"Come, let's sit in the garden. The rains have stopped."

I follow her through rooms brimming with ornate European pieces surrounded by feathered *kāhili* standards in reds and yellows; ownership of this house came to the Queen through her late husband, John Dominis. He died leaving only a son fathered with one of her servants. She leads me out to the large covered patio, separated from the garden by white pillars. Trees surround us, throwing cloud-like shadows onto the patio's stone floor. The stone is so cool, a chill passes through me as we walk over it.

"This is such an oasis for me at the moment," she says as we step through oleander bushes onto the lawn. A medicinal scent hangs in the air. We sit at a table on the grass set for tea. "The missionaries can take away my palace, but they can't take away my garden, can they?"

"No, your Majesty. They cannot." I look down at my cup and saucer. Men stand guard dressed in matching black pants and white shirts. They keep their distance. A young Hawaiian girl dressed in black pours the tea.

"I want to say first that I am sorry for your troubles." She pats my arm. It is the first time she's ever touched me. I never thought she liked me. I once overheard her tell the King that Ka'iulani would forget all her Hawaiian if I was the only child she played with.

"The news of your child is heartbreaking," the Queen says now.

"Thank you for your condolences." I wait, my throat dry. I am aching to take a sip from my cup. It is rude to take a sip before the Queen.

"Eliza, your father has long been a friend of ours and I'm heartened he sent you." She tilts her head in a way that recalls the King. "I have to ask before we speak. Were you ever engaged to Richard Irvin? Or is that my memory playing tricks on me?"

"No. We...disagreed on many matters," I say. "He married Emilie Ahsang."

"That I know. I attended their wedding. She carried chrysanthemums in her absent father's honor. I gave them a parcel of land in Pahoa as a present, because her father was always so good to us. Now Richard Irvin says all the crown's lands will go to his Provisional Government. That's what they call themselves now. The PGs. But they are still the missionaries to me. May heaven look down on them and punish them for their deeds." She shakes her head. "These men. They are the same sort who put smallpox blankets in the hands of Indian children. They'll stop at nothing to clear the land for themselves."

She's right but wrong: Richard Irvin does not think Hawai'i should be in the hands of Hawaiians, but he is not immoral. At least he wasn't.

"They meant to deceive us all along. Richard Irvin, sitting and eating at our tables all his life. Clarke, telling us to send my niece away. People say this would not have come to pass if Ka'iulani had stayed home. They say she is too beloved to have her throne stolen." With this she stops to take a sip, replacing her cup on its saucer noiselessly, the hurt evident in her face. "What do you think, Eliza? Did they plot her departure?"

"Yes, perhaps." I say. "Had she stayed, she could not have stopped these men, but she might have caused others to rise up against them. She is a romantic figure for many. I hope you don't mind my saying that?"

"No. It's the truth. She is half white and their ideal of beauty—the sort of princess haole men want to honor. Want to fight for. They do not prize fierceness in women as Hawaiians do. As we always have."

"Yes," I say, thinking of Chiefess Ahina and Hannah and Clara, and how each successive generation of that family's women has been kept in tighter and tighter circles as Hawai'i changes, until what is left survives only in a tiny house, on a sliver of peninsula, surrounded by cliff and rough ocean.

"You are her closest friend. I once worried that a planter's daughter might make her too tame, too haole. But you two ran wild together, barefoot to the ocean, sitting in dust under that banyan with those peacocks of hers chasing you."

The Queen smiles, and I smile too. It is not an abandoning of grief; it is a smile of remembrance. Just as the Queen giving up her throne was not surrender but survival. To have resisted the PGs when they brought in the American marines would have cost too many Hawaiian lives and provided no victory.

"I miss her very much," I say, finally taking a sip of my own tea. "How does the Princess bear the news?"

"I have not received word from her yet, but I know my niece has been apprised of this illegal act," she says, sitting up straighter. The softness displayed only moments before disappears, and she is strident. "Talk of her taking my place will alarm her."

"Of course," I say, my eyes catching those of a guard scanning the house. So she knows. As I was leaving this morning, Father told me that some want the monarchy maintained until Ka'iulani gets home and takes the Queen's throne. Sanford Dole, a leader of the PGs, is trying to convince everyone that this is the answer. But Richard Irvin insists it is time to do away with the "vile" trappings of monarchy entirely.

"You've heard of this plan as well?" Her tone betrays her anxiety.

"Only in passing. I do not believe it's being taken seriously, your Majesty," I answer.

"Kaiulani's father says I ruined the throne for her, that I pushed too far, too quickly to regain our rights." Lili'uokalani shakes her head. "All this talk of pitting my niece and me against each other."

It is strange to think of them as rivals. I remember Lili'uokalani leading Ka'iulani through an entire room of presents on her birthday: Ka'iulani rushing from one to the other as they were opened by servants, Lili'uokalani saying the name of each gift in Hawaiian.

"My father does not agree with it," I say, bringing the letter out and tucking it in my napkin.

"Well, I should hope not," she says, gesturing for the young girl in black to go get something. I pass my folded napkin to her. It is heavy with bills.

"I need every friend I have in your race at this moment," she says, softly.

"Yes, your Majesty," I say.

"Anyone sympathetic to my cause, to Hawaii's cause, should know my door is open to them," she says, twirling the string of onyx beads around her neck. She releases the beads and tucks Father's envelope below her chair. "Thank your father for me," she whispers. "He renews my faith. All hope is not lost, Eliza. The American president received me at the White House during my last trip to Washington. He will not like this vile cluster of thieves." She raps my hand twice like a conductor calling musicians to attention. "Irvin and Clarke will come back with nothing. I have faith."

I notice a woman watching us from the porch. The Queen raises her hand in greeting. "Come, Fraulein," she calls out. She leans toward me as another chair is brought and the table is cleared. "You may stay to have your cards read, if it interests you. She is very insightful."

The Fraulein reeks of herbal oil. She is also dressed as if for a funeral, but once she takes her seat she wraps herself in an orange shawl wildly embellished with beads and tiny mirrors, then reaches into her satchel to fetch her cards. She begins to deal; I glance at the unsettling, violent images before me and turn away. I know my cards say death.

"Open your eyes," the Fraulein commands me rudely. I look back at the cards unhappily.

"Open her eyes to what, Fraulein?" the Queen asks, her hand finding mine. "She's lost her child. Can you contact him for her?"

"No," the Fraulein says. "He's not there yet." She looks at me and points down to the cards, her finger touching the faces on each of them. "Stop letting men take from you. Never trust what they tell you."

"She says the same to me," Lili'uokalani says in an urgent voice. "She's right."

I quickly hand the Fraulein a bill. "Thank you." I turn to the Queen. "With your permission, I will leave you to your reading."

The Fraulein keeps her eyes on the cards while the Queen stands and walks with me. "You must have faith that you will overcome what God has put in your path. Devastation is written all over you, my dear. But we both must rise up now, Eliza."

We bid each other a respectful goodbye. Then she hurries back to her German clairvoyant.

"You have a visitor coming today," Mehana says, putting coffee and the morning's newspaper beside my bed for me. I look at the lacy window trims and little girl's dresser of my room, realizing I may well become an old maid here, waking twenty years hence and trying to remember the feel of a babe in my arms. The shower tree taps against my bedroom wall: *Come out, come out.* I watch it press its round leaves against the windowpane again and again, the vines which hold it hostage clinging to every branch. I pick up the paper to read Kaiulani's words, addressed to the United States of America.

Four years ago, at the request of Mr. Clarke, then a Hawaiian Cabinet Minister, I was sent away to England to be educated privately and fitted to the position which by the constitution of Hawai'i I was to inherit. For all these years, I have patiently and in exile striven to fit myself for my return to my native country.

I am now told that Mr. Clarke will be in Washington asking you to take away my flag and my throne. No one tells me even this officially. Have I done anything wrong that this wrong should be done to me and my people? I am coming to Washington to plead for my throne, my nation and my flag. Will not the great American people hear me?

I put the paper down. "How alone she must feel, on the other side of the world."

"It's her father who is coming this morning to pay his condolences to you," Mehana says, and hands me the coffee. "Drink. Your father asked me to get you up."

Archibald Cleghorn, Kaiulani's father, arrived in Hawai'i from Edinburgh to run a dry goods store with his parents. Then, with the luck of a white man in the tropics, he ended up marrying one Hawaiian princess and siring another. Likelike loved to remind her husband of his lower status, sending Cleghorn to fetch her wrap from upstairs at 'Āinahau when a servant was easily at hand, and they fought often. He detested raised voices, dramatic words. She sought both. But when they danced, his tall frame against her voluptuous one, the gardenia in her hair against his cheek, one could see how two opposites had created beautiful Ka'iulani.

I dress in black and go to the window of my father's study to watch the tortoiseshell carriage come up our drive. Cleghorn is dressed in a formal black suit, holding a massive bouquet of torch ginger. He stands frowning at the disarray of our garden while a much smaller figure descends from the carriage. I can hardly believe my eyes. It's Robert Louis Stevenson.

My father greets both men.

"How did the Princess learn of it?" my father asks as they settle into their seats. Cleghorn's lanky frame fits awkwardly into our small lanai chairs, never replaced after Mother's death.

"By telegram. Quite disappointing for her," says Cleghorn, displaying his tendency to understate everything. "I have never given the Queen anything but rather good advice," says Cleghorn sternly. "But she has turned out to be a very stubborn woman, not satisfied to reign but wanting to rule. If she had abdicated earlier as I'd urged her to, the throne could have been saved, but she did not think they would do as they did. If she'd shown more patience, we might have held them off until my daughter could take the throne. Now my daughter's birthright has been squandered."

"It's not finished yet," Father says.

I wait to see if he will tell them of the errand he sent me on, but he keeps quiet. He'd quizzed me when I returned from Washington Place. *What exactly did the Queen say? Who was there? Do the missionaries post guards near her?*

"So, how did you convince our brilliant friend to come back?" Father asks.

"Oh, I'm only passing through." While Cleghorn's voice is clipped and dry, Robert Louis Stevenson, a fellow Scotsman, sounds like he's singing a tavern tune when he speaks.

"We can't get you to stay?" Father asks.

"There's too much civilization here. I prefer the life of a Polynesian village. Samoa agrees with me." Stevenson looks my direction in the study, and I wonder if he still remembers me telling him it is where I liked to hide. "I hoped to see Eliza. Though the circumstances are beyond imagining. I most certainly understand if she is not well enough to visit."

I shore myself up and walk out. The three men stand for me. "Look who's come to see you, my dear." Fathers says. He is solicitous, apologetic.

Stevenson opens his arms. It is like hugging a tall child; he's much frailer than he was four years ago. His velvet jacket smells of musty, lovely old books. Everything about him is worn, yet I'm sure I could warm my soul by the light of his eyes.

Cleghorn stoops to give me a peck on both cheeks. "These are from our girl," he says, handing me the spectacular ginger.

"Grown at ʻĀinahau; I'd recognize your work anywhere," I answer, for he is a devoted botanist. "You must be aching to take a sheers to our neglected garden." I say as soon as Father takes the bouquet to the kitchen.

"It looks bewitched and abandoned," Stevenson says, waving his floppy straw hat over me as if to enchant. "With our heroine kept hidden high up in the castle's keep."

"Nonsense," counters Cleghorn. "It looks as if your father's lost his man. I can send up one of our—"

"No," I say as I sit. "It is entirely by his own choice." I look back toward the kitchen. "You must do me a favor, sir. You must assure Kaʻiulani my heart was always with her. I was prevented—"

Father returns and begins to talk politics with Cleghorn immediately.

"Shall we stretch our legs?" Stevenson asks me. His forehead is more blue-veined than I remember. I take him past the vine-strangled shower tree and through the row of royal palms, across the stream to the mossy boulder Ben and I loved. He tells me of his town in Samoa, how they call him *Tusitalia.* Storyteller. Then we are quiet together, simply listening to wind and birds, and he asks, "Did your son have any favorite things?"

It makes my heart leap. He's the first person to ask me to talk about Samuel when he was alive. "He loved baths. The color green. Your poems." I smile. "I read him *Counterpane* on his last day. He was often sick."

Stevenson keeps his eyes on me as I talk. Those lantern-lit eyes, his illness consuming him even as he shines light on all those around him. "In Samoa," he tells me, "there's a little girl who reminds me of you as a child. A bit. She asked me to make up a birthday poem for her, because her birthday is on Christmas and so there is never a celebration. I told her, I'll do you one better. I'll deed you my birthday. And so, the 13th of November is now hers in perpetuity. I will not be needing it any longer."

"It is a generous gift," I say. Samuel's was November 11th. So close. I scan the valley wall for some sign of life. An escaped leper, fleeing the sentence of Kalaupapa, perhaps. I could tell such a man to embrace banishment. There is an immense kindness in people once they have stopped fighting for their own survival. I think of drinking opium syrup until I sleep forever, and how much it will or won't surprise those who love me.

"I'd like to deed something to you, Eliza, if you will allow it." Stevenson takes a fountain pen and notepad from his velvet pocket, "Eliza Knowles Dawson," I can't help but smile that he remembers my middle name, "is hereby deeded one R.L.S. voyage out of Counterpane."

He scribbles his signature and hands me the note. "I don't give them out lightly. I was only given so many myself."

I trace the ink of his florid signature with my finger. "You are so very kind, but don't waste it. My life is done. I know that."

"I'm not convinced. I could have based an entire book on that grandfather of yours. You come from hardy stock."

"My grandfather never lost a child." I stand, ready to go back.

Stevenson takes my wrist and sits me back down. "When I was sick of living in a bed, my father would say, 'You don't look it boy, but you come from a line of lighthouse builders. Don't wallow.' And don't you know, forty years later, I'd rather be drowned, thrown from a horse, aye, even hanged than to pass through that slow dissolution of defeat. Die with your boots on, dear. I always say, die with your boots on."

I slip my hand into his to thank him for trying to help. His fingers are so feather light I'm afraid I will hurt him. I let go to push back my unkempt hair caught in the forest wind. Stevenson's long brown hair falls against his blue-white skin. "I've monopolized you long enough," he tells me. “My mother always said I loved giving sermons but was never willing to listen to any.”

“No, I will think of what you've said. I will. Perhaps when you return next I will have used your note.”

He looks at me very clearly, his expression telling me there is no use in saving any words for a next time.

When we return, Cleghorn and Father appear to be politely disagreeing.

“If you bring her home now, she can sway people's feelings,” Father says. “They all see her as for more sympathetic than the Queen. She could save this Kingdom.”

“Bring my daughter into the eye of this storm?” Cleghorn answers as he stands up. “No, thank you. This group will stop at nothing to destroy the family that stands between them and their profit and power. Better she is uncrowned but unbullied by this heathen lot, eh, Eliza?”

“Yes. You are wise to keep her safe,” I say, shooting a verbal arrow at Father. It misses its mark, for he has started asking Stevenson about his next voyage to Samoa, and tries unsuccessfully to convince him to stay with us longer.

The four of us bid goodbye with promises to see each other again. I watch Stevenson step into the carriage, wishing to burn every last second of him into my memory. The carriage starts down the drive and then stops short.

“Eliza!” Stevenson calls, head craning back at us through the window. I step forward, unsure what he wants me to do. “Under the wide and starry sky,” he shouts, “Dig the grave and let me lie. Glad did I live and gladly die. And I laid me down with a will.”

“Cleghorn is hating this,” Father says under his breath.

“This be the verse you grave for me,” Stevenson calls up to the sky. “Here he lies where he longed to be; Home is the sailor, home from sea.” He blows me a kiss then, and holds his hat up as I blow one back. Cleghorn raps the side of the carriage impatiently, then raises his arm in a parting salute.

"Bravo, Bravo," Father shouts after the carriage. And they are gone.

K,

I have had no change of heart. My friendship is ever yours.

Please forgive my silence. There was an element of scandal and tragedy to my marriage. It will have to be a story for when you are home, but I promise you the truth. That was the reason for my absence from you.

I saw your aunt yesterday. My father is determined that we can help. I stand at the ready.

Your father and RLS visited me at home most kindly today. I could feel your presence in the combination of our souls brought together. Their gift to me was the reminder that kindness exists. That there are gentle souls at search of one another on this Earth when the darker forces surrounding us feel all powerful.

Perhaps you have heard about my son. I have suffered a great loss and do not yet have the strength to be a good writer, but it will come.

Forgive me,

Forever your friend,

E

The house has not yet woken. In the kitchen, Mehana's shears are on the chopping block. They smell of rosemary as I open and close them, walking down to the shower tree. The morning is charged with color, the sky's blue rich and soft. I snip the vines choking my tree at their base and try to pull them down. Even after I've snipped the same vine in three or four places, I only remove a small remnant off the trunk. I pull at the mass in frustration before giving the tree a good kick.

"That won't kill it."

I turn around. "Webster," I say, barely whispering it in my surprise. He stands ten feet away, his clothes rumpled, his face so open to me: I can see in his great blue eyes that he wants to find me well. I'm still in my dressing gown.

"You should be calling me John by now, I would think," he says.

"I like you as Webster." I close the shears. I see no buggy or mare in the drive. I look at him, confused how he's managed to appear in our garden.

He smiles. "I walked. The boat got in an hour ago and I found out pretty quickly where you live." He carries a small bag.

I don't know whether to hurry back into the house to dress or pretend nothing is amiss. He seems at ease, so I stay. "Who's minding your patients?"

"A new doctor arrived Wednesday." He walks toward me and takes off his hat. "It wasn't hard getting the Board of Health to send someone to replace me. I've been there beyond what they'd asked."

I dread mentioning Abram. "Did he—"

"Yes," Webster answers, using his hand to point out the chairs on the lanai. We take a seat. "He came down to the bottom of the path with that cowhand, Lopaki, and a gun," he tells me, keeping his voice low. "I was in the clinic when I got word from the sentry. I brought a dozen of the patients with me to face him. We met him outside the colony, where you and I found Ikaika and the horses that night. He didn't like that the patients were there."

Webster had empowered himself with Abrams' greatest fear: disease.

"So he kept his distance. He shouted at me to give you up. I told him he was free to search the entire place for you, and he didn't like that offer one bit. I told him you'd likely gone to Kaunakakai. He stayed for a while, turning his horse around in circles."

I can see it all too clearly. "Abram is demanding money for Lee. He wrote Father's lawyer, saying Lee is now the sole heir, and apparently he's right. My father was too deep in his drink to prevent the adoption being confirmed."

"Well, he screamed about Lee being left alone. He said he'd get back at us. Then he bolted. I knew it was time for me to leave. He's built up some good will in the settlement with gifts of meat and money; I didn't want this to be divisive in the community. They have little to survive on except the tranquility of their lives."

I picture Abram at the bottom of the hill surrounded by the sick. I wish the disease upon him. "I'm sorry my freedom cost you your work."

"There's always a place for my work. I needed to leave Moloka'i. I'd started to forget there is anything other than death." He puts his hand around my wrist, turning it upwards, his thumb on my pulse. "How have you fared?" he asks.

"I fight my sorrow."

He nods, releasing my hand, and we are quiet for a while. He turns his eyes up to the sky, which is lush and promising. "Let's take a ride," he says. "To the greenest spot we can get to."

I laugh. "You've just taken an overnight boat, walked up from the harbor, and now you'd like to take a ride?"

"Eliza," he says. "I need to see fresh, living things today. Good, unbroken creation."

"There's quite a view of creation from the top of this valley," I admit. "And the horses could use the exercise. Father and I…we haven't been out much."

Webster saddles both mares while I change. I pin my curls up under my riding hat, pulling its dotted veil over my face and taking gloves from my bottom drawer where I still keep the dance cards from balls. The top one bears the initials, B.A. I envision Ben on a ship to Asia, moving farther away from me with every nautical mile. He has no idea what we have lost. I move his dance card to the bottom.

Webster sits in the saddle holding the reins of the softer mare for me. He dismounts and helps me up, letting his hand touch mine. We ride out the gates and turn onto Nuʻuanu Road. It's Sunday and still too early for the parade of carriages heading to church. I take him past the great houses and give a brief account of the families in each, recounting scandals of mistresses and lost fortunes. He asks for more details.

"Aren't doctors supposed to be above such things?" I tease.

"I'll take entertainment wherever I can find it," he answers with a wink. "My father always said it's not gossip if you don't know those involved, and I'm sticking to that."

We leave the civilized portion of Nuʻuanu and enter forest, dripping and lush with small streams. The trail is wild with stones and sudden drops, but I've made this trip so often I could race through it, and Webster has mastered the more treacherous Molokaʻi trail. Like the path down to Kalaupapa, this one reeks of guavas thick on the forest floor, making my stomach flip as the memory of Samuel clamps down hard on me.

We work our way to the top of the Koʻolau mountains, following the lava rock trail through the gap of the Pali's sharp peaks until it opens onto a view of the other side of the island, an amphitheater of mountains around fertile land and then endless ocean. Tiny villages and small fields dotted with water buffalo are the only signs of man on this side of Oʻahu. Sugar hasn't succeeded so well in these rainy hamlets. But this time its beauty fails to inspire me.

Webster reaches out and takes my hand. The force of the wind at the overlook point is blustery enough that it feels natural to anchor each other as we stand on the jagged precipice that drops down thousands of feet from the crumbling lava rock walls. Thousands of O'ahu soldiers were pushed to their deaths from this spot by the invading army of Kamehameha I. That battle built the foundation for the Hawaiian throne, which has passed through five Kamehamehas, down to Lunalilo, then Kalākaua, onto Lili'uokalani. Next it should go to Ka'iulani. This is the spot where Hannah's ancestor was saved by an owl. Samuel's ancestor. How many generations ago would that be? Chiefess Ahina's father. He was five generations back from my son. I think of the cliff at Kalaupapa, of falling. Warmth flows from Webster's fingers. My shoulders drop slightly, and I close my eyes under the morning sun, lulled into a feeling of safety.

"Such a Garden of Eden," says Webster. "Whenever I've been in Honolulu I've spent my time at work and never made this journey. I'm glad we came here together."

I listen with my eyes still closed. He waits until I open them again.

"Eliza, I know that you have suffered a tremendous shock," he says. "I will stay in Honolulu for as long as I might be of some use or comfort to you. If you find you do not have need of me, I will make my way back to Melbourne. But if you think I might find some role in your life, I will stay on, to see if that day might come."

I look out to the ocean, knowing that from this point of the island we face America, not China. My back is to Benjamin. I look at this man beside me, this good man. His face is hit with a gust of wind, and he laughs and squeezes his eyes shut, bringing my hand to his chest as if needing me to save him, when I know it is him saving me. He opens his eyes and smiles in a way that says we'll be all right. This is the card Stevenson gave to me. *This be the verse you grave for me. Here he lies where he longed to be; Home is the sailor, home from sea.*

When the wind stops I lean forward and say, "I might imagine that role."

11

January, 1895

It feels strange to hold a baby again. Clarice is faultless, happy to lie in her bassinet peddling her feet in the air while I finish a book. "Early, but very healthy," Webster tells patients who stop us in the street to admire our baby girl.

"What a beauty!" Father exclaimed the day of her birth, watching Webster clean her in his competent, medical manner. Then he burst into tears. "I'm sorry, I didn't expect this," he'd said, looking at us and asking, "What is wrong with you two? She's healthy, isn't she?"

"I've just been through this before, Father," I said, hair crushed against my cheek. My daughter's delivery was easy: two hours start to finish, with Webster attending me throughout. I didn't think of Ben this time, just the long night of Samuel's birth. What his little body had been like to hold.

"Many mothers are hesitant until babies get a little sturdier," Webster told Father, keeping his eyes on the squirming pink girl he was wrapping in a yellow spun cotton blanket Mehana had hemmed for us.

Webster brought the baby to me to nurse in the dead of night, bathed her when he returned home from his rounds. With his labor came deep love for our daughter. It was Webster who guided Clarice through the lifting of her head, clipping of nails, first steps.

I am more circumspect with her, loving her, surely, but sometimes catching myself addressing her as one might a child one has been paid to care for. I keep her clean and well fed, on a perfect schedule. I keep myself ever so slightly distant.

"You're just afraid of losing her, too," Webster told me. "It will pass."

Clarice is almost a toddler now, and Webster has started to blame my unease on the frantic pace consuming Honolulu. Bicycle contests overrun horse races. Telephone lines cover up tree branches. Elaborate Gothic mansions erupt on hillsides and city street corners. Neighborhoods are rife with bitter feelings for and against the overthrow. Nearly two years on, history's verdict still hangs in the balance, keeping us all on its knife-sharp edge. The Queen's prediction proved true: Irvin and Clarke failed to impress President Cleveland. The American press accused them of stealing Hawai'i, and for one week, victory was ours when Cleveland decided in the Queen's favor and declared the PGs should turn control back to her.

But Sanford Dole, Richard Irvin and Lorrance Clarke simply refused. Instead they pronounced themselves the Republic of Hawai'i. Dole declared himself President. They made political hay by joining forces with the U.S. Republican Party to pillory Democratic Cleveland for "refusing to support American citizens." They filled the press with rumors, claiming the Queen was a barbarian, saying she'd behead them if returned to power. In reality, she said she'd banish them. Their political pressure keeps Cleveland from doing anything more for the Hawaiians. And yet America still does not offer annexation, and now the PGs hold onto their power tenuously through spies and arrests, predicting annexation will come with a future Republican White House. Royalists hang their hopes on rumors that President Cleveland will not oppose a Hawaiian uprising, even if he can't send troops to help us.

"An uprising?" asks Webster, "That seems very risky talk."

"Perhaps people feel now is the time for risk," I say, careful in my words. We sit on the little second story porch of our modest Mānoa Valley home, looking down on New England-style cottages surrounded by wild banana patches and tracts of bamboo, rain dripping off the pointed beaks of white bird of paradise. The house is fashioned from stone and beams with recessed windows. It sits on a little lane set blissfully off the social path of Honolulu, and I wake each morning to a view of Diamond Head crouching leonine beside the ocean below. We live happily, with no hired help and few visitors. I start each day with a coffee Webster brews with Clarice's assistance. He kisses me goodbye as I read the morning papers over her silky head, staring at pictures of those I grew up with taking bitterly opposing roles in the crisis. Ka'iulani travels from England through New York and Washington, pleading for the survival of the Hawaiian Kingdom to the American president and the public.

Her speeches are emotional and reprinted by the papers loyal to her cause.

> *Seventy years ago, Christian America sent over Christian men and women to give religion and civilization to Hawai'i. Today, three of the sons of those missionaries are at your capitol asking you to undo their fathers' work. Who sent them? Who gave them the authority to break the Constitution which they swore they would uphold? Today, I, a poor weak girl with not one of my people with me and all these 'Hawaiian' statesmen against me, have the strength to stand up for the rights of my people. Even now I can hear their wail in my heart, and it gives me strength and courage and I am strong—strong in the faith of God, strong in the knowledge that I am right, strong in the strength of seventy million people who in this free land will hear my cry and will refuse to let their flag dishonor mine!*

Opposite her elegant portrait is one of Irvin and Clarke meeting with Republican Senators on the stairs of the American capital. Richard Irvin is now second in power only to Sanford Dole. He and Emilie have taken over the Ahsang estate in Nu'uanu. I can hear their patriotic American ice cream socials when I visit Father, the band booming over the mock orange hedge that stands between our properties. When our paths cross on Nu'uanu road, Emilie calls, "Eliza! is that you?" from her carriage and offers a bob of her parasol. We never talk about Clara or Hannah or Samuel. We pretend nothing has happened.

I politely decline the invitations she offers, for I suspect Abram attends her social hours. He lives on O'ahu now. He remarried—his new wife is a wealthy, older haole widow named Jacinda Cassiday—and Richard Irvin appointed him to the Committee of Safety a year ago. When someone is arrested for speaking out against this government, it is by order of Abram Malveaux.

"Isn't that what Robespierre called his committee during the French Revolution?" Father asked Webster when it was announced. "When he sent everyone to the guillotine."

"It is," Webster said neutrally. My husband eschews fiction but will soldier through any tome on history. Still, he refuses to be caught in Father's political snares.

"It suits the situation entirely," Father says. "There is a Reign of Terror in these islands. Informers are everywhere. People dare not speak, even in their own homes."

Webster refuses to rise to the bait; he shuns any talk of Abram. I have studiously avoided any place our paths might cross Abram's and have thus far been successful. No small feat in a town of this size; I avoid a whole stretch of Beretania Street to avoid passing his mansion. I do keep in touch with others from Moloka'i; Joseph passed soon after I fled Kalaupapa, Clara survives still. Her letters are filled, improbably, with stories of the great love she's found at the camp. She's married a Hawaiian minister from Kaua'i who was struck down with the disease himself, and they have adopted several of Kalaupapa's children, including Ikaika:

Now that I feel this kinship of motherhood, I understand better your bravery that night you came here. Ikaika and I, we send blessings to your daughter and thank you for bringing us together. We pray for you with everything God has left us.

I send Ikaika soap, sweets and a new book each month. I am not sure they interest him now, but it is a comforting habit. He writes me about what he eats that day:

No fish wanted to be my friend today, so I came home with one empty sack. But we have so much mango right now on these trees. I can eat them until my arms itch from too much sap. I'm happy to give the fish another day in their ocean.

I write him of plans being made on O'ahu to build a sugar train on Moloka'i, like the cow train he once described to me. It thrills me to know he is thriving, that his strong spirit is rooting itself into the cliffs of Kalaupapa.

Keala found me by writing, using my maiden name. Abram forced her and Charlie off the ranch after my escape was discovered:

We were taken down to Kaunakakai; cousins agreed to take us in. Our daughter came back from O'ahu and they live with us now. There are fish, taro, and sweet potato every day for the five of us, and that is more than enough. Charlie does better here. The trauma of not saving your dear boy changed him, but we are at ease with our lives, and I pray you are too.

My life *is* good now, and I am thankful. There are still nights when I dream of Samuel trapped under the sea or behind a wall of our house. I wake unsure of where I am, then shake the nightmare off and set the kettle on. If Webster is up, I bring him tea and settle into a chair to read a book set far away from here. I jump at any sound outside. "Darling, Abram's not coming to get us," Webster assures me from behind his desk.

He has no idea how charged his words truly are.

Abram and his henchmen are raiding chapels and lūʻaus, accusing worshipers and dancers of holding royalist meetings. His crew denounces and jails newspaper editors who dare to print anything other than glowing reports of the "government" they've replaced our monarchy with. He's forbidden all large gatherings. Abram Malveaux fosters fear and protects Richard Irvin's good name while he does it. But Irvin knows very well what Abram does. I doubt they ever discuss what happened to me on Molokaʻi. I think about both their part in it each time I drive through the Queen's gates with my flowers wrapped in newspaper, my daughter's blanket tucked so well around her. The Queen brightens when she sees me brought out to her in the garden. As long as there are men like my father, men with money and sympathy to her cause, there is still hope.

"Eliza," she asks me as I pass her the flowers under the soldiers' stare. "Do you know the old chant?" She waves her fan and sings for me in that voice so like her brother's.

> *O ka makani, ia wai ka makani?*
> *The wind, for whom is the wind?*

Liliʻuokalani folds her fern fan into her lap and looks skyward toward the soldiers' lookout smiling at them. She is emboldened today and sings the chant entirely in English for their benefit.

> *The stars, for whom are the stars?*
> *The rain, for whom is the rain?*
> *The sun, for whom is the sun?*
> *The sea, for whom is the sea?*
> *The land, for whom is the land?*

Her musical taunts go unanswered by the soldiers, who watch us, bored. As I leave, one of them whistles as I step back into my carriage. He receives a slap upside the head by his superior for his troubles.

Southport

Eliza,

Your description of Washington Place is helpful to me, for my aunt's letters of late have been difficult to read. She writes continually in worry that I am receiving proposals to take the throne.

But how can she not grow fraught in the conditions in which she lives? How she must hate the sight of Central Union Church turned into a spy tower. She says PG soldiers are billeted there and at Kawaiha'o Church. I suppose it is the right symbolism of the fruits the missionaries have brought to bear on us. If my aunt is restored, I hope she will remember those who rejoiced and helped in the overthrow. If I were in her place, held captured and hopeless, I could not stand it. I am afraid I should pine away and die.

A friend wrote me in confidence of a family gathering. PG soldiers battoned down the door, hearing the music of their hula. They hit a father in the chest with a rifle butt and said all gatherings of Hawaiians are forbidden by the government; Abram Malveaux saw a framed photo of me and said, "This looks like a royalist meeting to me. I'll put it in my report, along with your names." He made a list of everyone in the room.

My aunt also writes suggesting a match for me with a Japanese prince, but I told her I feel it would be wrong if I married a man I did not love. I could have married an enormously rich German Count, but I could not care for him. I cannot become merely a woman of fashion and most likely a flirt. I hope I am not expressing myself too strongly.

I have been looking anxiously every day in the papers for news of home, but nothing seems to have happened. I have been perfectly miserable. I had looked forward to '93 as being the end of my "exile." But now we are entering '95 and the end is nowhere closer. People little know how hard it is to wait patiently for news from home. I am doing a lot of reading, sewing and gardening. I am simply longing to see you all. In the meantime, "il faut attendre."

This is my sixth Christmas I have spent away from my home. It seems as if I were fated never to come back.

I often call for my far islands and I swear I can hear something calling back to me. Is this normal, I wonder? Last night I dreamed I heard my peacocks crying in the night. So plaintive and lost they sounded. I awoke with my throat aching, because I couldn't let my feelings out.

K

I do what I do for K. I do it to revenge myself and Samuel. My father does it for the memory of King Kalākaua, for the Queen, and to settle a score with Clarke and Blackwell, his schoolboy bullies. They grew richer as their ships arrived with lumber and liquor and left with sugar-filled hulls. They used their newfound power to block Father from getting space for his cane on outgoing vessels, thinking to starve his business and force him to come around to their side. This backfired. He sold his plantation to a newcomer from San Francisco after declining Abram's higher offer, and put his money into shipping. That money funds the plot to undo Clarke, Blackwell and the rest. Father does not tell me exactly what is planned, for fear of making it even more dangerous for me if I am caught.

But I know something is coming soon. Abram's brought in hundreds of California recruits as added muscle to stem the growing tide of discontentment against the PGs.

I tell Webster nothing of our subterfuge because I know he would make me stop. He is devotedly non-political, moving fluidly across the lines of PG and Royalist, protesting in his still strong Australian accent that as a foreigner he has no dog in this fight. He tends gently to all: if the Queen runs a fever it is my husband who attends her. Emilie calls him for her headaches and fainting spells. When I am about town with him, women snap their fans and wave; men press his hand and show him their healing stitches. He sees through everyone's vanities and tends gently to them all the same, caring for the least liked because they need it the most. Loving people whom most do not is a powerful currency, and in all the greetings shouted from carriages to my husband, I can feel how rich he is in it.

K,

The PGs have demanded that everyone sign an oath of allegiance to them. Rather than sign, the Royal Hawaiian band all resigned. Their bandmaster (remember the German the

King loved to tease by sending champagne to the musicians mid-song to see if they could resist?), he told his players they would starve if they did not earn a living. So they call themselves the stone eaters. ʻAi pōhaku. They say stones are what are left them, the mystic food of their native land.

All the island is calling back to you,

E

I ride with Father through town and there is meaningful silence. A carpenter stops his work to give him a long nod. Hawaiians tip their hats slowly.

"At least tell me when," I whisper as he drops me at my home.

Father looks cautiously at the driver's bench. We took a hired hack, as Kepa has the day off. "Truly, is it always raining in Mānoa?" he asks loudly, then leans to my ear and says, "Kepa is with the others offloading weapons from one of my ships near Waikīkī. Safer than unloading at the harbor, which is guarded. They'll bury them in the shoreline until the time comes."

"*When?*" I ask. The PGs have a proper military. We have whispers and hopes, volunteers who have never fought a day of their lives. But there is no other way left than to fight. To rid ourselves of this oligarchy and get Hawaiʻi back, it must be by rebellion.

"Tomorrow. Tomorrow's the day," he says so confidently. He has not taken a drink since the day he first sent me to carry a message to the Queen. "There's nothing more for us to do now. The battle is for men," he says. "Younger men than I."

I slip out of the carriage up the lava stone path to my home. I need to warn Webster of what will come tomorrow. He will keep the secret; of that I have no fear. There is nothing more to do now but hope.

"Hello, darling!" I call out in the hallway, whisking the raindrops off my black cotton dress. They scatter across our ʻōhiʻa wood floor, speckling the bone-white wood with slate spots. I never resumed wearing color after Samuel's death; I married Webster in black, my maternity clothes were in charcoal and navy. I have a fine silk in hunter green from Webster that I wear at Christmas, but it is the brightest garment I own. From men's appraising looks I know I have kept my mother's fair looks, but I keep my hair pinned tightly back with her whalebone combs, only taking them out for my husband. I am as prim as any missionary woman was arriving in these islands. Yet as I stand in the hall, I yearn for Webster's kiss. I have fallen deeply in love with my husband.

"Downstairs, Eliza," Webster calls. He sounds grim. I walk down the twisted staircase slowly. My husband sits empty-handed and totally expressionless.

"What is it?" I ask. Webster's eyes are fixed on a chair on the other side of the room. I follow his gaze. Hina peers back at me, one side of her face brightly lit by the desk light, the other side dark in its shadow. She looks brittle, aged beyond her years. She must be 17 now; the age I was with Ben. The age I was married off to Abram. She looks at me haughtily, letting her eyes wander over my rain-soaked cotton dress, my plainly fashioned hair. Her dark brown dress was once fine, but shows too much bosom too early in the day. Patches of the silk have gone dull. Her hair unfurls thick and wild down her back, her knees are slack at each side of the chair.

"Why are you here? You came from Molokaʻi?"

"Iwilei," she says mockingly, as much as admitting to being a prostitute.

An image of her standing in a doorway under a lantern, sullen and bored, comes to me. I wonder if she holds Lee in her arms as she wanders outside between clients. No, he would be too old for that now. Nearly four, like Samuel would have been.

"Where's Lee?"

"Abram get him," Hina says. "I don't hardly see him now."

Her speech has changed. The pidgin is still there but some of the sounds have been replaced with something Southern. It is a strange mix. Abram's mark on her. With his name comes the old feelings of fear. I cross over to Webster and stand behind his chair. He rises for me to sit. "No," I say quietly, shaking my head, still stunned and queasy.

"Why are you here?" I ask her again, knowing it will be money. She has heard of Clarice and guessed she is Abram's. I have let two years of silence ease my worry. Webster again tries to give me his seat, but I prefer to have him blocking Hina. Now he almost forces me into the leather chair.

"You'll want to be sitting, Eliza," he says, putting his hand on my shoulder and pressing me down.

"I have goods and information to sell," Hina announces, reaching to the floor to lift up a box that makes me gasp. It is the one Father gave me the day I married Abram, its inlaid mother-of-pearl cover, the scent of jasmine long gone. "I need money for get Lee back from Abram. You need your things."

She opens the box. Inside is the jade pin. The tiny diamonds wink at me from a different life. I take it in my hand, the jade so cool. *Green*, I'd told Samuel. "You failed to save my son but you took this," I say.

Webster knocks his leg against mine under the desk. "There's more, Eliza," he cautions.

Hina slides back the box's secret compartment: My mother's locket.

My mind is reeling, calculating. "You left my baby to die in a fire." I hiss. "What did you do with the hundreds of dollars inside? Steal it too?"

"Eliza, Hina claims she knows where Samuel is," Webster says, his hands on both my shoulders.

"What are you talking about?" I ask.

"She claims Samuel is alive."

My mind closes up on me. I cannot form a thought, but let out a sound like an infant's startled call upon waking in the dark, the sound babies make just before they cry out.

Webster drops his voice, "Guard your emotions. It could very well be a lie."

"Fine, if you nevah gonna believe me, I gonna leave right now!"

"No, please," I jump up as Hina stands. "Tell me."

Webster beats her to it, as if he can't bear to hear her speak again. "She says that Samuel was not in the cabin at the time of the fire. She will tell you how to find him, for the right price." His disdain is palpable.

I can't imagine it. I have been carrying Samuel with me, in me, dead, for so long.

"Extortion very rarely contains the whole truth," he says, looking at me pointedly. But I can barely focus on what he's saying. Tears course down my cheeks.

"Eliza," Webster says. "It's all right. If it is true, it's a miracle. But you must protect yourself."

"Why?" I say to Hina, between gulped breaths. "Why would you have done this to me?"

Hina tips her chin up self-righteously. "You was so high and mighty to me. I lit your stupid books on fire so you'd come home and be angry. Burned fast. I got scared for Lee. I took him out. Men were burning garbage and I thought if Samuel was gone, you'd go too."

"So when you told me earlier it was Abram's idea, it was actually yours," Webster says angrily.

"No. When the fire started going for real and I heard Samuel cry, I felt so bad. I put Lee on the ground and I went back. I put Samuel in da rice sack so Lopaki can take him down da road."

"And why would Lopaki do that? It's insanity." Webster says.

"For get what every man like. I get one baby with him later on. She stay on Moloka'i with his family. I like her okay. Not like Lee."

"But Lopaki's sister was Abram's..." I don't finish.

"Everybody was Abram's. *Dat* girl?" Hina snarls. "She never even ask why da baby came from da fire. Nobody care what some haole lady want. Lopaki nevah care. You screaming at him all da time about fires by your house. We get plenty problems for ourselves. He nevah care about you or your baby."

The room falls silent. Hina's anger drains slowly into an invisible gutter between us, and when her voice returns it is sad, almost meek.

"Den I see da way Samuel act when I come by. I figure, we wait couple days and your rich father come get you since you so *lolo,* den somebody can find da baby and get money. Fair, dat. But Samuel, he wasn't good. We dropped him in da bag one time and he all bruised on da face."

"Oh," I gasp. Webster puts both his hands on my shoulders.

"He grab me, he cry and cry. So I tell Abram."

"To be clear: you're saying Abram didn't know you took Samuel?" Webster asks.

"Not till den," she says, like Webster is an imbecile. "And he say I so rash. I so stupid. He grab my arm hard and make me come for get Samuel. He nevah know what for do next. I tell him, we go give him back. We say we found 'em walking in the trees, like he got out. See? I was smart. I knew what for do."

"I really do wonder if there's one ounce of truth in this, as you clearly didn't return him," Webster says. He's started taking notes in fountain pen, his jagged doctor's script recording everything she's saying.

"Oh, yeah? You wanna know why she nevah get Samuel back? When we come for bring him back she gone. Lee all alone but she nevah even care."

I freeze when she says this. She is telling the truth. I did leave Lee. Webster has stopped writing.

"You so sad. You so destroyed. Den you nevah care about dis little boy you hānai'd. You say he your own and you lef him like dat. Abram threw Samuel against the wall, he so angry. He said, 'Tell Lopaki get rid of him.'" She turns to me. "That's why you lost your baby. You did it."

"Stop. Stop it," says Webster. "You stop saying these things to her, or you won't get a cent from us."

"I can get everything from her," Hina says, swinging her hair off her shoulders. "She gonna give me dis house if I can find her boy. I nevah have to get with another sweaty man ever my whole life."

She spits these words out, and she is right in all of it. The dream I've had, again and again, that Samuel is hiding, locked away, is coming to life before me. My nightmares were real.

"So then, if you are telling the truth, where is he?" Webster says.

"You gotta pay now. Dat's fair." She rolls her head left and right on her shoulders, as if easing a pinch.

"How much is it that you want?" Webster asks.

"Ten thousand," she says, tilting her chin up and saying it as if she doesn't even believe the sum herself. It is what we paid Abram to marry me. "And you get the locket and pin," Hina adds. "I coulda sold them plenty times you know. But they insurance."

I open the desk drawer.

"No, Eliza," says Webster, shutting the drawer. "Hina, wait outside the house."

She hesitates, looking to see if I might offer something better.

"Hina, go outside *now*," he says. We listen to her footsteps up the stairs. She pauses at the top before the entry table, where a photograph of Clarice stands beside a china vase. I pray there's nothing in that picture Hina recognizes. After a moment I hear her steps to the front door, and finally the opening and closing of it.

"Where is Clarice?" I ask.

"Thankfully asleep upstairs." He grabs my hand as I try to write a check, kneeling down next to me. "Eliza, what are you doing?" he asks. "You give her money and she will disappear, mark my words. She could just have a friend willing to sell a child who looks like Samuel might have. We need to go to the police."

"Oh, the police are worthless. They are Abram's—"

"Eliza, I urge you to take a breath and think. Control your belief in this story, much as you may like to have it be true. You have come so far in your mourning of Samuel," he says, trying to embrace me but I can't be contained. He lets me go and he sits down, drawing me onto his lap. My world has rotated, and my mind cannot yet chart it. We sit with the rain continuing outside. I turn and embrace him, then rise to open the desk drawer and take two hundred dollars from our house envelope. I walk up the stairs and out the front door. Hina is reaching up, trying to pick a tangerine from our tree; she freezes the minute I open the door, as if she's been caught stealing.

"Here," I say, slapping the bills into her palm. "It's money for my jewelry and to get you a meal tonight and bring you back here tomorrow night after dinner." When Clarice is asleep, I think to myself. "Let's say 9."

Hina takes the money, gives me the locket and pin, and looks as if she might spit.

"You still mean," she says, turning and half running down the lane.

I watch a lopsided moon climb up, up, and over Waikīkī. Kepa and a silent line of men are unloading firearms on the beach tonight, feet planted deep in wet sand. I dare not even try to sleep; if I dream, Samuel will be with Hina and Abram, dangled in a rice bag. I would rather sit at my window and imagine my son sleeping somewhere under the same moon.

Webster shifts in bed. We fought as soon as Hina was gone. He wants to write a letter to Dr. Wilson, his replacement at Kalaupapa, and ask him to find out everything he can about Samuel, providing the doctor every needed detail of the story but Abram's name. I think we should go to Moloka'i and ask questions ourselves. "Eliza, please, tame your impulses," he'd reprimanded me.

"Tame the impulse to find my son?"

"The moment you arrive on Moloka'i word will be sent to Abram! And then we are lost."

"And your Dr. Wilson is to be trusted?" I'd asked, both hands pushing against the kitchen table, my back ramrod straight as I tampered down my rage.

"Implicitly. We serve together on the Board of Health. He has proven himself to be one who thinks ahead—"

"He'll want no part in this matter! It's not enough, Webster—"

"Will it ever be?" he'd asked, standing up to go up to bed. "Our lives have become joyful. Productive. Think of how much we have to fear if Abram pays too much attention to us, to our daughter. He has left us alone. Please don't jeopardize everything to satisfy the emotions of this when we don't know if it's true."

I'd waited until he was asleep to come upstairs, half thinking I'd crawl into his arms and seek forgiveness, but instead I watch him from the window, his bare chest expanding and contracting as he sleeps with an abandon I envy.

Our telephone rings at 2 am. Webster sits bolt upright. Clarice screams in her room. "Just get Clarice," Webster mumbles. "It will be one of my patients."

I scoop Clarice up. She is very large for eighteen months. Early to sit up, early to talk. My father is sure she is a prodigy. I surprise myself by clutching on to her. It is Clarice who always clutches on to me, pulling at my skirts to prevent me from leaving, wrapping herself around my legs to stop my steps. She holds me tight, her happiness is so clean and clear on this confusing night that I begin to cry.

"No cry, mama," she says, squeezing me as hard as she can. I hear Webster downstairs asking for an address.

"Eliza?" he whispers from the doorway. I turn, hoping he can't see my face. He needs no more hysterics; he's got a long night with a patient ahead of him.

"It's a very odd thing. A man's been shot in Waikīkī, and he's dying. A group of Hawaiians have guns."

I bury my face in my daughter's hair. I meant to tell him everything tonight.

"Please be very careful, Webster," I say. "It could be the start of anything."

"Right…well, lock the door after me and don't open it. I'll take my key," he says.

Despite all the political upheaval, there is virtually no crime here. Our lives will change in the coming days. People will lock their doors now. I hear him hitch up our carriage and clatter down Mānoa road, sick with the knowledge that he is riding into what my father and I have helped create.

I take Clarice into our bed and let her fall asleep on my chest. I picture Samuel as a four-year-old who can count numbers and write his name. A four-year-old who can sing itsy bitsy spider by heart. Some four-year-olds read. I tell myself Webster will come home safe, that Kepa got away from the shooting. My mind spins and spins until it goes blank.

12

"Eliza?"

I struggle to wake. I'm dreaming of Moloka'i, of Keala and a little boy throwing rocks.

"Eliza? It's ten in the morning. Look at your vanity."

I open my eyes, amazed I slept. Clarice has taken my pot of lip color and drawn zig zags and circles across my mirror. She turns toward me. There are zebra stripes down her face.

"You should have a look at yourself," Webster chuckles to me.

In the mirror I see she's colored rosy pink circles on my face.

"I can't imagine I slept through it," I admit. "What happened last night?" I ask.

"Someone tipped the police that Hawaiians were armed and assembling near Diamond Head. Pro-PG haoles rushed over, one fired shots."

If someone tipped the police off there must be PG spies on our side. Of course there are. We have spies on theirs. We have lost the element of surprise.

"The Hawaiians returned a round of shots at them. I gave the dying haole man morphine for his agony. The police took some Hawaiians to the Reef. Others escaped."

The Reef. Prison. "Did you see anyone you knew?" I asked. "Kepa?"

"Ke-pa! Ke-pa!" Clarice shouts. Kepa loves to carry Clarice on his shoulders, he puts her on his lap to mudslide down the embankment of Nuʻuanu stream. He could be arrested or shot today.

"No, but I saw Abram. He was questioning the natives being taken to the Reef."

"Did he try to talk to you?" Clarice starts squeezing my face, her sign that she doesn't like the tone of my voice.

"Just a nod as I signed the death certificate of that poor man. I tell you, Eliza, what I saw looked like the start of a full scale rebellion, though not a particularly organized one," he says, heading to the bath. Then he stops. "I also met Benjamin Ahsang last night."

I'd had no notion Ben was home. "Oh?" I ask, in a falsely casual manner.

"It all happened near his bungalow. He came over to find out what had happened. He didn't ask my name so I'm not sure he realized our… connection. He had the whole group amused, recounting his bad timing. Said he left Hawaiʻi because of the overthrow, then he left China because of the upheaval there, and now, with a man being shot next to his bungalow, he's beginning to think he brings chaos with him wherever he goes."

"Is that what it looked like last night? Chaos?" I ask.

He heads into the bath. "It looked like a rebellion. The PGs are sending troops to circle the rebels at Diamond Head. I'm supposed to report to the hospital to help with casualties."

I hear the sound of water starting to fill the tub. "For which side?" I call after him.

"A doctor does not choose," he calls back. "I'll drop you at your father's; I'd rather you and Clarice were there today than here alone."

Yes, Nuʻuanu is better today. If they come for Father or me, Mehana can care for Clarice. But if they take me to the Reef, who will search for Samuel?

PG soldiers guard the Ahsang estate, swinging rifles on their shoulders like excited boys. They turn serious as they watch us turn up my father's drive.

"You'd think we're guilty of something," Webster scoffs.

"I suppose they aren't doing their job if they look friendly," I answer flatly.

Gunfire starts down the valley. Clara snuggles calmly through it, but every dog in Nu'uanu starts to bay.

"These Hawai'i dogs are so soft in the belly," Webster says cheekily. "An Aussie would run toward it to have a good look."

I smile, but he can tell I'm spooked. He kisses my forehead and says, "I'll be back soon enough to get you."

I find Mehana and Father sitting opposite each other at the kitchen table, coffee in front of them both. Our family has dropped all formalities between employer and servants; Father's eaten at the kitchen table with Kepa and Mehana since I married Webster. When we are all here together we crowd around it on mismatched chairs. The formal dining table that once served 20 now serves none. Handing Clarice to Mehana, I pour myself a cup.

"Where Ke-pa?" Clarice demands.

"Oh, how this little one loves men," Mehana says, happy to have something to laugh about.

"I shouldn't like it put that way," says Father.

"She does. I make her banana flapjacks, braid her hair, but it's always, 'Where Ke-pa?'"

"It's true," I concede, raising my shoulders in a shrug to my father. Clarice could spend an hour just rubbing her hand against the stubble of Kepa's beard. The adoration is mutual. Kepa refuses to let her drink her milk cold and carves apples into flowers for her lunch. "So where is Kepa?" I ask, leaning back against the counter.

"We're waiting to hear from him," Father says.

"You got him involved, Father, surely we can do more than wait?"

"It wasn't your father," Mehana says, shaking her head and raising her hand, always the peacemaker between us. Though we work together in the service of the Queen, simmering below our cooperation is always the shadow of Samuel. We never speak of it, and though I do love my father, I have not forgiven him. "Eliza, you *know* it was Kepa's church that got him involved. They are all Royalists. They want to fight, and he wanted to fight with them. It was his choice."

She is so sure of life, of choices. I want to tell her about Hina and Samuel, but there's the sound of an explosion down the valley, and Clarice starts to cry. Mehana stands and bounces her on her shoulder, walking toward the back of the house.

"That's the PGs using their cannon," Father says somberly. "It will get very hard now."

I pull up a chair. "If Kepa's caught—"

"If he's caught, he's done what he wants," says Mehana from the back door. "Enough already, what's happened to our people. I'm glad he's there, fighting. Give me baby girl's hat. We're taking a walk."

I give her Clarice's bonnet and watch the two of them head toward the stream. Mehana swings her upside down, and Clarice is now squealing in joy despite the cannon fire, so quickly used to the sounds of war.

"Last night was a terrible start," Father says, lifting his cup to me plaintively. I get up to refill it, trying to create the same syrupy brown mixture of coffee and condensed milk that Mehana does. Father consumes copious quantities of it in place of his Scotch. How he ever sleeps I do not know.

"The idea was to catch them off guard, but instead we've brought the full force of their militia down right at the start. The foreigners who promised to join in are keeping quiet because they're seeing Hawaiians dragged off to prison in chains, thrown into dirty cells without charges," he says, tapping his foot on the floor, his hand against the table.

"Is that what's happening?"

"Absolutely. They all got a bit sloppy. I understand some of our men were drinking." He stops here and makes a shrugging movement with his whole face and body. "Who can blame them, facing death like that? I'm proud I've given money to it. It's a just cause, and I'm not alone. There's another planter—an Englishman—paying for this too. We've done what we can. But now it's up to Kepa and the rest of them to reek havoc with the PGs. Enough so the populace feels safe to come out, join in, and overturn the bastards with sheer numbers. But we need to make the PGs look weak first. And we're certainly not doing that."

We listen to the sound of cannon fire together. This rebellion has been my secret for two years, but today my mind clings to Hina, to Samuel. I feel oddly distant from politics. Was my fight for this place, these people, only a substitute for revenge? A great double blast makes both of us sit up in our seats.

"I should have bought our side a cannon," Father says.

"Father, I need money," I say.

He looks surprised. Not displeased, but confused. "I've offered you money for years," he says. "Washing your husband's shirts when you could be doing something with your mind—"

"I don't need help in the house. I like our life. It suits me." He waits for an explanation. But I've decided he doesn't get to know Samuel may live. Not yet.

"One thousand? Two? Three?"

"One. Thank you. Thank you very much."

"You ready *not* to find him?" Mehana asks.

"Why would you say that?" The breath goes out of me. Already so much hope has grown.

"If you find him, you're blessed. You'll have your boy. And perhaps you will finally forgive your father, because he's lived with it too. But if you don't, what then?" She shoots a look at Clarice seated in the basin of our sink, playing with potatoes and metal measuring cups and the running faucet. "It will be as if Abram is doing everything to you all over. And she's his," she whispers.

"I can't think of this today," I say, regretting that I told her. "I only—"

"I'm ready to lose Kepa," Mehana says, grabbing my hand hard. "I'm ready. He could die of leprosy. Or measles. Or bitterness, twenty years from now. Better to die fighting, if that's what he knows is right. Otherwise I couldn't let him go the other night. Your soul has to not ask for any more than what you have now. You have her, you have Webster, you have me and your father for as long as his body holds up. Kepa coming home, Samuel coming home, those would be miracles." Mehana gets up and goes to Clarice. "Go, take a walk if you want. I got baby girl."

I cross into the forest, passing through the clearing that was mine and Ben's without even stopping, though it frightens me how often my thoughts have turned to Ben today. If I went to him, told him of his missing son, he'd go look for him, I know he would. There are rumors a customs agent was rude to Ben's wife when they returned from China. He had the man fired and sent back to the States. Even with the wrong people in power he has connections, legal and otherwise, throughout Honolulu. But going to him would be another betrayal of Webster. My husband, my son, my son's father, they stand in different corners of my mind.

I climb far up the valley wall, breaking branches, scratching my legs. Through the trees I see a low cloud of smoke drifting into the valley on the back of the ocean trade winds. I cannot see the Palace through the smoke, or Washington Place, where the Queen now waits for this battle's outcome under virtual house arrest. It's nearly dusk, when birds usually draw their curtain of sound around my father's house. But Nuuanu's green earth lies under the rancid, thick air of this conflict. and there's no natural sound, just gunfire. I listen for Hannah's owl, the '*aumakua* I should be asking Mehana to invoke for my son's protection. But the owl is either silent or gone; there is only the whistle of artillery traveling like fireworks across the smoky sky.

13

For two days the Hawaiian rebels are shelled at Diamond Head. They retreat up toward the mountains, bringing the fighting into our little valley. Mānoa is overrun with baying bloodhounds and armed militia. Dole declared martial law, and wagons full of PG soldiers rumble past our home, shooting as they go. An elderly man sitting in his home one lane over is killed by a stray bullet; every hour is punctuated by screams in the algarroba trees above our house.

"I can't stand it any longer. There are wounded men up there," Webster says, opening his medical bag. He is meant to have this day off at home.

"Don't go out until the shooting stops," I plead, instantly shamed by what I've said. I'm unwilling to let my husband take the risks Mehana allowed hers. I start again, more carefully. "Webster, you refused to voice support for either side. What's changed?"

He's counting syringes. "I'll go to the aid of whoever needs it," he says, putting rolls of bandages in his bag. "I'll go to the hospital and care for the other side this afternoon. I know that's not what your father would like to hear," he adds. He closes the leather strap and kisses Clarice. "I'll only hike up to the waterfall. That's got to be where they're taking their wounded for water. It's nowhere near the shooting."

I feel very lonely when he leaves, with one foot in my home and the other in this fight, while my heart is with Samuel, and I'm not doing a good job at any of it. Clarice buries her face in the fabric across my chest. She softly scratches my arms, up and down, up and down, in the same rhythm she has since she was a babe. It is her signature movement, as Samuel twirled my hair. It irked me at first, but I find it comforting now.

Within a few minutes of Webster leaving, there is a loud, continuous knock at the door. Every knock now could be the police. I pin my hair hastily and button the top of my dress.

Behind the door stands Hina in a weathered yellow dress that does not fit her bony frame. I bring her into the kitchen, shifting Clarice to my other shoulder, wondering how I can keep the two of them apart. But Hina shows no interest in my daughter. Her eyes are on our fruit bowl. I belt Clarice into her highchair and empty a packet of her favorite saltine crackers onto the tray. "Take whatever you'd like," I say to Hina. She quickly grabs a tangerine. I bring her a plate.

"I didn't know if you were coming back. I thought we said last night," I say. "I do hope you took the path behind the houses; it's safer than the road with all this."

Hina's eyes seem glassier. Once, I thought I saw Ka'iulani in those eyes, but her features have hardened into something entirely different. I must get her to start talking. "How did you end up on O'ahu?" I ask, my back turned as I pour Clarice her milk.

"Don't try to make friends with me," Hina answers.

She breaks the tangerine in two. Clarice reaches out for a portion, but Hina does not notice. I start to peel another for my daughter. "I just wondered why you didn't stay on Moloka'i?" I choose my words carefully, keeping my eyes on the fruit.

"Why should I?" she asks. "You didn't." Juice runs from Hina's hands. I fetch a napkin. When I hand it to her, she says, "Abram left," wiping her fingertips. "When he came back, he telling me Lee needs school, dat he moving to O'ahu. I had da baby by Lopaki, but she nevah really like me. She like her father bettah. So I tell Abram, you only gotta take me and Lee, not da baby. But Abram just take Lee. I was all bus up. I came myself to da boarding house, just gotta sleep with the owner for stay there. People at the house, they like opium. I get money with the other men. For the opium." She stops and shrugs. "So sad without my boy. It was da only happy I get."

I feel a sharp pang of sympathy, a shared knowledge of that trauma, but then anger. "Tell me Hina, when that happened did you feel sorry for me, thinking my son was dead for years?"

Hina laughs. "Hell no. *You* sign da papers. *You* left my son. I nevah felt bad for you. I felt sad for Samuel, and Charlie. He knew Samuel nevah burn in dat fire. Everybody call him the *lolo* old Hawaiian man. It made him crazy in the head."

I drive my fingernail into the bed of my thumb to stop myself from reaching across and slapping her. I place the fruit sections on Clarice's tray. "Where is Lee now?"

"Abram's house. That old haole lady he married calls me devil. I tell her Abram knows every Kanaka whore in town and she say she'll get the police. One time, I called up for Lee. She came to the window and threw water on me."

"So you haven't seen Lee?"

"One day, I saw him walking. Tall, in a little brown suit, like a prince."

Clarice lights up at the word prince, turning to me and starting a rambling version of a fairy tale I've read her. For the first time I think of the irony that Lee is a half-brother to Clarice. A fact I pray she will never discover.

"You got to speak with him?" I ask Hina.

She shakes her head, looking vulnerable. "No. When I get da money, I can buy a lawyer and I get my boy."

"And Abram? Don't you think he will fight you?"

"He gonna come back to me when I get da boy. I know him good. So when you gonna give me money? Fair is fair."

I sit stunned, then wonder if I should explain to her all the reasons she should never let Abram touch her again, make her understand how powerful and dangerous he is, but she supposedly sits with the knowledge of where my lost son is, and has done so for years. I get up and get the bundle of cash from the dish towel drawer. "Webster doesn't want me to give you all the money at once. In case you disappear. So for every bit of information I find helpful I will hand you some. It's a thousand dollars. You can earn as much as you tell. And if I get Samuel, you get the rest. Is that fair?"

I expect a no, but she focuses on the pile of green bills before her. "Okay, I gonna tell you something. You know what we did with Samuel?" She is smiling glibly. "We hānai'd him. We hānai'd him out to one Hawaiian family. Funny, yeah? After all dat?"

"Who is we? You and Abram?"

She shakes her head.

"You and Lopaki?"

She nods.

I pass her a bundle of dollars. She tucks them into her bodice.

"Which family?"

Her glib smile fades and there's panic in her eyes before she puffs up and acts insolent. "Oh, I not stupid. You gotta pay more first."

"Okay, which island?"

"Moloka'i," she says without looking at me.

I pass her money. She tucks it in her bodice without a smile, then looks back at the fruit bowl and rolls her neck.

"Where did you go on Moloka'i when you gave him to a family?" I ask.

"Down a road," Hina says. "A dirt road, with plenty coconut trees."

I pass her much more. "What else? Think what else."

"Was the first time I ever seen ocean, where we wen left him."

I give her more. "Who was there?"

She looks down at the money and then at me, a lost expression on her face. I know she has no more to sell. "He said stay in the wagon. I gotta think for remember. But you happy with me?" she asks, wistful. "Without me, he was dead."

"Yes," I say, defeat in my voice. Coconut. Ocean. I see how empty she is, sitting there, wanting her own son back. I push the rest of the money to her. "Get something in your stomach. Where do you live?"

"I nevah telling you," she says, pushing the rest of the money down her dress and getting up to leave. A moment earlier she clearly believed she wasn't getting a dollar more. Perhaps I've made a mistake. Clarice has become exasperated at not being listened to. "Hold you!" she commands, arms raised.

"Wait, baby," I say, as I try to catch Hina's eye.

"I not a baby. Why you say I a baby?" she demands. "No baby."

"Hina, I want you to come back tomorrow after you've thought more about this," I say, lifting up Clarice. "Bring me *any* other information and there'll be more money," I say, following her to the door.

"I gonna come Friday," she says.

"No, tomorrow. Thursday," I answer.

She shakes her head. "No. You not da boss lady anymore," she says before she shuts the door behind herself.

I go upstairs to the balcony with Clarice and watch Hina walk down the lane. The sounds of gun skirmishes are all around us, but she seems indifferent. She picks up a stone from a neighbor's drive and throws it against one of their windows, breaking into a run once the sound of smashed glass joins that of gunfire.

"Their fortitude got them through it," Webster says, describing over dinner how he took bullets out of two rebels. "I had nothing to numb the pain for them, just a bit of disinfectant," he tells me as Clarice tosses pieces of chicken on the floor for an imaginary dog. She's told us she wants one, and we should name it Coconut.

"Clarice, stop," I say quietly.

"He very hungwee," she says in rebuke.

“Hina came,” I say as I pick the chicken up and stare my daughter down. She retracts her outstretched hand and pushes chicken into her mouth as she stares straight back at me.

“Oh?” Webster says.

I nod. “She said they hānai’d him out to a family down by the water on Moloka‘i. I don’t believe she knows much more than that,” I say, wiping my hands with a dishtowel. “I don’t know what to do next.”

“Well, I wrote the letter. So we’ll hear from Dr. Wilson soon enough. Sounds like you know everything Hina has to tell you.”

“Webster, have you heard anything about Kepa?”

“Ke-pa,” Clarice shouts hitting her tray with both her palms.

“He left the day it started and hasn’t come home.”

Webster absorbs this. “I’m not surprised he wants to fight,” he says. “But I fear for him, Eliza. I really do. I’d say the rebels are down to a hundred fighters. The PG soldiers coming up the valley seem endless.”

We should have bought mercenary soldiers to bolster the rebel forces. “That idea’s been rejected,” Father told me when I’d suggested it. “We bring in outsiders and the PGs will claim it’s a foreign invasion of American-owned businesses and property.”

“Rebels are being thrown in jail,” Webster says. “He could be there. Others are going up into the mountains to try to find fruit. Many don’t have any food left.”

“We could give them food,” I say tentatively. I’ve abandoned the effort in the wake of the news of Samuel. I should be doing something, anything. “Emilie Irvin put on a fried chicken and waffle picnic for the PG forces at the palace grounds yesterday.” I saw a photograph of her in the paper, standing amongst them in a plaid afternoon suit.

Webster nods. “First medicine, then food. Next thing you know, we’re prisoners in the Reef ourselves.” He looks meaningfully at Clarice; she throws the rest of her chicken down for our dog.

I wake at 3am with the swirl of Hina and Samuel, Kepa and the rebellion filling my head. I can't stand it anymore and go down to the kitchen. I toss every breadfruit and sweet potato shelved in our pantry into the oven. I bake tray after tray of Mehana's cornbread. It's not nearly enough for fifty men, much less one hundred, but as soon as I've cleaned the kitchen and dawn begins to lift the sky I set off on the footpath behind our house and head to the waterfall where Webster attended to the wounded.

At first glance through the trees, the area looks empty. Once I emerge into the clearing I see a group of men clustered in a sleeping circle to the right of the waterfall. Their feet are caked with mud, and I see my husband's work in the bandaged hands they rest their heads on, trying to sleep on the hard ground.

A footstep makes me start. I turn to find a young boy with a rifle pointed at me. I see myself through his eyes: blonde, an intruder. I lift my two full baskets, steam still rising from the sweet potatoes. My fingers are burned from grabbing them straight from the oven the moment their skins popped and sweet purple juices oozed from their flesh.

The boy points to his mouth. I nod and put the baskets down. He is so small—like Ikaika the first day I saw him. He puts his gun down carefully then rushes to the basket to stuff a sweet potato into his mouth. I look at the rifle on the ground. How will this rebellion end for this boy? In the Reef? Home safe? Dead? What game have my father and I played at these years, leading a boy like this here, while the rest of us are safe in our homes, unwilling to join until the tide turns. Which it will likely not.

"Can you ask them if they know Kepa Akina?" I ask the boy, tilting my head toward the circle of men. He nods enthusiastically just as the rain starts. The newspaper says that winter rains will be the government's strongest weapon, flushing sick, exhausted rebels from the mountains. The men rise from their sleep to move under banana trees. The boy has brought the baskets to them. They shake their heads when asked about Kepa, but raise their arms to me in thanks. I start down the path with a strong feeling of someone watching me, and so back track to take another way which leads down to a different lane of homes, away from my own.

The rain comes down heavy with the smell of mountain. An older haole couple try to wave me into their grey-shingled home as I pass, "You'll catch your death!" the husband calls, a shotgun at his side, an American flag hanging above the porch. Fear has spread across our valley, with each defending his own. I smile my thanks but run past their rose hedges, past government troops coming up the road in wagons covered with tarps.

I'm home before my family has woken.

A riot breaks out among Japanese workers over conditions at Abram's plantation. I wonder how many of those workers have endured Abram's forced medical exams, or had their daughters touched. Richard Irvin diverts troops from the rebellion to deal with what the newspapers call a "sugar uprising." The riot gives the Queen's supporters a reprieve; her rebels come out of the valley and make small advances against diminished PG troops.

"News from Moloka'i," Webster announces when he comes back from the hospital that night, after treating the PG troops. Clarice is beside me in her high chair mirroring my happy mood by shaking her head back and forth while making buzzing sounds with her lips.

"I hate to show you this, as you look quite happy at the moment," Webster adds, tenderly running the back of his hand on my cheek once he's put the letter in front of me.

"The handwriting is so poor I cannot read it," I say testily, handing the note back. Webster waits, not wanting to be the one to say the words, and so finally I read them:

> *I fear I cannot become embroiled in this matter, and I daresay I would warn you to do the same. Are you aware of the role certain individuals play in our government? And this will remain our government.*

I stop reading and rip the note in half. "What a brave man," I say.

"Don't give in to the despair of it," Webster says as I get up from the table. He tries to take my hand but I pass him and toss a dish into the sink. It shatters when I did not mean it to, making Clarice cry. I throw the pieces into our bin.

"Hina has nothing to say. You have nothing to say. My father never fought for Samuel in the first place. And there is no possibility either of you will let me ask Ben for help!"

"Hold you! Hold you!" Clarice pleads, stretching her little arms up to both of us.

"You're shouting, Eliza," Webster says, picking Clarice up.

I start to walk toward our front door, with no plan of where to go.

"Don't walk out," Webster says. I stop. "Dr. Wilson is not a bad man; I shouldn't have asked him to get involved, you were right. I suppose only the insane would cross Abram at this point in their career. We've lived carefully, Eliza," he says, kissing Clarice on the crown of her head, which stops her crying. "We don't need to be rash."

"I am rash! I'm terribly rash. You don't even know."

"What does that mean?" He says too calmly for my taste.

I cross my arms. "I ran messages to the Queen for my father. He gave money to the revolt. We've been working against Abram for *years*!"

Webster looks dumbfounded. Clarice puts her head on his shoulder and closes her eyes.

"I wanted to tell you," I say. "Then everything happened with Hina and with Samuel. And you don't need to tell me I was reckless. I know that I was."

"Really, Eliza? Do you? You've committed treason in their eyes." Webster starts to walk with Clarice toward the stairs.

"Now don't you walk away!" I shout after him. "It's impossible to understand if you haven't grown up here—"

"I understand very well," he says, with force. "It doesn't take being raised here to see what's happening. But do you want to give Abram a reason for taking what we love?"

"No—"

"It's exactly what you've done," he says, taking Clarice up for bed.

I do the washing up and go out to our garden. It is a tiny speck compared to Father's, but it is my escape on nights I feel my grief rise up. I promised myself I wouldn't put that grief on Webster. I promised myself that the day he married me even after we knew I was pregnant by another.

The moon has grown full, and tonight it lights a path across the sea toward America and beyond. I think how small my life has been geographically. I've only lived on two islands on this Earth. But their beauty makes my life feel bigger; surprises me with its grandeur. A rustling sound starts in the vines across our lava rock wall. "Webster," I call hesitantly back into the house. "Webster?"

He comes down the stairs. "She's just gone to sleep," he says. "What is it?"

"Remember what I told you? About our wall?"

"No," he says, as if I have lost my mind.

"Just come outside," I say, waving my hand. I pull him down onto the bench to look at our night-blooming cereus. In strong moonlight, once or twice a year, from cactus-like green tentacles they make their noisy, rare appearance in the world. They crackle as their green spikes emerge, prehistoric-looking in their sharp symmetry.

"They bloom all night," I say as they open up before us, first bursts of white and then their yellow hearts. "Like cups of gold. The first drop of sun withers them; they've always been done by the time you come home."

We watch for half an hour in near silence, hands held but separate in our thoughts.

The scientist in my husband can't help but wonder at how the flowers function. He gets up close to the blossoms, putting his hand next to one as it opens against his palm. This flower and that of the dragonfruit are related and one and the same in appearance. I can feel Ben's lips on mine that day in the greenhouse, the fruit and flower of the plant so vividly red and white next to us. I force the memory away and say, "It must seem mad, what I've done."

"No," he says. "Our natures are different, Eliza. We see the world the same way, and the last two years have been the most meaningful of my life. But I'm cautious. If most people were like you, this rebellion would work. But more are like me, frightened of losing what we love." Webster pulls me into his chest. "When I worked in South Dakota, the Lakota children used to talk about the Ghost Dance."

"I never even knew you were in South Dakota before," I say.

"I was placed through a Christian medical organization. I told them I hoped for America, and that is where they put me. I don't often like to remember it."

I wait for more. He rarely talks of his life before Kalaupapa. I know he's an only child, like me. That his parents were upset he left Australia, hoping he'd follow his father into his medical practice instead. Letters are few between them. He does not care to talk much of himself, my husband.

"What was the Ghost Dance?" I ask him, though I can tell he's decided he does not want to speak of it.

"A ceremony that summons a cataclysm to kill the white man. They thought there will be a resurrection of their tribes, the living and the dead, and the earth will be returned to them, with all its bison and prairies restored. They told me this so happily. As if I would be included in their bright future."

He clears his throat and looks so unhappy, I feel badly I have prodded him to speak.

"All the Lakota I cared for were massacred, near Wounded Knee. The women and the children. I'd done an amputation on a four-year-old who would have died without it, and the father put his hand on my shoulder to show me I had his blessing." Webster swallows hard. "All that cutting and pasting up, and they go and get massacred by the 7th Calvary, soldiers who looked just like me. That's when I took the post at Kalaupapa. It seemed like a Sunday picnic after that. Leprosy and all. It really did."

"You never talk like this," I say.

"Because I came to Hawai'i for something different than that nightmare I left. It's my nature to mind my own business. I never say I think Wounded Knee was wrong. I never talk about the tide of suffering in my Hawaiian patients. Their slow march to extinction, body and soul. I don't because I'm afraid if I draw any of that fire, it will hit the ones I treasure. I'm a selfish man at the end of the day. But you're a rash woman when your heart takes hold. And it's not just you this could hurt."

"I know," I say weakly.

"When I said don't give in to the despair of it, I didn't mean don't look for Samuel. I meant that we have rebuilt our lives. Together. When I first married you, you couldn't hold our daughter without desperately wanting to give her back."

"She has never had a day she wasn't—"

"That is *exactly* what I'm saying. You've done it. You've risen above this. We cannot sink back in. I think Hina is telling the truth. Whether Samuel is still alive is up for debate, but I don't think he died in that fire. So we must look. But Eliza, it's not going to be as easy as simply running into this at full speed. Abram will want to destroy us if he catches wind of it. To have a real shot at this means fighting Abram on his own terms. Whether it's threats or money or just plain underhanded power—"

"Father doesn't have that sort of power anymore." As I say this I realize I've worked at cross purposes. If I'd known Samuel was alive, that I would need to find him, would I have curried favor with the people in power, people who can counterbalance Abram? Would I have accepted Emilie's invitations and forgotten my distaste for what she and her husband have done?

"I wasn't talking about your father," says Webster. "And we both know I'm the man for many things, but not underworld dealings. I'm talking about someone who would be motivated to take this on and fight Abram," Webster says. "I'm talking about Benjamin Ahsang. I think it's time he knew he had a son."

14

Webster drives me through town; we don't speak of Hina or Samuel or Ben, only chatting about which patients he will be seeing. The smell of sawdust from new homes and stores and warehouses floats everywhere. I cough and sneeze, noting the PG troops posted at every street corner. The rebels are holding firm in the back of the valley; I left food at the waterfall earlier this morning, baskets wrapped tightly in clean sheets. No one was there.

He stops the carriage and kisses me on the cheek. An acquaintance calls out for him from the sidewalk and he waves bashfully. "You're a popular man," I say. "You could have been a politician."

"More likely a barkeep," he answers. "It's the same work I do now, without the hernias and tonsillitis. That's one of the Bailey boys. He works down at the harbor marking the boats that come and go. A perfect job for someone who likes his drink as much as that fellow does."

As if on cue, the man makes a quick turn into one of the block's four saloons. For a town built on missionary zeal, Honolulu has never managed any pretense of temperance. I lower myself carefully down to the street. The sidewalks in town have improved, but not by much.

"Are you sure you don't want me to come?" Webster asks. We've left Clarice with a Portuguese woman from down the road who misses having her six grown children at home.

"I don't think he would have the conversation we need to in front of you," I say.

Webster agrees, nodding, but I struggle to find the right way to part. "You'll be home for dinner?" I ask, shading my eyes as I look up at him.

"Barring any disasters, yes," he says. "I've got Mrs. Obemeyer today. She keeps saying she wants to die this week because it's her wedding anniversary."

"Is her husband that unbearable?"

"No," says Webster, laughing, "he died last year. She'd like to join him." His face becomes serious. "You tossed and turned all night and I did not do much better," he says, putting a hand on one knee to lean down. "I want to help you find him, if he's out there."

"I know. Thank you, Webster. Truly."

I watch him go down King Street with a deep feeling of gratitude for his decency.

Once he's turned out of sight, I start nervously toward the Ahsang store. Mauna Kea Street has lost a spot of what Father used to call its "frontier" air. There are the familiar stores selling their dry goods, oil paintings, and men's attire, but there has been a change. Women in kimonos now stand behind the counter in their husbands' stores, selling their foods and fabrics. Signs I cannot read hang above these shops, in spots formerly announcing their goods in English and Hawaiian. Japanese workers are leaving the fields as the Chinese did before them, and they are making a good living of it. I reach a quiet spot across the street from the red door. An elderly Chinese man smokes his pipe outside. I glance up at the second floor to see if Benjamin is by chance staring down. I'm watching workers unpack watercress bunches into sidewalk bins when the hair stands at the back of my neck, and Ben steps out of the store. He looks up to the sky to see if it will rain, then lights a cigarette and glances toward a small coffee shop across from his father's store. I imagine what it would be like were we to go for coffee together, what it would be like to tell him across a table.

I stare with the abandon of a street urchin. Benjamin wears spectacles now, and the set of his face is sharper, his cheekbones tools rather than ornaments. His new face demands respect.

I still dream about him. We no longer love each other in my dreams. Instead I chase him, spurn him, help him, beg him, all depending on that evening's plot line. Last night, I dreamed we'd found a dead woman's body together, floating face up in the ocean. But never in these unconscious journeys do we end up together. Does he ever have dreams of me?

He turns and goes back through the red door. I follow. There is no light in the stairway; it smells slightly off and moldy. It amazes me that a family with so much money hasn't yet built a fine office of wood and light and pleasing views. I make my way to the second floor. No door separates the stairwell and the office. Years of cigar smoke cling to the yellow walls and there are sacks of rice lying in the corners. One calendar in Chinese and another in English are mounted with dates circled and crossed. The low, undistinguished sounds of the street below make the room feel secluded and drowsy. Three men sit before ledgers, surrounded by boxes and bags marked in Chinese. They look up at me indifferently. In the corner, Benjamin sits at a desk pushed up against the only window. He works on an abacus, a skill he tried to teach me once. He'd rolled my fingers over the wooden beads, kissing me if I got the sum right, or wrong. The men have gone back to their ledgers. I walk across the room. Ben puts down the abacus to write out a series of additions. By his left hand is a photograph of a woman, her bone structure cut like the facets of a diamond. Mei Ling's elegance is set off by two grinning little girls with pointed chins and peach cheeks under each of her arms.

"Hello, Ben," I say.

He looks up at me, the face I see so often in the course of my nights. He puts down his pen clumsily, and the ink begins to spread on his calculations.

"The ink," I say.

He picks the pen up but knocks over the inkstand. The men who had ignored me come forward with a cloth and mop the ink up before retreating once again. Ben keeps his eyes on his hands.

"Something has happened," I say in a low voice. "Is there another room where we might speak?"

"There's a small garden in the back," he says brusquely.

I follow him past the men, down the dark stairs and through a door I would never have guessed existed. The light outside feels glaring. Garden is too kind a word for the space, a patch of brown grass with empty crates crusted with old produce piled along the walls. Two men crouch low to the ground eating noodles. At Ben's arrival they stand and take their bowls behind another door at the opposite side of the space.

"I've often wondered how this would happen. What we would say," he says. There's a deep flush of red across his cheekbones, the way he used to look after nights drinking with the King, wine coloring his skin like a burn from the sun. He called it the Chinese fire alarm to alcohol.

"I have something to say, but I'm so nervous I can hardly stand," I tell him.

Ben raises his arm toward a careworn bench. We sit at opposite sides of it.

"You're married now, with a daughter," he says gently.

"And there was a son."

"I lit a candle in a temple the day I got the letter from Clara telling me you'd lost a child in a fire," he says, his eyes downward.

"You lit it for your own son then, Ben," I say, covering his hand with my gloved one, a surge of compassion for how he will receive this news surprising me.

The crush of pain in his face wipes it of any strength. "A son?"

"I didn't know until after you'd left."

I pause, staring at a paper lantern painted with the pattern of bamboo shoots hanging in a window behind him. "I had to marry and go to Moloka'i. It was that, or give him up. He looked exactly like you—such a beautiful boy—and, all these years, I thought he was gone. But someone I knew there recently came to my house." My hands are shaking. "This woman claims that Samuel, our son, is alive. That he was stolen from me under the guise of that fire. And that my former husband was involved in taking him from me. Abram Malveaux."

That name wipes the vulnerability from Ben's face. "She's telling the truth?" he asks me. His voice—there is a touch of something foreign in it now, as if his years in Macao made him forget the cadences of Hawai'i. But the swiftness of his interest is exactly what I had hoped for.

"I believe her. But I don't know if that's because I want it to be the truth."

He looks into a window that connects the courtyard and his crowded store. While my hands still shake, he is perfectly still. We are quiet for a long time. He still smells of lime.

"Has she made a demand?"

"She wants ten thousand dollars. I've already given her one. But I suspect she doesn't know much more. My thought is to track down a cowboy on Moloka'i named Lopaki. She had a child with him. And he's the one she claims hānai'd our son out. I need to keep her strung along—"

"Or she'll go to Abram Malveaux." He speaks bitterly. "Does your husband know you're here?" As he asks this, he takes me by the shoulders, his hands still stained with ink, and urges me toward him, further away from a doorway opening to a long hall. "People love to listen in this building."

"It was his suggestion. My former husband can be a frightening man." I open up my envelope. "I have no photograph of Samuel, but I sketched him as well as I could." I watch Ben's stunned reaction as he takes in the likeness of himself.

"He does look like me in this," he says softly.

My heart leaps. "Of course, he is older now. This is a letter from a friend on Moloka'i. I asked her about something she'd written me a year ago, on the anniversary of Samuel's death. She saw someone who looked like him."

Eliza,

What hopeful news. I will keep it a secret as you asked, though I am sorely tempted to tell Charlie and would ask your permission to do so. He's never been able to forget what happened.

That day I saw the child, we were walking along the ocean at Kaunakakai. We'd come to town to sell papayas and sweet potatoes. A child was playing alone in the shore break, and I thought it dangerous. He was three or so. Tall and well-formed. Fair, with reddish tints, so he stood out. I looked for the mother. The boy was throwing rocks in the water. I went to move him to a safer area. At that moment another child—8 or 9 years old, ran past me and lifted the boy, carrying him to a cart. It was then I saw a bit of his face and thought, that is how Samuel may have looked. I did not say anything to Charlie as the subject so upsets him, and he is truly blind now. The older girl put him in the back of the wagon with other Hawaiian children. They left. I cannot say I saw or remarked on the adult driving the cart. The missionary children change out often here, so I did not think anything more of it. Do you want me to start to ask? Will you come to Moloka'i?

"Don't go to Moloka'i," says Ben. "We need to be invisible. I'll find this Lopaki. I'll send agents dressed like laborers and have them ask for work around the island."

It is thrilling, his decisiveness. I find myself strangely comforted by the idea that his agents might be thugs. It may take a thug to sort out Lopaki. And Hina.

"Hina says they brought him to a place down a long dirt road. With palm trees and ocean."

"Where do I find Hina?"

"Iwilei. But she's coming to my house today at four. I hope."

"She's a prostitute," Benjamin says matter-of-factly.

"Yes. She was drawn to it with opium," I say gingerly, remembering that his father once sold the drug.

"She is walking, I assume?"

"She did when she visited yesterday. Ben, she hates me. She may turn us in to Abram, tell him that we're looking."

"She won't get the chance. I'll find a place for her to fuel her habit."

I imagine Ben's carriage waiting at the side of the road. Him smiling and leaning out to call Hina with the same smile that always got me. She'd get into his carriage very pleased. I look at him, wondering if he is selling the drug. Webster sometimes treats those who take it.

"I don't have any," he says, reading my expression, "but I know those who do. My father still has a great deal of goodwill here, with the gamblers and the opium den owners. I suppose he owes us this." He lets his eyes wander to the crown of my head and then down to my lips, just as Samuel used to when he was learning my face, and he lingers there for a second. I feel my heart tip toward him.

"And your wife, what will you tell her?" I ask.

"There will be no more children for us," he answers. "Her last delivery was her final child, everyone has told us. For me not to have a son is a disaster for my business, here and in China. My father has many grandsons through his first wife. One of them will get the business here if I have no son to teach. She will understand. She will need to. I could take another wife, but I will not do that to my daughters. Or Mei Ling."

He looks at me appraisingly. "Sometimes, when I'm with my family around the table, I feel the strongest sense that someone is missing, like one of my children is in another room. I thought it was my dream of a son playing tricks in my head. Now I wonder if is the presence of this son, this Samuel." He squeezes my hand and stands, leading me to the door with his hand at my back. The smell of the dark hallway makes me cover my nose and mouth.

"You don't like it?" he laughs. "Dried herbs and mushrooms we no longer carry. But the smell will last forever."

Somewhere in the smell is a memory I can't place, and then I find it: Moloka'i. The herbs share the same dusky scent with the red dirt on the ranch.

"I heard Kepa was fighting with the rebels," Ben says in the dark. "His name was given by a man the PGs captured. They're looking for him. And because of Kepa they've started asking all the captured rebels questions about your father." Ben's hand goes around mine. "It would be a good time for him to find a berth on one of his own ships out of here."

"Are you with them, Ben? Because of Emilie?"

"I'm with no one. I have my own sources within. Not Emilie. I give the PGs what they want from the store. You can probably guess what I think of the rest of it."

"My father won't leave," I say, already knowing it's true.

"The royalists are doomed, Eliza. They counted on *haoles* to rise up against their own. There weren't enough willing to do it."

In my heart, I know this already. I knew it the minute PG troops returned from the sugar rebellion. But hearing it from Ben makes it so horribly final.

Ben rubs his thumb over my hand. "Eliza, what is he like? Is he a smart boy?"

"He's a little you. Though by now, who knows what he might be. Ben, if you tell Mei Ling and she tells Emilie—"

He interrupts me by placing a finger to my lips. "I told you, it will all be handled. Warn your father to go. If it weren't for this, I'd say you should go too. But I know you. I know you won't." He presses his cheek against mine, not kissing my face but whispering against it, "I have long regretted our last moments together. Let's hope we remember today as a new beginning."

He opens the door and gives my elbow a final squeeze. I step out through the closing door into the sun-bleached street. PG soldiers pass, rifles on their arms. They have two civilians by the arm, marching them down the street. One of the arrested men walks with just one shoe, hobbling unevenly.

I take a hired hack straight to my father's house, my mouth dry. My heart overwhelmed by what I've started.

The soldiers at the Ahsang estate don't look up as the hack passes, but once we pull into my father's I sense something is very wrong from the posture of his body on the lanai. He looks drunk. "Let me off down here, please," I ask the driver.

"It's done," Father says. He sits on his balcony with a glass of Scotch, the first I've seen him take since I returned from Moloka'i. My body tenses watching him gulp it. "Abram's gone and dug up the Queen's garden."

"What does the Queen have in her garden?"

"Apparently bombs made of coconut shell, rifles, pistols, and swords. I don't know if they were planted or put there in case of the battle escalating. But the Queen has been arrested. She's being held prisoner at the Palace."

I sit down next to him, tempted to take a sip from his glass.

"Where is Mehana?"

"She's gone to the Reef. Looking for Kepa. Rebels are walking down from the mountains because of the news, giving up. Being arrested."

"I doubt going back to the bottle will help Kepa. Or the Queen."

Father shrugs. "What's to be done now? Jesus, I thought there'd be more of us. Young men. I thought the firefights would give the royalists in town a chance to rise! But they've started arresting journalists and carriage drivers. Malveaux has got this town by the throat.

The mountains are the place to *stay* now. Kepa should disappear until things die down and they lose track of him. It's all a mess."

I do take a sip of his whisky. He takes it back, unhappy to share.

"You and Webster should take Clarice on a ship leaving tonight. Make your way to Australia, for God's sake." he says. "I'm far too old, but you should go. Come back when things have calmed—"

"No. I won't be sent away," I say, not looking at him. "I'll face my future here. You must go, Father. You have to. I've heard they've started looking at you."

He drains his glass to the bottom. "Can you imagine, the Queen a prisoner in her own palace?" he asks. He either hasn't heard me or doesn't care. "When our families rounded South America, all crammed together on that boat, the Dawsons, the Irvins, the Clarkes, all reading their Bibles in their hammocks, sick on the deck, they had no clue what they were unleashing on these islands."

He is already drunk after years of abstaining, and I cannot bare to watch.

"I asked my father about the voyage out, Eliza, and do you know what he told me? That he'd had a ship hand whipped for singing during prayer time. A sixteen-thousand-mile voyage, one hundred and fifty days at sea, and that was the only thing he cared to tell me of it. The one and only thing."

I stand up and touch my hand to his shoulder as I leave for home.

In Mānoa, I pause for a second at our front door and turn back to scan the valley walls for any sign of humans moving on the paths. I see no one; the valley is silent, the gunfire gone. I push into my house looking for my husband, my daughter. They sit at our kitchen table, a letter before them. It is from the Provisional Government. Richard Irvin's signature in the corner of the envelope. I open it.

Come alone to the Palace to speak to me about your father.

15

I stand outside the Palace on the same patch of earth where I waited for Ben Ahsang five years earlier, the night of the ball. There are no longer flower bedecked carriages. No Royal Band on the veranda playing waltzes. Two brass cannons grimace from the lanai now. The government band on the lawn is playing *Marching through Georgia*, which the PGs have adopted as their anthem. Their troops lie on the grass outside their hot tents, showing off small bandages over their eyes where their rifles have retracted back and cut their skin. They practice the stories they will tell for years to come: the time they put that native rebellion down.

A single soldier who'd been sitting on the steps reading Mark Twain sprints to open the palace door for me, my coloring sufficient proof of my allegiance. The moment I'm inside the familiar cool of the Palace I hear the unwelcome ruckus of PG troops coming up from the basement rooms below. An officer stands at attention at the base of the koa staircase.

"Richard Irvin?" I ask.

He looks me up and down. "President's office," he says, pointing upstairs.

I am surprised. I thought I would meet with him downstairs, in the blue room. Or that they would have crammed all their desks into the ballroom, like a telegraph office. Upstairs has always been private, the royal family's bedrooms.

I walk up the stairs slowly. Will Abram be waiting for me, too? I keep my hand on the bannister. At the top I see Richard through the first open door. His office is the King's former bedroom. I've never seen the inside of it, and it feels such a trespass.

"Eliza," Richard says pleasantly. A portrait of President Dole hangs behind him. Dole's desk is massive. Richard is sitting at a small writing desk, looking like a secretary awaiting dictation. When the King slept here he had singers stand outside every morning to wake him with his favorite Hawaiian hymns.

"Come, let's go next door," Richard says, taking me into what had been the King's study. The room makes me weak with nostalgia; it smells of koa wood, as it always has. They've kept the King's books and lithographs, his green felt-topped table on which K and I played cards with him during visits. He'd cheated outlandishly, discarding bad cards behind his ear, peering over our hands while twirling his mustache for effect. He'd served us guava juice in champagne glasses and taught K little strategies. I run my hand along the back of his chair.

"Memories?" Irvin asks.

"Of course," I answer crisply.

He closes both doors to the room. "Malveaux's office is down in the basement. I didn't want you to feel any less comfortable than you need to."

"I suppose a basement is the right place for the sort of meetings he takes," I answer.

Richard looks at me hard. "I'm not sure what you're implying."

"Nothing," I answer. "Thank you for considering my comfort."

"Well I haven't anything else to offer you. No food or drink. No wasting money the way the royals did in the old days. Sit, please," he says, indicating a chair.

I wait as he skims the pages of a ledger without explanation. Five years ago, we sat next to each other exactly below this spot at the

King's table, eating oysters and pigeon pie. I'd felt sorry for him because I chose Ben over his offer of marriage. But now, here I am, caught in whatever web he is busy spinning for me.

"So, we've arrested 300 Royalists," Richard announces, looking up from his pages. "Your father is next. And he could be sentenced to hang, at the time and place of our choosing."

I wait for his assurance this will not in fact be the case, but none comes, and it feels as if the breath has been knocked out of me.

"Have you brought me here to beg?" I ask.

"No," Richard says, shaking his head back and forth. "I couldn't stop the arrest even if I wanted to. We'd be hypocrites to let off a man so clearly guilty. We have intelligence that he funded half of this entire debacle. The guns you've heard day and night, disrupting lives and businesses? We have your father to thank for that terror. People want the death penalty for all white traitors. Hawaiians can plead lingering allegiances. Whites? They're Benedict Arnolds."

Richard says this sitting in the stolen seat of the King. The oceanfront portion of his family's plantation was a gift from the royal family for his grandfather's efforts on a state matter. "And the Queen?" I ask.

He looks back down at a ledger he's opened and points a thumb toward one of the closed doors. "Across the hall," he says.

"What sentence do the *people* want for the Queen?" I ask.

He bunches his lips to one side. "Banishment?" he offers. "Here. Here is your father's name." He turns the ledger around so I can see it. "William Dawson" is entered into the far left column, one of a scattering of *haole* names amongst so many Hawaiians. Next to the others are dates of their arrest. My father's is blank.

"If your father would like to turn evidence—give us any knowledge the Queen had of events, it could greatly help his case. You may convey that message."

"My father will want to stand on his own two feet at trial," I say. "But I ask for your mercy for Kepa. He is either in the Reef or being chased by your forces now—"

"Kepa?"

"Kepa our coachman? The one who pulled us both out of the stream when we were, what, 10 years old and trying to cross it that Christmas it was too high."

Richard reddens at the memory. That day he ran shaking into Mehana's arms, his hair matted into a fiery clump after being pulled under the water. It was a year after his brother died falling in the boiling sugar pulp during a game of hide and seek.

"This sort of thing won't work anymore with me, Eliza," Richard says harshly. "This is no longer a little kingdom where everyone owes someone something from a generation ago. It's going to become part of a big, mighty country."

It's going to become. The PGs are still wooing the U.S. to meet them at the altar. "Father retains his American citizenship. He has both. How will that mighty country feel about you hanging one of its citizens by the neck at the time and place of your choosing?"

"Ah, but his Hawaiian citizenship was the more precious to him, clearly. And a traitor is a traitor."

"He took no steps against the U.S. government. We both know Washington has absolutely declined to be a part of all this." I wave my hand across the stack of log books between us. "They might think you are the barbarian you told them the Queen was."

His face tells me others have also raised this risk. Richard sighs, as if I have him beat. "Eliza, I will do what I can for your father. Our history as families does mean something to me, even if I fear we have taken paths that will lead us to very different places in this community—"

"The prison verses the palace?" I say.

"In a phrase, yes." He shakes his head and looks out the window. "At times, I think you put me in the Palace. I know it was not your intention to humiliate me. But that was certainly the effect. Nothing drives the desire for power like humiliation. I certainly can attest to that."

"That's a terrible thing to say to me, Richard." I am genuinely sick at the thought that I am an inspiration to him in this.

"But it's true. When I offered you everything, thought you the fairest thing, you treated me like your fool."

"I was a seventeen-year-old girl who had nothing but good will for you. I simply wasn't in love. With you. So now you threaten to hang my father? Surely if our families came here together to serve God this is not what they meant for us."

Irvin closes his ledger. "I suppose I might rightly be accused of pride." He runs his hand along its edges. "I will see what can be done for your father. He's never tried very hard to make friends though, and that is now catching up with him. There is one thing you could do to help his cause while you're here. The former Queen is very lonely. Why don't you pay her a visit before you go? I know it's something you have done often these last two years. I've even heard you brought food to her rebels. Though I'm sure that was done in the name of the Christian values which, as you've reminded me, once bound our families together."

"So I am on notice, as well," I say.

He puts his hands up in surrender. "I have no interest in prying further into your conversations or tea parties. We will not make it a habit at this crucial time in our country's history to harass a young mother and the wife of a useful doctor. Rest assured. But I would like you to pay Mrs. Dominis a visit today."

It takes me a moment to understand what he means. The Queen, reduced to her dead husband's last name. It never ends with them.

He stands and indicates the door. My heart beats wildly as I follow him across the hall, my eye seeking the crowns and flowers in the ceiling plaster to avoid seeing the gashes and grime on the palace floor. It's been stripped of its silk carpets.

Two soldiers step back, allowing Richard to open the Queen's guarded door. I dread the awkwardness of his bringing me to her. But he stands aside for me to pass, shutting the door behind me.

My eyes adjust slowly to the gloom. The curtains are drawn, and the room once filled with Ahsang's gift of orchids reveals itself to be morosely furnished. The Queen sits on a single bed in the corner. There is a tiny square table, a chair, and a bureau.

"I would have gone mad if I have to spend one more hour listening to those guards pace outside," she says. "How did you convince them to let you visit?"

"I did not request an audience, your Majesty," I say, pulling up the small chair so we can speak quietly.

"Have you not heard? I am to be called Mrs. Dominis. You are my first visitor, aside from the women attending me."

"You could plead headaches and send for my husband," I suggest.

"I will not give them any more evidence of weakness than I am forced to, but it is a joy to see someone kind. How did you end up here?"

"Richard Irvin summoned me to discuss my father. He told me to pay you a visit. Perhaps his conscience is troubling him?"

Her brown eyes narrow. "No. I know what this is. They are pressing me to abdicate. I told them I cannot possibly without the advice of my supporters. I've been using this as an excuse to stall them. They'll say you are the supporter—a longtime friend of the throne. From a prestigious family."

"Not so prestigious if they hang my father."

"I saw his name. They gave me a list of those they will kill. If I sign the abdication, they say my supporters will be released."

We sit together listening to the guards' footsteps outside.

"They never stop," she says. "All day, all night, the same steps. The same pace. They allow me nothing to read but my Book of Common Prayer. No paper to write music. I compose in my head. I turn their footsteps into my tempo." She claps her hands soundlessly in time with the guards' steps. "All my retainers were arrested. Forty people. All my papers and my late husband's papers have been taken. My diary. The only paper I have held since they brought me here was the one for my abdication.

The Queen's voice catches and she hangs her head. I turn my eyes away, as I know she would prefer. By her pillow there are ti leaves half woven together. She was always one to fashion wreaths for the graves of loved ones. For her husband. For K's mother, the Queen's sister, Likelike. Was she still weaving them in here? Asking guards to pick something from the garden for her? At least they allow her that.

"I would choose death rather than sign their abdication papers," the Queen says quietly. "But for those who suffer by reason of their love or loyalty for me, like your father, I must sign. Unless I do the will of my jailers, they will be put to death. I do not want their blood upon my soul."

I am relieved she will sign to save my father's life. She is strong-willed; I would not have been surprised if she'd refused. For all of the hopes of the last years to come to this little room, this forced abdication. It is a bitter end.

"They are so falsely gallant. 'We will not ask you to be at your trial, Madame. It would be humiliating,' Irvin said. 'Humiliating?' I said 'What have I left?" She runs fingers under her eyes. I look down, knowing she does not want me to see her tears. "The bombs in my garden were planted, of that I'm sure. The rest was my husband's collection of firearms; an old curiosity shop of obsolete warfare."

"Surely that will come out at trial?" I say.

"The truth of my crime is that I knew my people were conspiring to re-establish the constitutional government. To throw off the yoke of the stranger and oppressor."

The guards' footsteps pass, back and forth. Back and forth.

"In the beginning, I wanted my throne back. For me, and no one else. Then I wanted the Kingdom saved, whether for Ka'iulani or myself, it did not matter. Now, I just want to go home. To be among Hawaiians under the shade of my trees away from the PGs' deceit in all things." She stands. "Will you pray with me, Eliza?"

"Oh, your Majesty, I hardly know my prayers."

"Surely, the Lord's prayer?"

"That one. Yes," I say, and we laugh.

She takes me into the little corner alcove. There is one off each of the palace bedrooms. K and I spent hours hiding in them, dreaming in them. *What would our husbands look like? What flower would we carry at our wedding?* The Queen and I kneel. She looks up through the little window. In the corner of the glass panes I see streaks of dark blue—the reflection of soldiers' uniforms below. She takes my hand and closes her eyes. We say the Lord's prayer, the backbone of the religion brought to these islands by the grandfathers of those across the hall. By my own grandfather. I pray for Samuel. *Please let it be true. Please bring him home. Let me be his mother again.* The Queen squeezes my hand harder, and I pray for her people, her kingdom, my father. "Lord, we are not frightened. Help us to remember that," she says.

We rise. "Will you come to my trial, Eliza? They will not allow Hawaiians. It would help me to have a friendly face amongst my accusers."

"If they will allow it, I will be there. I will pray you are released."

"They have told me nothing of what they have in store for me, Eliza. This could be my future," she says lifting her finger to point to the footsteps outside. "At least he keeps his timing. If I can get some paper, I could compose something to that beat."

We walk to the bedroom door. "You know, it's a terrible sign that they've let us talk this long," she says. "It means they know I have no cards left to play."

I emerge from the room. A guard pivots from his pacing to fetch Richard Irvin. Then soldiers salute Richard as he escorts me out of the Palace. I watch him gaze at our surroundings like someone who's purchased a property and cannot believe their good luck. "We truly would have made a terrible couple," he tells me. "You were right about that much."

I cannot help myself. "Tell me, Richard, when you sent Abram Malveaux my way, did you know what a monster he was?"

Richard blushes scarlet. "I hardly knew him then. And you were a desperate girl in need of a solution. That's the thing, Eliza. You waste your gifts. You sabotage yourself through impulse. Keep on my good side. You'll certainly need fewer enemies to survive what's coming. If you want to see your father before he's sent to the Reef, head to Nu'uanu now."

❧

Father was drunk when they took him in. "Such a lot of fuss for such a little rebellion," he'd said as he let them lift him into the wagon. He had the air of a vagrant, like the sunburned alcoholics who veer along the Fort Street sidewalks, cutting dangerously in front of carriages to cross over to another saloon. The sort of man who, people note sadly, once held a higher station in life.

Soon after, Richard sent a personal courier to inform me that Kepa had joined Father at the Reef. They'd caught him on the mountain paths crossing back to Nu'uanu, trying to get home. He'd been put in a large holding area with other Hawaiians. Father shares a cell with another royalist plantation owner from the Big Island, an Englishman named Brickart. Haole or Hawaiian, word is that all prisoners sleep on hammocks and keep buckets for sanitation.

The Queen abdicated, yet not one of her supporters has been released. Instead they started the trials. To save time, the commission tries the accused rebels in batches.

❧

Kepa's group goes first. Webster and I stand outside the Palace with Mehana. We see Kepa loaded off a cart, his hands in cuffs, cuts on his face, his arms. There are stories circulating of men being stripped and held in a dark cell for days to force them to confess something against the Queen.

"Barefoot? Dirty? They take him to trial in a ballroom like that?" Mehana fumes.

Kepa is pushed with five other prisoners up the stairs through the palace doors. Guards are allowing Americans through to watch. I turn to Mehana and say, "Wait for me here."

Webster reaches out for me as I move into the surging crowd, but I keep going. The guards don't give me a second look as I squeeze into the Palace, pushing my way past the koa staircase and along the wall until I can crouch in the doorway and see a sliver of the throne room. A lawyer within is already addressing the military tribunal, which sits at a long table, Richard Irvin at its dead center. Blackwell and Clarke are nearly out of sight at its end.

"The white men who started this thing," the lawyer says slowly, "were not there to meet the government forces. After two years of plotting they put everything on these people and then tried to cover up their tracks. But now, what is to be done?"

The lawyer's accusation is just. My father, people like him—me—we all played at revolt, but had not taken up arms, like Kepa. We were guilty not of treason to Americans, but of half-heartedness to Hawaiians.

"Do you understand any English?" the lawyer asks the line of prisoners. He focuses in on Kepa, the roughest looking of the bunch. "Yes," comes Kepa's answer.

"What is the word for gun?" the wiry, small lawyer asks. "In your native tongue?"

"*Pū*," Kepa answers warily. I remember how he'd bring his English Bible into Father's study Sunday afternoons. When he found a word he did not recognize, he would copy the definition from father's dictionary into his Bible's margin in his surprisingly delicate longhand. The missionaries had taught nearly every Hawaiian to read and write. That, they had done.

"What is ship?"

"*Moku*," Kepa says. He is feeling teased. His hair seems to grow wilder on the stand, his missing teeth more menacing as his mood darkens. I have never seen Kepa's temper, but I know he nearly killed a man who stabbed him, smashing a bottle into his face again and again in a dank saloon before my birth. Only the thought of the Reef stopped him, the desire not to rot there. It was the fate he faced again today.

The lawyer thinks better than to ask Kepa for more translations, turning instead to ask better questions of the other men. They do not dispute the lawyer's accounting of pistols being unloaded on the beach. They nod when asked if they all were there that night. Then the lawyer decides he has not included Kepa enough. He turns to him and asks "And is it true that certain among you used as a password for the evening the word 'missionary?'"

"That was the word," Kepa answers, as resigned as the others. We all know today has a forgone conclusion. The whole town expects that these poor men will be found guilty but spared the death penalty. That is only on the table for white offenders like my father, the men who make the PGs far more angry.

"Did you understand what a missionary was?" the lawyer asks Kepa, his tone snide.

Kepa tilts his head, as if trying to understand what this little man is looking for. "Yes," Kepa says quietly, "Keep thy tongue from evil and thy lips from speaking guile. Psalm 34."

"Good, very good." the lawyer says, "And did—"

"Search me, O God," Kepa says quietly, "and know my heart. Try me and know my thoughts, and see if there be any wicked way in me. Lead me in the way everlasting. Psalm 139."

"That is enough," a voice says from the long table holding the military tribunal. It is Richard Irvin. "Today is not Sunday. This is not a church."

The courtroom laughs heartily; Kepa looks sidelong at Richard, his nostrils flaring.

"As ye would that men should do to you," Kepa bellows. "Do ye also to them. Luke."

"No more, witness!" shouts the lawyer, rapping his hand twice against the arm of Kepa's chair. Kepa laughs, his missing teeth exposing the dark red roof of his mouth as he tosses his head back. "Judge not!" he shouts, clenching his fists against his long hair. "That ye be not judged. Matthew."

"Remove him," Lorrance Clarke says.

A guard moves toward Kepa, who stands, looking straight into the faces of his co-accused: one is crying, another is making the sign of the cross. Kepa shakes his head back and forth before turning to the transfixed throne room. "Go ye, therefore, and teach all nations. The wicked will not stand in the judgment."

"Out!" Blackwell stands and says. He is the oldest, the most publicly devout of the missionaries assembled today. He is the one for whom these words burn the hottest.

It takes three guards to push Kepa toward the door where I am crouched, but he does not see me as he is brought through the silent crowd which parts for him. The group is immediately sentenced to five years' hard labor and a $5,000 fine.

I rush out of the Palace to find Mehana. A crowd of Hawaiians are screaming as the men are loaded back in the cart.

"Kepa! Kepa!" Mehana cries.

He lifts his head, the fight totally gone from his face. She puts her hand to her heart and lips. He nods and closes his eyes.

On the day of the Queen's trial, the former throne room is under heavy guard, filled with orderly California reporters, the consuls from Japan, Portugal and France, and a host of British and American dignitaries. Richard Irvin has allowed her request that I attend.

We silently watch as a reporter from San Francisco approaches two men sitting in front of us to ask for their opinion on the trial. The California press has written that the Queen's private secretary,

Joseph Heleluhe, was stripped and placed in a dark cell without light, food or water. They write that forced confessions have been made in tanks of ice water.

"Go find your lies elsewhere," says one of the men to the reporter. "It's the American and British ministers that are the real problem," says the same man after the reporter returns to his seat. "They are against the execution of sentences."

"The guilt goes back to President Cleveland," answers his companion. "He's the one that made Hawaiians believe the monarchy should be restored. Damn him for this mess."

"The bottom of your skirt could use an iron," Emilie whispers to me, taking the seat next to me. "You should have a word with your help."

"I'd have to rebuke myself," I answer.

"When Richard and I went to Paris, everyone was so well turned out," Emilie says. "It made we wonder if most Yankees dress poorly just because it was only the peasants who left Europe for America. Don't you think?"

Just then, the Queen enters, dressed in black, carrying a woven *lauhala* fan decorated with ferns. We lock eyes for a split second. Native policemen are posted behind her high-backed chair, no doubt so that the San Francisco press might sketch them into their newspaper illustrations, giving the impression that Hawaiians support this trial.

"Let us come to order," announces a man I do not recognize from the military commission. "This tribunal has been convened to try Mrs. Dominis for misprision of treason for concealing her knowledge of a treasonous plot to overthrow the Republic of Hawai'i."

The Queen gives all her testimony in Hawaiian, answering most questions with "yes" or "no." She makes no effort to be sympathetic.

Emilie raises her fan and says, "Haughty," under her breath.

Had I not sat with the Queen, prayed with her, I may have found her haughty too. How little we know of the inner workings of each other's thoughts. Her attorney stands to read the Queen's statement in English.

"I owe no allegiance to the Provisional Government established by a minority of the foreign population nor to any power or anyone save the will of my people and the welfare of my country."

The American Minister, Willis, nods his head vigorously.

"The wishes of my people were not consulted as to this change of government. To prevent the shedding of the blood of my people, native and foreign alike, I quietly yielded to the armed forces brought against my throne and submitted to the government of the United States the decision of my rights and those of the Hawaiian people. As for my supporters you hold as prisoners, as you deal with them, so I pray that the Almighty God may deal with you in your hour of trial."

The prosecution takes its turn, calling the Queen "the prisoner" or "that woman." They call her a dictator and she counters, "You argue for freedom and democracy and yet you are not willing to put your annexation to a popular vote. I am. Who is the dictator? You have converted Hawaiians into Christians and our lands into cash."

There are mumbled objections rumbling through the crowd. The mood in the former throne room is threatening. I feel real fear for the Queen, for what they will do to her. K's father, Cleghorn, was right to keep his daughter far away from all of this.

The Queen's expression does not change as she is sentenced to a fine of $5000 and five years' hard labor. Then she is taken upstairs and shut off from the world again.

Eliza,

My men have been sent, though as you may know travel has become so monitored with these trials that we needed to wait two days for passage. Perhaps I should send these notices in a different manner as your father's court date draws near. I hope for the best for him. Of all of them, he was the fairest to my father. Tell him that.

Ben

Father is tried two days later.

Again I have Emilie at my side, for Richard denied a seat to Webster.

When he enters, I see Father's lost weight. Mehana and I have delivered hot meals and jerky every few days, but we suspected nothing was getting through. Without his glasses, he walks into the corner of the commission's table. Some laugh, I know, because of his reputation as a drunk. He can't see far enough to know that I'm present. My nerves are running so high I'm trembling. There's been no drink at the Reef. He isn't shaking at all.

They seat him next to the other "traitor," the British plantation owner named Brickart, and four other wealthy haole men accused of financing the rebellion. As the commission runs through each man's name and the charge, Father winces in pain. I'm not sure if it's from bumping into the table or something more serious.

When his own name and charge is called he springs into extraordinary and disastrous action. "Treason?" he demands, standing. Even as the Hawaiian police try to seat him, he keeps shouting. "My American president worked toward restoration, even if he does not hold the power with Congress to act on it. My Queen has been illegally dethroned. I have been loyal when others have been thieves!"

"You're going to come into your inheritance very early if he keeps this up," Emilie smiles.

"Watch yourself, Dawson, or we'll see what else is rotten in your household. Your coachman's already been sentenced," says Clarke.

It's quiet then. I study Emilie's fan. How many here know I am involved? Abram has been absent at these trials. Irvin no doubt wants to keep everything untoward far from the American press.

Father sits back for the rest of the proceedings. They call out the sentence for the whole group of men. "…hung by the neck until the time of your death."

I'm stunned; even Emilie gasps. "Richard said it wouldn't come to this," she says as we watch Father led quickly from the court.

I try to stand. "I am not sure my legs will carry me," I admit. She helps me from my seat and walks me out, fanning me as I collapse on the koa staircase.

Richard is coming toward us. "I'll talk with him," Emilie whispers. She snaps her fan back into place and rises.

"Go home, Eliza," Richard says. "Webster is waiting outside. I'm sorry I couldn't—"

"Richard, you have to do something," I say.

Emilie is shaking her head "no" to me from behind her husband.

"It is necessary to make examples of some. Dole is saying he'll resign if it's carried out, but honestly, Eliza. I have warned your father he's picked the wrong side for years now. With his behavior today, I don't know how much more I can do. I'll let you see as much of him as you like for the time he has left."

16

That Sunday, I am trying to calm Clarice as I leave our home to go to the Reef when a deliveryman comes to my kitchen door.

"We did not order anything," I say, handing back the box.

The man says what sounds like a curse in Chinese. He drops the box to the ground and splits it with his knife to reveal half a dozen dragonfruit within, their skins taut, spines chartreuse. My hand goes to my throat and I laugh, giddy as I take the box inside.

"Mama laughing?" Clarice asks. It's sad these trials have made the sight so remarkable to her. "Fruit," I answer, which only makes her more puzzled.

"Give you?" Clarice asks, pulling on my skirt. I hand her one.

"Oh, bad fruit!" she says, stepping back from its green spines.

"Oh no, Baba. The prickles don't hurt."

I put it down on the table and I open the drawstring of the burlap sack inside. There is a note: *I think we've found him.*

Sun glints off the fishponds and ocean surrounding the Reef, making the prison appear as if it is floating out to the shimmering sea. When Kalākaua was king, visitors strolled along the Reef's high walls to take in the views. Now the coral fortress is entirely forbidden to outsiders, unless Richard Irvin allows an exception.

"I was hoping you would bring Clarice," Father says as I enter his cell. The smell of sewage is everywhere in the building.

"It's a miracle I'm here," I tell him. I unwrap a collection of jerky and biscuits from Mehana. "They haven't allowed us to visit Kepa." At least there will be food for them to share. Father rolls his eyes at the sight of the basket; there is no use in trying to force his appetite amidst the stench. There are yellow crystals along the ledge of a boarded up window, and for a second I hold my hand over my face thinking it's dried urine.

"I haven't quite gotten that desperate, my dear. It's salt water crystals from the ocean air sneaking in through the tiny crack they didn't manage to cut off. Otherwise they've been very convincing in their enforcement of misery. Try them. They are like a human salt lick."

"Very funny. I didn't even ask permission for Clarice to come. She thinks you're on a sea voyage. It's impossible to explain."

"Yes it is," Father says. Then he starts to cry. "I'm trapped in this room, thinking of my life ending and what I did to you and Samuel. I cannot escape my failures."

I take his hand. "Let's not use this brief visit for that."

"So you'd rather I go to my hanging with this unspoken between us? Dammit, just speak your mind!"

"All right. I cannot fathom that you sent me away to that place. Especially now that I have a daughter of my own. Let alone the rest of it."

"Most of the world's woes come back to pride, Eliza. Pride made me send you there. Drink made me forget you. And him. Now he's dead, and there's nothing I can do."

He is sobbing. I put my hand on his back, feeling almost motherly. I had not wanted to tell him until my son was home. But now his return is only a matter of time. "Father, Samuel is alive. A woman from the ranch lied about his death. Ben's helping me—"

Father pulls away from me. "Webster agreed to this?" he asks, voice booming.

"I tell you that the grandson you weep for is alive and you ask if I have my husband's permission to bring him home?"

"I'm asking if you have allowed the man who ruined you to play your husband for the fool!"

A cold silence falls between us. He always returns to his missionary ideals when he thinks he is the antithesis of them. It is not the time for that, I tell myself. I speak calmly.

"It was Webster who decided we need a man who can take Abram on—"

"Well, I hope Ben proves his worth this time around. You actually believe —"

"I believe you and I are no good at consoling one another, Father," I say tersely, pulling my gloves on. "I'll send word of Jensen's progress on your appeal."

"Don't bother. I'll see you at the gallows," Father answers.

I stop at the door. That could be where I see him next. I turn back. "I don't want to leave you in this prison cell with those as our final words."

"Don't let Benjamin Ahsang lead you astray again, Eliza. Don't let him distract you from the man you were so very lucky to marry. Benjamin Ahsang will never stand up for you. Not in front of his wife. Not in front of all of Honolulu."

He is still ashamed of what I did. Afraid I'll do it again. "I am hopeful now, Father. My son is alive. Your grandson is alive. Be happy for me. And when Samuel returns, be proud."

"If I live to see your son, Eliza, I will shout his existence from every corner. But it would take a double miracle for that to pass, my love. I'm proud of the family you have now, the one you've built. I should say these sorts of things before they string me up."

"They will not string you up. Just try to behave yourself better until Jensen can get you out of here. Hold that temper for all of us."

I walk up Iwilei Road looking for a hired hack to take me home. *What if Ben does fail me again?* Hope grows in me now, a third pregnancy. I push Father's comments from my head for fear of losing that hope, our child. Prostitutes watch me from their balconies, their cooking utensils and dishes drying in the sun before their lives change over into the evening hours. They must wonder what a missionary lady is doing on their street. *This missionary lady has born two children to the wrong legal fathers,* I think. *She is not so very different from you.*

"Are you lost? I suppose we couldn't avoid each other forever."

His curls are cropped close to his head, and there is grey in them. Deep lines run at the sides of his mouth and the corners of his eyes. Abram looks like a rich man now. I could be sick right in the street. I turn to keep going but he follows me.

"I want to know why you've got your lover snooping around, using my name in places it doesn't belong."

"You're mad," I say, heading for a carriage at the corner.

He yanks me back. "A little bird told me yesterday that Ben Ahsang's got Hina holed up, having her tell lies in exchange for a pipe. Asking her about your bastard. You leave me out of this. I've got real business here, and I don't want you messing with my name."

"Your name?" I snap. "It's too late for your name. We've found him. Soon you'll be the one inside this prison for what you've done."

"Maybe you ought to spend less time worrying about me and start worrying that the next time I see you your father's going to be swinging high from a rope." He walks backward and smiles at me. "And your boy's dead, Eliza. Still dead."

"Why in the world did you tell him?" Ben asks.

"It just came out my mouth."

"Now he needs to make our son disappear." He looks at me in frustration and I sink down onto the small bench against the wall in the hidden "garden." After a moment he joins me, putting his hand gently on my knee. "I wanted to get him before Abram did."

"I know," I say sorrowfully, not believing what I've done. "Where is he, Ben?"

"Close to where your friend saw him, outside Kaunakakai. They were at a house down from the coconut grove and saw a child sitting alone tracing something into the mud. He looked up and ran. But they said our resemblance was eerie."

Ben looks at me bashfully, aware of how much pride he is showing. He beams the crooked smile of his youth, and leans forward to kiss me on the forehead. I wonder, if I kiss him now, will his hands be in my hair, the bodice of my dress? A door swings open into the courtyard and we part. A harried cook carrying a pole dripping with freshly cut noodles runs past us into an alleyway trailing flour behind him. "What happens now?" I ask when the man is gone, relieved when Ben doesn't touch me again. I don't want to dishonor Webster. This friction between Ben and me, it's the rekindling of a lost world.

"I gave them cash to bribe the family into letting him go. I wanted to avoid raising a fuss and being seen. But now I wonder if I should go to Moloka'i and handle this myself. I'll tell Mei Ling there's trouble at the Maui plantation."

"I thought she knew?"

"Not yet. No need to stir up those emotions until he's real."

When I step outside into the world, those words come back to me. And the lines of Samuel, so crisp only an hour earlier, blur before me.

I ask my driver to detour to the cemetery at Nu'uanu, where my mother is buried. I have visited often these past years. Mammoth carved

headstones make death look rich and expensive here. Angels swoop down over the names of men who abandoned God's work to make a business out of these islands. Now they sleep in this valley, overlooking the town they built into a city and the land they secured for their families. My heart seizes up at the idea of Father buried here. Surrounded by the families who made him so uncomfortable.

My mother's tablet is carved with a child-like angel. Father ordered it to look like me. I take Ben's note from my sleeve to check on it again as one does for a key in the pocket, needing to know that, yes, it is still there. *I think we've found him.* It still says clearly in ink that Samuel is found.

"I saw you in your carriage," Emilie calls, marching up the graveyard path, winding between wizened trees with extravagant yellow blossoms. Her mother's family is buried here too. Not the Hawaiians, but the American Yankees who were Hannah's haole line. "Richard's reconsidering your father's sentence," she announces when she reaches me.

"Oh, Emilie, I am so, so grateful—"

"I said considering," Emilie says, looking out across the gravestones.

Her mother rejected her European bloodlines to embrace only her Hawaiian. Why do I find that benign, yet judge Emilie so harshly for choosing to be only haole? Ben chose his Chinese line, Clara the Hawaiian. Emilie had just as much right. Yet if the Queen still reigned all powerful, I suspect Emilie would be standing before me in a *holokū* dress and feather lei, just as she used to sport her father's jade when he was the one taking her to the Palace. Today, the jade has been abandoned for a polite strand of pearls. Her sleeves are puffed and starched like a Boston matron. Her eyes, I realize, are light and wild with anger.

"Abram Malveaux came to have a word with me."

She was kind the day of Father's sentence. I pray our old ties get me through what lies ahead in this confrontation. "He is neither a good nor honest man, Emilie, I know that better than anyone, I can assure you."

Emilie's cheekbones shift as her eyes narrow. "He says you are going around claiming there's a child of sin between you and my brother? Are you? I forbid it."

This means Abram thinks he's alive. "You can't forbid a child who exists, Emilie." I can't stop myself from smiling, which enrages her.

"I won't have him exist. Not here," she says. "I won't let you ruin everything. Richard needs no scandal, no association with you. Who behaves like this? I thank God my father and Clara were spared this knife in our back."

"Clara knows. I told her in Kalaupapa."

Emilie steps back; power shifts to me.

"Your mother probably knows; I saw her too. I'm not sure about your father. Ben may have written."

My words hit her hard. Her eyes fill, "Were you ever truly our friend, Eliza? Or were you just trying to capture my brother?"

"Emilie, I loved you all."

"Well I certainly don't love you," she says, taking the power back. "I'm going to tell his wife everything. Because I know for certain she has no idea."

The wind starts up, swirling yellow petals around us. Could we truly be the girls who'd played mahjong for hours in the bungalow, our feet tucked against each other's hips on the daybed? "You don't want to hurt your brother. Let Ben be the one to tell her. Please," I plead.

"No. I'll see your father gets no mercy either if you continue with this business."

"Are you blackmailing me? Has it come to that?" Emilie once courted my friendship, asking me to take her to 'Āinahau to visit the Princess. But that was it, wasn't it? She'd pursued me when I provided access to the hearts of the royal family, the family she had no use for now.

"I'm telling you to stop ruining our lives the way you have your own." Emilie steps toward me. "So prim and quiet, in your grey smocks and your schoolmarm hair," she sneers. "Just a trollop in disguise. How common you are, falling pregnant right and left."

In another life, one in which the King did not die, where Ben and I had wed, we would have been sisters, commiserating about life's disappointments together. She married Richard three years ago, yet they have no children. It's been nearly two years now for Webster and me, hoping, waiting.

"All the town will know what you truly are, if you continue," she says. "That child should have gone to an orphanage. Look at everything you could have saved yourself. All accomplishing nothing. Except angering my husband. Maybe your father does need to serve as an example."

"When your brother and I find our son," I say coldly, "he will become heir to your father's business here. I doubt he will take kindly to an aunt who pushed for his grandfather's hanging. I will not trade Samuel's life for my father's. If you let my father hang, it will be for you to explain. It will be on your soul, not mine."

17

Annexation Day, 1898

We march toward the Palace in lock step, the air around us charged with the feeling of an execution. Rather than a hangman's noose atop the palace scaffolding, there is a speaker's podium. Richard Irvin stands before it, his arm placed protectively around a pregnant Emilie.

America has finally accepted his proposal, and this is their wedding day. 'Iolani Palace sulks behind him like an overdressed woman, decked out in red, white, and blue bunting. Swarms of men, red-faced beneath their top hats, move past us making an effort to show themselves to Richard before the ceremony begins.

"I should probably say a word or two," Webster says apologetically, moving up to the scaffold to congratulate President Sanford Dole.

Dole stands a full head taller than the rest, with a foot-long beard. Clarke poses next to him for a newspaper photograph, his eyebrow arched. All the puritanical laws the King had overturned are now back in place by Clarke's hand. Hula is forbidden. Sunday concerts are allowed only in the case of European music; a band in Hilo asked for permission to play Portuguese music at Easter and was denied, perhaps because so many Portuguese have come to work the sugar fields and so get grouped in with the Asians and Hawaiians rather than the *haole* masters.

"We ought to show Richard a map of Europe. Portugal is still that bit at the end," Webster said, sketching it for Clarice over breakfast.

Mehana asked me to reread to her the news that Hawaiian is henceforth banned in classrooms because she was sure there was a mistake. She'd thought the Hawaiian newspapers were exaggerating the threat. But there it was, in the English papers too. "How can they kill our words?" she asked, the paper crumpled in the sink as she ran water over it like dirty produce.

I still hear parents speaking Hawaiian in the streets, but their children answer in English. Hawaiian is becoming a tongue for the old.

Hawaiians are not at the Palace today, save for the musicians. I look down Richards Street to watch as carriages carrying the Queen's supporters arrive at Washington Place, knowing they can offer her only kisses and tears, prayers and anger. I would prefer to be in their company, but a curtain has been drawn. The age of *haole* royalists has forever passed. My place is here now, whether I like it or not. This morning divides us into two separate camps in one fractured Territory.

There are no Chinese here today, either, unless one counts Emilie. Which, of course, she would rather one not. I didn't expect to see Ben. We have crossed paths only rarely since he returned from Moloka'i three years ago without our son. He found the house Samuel had been seen at: it was empty, the large family who lived there gone. I believed Ben when he said he tried everything to find our boy. I'd told him everything Emilie had said to me in the graveyard. "My sister denies talking to Abram about it," he'd said. "She's lying," I told him.

Now I see Webster doff his hat to her. Like every woman here today save me, she wears a puffed sleeve, dotted white muslin dress with a pale silk sash riding high above her rounded belly. They all look as if they are brides. I wear my lightest grey; the ladies at Washington Place grieve in their black holokū with feather lei in orange and yellow. Black has become the Queen's permanent color. Ka'iulani is with her today. My friend returned home after nine years with two parts of her late mother's death-bed prophecy already fulfilled: she was gone from Hawai'i for a very long time and she will never see her throne. Today's ceremony makes that official. Final. We have joyfully rediscovered each other's older, more somber selves. This afternoon we have a date to swim in our old mountain pool together.

There is a tug at my hand. "Momma, why must I still wear a hat when it's cloudy?" asks Clarice. She is a contrarian, my daughter, bright and questioning.

"You'll be happy you're wearing it if it rains again," I say. It's the middle of August, yet it feels like winter.

"Why is that lady talking to Father?" Clarice asks suspiciously. Emilie is pressing her bump while telling Webster something. We have not spoken since that awful day in the graveyard, and my own belly has stayed empty these years. "It must be something I was exposed to at Kalaupapa," Webster apologizes to me. But I know it is Samuel: he is the phantom pregnancy that fills me, that I carry everywhere. I did not even offer condolences to Emilie when the news came from Kalaupapa that Clara had passed. Hannah stayed at the settlement, quietly cared for by Clara's widower. I'd written Ben a note, but not Emilie. I wrote Clara's widower, too. He answered my letter saying Clara wanted to leave her unused dowry to Kalaupapa for the children, but someone in the Ahsang family had refused. "It would make Clara's presence too public," surmised Webster.

My husband rejoins us. An older couple I recognize as distant neighbors in Mānoa give me a severe look as we stop to take a program decorated with an image of Uncle Sam holding the American flag.

"Why are they staring?" Clarice asks. The couple averts their gaze. Soon I'll have to explain that her grandfather is the example everyone uses for an American traitor.

"Because your hat is so very pretty," Webster says, taking my arm as an attendant waves us up to the Palace's second story balcony. We join the hundreds of feet moving across the palace floors, the noise near deafening without any rugs or art left to absorb it.

"I don't think anyone gives two pennies about this silly hat," Clarice nearly shouts.

It is for Clarice's sake that my father insisted we make an appearance today. He is bedridden now. Richard Irvin commuted his death sentence at America's urging, but prison splintered his health. He stays in his room except for the days he's helped down to the patio to watch light move through the valley. His physical condition keeps him from drinking, and he sees the world in a clearer fashion now. Some days the roar returns to his voice. I heard it when he learned I had no intention of attending today's ceremony.

"Clarice is the future," Father said. "We must show ourselves in this new world. Our side has lost once and for all. Let's get on with it."

"She's five years old, and you haven't got the plantation to worry about anymore," I answered. His skin is yellow and sags at his jowls, but his hair holds its dark color. In business he is a rich and vindicated man, buying up boat after boat so that the sugar men are now forced to book space on his vessels.

We pass by the room where the Queen was imprisoned for eight months after her trial before being released to Washington Place—but forbidden from travelling. As we take our seats I hear my father's name being murmured.

"Stop. Staring," Clarice says in a theater whisper to someone on our left.

I keep my face fixed on the podium below. Webster covers his face with his program. We never know what will come out of our daughter's mouth. I suspect Webster thinks she gets it from me but is too polite to say so.

The ceremony begins, quick and hollow. They pull down the Hawaiian flag—red, white, and blue stripes surrounding the Union Jack, a remnant from the days of British influence—to a melancholy rendition of Hawai'i Pono'ī, which the musicians obediently finish, their pain evident in every trembling note. The old flag drops to the ground. A gigantic American flag is raised, and a double twenty-one-gun salute sounds from the harbor.

It lasts forever.

I do not feel the ceremony in my bones as I thought I would. This world disappeared for me years ago, along with my dream of recovering Samuel. When he returned from Moloka'i, Ben hired a spy to visit Abram's ranch as a fisherman; we thought Abram might have taken him across the channel to Lāhainā. That would have been easy, on a worker's boat, so we searched Maui too. But Samuel had vanished. One detective suggested that Abram drowned him in the channel to Maui. So all I wish for now is to survive this new Hawai'i in the cocoon of my little family. "It's done," I say, taking Clarice's hand and steering her toward the palace steps.

"I didn't like that church service, Mama," she yells over the cacophony of the crowd.

"It wasn't a service," I answer, trying to move her along. A man jumps down the stairs and hits me with his elbow. I'm 25 this year, but feel 52 years' worth of annoyance that such manners are now allowed in this palace. Webster picks Clarice up in his arms, then stops still, lowering her quickly down and out of sight.

"Look," he says. I follow his gaze, and there is Abram, dressed like a dandy. He is within a circle of men smoking cigars. I turn us the other direction in the crowd, which suddenly presses in on me.

"Are you all right?" Webster asks. I nod. "Surprising Abram wasn't on the podium," he adds.

"I'm sure they want to forget his contributions now that it's done. He's busy buying up sugar lands. No doubt with my money," I say.

"Better your money than you," Webster answers.

Abram kept my father in prison a full year after his sentencing. Kepa returned home six months after the trials, emerging from prison more devout and silent. I only hear his voice when he sings now. "He lives his life internally," Webster says. "It's not the worst way to live."

We pass the throne room where Emilie is instructing a group of women to roll out yet more red, white and blue bunting between the chandeliers as workmen crank open the windows behind her. Tonight is the Annexation Ball, and I realize they are throwing open the windows so guests can listen to the band play through from the lanai, just as we used to in the old days, when ropes of maile leaves and pikake decorated the chandeliers.

A barefoot Hawaiian man waits next to her with a ladder. His eyes are swollen. I remember Ka'iulani in this room when her mother lay in state for three weeks. Everything in the room draped in black. Every eye red. Today, it's as if a whole nation has lain in state for three years, and the burial finally came.

Ka'iulani drifts next to me. We float side by side, quiet and drained after the day's events. Clouds are trapped in the corner of Nu'uanu valley, enveloping us in their mist. It is cold, and though I wish I could last longer in the shivering clear water, I pull my wet mu'u mu'u up around my knees to navigate my exit across the pool's moss-covered rocks.

"You are the Lady of the Lake," I tell Ka'iulani. She drifts in the clouds, her eyes and lips blooming full and lush in her dainty face, a face that has been canonized in Western papers: Ka'iulani, the beautiful "barbarian" princess, they call her. How little they know.

"Ah, so where then is Excalibur when we need it most?" she asks, raising herself to stand neck deep. "The Lady of the Lake gives Arthur Excalibur. How nice it would be to have an Arthur right now."

So many romantic dreams are pinned on my delicate friend. The Hawaiians still hold onto a sheen of hope: she is their Ghost Dance, their improbable dream of freedom and victory.

Ka'iulani looks up the valley wall. Short, thick waterfalls cut across it from the day's rains. "If I'd been here when it all happened. Perhaps..."

"Webster says there was no way some larger country wasn't going to swallow this one, eventually. You can't hold off the entire world," I say.

"That's the most helpful, saddest thing one could say." She floats again in the water. "They wanted twelve native girls to raise their new flag today. They thought it would be poetic." She laughs. "They could not find any willing girls. Emilie came to 'Āinahau to invite me to the Annexation Ball tonight. I told her, why didn't you ask me to pull down Hawaii's flag, too?"

"What did she say?"

"She told me she thought I'd be happier. I told her I thought I'd be Queen. 'I thought you'd be Queen too,' she said. Ka'iulani impersonates Emilie, trying to look sad. I burst out laughing, and she laughs too. I love her laugh: brazen and loud, with no apologies made, no hand covering mouth. It hasn't been spoiled by English boarding schools, though her voice is now faintly British sounding and crisply embroidered.

She skims her hand along the water's surface in a circle. "She behaved as if Richard had nothing to do with it," she says with disbelief. The day's events sit between us for a moment, and then she disappears as she dives. I wait, the sound of the waterfall my only company. I've told Mehana I always feel watched at this spot. She claims the cliff side holds a cave that hides the bones and canoe of a long buried chief. I'm searching for the cave, wondering how they managed to hoist a canoe so high up the valley wall, when Ka'iulani surfaces, the fabric of her dress bubbling up with her. "It wasn't just Richard, though, was it? Our royal house failed its people," she says calmly. "One by one each king gave a bit away, until there was nothing left."

She looks so alone in the water, so bereft. "Come out, it's cold. You'll get sick."

She appeases me, coming out across the rocks, her mu'u mu'u sticking to her body. I glance quickly around to ensure that we are in fact alone. I lift the blanket around her shoulders, wishing we had a campfire to share, too.

Ka'iulani squeezes the water from her hair and smoothes it into a low bun, her eyes on me. "Eliza...your son. I was thinking, couldn't your father have Abram arrested? Questioned? Perhaps there'd be a lead to follow from that?"

"Oh, those days are long gone. My father has no friends in power. And Emilie works against us. She doesn't want the scandal of Samuel. I think she may have helped Abram hide him. Or worse." I rest my forehead on my knee, pressing it down. "But, Samuel doesn't feel dead to me. I went myself with Webster to look through Lāhainā. I forgot how bright the sun is there. I burned my skin walking up and down each little lane. After two years of looking, everyone tells me to find peace with it. Again."

"Find peace with what? *Murder*? Not knowing?" Her eyes flash, her voice shoots up. Then the fury she holds for what happened today bursts open. "That is what they all tell us. Be quiet, be good. Behave. Why shouldn't you rage? Why shouldn't you scream in mourning? Why must we hide our very selves for their comfort?"

This is her mother in her, the strength beneath her smooth exterior that so few get to see. Miriam Likelike was a dancer, a singer. About town one still hears songs she herself composed and sang on Sunday afternoons when Kalākaua and Lili'uokalani came for singing competitions with an autoharp on the porch or around the piano in the parlor. The entire family could draw out melodies from thin air.

But if Likelike perceived any slight to herself or her daughter, she released such rage the servants took themselves to the kitchen to avoid it.

"Don't *let* them tell you to sit still and do nothing, Eliza," Ka'iulani commands, and I love her for bringing my grief under the umbrella of her righteous anger. "Look at me," she says, lifting her wet mu'u mu'u from the flesh of her thighs. "In my grandmother's day no Hawaiian woman would wrap herself in this tent to swim. I've played by their rules. I'll throw the Americans their lū'au next month and show them how 'civilized' I am. I've learned French and German and made myself to their liking and look what it has brought me, and the rest of us. Nothing." She raises her head up, cups her hands round her mouth and cries out to the back of the valley: "NOTHING!"

Her words echo back to us, sounding exhausted and spent.

18

The sunset is vivid tonight. We drive with the top down to enjoy the pink sky. Webster's hand is on my knee as we pass the Waikīkī Villa, its two stories lit up corner-to-corner with white lights that flood the ocean below like an unnatural moon. It is a popular bathing villa now, drawing the growing crowds staying downtown at the Hawaiian Hotel for a day at the beach. The Ahsang bungalow comes next, dark and barely distinguishable from the grove of monkey pod trees around it.

I suppress a case of nerves as we come down the drive at ʻĀinahau. The row of date palms that were my father's height last I came are now tall enough to form a tunnel. This place was a second home to me once. I'd last visited with the King, to lift Kaiulani's spirits before her departure to England. He explained snow to me on the ride into Waikīkī, using his walking stick to draw the angles of imaginary flakes on the carriage floor.

"Ku'uipo, darling," he'd said gently when we'd found Ka'iulani alone among her family's portraits and wood calabash set high on pedestals. "Will you show Eliza and your Papa Mōʻī your garden? Your pony wants you to take her for a ride. Your peacocks are lonely for you. I hear them crying."

Ka'iulani had walked between us through the grounds her father had landscaped entirely for her happiness, through the deepening shadow of afternoon, the groves of coconut and spice trees. We fed an apple to her pony, Fairy, and sat with our legs dangling off the footbridge while turtles made their awkward chomps at their lunch on the edge of the fishpond. The King sang two songs, one sad and the other rousing, asking Ka'iulani which she preferred.

"I don't think I like music so much right now, Papa Mōʻī," she said.

"There will be time for music later," he said. "Pick me a flower for my buttonhole so I look handsome in my carriage ride home."

We picked tiger claw hibiscus. Ka'iulani placed the red ruffled flower into the buttonhole of her uncle's jacket. Three peacocks stood guard at the King's carriage, their tails fanned out, side-by-side, covering a span of fifteen feet with their iridescent feathers. Ka'iulani took my hand at the sight, her finger to her lips. They posed for their Princess, until another bird cried deeper off the path and the fans shuttered and folded, the birds running into the shadows.

"It's only one year in England. Promise?" she'd said as her uncle climbed back into the carriage. "Any longer and my peacocks will not know me."

"There must be at least three hundred people here tonight," Webster says.

We leave our carriage and survey the grand lūʻau set out before ʻĀinahau. Sunset is fading. Peacocks cry from the branches of the banyan tree, and in the purple dusk everything seems a mirage. A band on the lanai is playing a popular American tune under blue lanterns. The lawn blooms with white flowers planted by Cleghorn for just such a moonlit night. Kaʻiulani is seducing foreigners this evening. Guests from New York and Washington will roam the grounds slightly dazed, lured into forgetting the social armor they wear in their own cold cities. She will be their exotic dream; they can give her people back their vote in return.

I see her moving among them, wearing yellow satin and so many ropes of jasmine that I can smell them from where I stand. Jasmine is her preferred flower, the way her mother wore gardenias. She is so associated with it that lei vendors call the flower *pikake,* the Hawaiian word for peacock, in honor of her favorite pet. "I had peacock nightmares as a child," I tell Webster. "From one biting me here."

"Now that is an exotic phobia. I never dreamed I would marry a woman with such elegant nightmares."

I watch as Ka'iulani kisses wives on the cheek. Gentlemen who swore royalty was evil bend low over her hand, looking a little in love. She looks flushed, her eyes glistening.

She makes her way to us, kisses me, rubbing her hand on the hunter green silk of my sleeve. "Eliza, look at you. We are cutting such figures tonight. Hello, Eliza's doctor," she says to Webster mischievously.

"A title I bear proudly," Webster answers, with a quick bow.

"Eliza, may I?" she asks, as she reaches up to pull the whalebone combs from my hair, letting my curls free the way she wears her own hair tonight. "There. That is the Eliza I remember. Do you approve, Dr. Webster?"

"Wholeheartedly."

She gives them to Webster to put in his jacket pocket. "I've seated you both next to a commissioner. If you bring up the vote for Hawaiian men after they've had their drinks, I would be thankful."

"Why stop at the men?" Webster asks. "We could ask for the ladies too, I should think."

"One day," I say. What a thing that would be for Clarice. And Mehana. And me.

"Perhaps after a few more lū'aus. Or a few more bottles of gin," she says with a little punch in the air. We laugh. "Father and I have quite a place to lick our wounds in, haven't we?" She looks back at the house her father finished while she was away, when he realized she'd never have a palace to come home to. "Would you like the grand tour? My father is very proud of it."

Ka'iulani takes me up the stairs and puts me in her father's hands. Cleghorn leads me around what I recognize is a love letter from a Scottish father to his Hawaiian princess daughter. The drawing room's enormous windows look out onto the botanical paradise he's tended for her since her birth. Every light fixture and tile appears to have been discovered upon his travels and collected like rare plants. Cleghorn takes me through a suite upstairs, decorated with patterns of the kāhili and the Hawaiian crown, symbols of a lineage now deposed. We stand together, staring at the crowns in silence.

"Yes. It's a bit hard to bear, sometimes." He turns toward the door. "I suppose we should get back down to take care of this vote issue."

When we are all seated, the commissioners' wives press their lei to each others' faces, breathing in the soapy scent of pink carnation. Their men dip fingers into the poi and then scrunch up their noses. I tell my assigned commissioner, Mr. Paul, to try the raw salted fish, the slabs of kalua pig, but he eats only the roast chicken and speaks almost exclusively to his wife. The moment I speak of the Hawaiian vote he stands and proposes a toast to Ka'iulani, a move widely applauded by the other tables.

Ka'iulani stays seated. Her kāhili bearers, two fair and small-boned native women, wave their white feather staffs continuously above her head, a clear reminder that the Kingdom may be gone but the Princess remains.

Flush with the success of his toast, Mr. Paul starts to wander away. I catch him by the crook of his elbow. "Sir?" I say. "May I say, how important your work is? My family came here from New England. The Hawaiians, their hopes are entirely with America now. They believe it a good country that will right the wrong of their stolen vote."

"Spirited thing, aren't you?" the commissioner says, putting his cigar in his mouth and leaving me without another word.

I cringe as I sit back down. I'm only half listening to Webster speaking to the woman at his right about a place they've both been to in California when I see a woman glide between the tables. She walks right in front of me wearing a fitted red silk dress with a high collar, and I know she is Ben's wife. Jade and gold dot her neck and wrists. Her hair is a curtain of black, her face sharp, perfect angles. American men stop their laughter and back-slapping to stare at her with longing. I look for Ben, but Mei Ling appears to be alone.

"Your home, it is enchanting," Mei Ling says to Kaiulani's father, speaking clearly enough for all to overhear.

Cleghorn stands, his tall frame making her look even more delicate.

"I recognize some of the touches as being the finest work of Shanghai and am honored it met your standard," she tells him. Others would have lingered too long; Mei Ling excuses herself immediately, kicking the pleat of her dress outward as she makes her way from the drawing room, all eyes following her rustling silk.

"I'd say it was cigar time," says one of the men under his breath. A few of the others smirk, and three men rise to follow her out onto the lanai.

The Princess is clapping lightly as one of the commissioners sings some sort of railroad tune to her. I lean in low to ask, "Is Ben here?"

"No, nor Abram. Ben could not attend. And they didn't ask for an invitation for Abram, thank God," she says, keeping her eyes moving about the room to smile at those who walk by. "I should have warned you she was here. It was necessary. The Chinese merchants are being so helpful with the voting issue. But—"

"No, it's fine. That's all in the past now."

"Do you think it's going well, Eliza?"

"Wonderfully," I say, "though I was rather unsuccessful with Mr. Paul."

"Oh, he's the worst of the whole lot. At least Auntie looks happy," she says, glancing at the deposed Queen, seated safely between her adopted nephew, Prince Koa, and a former lady-in-waiting. I bow to her from across the room, and she blows me a kiss. She's gotten two years of peace under her trees now, just as she'd dreamed of in captivity. She composed beautiful music in jail, music the band is playing tonight, though I'm sure the Americans have no idea of its significance. And if Irvin and his lot know the songs are being played as a protest, they are not rising to the bait: now that they don't have to answer to her, the men who vilified the Queen like to sentimentalize her in doting pieces in the newspaper.

"It amazes me that everything depends on our being in the good graces of these people," Ka'iulani whispers. I follow her eyes and see the men she is watching. With their sunburns and meaty jowls, they could be American farmers if not for their fancy dress. "Things will go from bad to wretched if we can't get these men to give my people some sort of chance here, some say."

A group of men start singing the Star Spangled Banner. Richard Irvin and Emilie join in. Ka'iulani watches them. Is she remembering Richard at her birthday parties? Emilie presenting the tiger cub to the King? She smiles brightly at Irvin when he raises his glass to her, as if nothing could delight her more.

"They make a good match," Ka'iulani says.

As if she's heard us talking, Emilie gets up, tapping Mei Ling's shoulder. They cross the room to us and bow to Ka'iulani. Emilie acknowledges me with a small nod. Mei Ling remains fixed on Ka'iulani, as if I do not exist.

"What a night. Everything is beautiful. Like it used to be. I miss it," Emilie says.

"Richard isn't quite sure the Hawaiians would know what to do with the vote yet," she says sweetly. "But no one can argue the evening hasn't been a success."

"Emilie, introduce Eliza to your sister-in-law," Ka'iulani says flatly.

"Eliza Webster, the doctor's wife," Emilie says, brushing the fabric on her hugely rounded stomach.

"Eliza. That is a new name for me," Mei Ling says in coolly accented English. "Your home is beautiful, your Majesty. I was telling your father that parts of it remind me of my family's home, though ours of course cannot compare with this. The grounds are inspiring."

I had expected her to seem more foreign and out of place here. Yet her ways are in perfect sync with island society.

"Ben so wanted to be here tonight. But he did choose my dress. We are staying very close by, in the family's beach house."

I decide to let myself truly suffer. For a second I lay on rumpled sand with Ben, I smell the leather on him and think of phosphorous water. Was he truly too busy to come tonight, or can he not face me and Emilie at once?

"I'm going to find Webster," I say. "We should be getting back to our daughter."

"Oh, I'll come with you. I should dance with some of the guests," Ka'iulani answers. Emilie and Mei Ling drift off into the party as we walk toward the lanai.

"Emilie was always a bit like that, wasn't she?" Ka'iulani says.

"Richard isn't quite sure what the Hawaiians would do with the vote yet," I say in my prissiest voice. Ka'iulani lets out her great whoop of a laugh, taking a few nearby commissioners by surprise. "Chiefess Ahina must stomp in her grave to see her bloodline carried around in that one." I say quietly while their eyes stay on us.

"Just wait. Richard doesn't get to tell these commissioners what to do. That's the beauty. Now that we are American, her husband's little group no longer runs the whole show. And if we get our way with the vote they will be voted out." Her flushed, excited air turns sad. "It isn't the way we wanted it. But it's certainly better than it's been."

I thread my arm through hers and clasp her hand. "I think you've summarized both of our lives," I say.

"Eliza," Ka'iulani says. "Do you think trying is the part that hurts the most?"

"Are you asking whether you should still do nights like this, when seeing these people opens the wound? I would say yes, because the vote is something you can't forget. If I could find a way, I would look for Samuel every day of my life rather than accept that he is gone. Is that what you meant?"

"Yes," she says, looking at me as if there's more to tell me. "You've answered my question."

She nods her head at someone, and I see it's Webster holding up a hand to me. He has called our carriage. I raise my hand back.

"It's funny how our lives keep turning down the same paths. Our mothers and then all this," Ka'iulani says, lifting her shoulders and breathing deeply. "Go to your lovely husband. I must dance."

I lean against Webster's chest in the carriage ride home and cling to him as we sleep that night. I dream of Mei Ling emerging from the Nu'uanu stream, black hair dripping wet nearly to her knees, not caring that I see her unclothed. She walks into the ginger, and in my dream I know Samuel is in there. I try to follow but the green stalks turn into a red lacquered door through which I cannot pass.

19

The lanterns are still strung between the trees when I return to ʻĀinahau the next afternoon. The peacocks abandon their spot underneath the banyan's dusky circle to run squawking alongside my carriage, their train of feathers rippling like sheets caught in the wind. One pesky fellow follows me all the way to the house, pecking at my ankles as I walk to the stairs.

"Oh, they have such horrible manners sometimes, haven't they, Eliza?" Kaʻiulani calls out from the lanai. She throws a biscuit in the air to bribe the peacock; the bird stops harassing me. I kiss her on both cheeks. A bowl of poi and shredded pork sits nearly untouched on the koa table. She usually devours such a meal. Servants are bringing packed luggage out of the house.

"Are you off somewhere?" I ask.

"Remember, the Parker wedding on the Big Island?"

"Oh, that's right," I say, watching her more closely. "Is everything all right? You seem at odds and ends."

"Oh, it's just this place, as beautiful as it is. It grows dark because it's so dense with plantings. One could get lost in it. I walk through it and come across a corner I'm not sure I've ever been to before, and it reminds me of how uncertain the world is. And how little keeps me here now, except for Father, really." Kaʻiulani summons the smile she gave the whole night before. It slips quickly away.

"Would you want to go away?" I ask carefully.

"No, I don't see myself leaving." Ka'iulani begins to cry.

"Are you all right?" I ask, startled.

"I'm sorry. I'm sorry," she says, tapping her brow as if she has a headache. "I am just out of sorts at the moment. I've felt terribly odd this week. It will get better. I'll try to take some fresh air in Waimea." She rests her head in one of her hands so that I can't see her face, and then she looks up with such a broken smile that I can't resist putting my hand to her cheek.

"I cannot shake this grief," Ka'iulani says, breathing in deeply. "I suppose the wise thing would be to travel, to find a foreign noble who would make life grand somewhere I can forget all of this. But that seems like a coward's path to me."

"You could be married by the summer to any man you choose. By this time next year, you'd be preparing for a child's birth."

"It is not that I fear it cannot be done." She rubs her collarbone as if in pain, taking a deep breath before continuing. "It is that I know it will not be. The Hawaiian in me, I fear it knows that the end will come without any new beginnings for me or mine. This short life has passed in preparation for a throne which disappeared, and that is all I will have."

"That's just your nerves," I say, but I think of Mehana's stories of Hawaiians knowing the hour of their own death, walking up into the mountains to find the cave they'd always known would be theirs to die in.

"I sense it as my mother sensed it," she whispers. "Her prediction for me was not given out of malice. She was preparing me. It was the last thing she could do for me."

"She was ill," I say forcefully. "She was unable to think clearly in those final hours, and besides you can create whatever destiny--"

"Ah, that is the American in you, Eliza," she interrupts, "Keep it. It is not in us all. Perhaps my family and my people, we were meant to pass into another life entirely and we are all leaving together now, night marchers, all of us. Maybe it was always written somewhere, and there is nothing my family could have done to change it. I must let go of this remorse, this weight of guilt for what could have been. I think sometimes I was simply born under an unlucky star."

"You are young and beautiful."

"But is that all?" The Princess shakes her head impatiently. "I think I am simply the end of a line, not meant to rule, to mother, to continue. Sometimes, I am sure. Do I sound crazed?"

"No. I am sometimes in that same prison of sadness. My husband is so good to me. My daughter loves me. I pretend by day that all is as it should be, but there has always been that lingering doom you describe. There is always Samuel."

"Eliza, I did something." She looks at me, then pulls out an envelope. "I wrote a letter to someone without asking you. I was afraid to raise your hopes. But this came yesterday." She puts the envelope in my hand. "It's why I asked you to come back today."

I open it half unwillingly. The top sheet is a letter written in Hawaiian with a Maui address at the top. As I'm trying to make sense of it, I see the corner of a photograph—a face in black and white, and I know. I simply know. And I try to stop the tears, but they come. "How?"

"I wrote the Reverend Kauko, at the church in Lāhainā. I asked for him to look for your boy as if he were mine. With all the love he has for me. He says the warden of the Lāhainā prison has taken in many children. The reverend sees them when he ministers to prisoners. He had this photo of some of them taken six months ago."

The prison in Lāhainā. Hale Paʻahao, the stuck-in-irons house. I'd leaned against its thick coral block walls, seeking the shade of its towering mango trees. I can picture the gatehouse between its walls, the house that served as the warden's home, with laundry hanging from its window, the smell of fried onions from the kitchen built over the open prison gate. Webster and I had peered through it while on our search for Samuel. The imprisoned sat in circles on the grass, men separated from women. "They built it to have a place for drunk sailors from the whaling ships," I'd told Webster, running my hand along the bumps of the coral wall. "My grandfather would come here to find his men smoking cheroot and playing cards on the grass. They'd want to stay for the next meal before he paid their bounty." Webster had pressed a wet cloth to my burned neck. I'd told that story while Samuel may have sat above us in that kitchen.

"We never thought to look there—"

"What do you want done? Tell me, and he will do it. He awaits my instructions."

"I think, I think I need to tell Ben. And Webster. I will not breathe a word of your involvement." I throw my arms around my friend and squeeze. "I promise. I do not want you to suffer for me."

Ka'iulani guffaws, bringing her hands up to cup my face. "Oh, Eliza, what more could they possibly do to me?" She rolls her eyes, laughing and crying, suffering and joy spreading across her face.

"You'll be too tired to greet him properly," Webster says from the other side of the bed. It is three in the morning. In a few hours, Ben brings our son home. The letter arrived today.

> *I saw the boy under one of the mango trees at the jail. Even with the light behind him, just the way he held his head was familiar. You were right. He is a younger me, if a little white washed. I have not yet heard him speak or gained any true sense of his thoughts or person, though that is likely due to the circumstances. The home is purely Hawaiian speaking. He is very close to his siblings, or those he'd thought were his siblings. He seems rather sad now.*
>
> *The warden was told Samuel's mother had been crazy and abandoned him, the father unknown, and no one wanted the child. He's never heard from the man, whom I believe to be Lopaki, again. I fished for any ties he had to A.M. I*

believe he has no knowledge of the man's involvement and so I left it alone.

The warden and his wife are both Hawaiian-Chinese. The family has five other children, some hānai'd, some their own. They thought someone might come someday, that the child somehow did not match the story. He asked everything about the circumstances of the child's birth. I was truthful in all my answers without using AM's name, and he is satisfied. Thank God for the Princess. They would never hand him over if it were not for her and the minister's word.

We leave by ship on the SS Princess Likelike *from Lāhainā. You'll soon hold your boy. I've told no one, as silence appears to have allowed us to put this finally to an end.*

"Do you think Ben's already told Samuel he's taking him for his first night? I should have insisted the first night be here."

Webster sighs. "Aren't mortals funny? As soon as I tell a patient they will in fact live, they remember the mundane. Why their dear wife let the good skillet burn. When in God's name will their children ever keep the noise down and be useful."

"Where my son spends his first night is not mundane—"

"It is not," he says, kissing my hair. "And all this will come to pass as it will be." He rolls me onto his chest. "I promise Samuel's more nervous than you are."

I surprise myself that night, wanting my husband, able to put Samuel from my mind while in Webster's arms. After, in the hours before dawn, I watch Webster sleep and imagine Samuel in the berth of the ship. How has Ben explained everything to him? I try to picture him sleeping soundly, kicking off his blanket as children so often do. I tell myself that a seven-year-old still sleeps like a puppy, even when he's scared.

In a few short hours, Webster is helping to rouse and dress Clarice. "Where are we going?" she asks drowsily.

"Remember, you have a friend coming today?" I say.

Clarice falls asleep the moment the carriage begins to move toward the wharf. I am so nervous I think I will be sick, and I have to ask Webster to stop twice.

"That must be it," says Webster as we spot a ship tacking across the harbor. Ben's carriage is already waiting. Webster and I let Clarice sleep; we get out of the carriage and walk to the water's edge. Peering through the binoculars he confirms, "It's the *Princess Likelike.*"

I breathe deeply, looking toward Ben's carriage to see Mei Ling staring at me, wrapped in a black blanket. She turns her head away. "He said he hadn't told anyone," I mumble.

"Perhaps he meant no one outside of his marriage."

"Fair enough."

"Don't be grumpy on such a momentous day." Webster takes my hand.

"I don't feel grumpy. I feel scared to death," I say, wrapping my shawl tighter and glancing back at our carriage. Clarice's stocking-feet poke out on the side of the seat.

"Perhaps you could go make her feel welcome? Mei Ling, I mean."

But I stay where I am. This is my morning, and the ship's crew is already casting down the lines. I scan the deck where passengers wait for their turn to disembark. A Hawaiian man has his ukulele held up almost to his chin, singing to himself to pass the time. A child runs to the front, dangerously close to the edge of the boat. I catch my breath but realize the child is too young to be my boy.

Ben appears at the ship railing, peering down with his arms crossed. When he sees me, he turns and reaches his arm out, and a child comes forward.

And there he is, his sweet, worried face scanning the wharf for anything he might recognize. His face is just the same, his hair wildly unkempt. I see he's dressed in a thin shirt. At the sight of the shore he pulls the sleeves down over his hands.

"Oh, Ben should have gotten him traveling clothes. He must have been so cold all night."

"There probably wasn't time," says Webster, speaking as if in a trance.

The little boy walking down the plank has the reddish gold of baby Samuel in his skin and hair, but not the smile. He looks around forlornly.

"Samuel?" I call, and he looks startled.

I walk toward him; he stops in his tracks, wide-eyed. They are still that green-grey they'd promised to be when he was little. "Samuel." I kneel on the ground and put a hand out. He starts to walk toward me and I laugh a little. "I'm your mother," I say, arms outstretched.

He bolts, running past me and Webster, who tries to stop him. He is charging up the street when Mei Ling jumps from her carriage and plucks him up into her arms. He bursts into tears and by the time I reach them his head is on Mei Ling's shoulder, and she is patting him on the back and making soothing sounds.

"Please give him to me," I say, putting my arms out.

She makes no move to hand him over. I begin to pry him from her, and he starts to cry again. Webster says, "Give him a second to calm down."

Ben now stands beside me, studying our son in his wife's arms. Samuel's body is limp. He rubs his eyes and lays his head back down on her shoulder.

"Don't be hurt, Eliza. I don't think he's seen many haoles," says Ben.

How that word cuts me as it never has before. Haole. *Stranger.*

"It appears both the children need more sleep," Ben says, nodding toward Clarice still sprawled out in the carriage. "Who shall take him home?" he asks.

"I must," I say.

Mei Ling mutters something in Cantonese under her breath; Ben shakes his head at her. "With your permission, I will call on him this afternoon," he says, moving to lift Samuel from Mei Ling's arms. She lets go of him unwillingly.

Webster steps forward quickly, reaching for the boy, whose eyes are wide open but unfocused. Webster puts him on the seat opposite Clarice.

Mei Ling turns and Ben tips his hat, walks away, and then returns. "He hasn't spoken a word to me yet. He seems happy in…repetitive tasks. If he's upset, give him something to throw. We tossed coins from the boat to get him away from Lāhainā."

The two of them drive off. I sit next to Clarice, watching Samuel cowering in the corner of the carriage. He falls asleep almost immediately once we start moving. In the body of this seven-year-old boy I search for the lines of my baby. I try to imagine him at three, four, five years old. His first sentence, which foods he loves. We reach home and Webster and I each carry a child inside. Webster takes Samuel to the room we made up for him, converting what had been a corner storage room. All week, I cleared it out, hopeful, Webster dragged the settee in to give him a place to sleep.

"This is not going to be easy," Webster whispers as we stand together watching Samuel sprawled out on his makeshift bed. He makes a clicking sound with his tongue, soothing himself. I bite my lip, remembering him as a baby making his rolling R sound when he was happy or hurt, even then knowing how to comfort himself, somehow knowing he would need to.

"I'm a stranger to him," I say, letting Webster reach around me to close the door softly and lead me to our bedroom. We lay down to rest up for what will come next.

When Samuel wakes, he lets out a cry.

"I'm here, I'm here," I say.

He sits up, looking terrified. I put my arms around him, preparing myself to be thrown off, but he stays still. My hand rests in his hair, damp with sweat.

Samuel has yet to speak. It has been 8 days.

I try in Hawaiian or English. Ben tries Cantonese. Webster brought home a new bicycle to tempt him outside, but he stays almost exclusively in his room, often under his bed. Or he sits in his wardrobe and bangs his head softly against the wall until we stop him. All those years of dreaming and dreading the vision of him lying on my bed, crying as the flames come closer, and here he is, safe and sound, and mute.

"Is he slow?" Ben asked. He sat in Samuel's room for a good hour, speaking of his daughters, his father, the wonders of China. He showed Samuel where the family came from, the property they held from Maui to Macao. "Is this what he was like as an infant?" We'd stood at the bottom of the stairs, Ben with his hat in his hand.

"No. He was splendid," I say, looking upwards to the closed door of Samuel's room. "Hina said he was dropped very badly. I don't know if—"

"She said what?" he grabbed my hand as I lifted it to smooth my hair. He held it up, as if we were dancing together.

"She and Lopaki dropped him hard when they stole him."

"Whore. I shouldn't have given her a thing," Ben says.

"You gave her more?"

He takes a deep breath. "I promised her the full amount if we ever got him back. But it's as if he isn't back at all."

"I know," I say.

I wrote my father and he's rung twice, pleading that I bring Samuel to him, but I want Father to see Samuel as sound. I wrote to Mehana too, a private letter, telling her of Kaiulani's involvement, promising to bring Samuel when he's recovered from the shock, saying more new people might not be the best solution, admitting that all is not as simple or purely joyful as I'd hoped it would be. To Mehana I admitted my fear of my son never healing, because I uprooted him from the family he thought was his.

⸙

Clarice takes ballet class on Fort Street, in a dance studio with cut velvet wallpaper and a crystal chandelier. I watch my daughter pirouette to Russian piano music while vendors holler in Japanese on the street below. When the lesson ends, I promise her an ice cream, and brace myself for the heat and noise of the street, for the return home to Samuel, silent in his room despite all of our efforts. We've only just stepped onto the sidewalk when I am grabbed by the arm. I look up, thinking it's Ben, but it is Abram.

"Let go of me," I hiss in the quietest of voices. Other mothers come out, and I stand very still, hoping they will not notice us. The last of the class moves down the street, some of them stopping for the ice cream Clarice is expecting. "What do you want?" I ask, wincing as my daughter squeezes my hand hard. She feels my fear.

"You tell your chink to stop messing with my son," Abram says.

"You're mad," I say, walking away. He yanks me back.

"Ben Ahsang's given Hina money for a goddamn lawyer. You tell him he shuts her down, or that boy you think is yours? He'll have the shortest spell on record in Honolulu. I'll make sure of that."

Clarice starts to cry. I pick her up. "Someday soon you'll get everything you deserve," I tell him.

Abram laughs so loudly that people speaking to one another on the corner actually stop to look at him. A short thin man stops a few feet from us, looking at me to see if I need help.

"Really?" Abram says. He reaches out to stroke Clarice's hair. A cold look rolls over his face—my grandfather once described a shark preparing to eat, its eyes rolling back, mouth opening, and that is the image that comes to my mind now. "You could be my sister's child, the way you look, little girl. How old are you?" he asks Clarice, catching her chin even as I brush his hand away.

"You know who her father is. Come near us again, and I'll have him set you straight."

"I hear you have your Chinaman do your dirty work, not your husband. Well, you take care, pretty girl," he says, patting Clarice's cheek. "Clarice isn't it? What's your birthday, sweetie?"

"Don't talk to this man, Clarice."

"Doesn't matter. I can look it up."

"Is there a problem here?" asks the small man. He appears to be a newcomer in town. His clothes look too warm, his skin too pale. He doesn't relish the trouble he is bringing upon himself and backs away as soon as Abram says, "No problem here. Thank you."

Abram shouts for a carriage, and I stand still a second more and then bolt the other way, keeping Clarice in my arms for two full blocks, until I have the presence of mind to turn back around toward Mauna Kea Street.

Ben watches Clarice, still in her tutu, bounce coins onto the pavement stones. They are the old ones bearing the face of Kalākaua, our kind King now left abandoned on street corners. The monarch looks up at us as Clarice's aim improves and the coins come closer to our feet.

"Sweetheart, try to bounce them over there," I tell her, pointing to the far side of the courtyard.

Ben unbuttons the cuffs of his shirt, rolling his sleeves as he speaks. "If she's hired a lawyer with it, that's her doing."

"Why is she doing this now? She could have done it when I gave her that first thousand. Did you suggest it?"

"Never. She simply wasn't in the mind to do it then. She spent all your money on the pipe," Ben says. "The time she spent in my custody didn't help her with that habit. But she's reformed herself, as far as I can tell. She was cooking and cleaning for a boarding house when I found her to give her the balance."

"I wish I could finally rid myself of both of them in my life. In Samuel's life."

"Neither of them can do anything to us. Abram's having an affair with a very young girl, a former minister's daughter no less. That has won him no friends. And we have Samuel safely under our roof. Roofs."

"He's threatened to look up Clarice's birth records."

Ben's eyes widen with surprise at what I've revealed.

"Her conception was by force," I whisper. He looks away, and I wonder if he is thinking poorly of me. "She is our darling. We couldn't bear losing her to Abram."

Ben shakes his head. "God, Eliza. You lived in misery there," he says. He blows air through his lips, pushes his hands through his hair. "These last years, not being able to bring him back...I so regretted what I did to you. I'm sure your father thinks I'm guilty of the same crime."

The man who ruined you. That's what Father calls him. "Ben. I wanted you so badly then. I was in love with you."

The bells at Kaumakapili Church ring outside the courtyard walls. Clarice is happily running up and down the far wall.

"The first months in China," Ben says, taking my hand, "I was destroyed. I worried about you. I was still in love with you. So angry with my father. I brought that on Mei Ling. I wasn't cruel to her, but I was cold. Then she became pregnant with Lian, and my feelings grew into something else. She's a wonderful, truly wonderful mother. And as I've become more like my father, she understands me in a way I think would have been difficult for you." He stops, looking to see if he is hurting me. "Eliza, you were my first love. I can feel it still when we're together. I think you can too."

"Yes." There it is, the truth. I love Webster, but there is always this, no matter how many times I've assured myself it is gone.

"If we had married I believe we would have had a happy home. But I was incapable of fighting for you then. Our worlds were close, but not close enough. It was based on a dream that ended. It's good that my home is with Mei Ling now. And yours is with Dr. Webster."

Clarice runs back to us squeezing a gecko lizard clasped in one outreached hand. "I could squeeze its stomach out," she says.

Ben lets go of my hand and laughs. "Clarice, let the lizard go," I say, gathering my hat and gloves from the bench in case I need to take her home. She squeals and drops the lizard, which seems dead for a moment but then runs to hide in a gutter.

"This is not to be repeated, but Abram's been relieved of his powers by Richard," Ben says.

"When?" I ask.

"Days ago after that affair came to light. My sister is not one to welcome any threats to her husband's reputation. She had Richard cut ties."

"Does she know Samuel's here?"

"No. Sadly, I cannot let my sister have much to do with my children after all that has passed."

"You do believe that she helped have Samuel hidden?" I ask. "You believe that now, don't you?"

"After finding him in a government prison? I suspect she may have," he says. "If we'd found him three years ago, imagine how well our boy might be today."

Our boy. He is home with Webster now, probably being coaxed out of the wardrobe in his room. "I should go," I say.

"Take Clarice home and keep her safe there. Abram still has some of the police in his pocket," says Ben. "I'll see what I can do that will keep him away for good."

That evening is surprisingly calm. Samuel comes downstairs to play in the garden at Clarice's invitation. She has accepted all my vague explanations as to his identity without argument. She has been kind.

But the next afternoon, the police wagon comes to our home with an officer asking to see my daughter's birth certificate. "Abram is with him," Webster says to me as he walks to his office to retrieve the document.

"I've checked the birthdate. October 7, 1893," Abram shouts through the door.

"Momma. How does he know my birthday?" Clarice asks, peering out of her room. Samuel is with her.

"The child was conceived on Moloka'i. When her mother was my wife. She's been stolen from me."

Webster hands the officer the certificate of birth bearing his own signature.

"Her name should read Clarice Malveaux on that document. That's her real name!" Abram's voice explodes up our stairs. Samuel starts to knock his head against the wall.

"Samuel, stop it. Please, stop. You'll hurt yourself."

"Mrs. Webster," the officer calls out. "Could you come down here please, ma'am?"

He sounds like a cowboy from the American West; I suspect he's one of the California recruits the PGs brought in three years ago during the rebellion. I tell the children to stay in their room and go down to face him.

"I'm afraid you're going to have to come down to the station with the birth certificate and the girl," the officer says to me, bypassing Webster entirely, as if he already has no claim.

Webster, Clarice, Samuel and I sit in a whitewashed holding room at the police station, waiting. Her birth certificate has been taken away to be discussed. “He can take me? That mean man?” she asks. “He really can?”

“No. He cannot take you,” I say adamantly.

Webster looks at me almost angrily. He prides himself on never lying to Clarice. He’s telling me, yes, Abram might take her.

The door opens, and a higher ranking officer enters. I’ve seen him before: he is one of the officers who stood behind the Queen’s chair at her trial. He is part-Hawaiian. “The children can wait outside while we talk,” he says, indicating another officer at the door.

“Where is he taking her?” Webster demands, standing. Clarice clings to her father’s leg.

“Just out in the hall. Not to worry. Officer Hadley gonna make a quarter disappear a couple times for you two and then you get your parents back, okay?” the officer says to Clarice. She nods and takes Samuel’s hand to follow the man out. Samuel seems utterly comfortable. Webster stares at the door.

“Dr. Webster,” the policeman says. “You cared for my uncle in Kalaupapa. Makua was the name.”

“Clifford?”

“Yes,” the officer says. “My mother was his *kōkua*. She wrote about you.”

“Your uncle taught many to fish at the settlement,” Webster says, though I can tell from his voice he’s having a hard time speaking. He’s talking like this because he senses it will be good for our case.

“He taught Ikaika,” he says to me.

The officer nods. He puts Clarice’s birth certificate in front of us. Then he pulls out another document. It’s my divorce certificate. I am certain it is Abram’s copy.

“Any judge I know is gonna look at this date,” he points to May 31, 1893, the divorce, “then look at the other,” he taps on her birthdate, October 7, 1893, “and he’s gonna say that girl out there belongs to him." He gestures toward the door. "So I'm gonna send your girl home with you right now. But I'm telling you, you better get on a boat soon, because it's by accident I'm here today, and the next time, could be somebody else who's captain on duty. Somebody without an uncle at Kalaupapa."

"Thank you. Thank you so much," Webster stammers.

When we leave the station, Abram is glowering outside. He stops shouting at the officer who brought us in to smile at Clarice. "I'll see you soon, baby girl," he says, pretending not to see Samuel at all.

It has just fallen dark when Ben knocks on the door of our Mānoa home. Webster is upstairs reading to Clarice. "Abram had us taken in today," I say as I let him in.

"I know," Ben's eyes scan the room. He takes off his hat and sets it on the entry table. "Makua's my cop," he says. Reading the surprise on my face he adds, "It's loyalty to my father. We always fill his family's bag at the store, but he's just as likely to bring us fish. I'm there if he needs me. The same is true in reverse. We're lucky. He heard what Abram's cop was doing, and he knew about you from me..." Ben's voice fades as he says this.

Webster is standing above us on the stairs, hesitating.

"Come down," I say to him, pointing Ben toward the kitchen table. In the strangeness of having him here, I forget to offer anything, and the three of us sit awkwardly together.

"You have a pleasant home," Ben says.

Webster studies Ben's hands. They have clearly never known labor or the stench of camphor soap. Ben wears a signet ring with his monogram on his left pinkie. It's a ring I have not seen before. It must be from Mei Ling.

"The day Abram threatened your daughter," Ben gives a deferential nod to Webster as he says this, "I spoke with a man who wants him—in fact, is waiting for him. A man whose gambling hall he frequents too often and not respectfully. He likes to play cards."

I remember Abram at the campfire, egging his hands to throw in money as he threw the dice and always came up lucky. The cowboys would want out. They'd walk away as Abram bent to collect, but he'd call them out by name, goad them back to the circle and tell them to try again. "No more, boss," they'd say, turning out imaginary pockets to show him they were dry.

"Don't worry. I know you're good for it," Abram would say with his wide smile, his good teeth, and they'd have to give up two weeks' wages to his next roll.

"Gambling debts," says Webster dramatically, his unfamiliarity with Honolulu's underworld clear in his voice.

"Not debts. The opposite. Abram is too lucky. The polite thing to do once you've cleaned out a house is to stay away, not be greedy. But Abram comes back, and wins again, and again. He threatens to call the police and have this man deported back to China if he doesn't pay up. The owner has come to me for help. It would be good to harness his anger."

"Makua warned us we should leave. That Abram will succeed in taking Clarice if it goes to court," Webster says.

"Abram's corridors of power are collapsing," Ben answers, "but not quickly enough for this matter to be beyond his ability to influence. He knows that the judges now in place are all fervently against those who participated in the rebellion."

Webster looks at me grimly, adding the bitter pill of my father's prison time into the equation of fighting for Clarice.

"Did Makua also tell you there are a few fathers who would like revenge on Abram for his...activities?" Ben adds. I can tell he knows Makua never told us this. He wants to broach everything as a question to Webster to avoid seeming superior. He's so like his father.

"No. What exactly are we working up to here?" Webster asks, giving me a sidelong glance. I realize I've been smiling at Ben and stop. I look down at the table.

"Abram represents a problem for Clarice and potentially Samuel. So if Abram were to be put on a ship by men not afraid of the law, if he were forced from these islands in the middle of the night, many problems would be solved. But if we are ever asked after the fact, there is no reason to share the story of Samuel or Clarice, since there are so many reasons for Abram to have disappeared. Don't you think?"

With one uncertain look at Webster, I jump in, "Yes. I would have to say, while I hope there is no violence, I feel it is not unjust for Abram to leave Hawai'i."

Webster nods as well. "This round with Abram started with Hina trying to get custody of Lee," he says. "So what will happen with that?"

Ben nods. "After Abram vanishes, she'll probably get Lee."

"How could a woman with her history have Lee?" asks Webster. I think back to the documents we'd paid Abram to sign, resolving me of the adoption, of Lee's body asleep in my bed. *Please have a good life.*

"She is his mother," Ben states.

"That poor boy," says Webster.

"Anything is better than Abram," Ben says.

The three of us sit in silence.

"How is your wife faring through all of this?" Webster asks. I straighten uncomfortably.

"She is honored to have a son."

"He is my son, Ben," I say, thinking of the year I had Samuel, bathed him, walked him through sleepless nights, lived for him. I look upstairs hoping he is sleeping peacefully.

Ben leans in. "Mei Ling saw the sadness in me these last years, when I believed there would not be a son. She offered to let me take a second wife. That would be too strange for my daughters, and I was raised here, where such things are frowned upon. So Samuel's return is a gift to us all. Mei Ling is happy. Samuel will protect our daughters one day. If he succeeds in… adjusting."

After a moment, I say, "There has been small progress in the last few days. He's been coming out of his room unbidden to play with Clarice. Webster got him on a bike."

Now it is Ben's turn to be jealous. "He is more open to you than me. You'll have to teach me how to reach him."

"Well, I will certainly never be the boy's father," says Webster, "but I cared for him his first year, and care very much for him now. I hope you both know that."

I take his hand. The moment feels intimate, and guilt-laden.

Ben looks at my husband with real kindness. "We all have a lot to teach him, a lot to make up for. He's lucky to have all four of us," he says, taking a cigarette from a silver case in his pocket and offering one to Webster, who shakes his head. "We should not be so somber. If the fates continue to cooperate, Abram will soon be one less problem for our children going forward. I owe you both that, at the very least."

Ben stands to go, his hat halfway to his head when Webster stands up and sticks his hand out to shake. Ben seems taken aback, but then puts his hat down on the table and squares up to my husband. They clasp hands quickly, eyes directly on one another.

"I'll see myself out," Ben says when it is done between them.

E,

All is merry here. Quite a few of the natives in Hamakua called on me, singing so well. We had some dancing and did not turn in until midnight last night. This morning we took a great ride over to Waipi'o to take a look around the valley. Unfortunately, it began to rain and we had to hurry because of the Pali being too slippery. I never rode up such a place in all my life. I was simply hanging on by my teeth. We had a splendid ride home, jumping logs and pig holes. My goodness the rain cut one's face like hail and it was blowing like cats and dogs. We got home wet to the skin, but thanks to a warm bath and warm drink with our dinner we were none the worse for it.

I've asked Father to send my headache powders and Bromo Quinine pills as well as a few holokūs. I've stayed longer than I had planned, but it is so good to be here where I can pretend nothing has changed.

In Honolulu, I sometimes feel they haven't left me much to live for, that I can't be much of a real Princess. I try not to grieve in front of my father who watches over me so devotedly and is always seeking to make up to me for all the love I have lost. For his sake, I try not to mind and to appear bright and happy. But I think my heart is broken and that is why my headaches, the nervousness and exhaustion, they are my constant companions there.

Seeing the Hawaiians here, so many poor but proud, I feel we are a great race subjected to such misery. The more I see of the American soldiers about town on Oʻahu, the more I am unable to tolerate them. It is enough to ruin one's faith in God. Before I left, some Americans came to ʻĀinahau and knocked rather violently at the door, and when they stated their cause they wished to know if it would be permissible for the Ex-Princess to have her picture taken with them. Oh, will they never leave us alone? They have now taken away everything from us and it seems there is left but little—and that little our very life itself. I wonder, to what purpose is my life?

I do hope the purpose in yours is clearer than ever. I am afraid to ask what you know I must be dying to hear of. Please write if there is something you can bring yourself to say.

K

20

I make my way down the drive to ʻĀinahau in a hired hack. I pass Kaiulani's peacocks, sitting under the banyan's circle of shade, unable to rustle up any interest in me. Cleghorn stands on the lanai. He puts his hands in his pockets and walks down to greet me.

"Eliza."

"Is everything all right?"

"Not entirely, no," Cleghorn says with a crestfallen face. "The doctor's up there now," he elaborates. "She went riding in the rain in Waimea and hasn't been well since. She was carried by litter down from the mountains to a ship, sick the entire way. I was actually going to see if perhaps your husband might come? I wouldn't mind if he took a look at my girl as well."

"Of course."

When the doctor comes down to report, Cleghorn sends me up to Kaiulani's room, which is filled with white flowers and yellow light like a child's nursery. She lies propped up in bed, her hair matted on the pillow. "I've gone and gotten myself into a state," she says wearily, patting the edge of her bed.

"Webster will come over and set you right," I say, sitting beside her and propping up the roses that have fallen lopsided in the vase beside her. I look at her half-mast eyes, unsure if this is the time to thank her for my son. "Is the light bothering you?" I ask.

She nods yes, closing her eyes.

I shut the louvers. It is a spectacular Hawaiian morning, the sort visitors think they will find every day here. The sound of surf reaches me at the window. How I wish I could put Ka'iulani on a litter and take her down there, to the sea. I turn back to the darkened room, and it looks as if she is asleep, a slight frown on her face. Her expression worries me.

"It hurts so much at the moment. The headache," she says.

I join her and take her palm, pressing into it as Webster does for me.

"Good or bad?" I ask.

"Good," she says, her voice husky. "Eliza?" She starts to cry. "I think I'm dying."

"Rubbish," I say, kicking off my shoes and sliding in next to her, pulling her head into my neck, our brown and blond curls mixing as they did so many times when we were little girls, hiding under sheets from the governess, swimming underwater. "You just got home. You're staying put," I whisper against her hair. I can hear a huge set of waves booming down onto the beach. "There are miracles everywhere. Your miracle has worked for me." I squeeze her hand, my voice trembling. "Samuel is home."

She gasps. "I feared nothing had…" She is struggling to speak. "You—"

"I was waiting for him to get a bit better," I swallow. "It's been a shock."

"Bring him."

"Tomorrow I'll come with Webster, then next—"

"Eliza, bring him."

I nod, and she presses her forehead against our clasped hands. "The pain is that bad?"

She nods. I stay very still, the way one must when a child needs to sleep, to slow everything down. The palms outside scrape her window like a rocking arm. The sun breaks through closed slats to cast thin lines of light on the wood floor. She sleeps.

Samuel and I prepare to make our way to ʻĀinahau. He is silent and compliant as I dress him, pulling up his brand new trousers, buttoning the beautiful linen shirt Ben bought him. He lets me comb and smooth his hair. But when I ask, "Does that feel good?" he backs away.

Webster returned from ʻĀinahau earlier that morning saying, "She is in good hands. There is no other treatment I can recommend."

"So you'd say she's doing well?"

"It's pneumonia, Eliza. And it's very advanced."

"The princess is sick, so we must be very gentle and quiet when we're there," I explain to Samuel, though the warning is comically unnecessary. I've taken to talking to him for twenty, thirty minutes at a time, as if my words can fill his head and overflow through his mouth.

When we arrive, a priest sits next to Cleghorn outside her room. At the sight Samuel brightens, putting his arms around the clergyman. "Hello, little man," the priest offers.

Kaʻiulani is mumbling when I bring Samuel to her. She seems not to know either of us are there. Samuel comes closer to her bed and puts his hand on her forehead. I am about to move his arm away when I realize she seems soothed. I move a glass resting on the table near his elbow further back. I am still not sure she sees him, but Samuel seems to recognize her. He has clearly seen her photo before. In this room so heavy with convalescence, he is happier, more whole than I have seen him yet.

"Bless me. Please, bless me," Kaʻiulani says. Samuel darts out of the room, bringing the priest back by the hand. The priest sits at the edge of her bed, his head bent close to hers.

"Victoria Kaʻiulani. The Lord bless and keep you. Our Father, who art in heaven, hallowed be thy name."

Samuel keeps his head bowed, and I understand who he takes after. It is not me. It is not Ben. It is Hannah. He is spiritual, this boy of mine, more than I have ever allowed into my home. More than I ever thought I would need to bring into my life.

Samuel stays at the foot of her bed while she sleeps. Cleghorn and I sit in the hall outside her door, under the alabaster crowns molded into the ceiling.

"She believes she was born under an unlucky star," Cleghorn tells me, passing me photographs from her memento box, which he's brought out to pass the hours spent watching his daughter around the clock. I hold a photograph of Ka'iulani as an infant, surrounded by her parents, as well as Lili'uokalani and Kalākaua. The King looks beyond proud, his hand reaching across his sister, Likelike, to hold Kaiulani's little fist. The rest of them look elated. The Princess herself, barely a year, looks mature beyond her age.

"No child was born more adored," I say.

Cleghorn says, "Quite so. Quite so," and pats my arm to thank me for saying it. He needs every bit of happy thought now, and we sit in a cloud of intimacy impossible to imagine without our shared worry.

"Her body will fight this," I say, dropping my voice. "My son's fate looked just as unlucky, and it has turned because of her. Did you know she found him?"

Cleghorn looks at me sheepishly. "I told her not to write that letter. Can you imagine? I have always preached caution, not confrontation. I worried getting involved would draw his ire out against her."

"I would probably have counseled my child the same."

"This is what I've feared most in my life. Losing her. When those men seized the Palace, I told her, bide your time in hiding. Yet she spoke to newspapers. She pleaded with the American president in person. Oh, she would have made a good Queen, I should think. This is what reached her in London." He gives me a telegram. "I hadn't known she'd kept it,"

I read it. "Queen Deposed', 'Monarchy Abrogated', 'Break News to Princess." I place it back in the koa box, unable to think of anything comforting to tell her father.

"I recognize this." I smile as I pull out Kaiulani's red autograph book, turning it to the back page, where I scrawled a message of eternal friendship under the shadow of her departing ship to England eleven years earlier. I know exactly what came on the page before my own inscription. The poem Robert Louis Stevenson wrote for her. Its ink has faded to a ghostly, beautiful blue.

> *Forth from her land to mine she goes,*
> *The Island maid, the Island rose,*
> *Light of heart and bright of face,*
> *The daughter of a double race.*
> *Her Islands here in Southern sun*
> *Shall mourn their Ka'iulani gone.*
> *And I, in her dear banyan's shade,*
> *Look vainly for my little maid.*
> *But our Scots Islands far away.*
> *Shall glitter with unwanted day,*
> *And cast for once their tempest by*
> *To smile in Kaiulani's eye.*

Tears start in my eyes as I read Stevenson's note below the poem.

> *Written to Ka'iulani in the April of her age and at Waikīkī within easy walk of Kaiulani's banyan. When she comes to my land and her father's, and the rain beats upon the window (as I fear it will), let her look at this page; it will be like a weed gathered and preserved at home: and she will remember her own Islands, and the shadow of the mighty tree, and she will hear the peacocks screaming in the dusk and the wind blowing in the palms and she will think of her father sitting there alone.*

Samuel appears and pulls me from my chair. Cleghorn and I enter Kaiulani's room and find her with her eyes open, staring at the shadow of palm trees moving on her wall. Her mouth is open as if she is finding it hard to breathe.

"Darling, I'm going to have them bring you up some broth. It will do you well," Cleghorn announces, first moving the hair off her face and pulling the blanket around her.

I sit on her bed and my boy sits on my lap, the first time he's done so of his own accord. Ka'iulani swallows hard and looks at him.

"Samuel," she says. She mumbles something long I cannot understand but I nod as if I do. She shakes her head and looks pleadingly at me. I press my ear to her lips. "All our races. In his little body," she tells me. I stay, my cheek to hers until I hear her breath settle into fevered dreams.

I cannot control myself as we leave 'Āinahau, crying in deep, pained breaths. Samuel is leaning back, watching the great palm fronds pass above, seemingly oblivious to my ugly tears. Each time the carriage passes out of shade into sun he closes his eyes, rhythmically opening them for the next band of green we move through. He wiggles his small hand into mine. He pulls my shoulder so I too can lean back and move in and out of shadows. He wants us to do this together.

I fair poorly that evening, unable to eat or speak. When Ben's carriage pulls in front of our home I am, for the first time in my life, unsure I want to see him. I go upstairs to lie down, leaving Webster to talk to him.

"I think you need to come down, darling," Webster tells me. "He has a lot to report. I've heard all I need to. I'm going to go read the children a book."

I join Ben unsteadily, gripping the kitchen table as I sit across from him.

"I realize my timing is awful," Ben says. "Webster tells me there is no good news."

I shake my head no.

"You married a good man."

"Yes," I say. "He said I should come down to hear your report."

"I came to tell him, and you, that you have nothing more to worry about with Clarice. Or Samuel."

I raise an eyebrow. "He's gone?"

Ben nods. "Do you want to know? Webster didn't."

"You were there?"

"I was," he says, crossing his arms across his chest like his father. He tightens his jaw while he collects his thoughts. There are dark circles under his eyes, as if he hasn't slept. This is how we grow old, and strong, I think to myself. Stories like the one he's about to tell me.

"It was very late last night. Well—very early this morning," Ben says. "I brought my cop, Makua, and the gambling hall owner had his own men. Abram was walking out of a place of ill repute, shall we say. We grabbed him, and he gave us a tongue lashing, called us every vile thing one can call a Chinese man. That earned him a few more kicks than I'd planned on him getting." Ben smiles. Not his crooked, young smile—this one is world weary and triumphant all at once. "We threw him into a carriage and took him down to the wharf. He's very strong. Makua pistol whipped him, but Abram kept fighting until the carriage opened and he saw all of Makua's men waiting. We brought him out, and he focused on me. 'You're Samuel's father,' he says, understanding, and I say, 'I am.' I gave him my handkerchief to wipe the blood from his mouth, because I couldn't make out what he was saying. 'Wasn't me who started this. It was Hina, all along,' he tells me. 'You know the culprit. You already got the boy. Let me be. I'll make it worth your while.'

'This already is worth my while. Just the way it is now,' I told him. 'You could have returned my son anytime in the last six years. And you didn't.'

'Eliza left my boy, Lee, like a piece of trash. When you're a father and you see your son treated that way, you can't think straight.'

'But you see, I can think,' I told him. 'I think you're going to get on that ship and never come back here. Your lands will be Lee's. I promise you that.'

'You don't get to promise me anything,' he tells me.

'Then I'll let a few other men board this ship with you. There's a long list that are interested in your voyage,' I told him. And that's when he gave up. He started bawling, saying Lee's name again and again. He finally got up and said, 'Just get me to California.'"

"So he left?" I say.

"Almost a day go," Ben answers, watching my face.

"He'll return crueler and richer. He will chase me all my life — from San Francisco or some gold mining town where he'll end up being sheriff."

"I don't think so. The ship went to Chile. If he makes it to Valparaiso he will have many young, dark girls to prey upon, and a good chance to remake his fortune. But it was a very tough crew of men taking him there. And strange things happen at sea."

The telephone rings after midnight. Webster gets up to answer it. He shakes me, but my mind is slow to wake, still dreaming that I'm calling 'Āinahau to tell Ka'iulani that the night-blooming cereus are opening, and to come, come quickly.

"Eliza, it's a call from 'Āinahau."

I sit up and look at Webster, swinging my feet onto the floor and padding downstairs in bed slippers to the telephone. Webster follows close behind. I pick up the receiver, registering how serious he looks.

"Mrs. Webster speaking."

A young man answers. "Mr. Cleghorn has asked that I inform you the Princess has taken a turn for the worse. You may come down to 'Āinahau." His voice is tediously professional.

"Of course," I answer, looking up at Webster.

The man gets off the line without another word.

"I'll stay with the children. Can you manage the carriage?" he asks.

I think through the route in the dark. "Yes," I say. "Can you harness it while I dress?"

It is the beginning of March, windy and moonless, with no light showing from any of the houses. The only noise comes from the tree tops, branches twisting and slamming against one another. Some knock against the homes they usually shade, thumping like a heartbeat. I pull the reins sharply as I approach a large tree limb across the road, but the mare stays steady and works a path around it. We make it down the rest of the valley. Once on the wide road to Waikīkī, it is a straight shot to ʻĀinahau.

We waited for him that afternoon at the bench beneath the banyan. He arrived again in that jacket of worn brown velveteen, looking frail, as if he'd had the flu for a year or more. He told us he'd spent his childhood in a sick bed, and that he was traveling through the Pacific to outrun the grim reaper. Kaʻiulani reached out to squeeze his hand. "Are you very lonely?" she'd asked him. "Don't be lonely."

"Oh, with books at my bedside, I'll never be lonely. Tell me a story, Eliza. It's your turn."

"I don't know one," I said, unsure of his attention. It belonged on the Princess.

"The night marchers. You're good at that one," Kaʻiulani said.

"They are the aliʻi - royalty - and they walk the ancient paths on moonless nights at the height of the tree tops. They do not touch the ground, but people hear their drums and see their torches and then you must prostrate yourself and shield your eyes," I said, bowing myself low on the ground and spreading my hands across my eyes just as Mehana had made me practice doing on the lawn behind our home facing the mountain.

"Otherwise they will strike you down. They will kill you," Ka'iulani said. "Unless you are their own. They are from all the generations past and my mother said even those from hundreds of years ago would recognize me as theirs and protect me from death. And I'll protect Eliza."

"Will you not tell these night marchers you know me too?" Stevenson said, comic desperation in his face. We laughed, but the Princess warned him again that he must hit the ground if he heard the marchers coming. "I don't know how many I can protect," she explained, looking at us both, unsure.

The house blazes with light, a group of servants crowding on the patio, some still in nightdress. I recognize the kāhili wavers from the commissioners' dinner, both women praying in unison in Hawaiian.

No one seems in charge. I make my own way up the stairs. Cleghorn is deep in conversation with a doctor in the corner. His daughters by a Hawaiian woman before his marriage to Likelike, Helen and Rosie, stand beside their father, holding hands. I move among them toward Ka'iulani, who struggles for breath.

I take her hands. They are hot and limp and years of images flood my memory: Ka'iulani grasping horse reins on the beach, holding a prayer book at St. Andrew's Cathedral, pressing her hand against mine underwater, pulling her wet mu 'u mu'u from her body, handing me the envelope that held Samuel's photograph, the letter that gave me my son back. I remember what it felt like to be twelve years old together, standing in the wet groves of Nu'uanu, when her mother insisted we get out of the carriage to pick wild ginger. We stood in the wet and laughed, pulling the thick plants down and snapping off huge heads of white silky blossoms that smelled of spicy liquid mist.

"Stay with us," I say. Her face is waxy and retreating. She begins to speak, but it is gibberish. Cleghorn kneels down and puts his cheek to his child's face. A sob begins in me. She takes in a great breath, a look of pain on her face opening up into peace.

Minutes pass, and she is gone.

"Goodbye, my darling," Cleghorn whispers in the quietest of voices. "May the next world treat you more kindly."

A terrible screeching comes from beyond the open window. The peacocks make horrid cries that sound like a baby in the worst sort of distress, and the wind carries the sound up into her room and through the treetops of 'Āinahau, out across Waikīkī.

In the days that follow, people will claim they knew the moment the Princess died because of that sound. Doubters will argue the birds cried in reaction to the unusual activity, the house lights on at such an odd hour, but I was there. They knew.

I sit numbly on the veranda in the dark, waiting to be told how to help and watching Hawaiian society arrive to give their condolences. 'Āinahau is lit solely by candles after her death. As the birds start their dawn calls in the still dark treetops, people have their carriages brought around. Couples step down from the house, husbands putting wraps around their wives' shoulders as if they're leaving an all-night ball after breakfast has been served. I doubt the remnants of this elegant old world will survive even a year. She was its belle, and 'Āinahau its dream. Cleghorn will spend the rest of his days here, I feel certain, in the shadow of that banyan, wind blowing through the palms, peacocks screaming in the dusk, thinking of her.

Dawn is coming. The children will be waking up. It is time to go home.

21

March 12, 1899

Two hundred and thirty men dressed in white trousers and hats, blue jerseys and yellow capes will pull Princess Ka'iulani on the two-hour journey up to Nuuanu's Royal Mausoleum. The afternoon is bright, and we ride with carriage tops down, on view to the thousands who watch along the route. I pull Samuel's collar straight and dust the sleeve of his shirt. He has brushed against what looks to be hibiscus pollen. I put an arm around him.

"Look, they're starting to pull!" says Clarice, standing up to see the army of men lean forward on their black and white ropes and begin their sad parade. Richard and Emilie's carriage is several before ours. He is met with silence and even scattered boos. Kaiulani's death has been met with rage; people blame the PGs for breaking her heart.

"Can someone truly die from a broken heart?" I ask Webster. My lips feel slightly numb. He has given me a sedative to get through today.

"It can add to what is already weakened in the body." He lowers his voice. "A healthy body survives loss, as you did on Moloka'i. You are the strongest woman I've ever met."

I look at him, thinking that after this is all finished I must do something for him, to acknowledge all he's done for me.

We pull onto the green lawn of the mausoleum, its gates hung thick with ropes of orange ilima and jasmine. The number of people here is staggering. The Queen stays in her carriage under a royal palm, private in her grief. As the pallbearers lift the white coffin to lay it in front of the crypt, Clarice asks Webster to take her up front where Ben and his daughters stand. I beg off and stay back with Samuel, unsure I can keep my composure, even with the medicine's help.

Emilie and Richard come through the gates last. Emilie holds their daughter, Betty. She stops to show the baby off. Women coo, and I realize I am standing in the wrong place. The true mourners are further in front. The Hawaiians lining the route had called out in wails of grief, but this part of the crowd thinks they're at a garden party.

I stare at them. The Doles, the Clarkes, the families who broke my friend's heart have come to her funeral to participate in the event of the season. They are chatting about babies and business. The U.S. naval base will open this year at Pearl Harbor. The fishponds there will be filled in for more sugar land. On and on their lives go. None of them understand the sky has fallen. My friend is dead.

Emilie stares back at me, looking at Samuel. I know she recognizes exactly who he is. Others start to stare, whispering, causing Samuel to tuck his face into my skirts. I feel a hand on my elbow. It is Cleghorn.

He smells like his daughter, and I think for a second that she stands behind him until I see the ropes of *pikake* on his arms and remember that the flower is all I have left of her presence now. His eyes are bleak with tears cried in private. The chatter around us ends entirely. Everyone is looking at me, at Samuel, at Cleghorn. He looks straight back at them, his white beard tilted, his full height drawn, reproaching them. *You did this*, his face says. *All of it*. President Dole looks mortified. Clarke looks down. Richard takes the baby from Emilie and pretends she needs fussing over. The crowd stays utterly silent.

"Let's go and say goodbye," Cleghorn says to me. Samuel is clutching at my skirt, and I clutch back. Cleghorn moves us forward through the crowd, up to the crypt door, his surviving daughters joining us on his other side, and we say the 23rd Psalm as Cleghorn rests a Bible on his daughter's casket. *Thou preparest a table before me in the presence of mine enemies: thou anointest my head with oil; my cup runneth over.* Kaiulani's half-sisters put nosegays of gardenias at the corners of her casket, and Cleghorn turns to me with the ropes of *pikake.* He hesitates, then gives them to Samuel and nods. Samuel understands perfectly, placing Kaiulani's last *pikake* over her casket, which is then lifted and taken inside the tomb. She is joining Papa Mōʻī, with his cigars and hula dancers, and her mother, fulfilling her prophecy. The doors close.

"Thank you for always being very careful with my daughter's heart," Cleghorn says to me so softly that afterward I am not sure I heard all he said. There might have been more, but he squeezes my hand, and then he is gone. The crowd moves thickly around me and Samuel. Clarice finds us and shouts, "I want to take Samuel to Grandfather's house."

I pick her up and press her to me. "Yes, let's go," I agree. I want to find Webster. I want to have Father meet Samuel and say whatever it is he is going to say. I want to sit in the kitchen with Mehana and tell her everyone now knows that Samuel is mine.

The front door is locked when we arrive. The four of us trudge around to the back. Webster takes Clarice down to the riverbank, letting me take Samuel through the kitchen door for a tour of the downstairs, still too nervous to take him straight to Father. I keep up a running monologue, pointing out items in Father's study. I tell him about Father being naughty at his age, singing under his breath in church.

"Your grandfather was a rascal at your age, you know, *kolohe,* and didn't care that it was naughty to sing during the prayers."

Samuel laughs. It catches me so off guard that I stop on the stair and look down at him, amazed. He must have been called *kolohe* before, by someone who made him happy.

When we open the door to Father's room he is sitting up with his papers. Samuel hangs back, uncertain. "Why look at you," Father says, shaking his head. "What a miracle." He tries to take Samuel's hand, but Samuel recoils. Father holds his hand up as if in peace and says, "You must be very happy to be back with your mother."

Samuel opens his mouth, but he only steps forward and presses his face into my skirts. I bend down to kiss him. He puts his face into my neck, breathing the scent of me.

"Do you like that smell? It's the same soap I bathed you in, years ago." He pulls away, studying me; I try to pull him into my neck again, but he looks down the hall to my old room.

"Go explore. I'll come along in a minute." I say. I sit down at the foot of Father's bed.

"I had to reread your letter three times before I could believe it," Father says. "You'd told me it was possible, but I never thought it could be. I hope I wasn't the very last to know?"

"Well, Emilie stared us down today. Everyone knows now."

"Doesn't matter. No one's going to stop sailing my ships. No one's going to stop being cured by Webster. Or buying food and whatever else it is Benjamin Ahsang sells in that store these days."

"If only you'd thought the same seven years ago," I say.

Father shrinks into his pillow as I think about how different life would have been, raising Samuel through the ages of two, three, four, five and six, but just as the sadness of missing those years starts, I think of my daughter and Webster, and I cannot fathom not having them. "I'm sorry. I will not bring it up again."

"Really? *Ever*?" Father asks, the fight back in him.

"Not unless you bait me into it," I say. "Please no teasing today."

"I know," he says. "I doubt you want to talk about it. I certainly can't bear to. Poor Cleghorn."

I shake my head, meaning there's nothing more I can bring myself to say.

"Bring Samuel back in after he's looked around a bit. No hurry. Send Clarice up to entertain me until then."

"All right," I say, leaving.

"Eliza," he calls. "Am I truly forgiven?"

I look back at his tiny, bed-ridden form. What a force this man has been in my life. "I forgave you as soon as I heard he was alive," I say. "Just treat him as you do Clarice. In everything."

"That is my intention," he says, holding up a paper. "Everything is changing."

"That's good."

I join Samuel in my old bedroom, where he holds my grandfather Caleb's Bible. He is reading the smallpox list, his lips moving in the shape of each name. I wait breathlessly, expecting one of the names to fall from his lips. He stops, looks up at me.

"Did you find that under the bed?" I ask, thinking of the seven years it lay hidden there. Seven years of love and death. Seven years of waiting, now come to an end.

He nods, handing it to me and going to the window.

"That's your father's house down below," I tell him. Something good is being cooked in the Ahsang kitchen, stirring my hunger. "Let's go find everyone and get something to eat," I say. "And your grandfather wants to see Clarice."

In the kitchen, we find Webster and Clarice. She heads up to Father; my thoughts return to Ka'iulani, and I sigh so deeply that Webster comes behind me and wraps both his arms around my waist, letting me go only when the back door opens. Mehana enters, dressed in her best *holokū*. Kepa walks dutifully behind her.

"Did you go down to see it?" I ask.

"We did," Mehana says. They both look wrung out. "We saw you pass by the cemetery. We saw your handsome boy and Clarice." Mehana crouches down and opens her arms to him as I remember her doing for me when I was little. After a moment of shyness Samuel walks toward her and lets her envelop him.

She whispers in his ear, and I hear *makuahine,* "mother." He listens and then puts his hand to her lips, like a blind man feeling a loved one's face. She smiles down at him and catches my eye.

Kepa fetches a ball and starts to bounce it on the kitchen table until Samuel's interest is diverted. Mehana looks annoyed and says, "Oh go on. Take him outside to play. I'll visit after."

Without a word, Kepa and Samuel go out back.

"Well, Samuel is the only person I know who speaks less than Kepa, so they make a good pair," I say. "He has yet to say a single word."

"Remember what your greatest dream was a year ago, and think of the angel who helped you find him," Mehana answers.

I will. I will think of her every day of my life.

22

1900

"We Hawaiians have confidence and trust in the justice of the American people. We believe they will not wish to wrong us," Father quotes Wilcox from the morning paper, bellowing the words to Samuel.

Robert Wilcox, one of the failed rebellion's leaders, has become the strongest voice arguing for the Hawaiian vote in the great cities of America's East Coast. Kepa and Father served time with him in the Reef, where he was called the Iron Duke and shamed the guards in both languages to bring poi and blankets for the miserable prisoners. Samuel makes a 'yes' motion with his head as Father punches his age-marked hand on the mattress.

In Washington, lobbyists for the PGs are fighting to keep Hawaiians without property from voting in their first American election. Hawaiians—supported financially by men like my father and Ben—are battling back.

Ben hopes Wilcox will get the vote for both the Chinese and Hawaiians. He's allowed to vote because of his mixed parentage; pure Chinese are not.

Webster is following these events for the sake of the patients of Kalaupapa. The PGs took their vote away too, property or not, and now Wilcox is fighting to allow them to cast their ballots again.

The day news of the vote is due, we turn into Father's drive and see Kepa draping an American standard from the attic window, for all of Nu'uanu to see. He has faith that America will be fairer than the PGs, and looks up at us to wave. I wave back, far less sure.

Father insists on being brought down to the lanai to hear the news as it comes up the drive in the form of a note from his lawyer.

"The Chinese have been denied," Father tells our silent circle, scanning quickly. "But Kalaupapa has the vote."

"Yes," says my husband.

"And Hawaiians have carried the day. Every Hawaiian shall vote if they can pay a poll tax of one dollar."

Kepa kisses the cheek of a beaming Mehana, then lifts Samuel on his shoulders and does a victory lap in the garden.

"Oh, but listen to this," says Father. "A statement given to the press from our friend Richard Irvin. 'The striking out of the property clause places power in the hands of haters of all things American. At least our sugar can never be removed from the tariff free list.'"

"Well, they asked for annexation," I say. "Now they've got it, with all that comes along with it."

"She's definitely your daughter, William," says Webster. He kisses me on my furrowed brow and says quietly, "Ikaika will be casting a vote in three years."

"If he lives," I say cautiously.

"He'll live. A child who grows into a man at Kalaupapa will live to see many milestones."

I walk back to the kitchen with Mehana. She's folding cubes of taro and fish into the bright green ti leaves Kepa's brought from the yard. A bamboo basket sits atop her boiling pot of water, ready to steam her perfect folds into lunch. The night marchers come less now, she tells me. The 'aweoweo do not pool in the harbor. But Kepa tells Samuel his scar is the birthmark left from his shark brother. Mehana is determined that my boy will not lose his taste for briny seaweed or the starch of steamed purple taro and pounded poi.

"They're saying at church, even if we get the vote, they can take it back if we don't vote the way they want," she tells me, putting the *lau lau* on to steam.

"They can't, Mehana. It's American law now," I say. "Richard Irvin will have to woo Kepa to keep himself in office from here on in."

"Just you watch," Mehana says, picking up a large platter to dry with strong sweeping motions. "They'll stop all their talk about the evils of gin and hula and start throwing drunken lūʻaus to try to get the Kanaka vote."

"You're probably right," I say. What a thing it would have been for Kaʻiulani to see today's news. We look out the window for the children.

"Looks like Clarice took Samuel next door. To play with the Ahsang girls," Mehana says.

I scan the mock orange hedge toward Ben's home. For some time, I'd kept my eyes on Mei Ling's every move, noting suspiciously the lovely clothes she returned Samuel to me in, the way she pinned Clarice's hair in the same bows her daughters wear, making my daughter fall in love with her. But we have a truce between us now. She sends servants over with huge pots of oxtail soup when my daughter tells her I am sick. I buy her daughters, Lian and Violet, the books I loved at their age and receive thank you notes in their perfect penmanship. They are brilliant, and I suspect they will be the ones running the Ahsang business in Hawaiʻi one day, not my Samuel. But I am happy to find that I do not care. He is enough for me already, as he is. There is no drive within me for more power, more wealth, more prominence. I know that is likely what has kept me sane through everything.

"It's nice those girls don't ever tease Samuel for being mute," Mehana says.

"He's not exactly mute," I say. Mehana looks at me skeptically.

Every doctor confirms that Samuel's is not a medical condition but one of the mind, and there is nothing for us to do but wait. I found the name *Samuel* written in the mud of the riverbank. When I took him there by hand and pointed to it, he wrote his name again. Mehana nods as I tell her this. Then she says, "I hear

Emilie's coming to dinner tonight," handing me the platter to put away.

"Well. Mei Ling can manage that. Now I'm really glad I didn't marry Benjamin."

"Are you, Eliza?"

"I truly am."

"They say he hangs on his wife's every word."

"As he should," I say. No matter how many times he touches my face as if he misses me, what I hear through the mock orange hedge when I visit Father is a family laughing; on still nights I can hear him talking to Mei Ling on the ceramic stools by the river. Their arranged marriage is undeniably now one of love. And I am at peace with that in a way I was not before Ka'iulani died, though I cannot say I understand exactly why.

There is much I am not sure I will ever completely fathom in how this Earth works. I cherished my son above all things, and the jealous gods took him. My best friend gave him back to me and she lost her life. Did my joy in his beauty, the boastfulness deep in my soul draw the gods' ire as Ahsang believes? Did her protection of Samuel demand a price? I am not sure. I do not know. I can only hold my children close to me and try to be worthy of the second chance she gave us.

Nuuanu's mountains look artificial the next morning, like a stage set. "Clarice, it's all crisp sunshine today. There's not one cloud in the sky," I say, leaning down to bring my face level with my daughter's and point out the window.

"Not a cloud!" Clarice repeats, swinging her legs and throwing her weight against my body. "Grandpa says sunshine turns your brain to mush," she announces, and I smile despite myself. He'd said the same thing when I was five. In his plantation days he said it when his workers were moving slowly. In his docile years it is simply one of a hundred bits of wisdom he feels obliged to repeat to Clarice on nearly every visit. She absorbs them all, parroting him with perfect timing. He needs to somehow teach Samuel them too.

Ben finds me kicking a ball with Samuel along the aisle of royal palms. It rained the night before and my shoes are green with wet grass. A governess works with Samuel now in the hopes of getting him to catch up, and I send Samuel in to wash and wait for her in the study. He walks toward the house, running a few steps and then slowing down to turn and give me a shy wave. It is hard for me not burst with the delight of his being mine.

"Handsome boy," says Ben. "I'd like to take him to the bungalow this Friday."

The bungalow, unchanged in spite of all that has passed. I recall the smell of fine wood and woven mats exactly; it is the scent of abandonment. The flagpole, the beach, the water where Hawaiians still surf with a joy that refuses to believe the shore is no longer theirs. The girl I was in that bungalow, the girl who wasn't afraid to swim in the dark ocean, who lounged unclothed on a daybed looking at Ben's golden skin. I have survived things that girl could not have imagined, but I have survived, and most miraculously, so has my son.

I step closer to Ben. "When you first take Samuel to the bungalow, take him alone. Please."

Ben's face curls as if to argue, but then he stops. He will give me this. "Yes, I'll make it a man's weekend." We stay like this for a second more, remembering, then the moment passes and he makes a joke. "Let's just pray he starts to speak to me down there, or it could be a long weekend."

"He's still settling in."

"Eliza, it's been quite a while now."

"I know. He just needs a little more time. Let's be happy having him with us."

"I am. Very," says Ben.

I feel proud and relieved that he has claimed Samuel as his even though many in town gossip about the scandal of our son, the damage they no doubt whisper it has done to the child's mind. Ben leans forward as if to whisper into my hair, but I pat his arm and say thank you and then head into the house. Ben still appears in my dreams, sometimes even playing the role of husband. But I know the difference between dreams and the pleasant reality I wake up to.

Webster comes back from his rounds that night to find the children frosting red white and blue cakes with Mehana and Kepa, who are feeling a burst of patriotism over gaining the vote. Samuel and Kepa are perfect mates in their silence, exchanging short looks as Kepa guides Samuel's hands to improve his skills. Mehana and Clarice speak over and under each other in a loud, happy, singsong that sends Webster and me to the drawing room for some peace.

On a side table is a picture of our family I had taken at Father's request. Painted backdrops have passed out of fashion so we posed simply: Webster and me on chairs with Clarice at his side and Samuel at mine. Clarice is lifting one shoulder and beaming like a cabaret girl, which put Webster in stitches. I hold Samuel's hand, my face angled toward him but my eyes on the camera. I was explaining to him how the contraption worked. He was interested, and afterwards the photographer had taken ten minutes to explain its operation.

An outsider might see the picture and remark that the boy looks nothing like the father, and the girl doesn't much either. Our family is not a cohesive match, but the picture tells my story, and that is pretty enough for my tastes, though soon enough it will need to be updated.

"I thought I might take Samuel to the bicycle races this weekend," Webster says. "Perhaps Kepa could come as well? They seem quite comfortable with each other. What do you think?"

"I think the following weekend would be perfect. Ben's taking him to Waikīkī this Friday."

"Oh," Webster says quickly.

"Which means we can have a weekend to ourselves. We could leave Clarice with Mehana and go to the Hawaiian Hotel for our own holiday." I slide off his shoe and put his socked foot on my bent knee to rub it.

"That would be nice. But let's take Clarice. She deserves a reward for adjusting as well as she has to not being an only child."

"Clarice is going to have to get used to sharing your attention even more."

"I know, I know. It's hard when his real father is sharing him," Webster says.

"Not Samuel. I'm talking about someone new." It takes him a moment to understand, but when he does I'm almost embarrassed by the kisses he gives me.

"Yes, my third child," I say, leaving off, "by a third father."

But Webster can hear the self-mocking in my voice. He tilts my chin and says, "*Our* third, and our *first*. Our very first."

Samuel leaves with Ben that weekend, and Webster, Clarice, and I visit the Hawaiian. The hotel sits on Richards Street, across from the stripped palace. The salon buzzes with fashionable families. They look up as we enter, and I wonder which scandal they will sink their teeth into. My father's imprisonment? Samuel's birth, or Emilie's disdain? They turn back to their own parties and carry on. My family sits drinking lemonade in peace, and I feel a rush of appreciation that everything in my life is now in the open.

Clarice doesn't share my sentimental mood, instead remarking on whose hat looks expensive and which she'd like to have herself. "That's an awful one, like a dead animal!" she nearly shouts. Webster and I both clap our hands over her mouth and sink into the settee.

The hat she is speaking of is traveling past the high-backed chairs directly across from us. I pray it belongs to a casual visitor. But when the figure turns, it's a familiar one. Hina is dressed head to toe in a pricey black silk dress, paired with a hat boasting such a profusion of feathers that I have to concede Clarice has a point.

Hina recognizes us, and her expression changes into something like delight. I tighten to take a blow. Webster stands up protectively and then we both see a little boy at her side.

"Is that Lee?" I ask, amazed. He wears a dark suit, but his hair stands on end like Ikaika's.

Webster smiles broadly and says, "I was your doctor when you were a little fella."

"I'm going to be a doctor. An animal's doctor," says Lee. He leans forward to shake Webster's hand. I wonder how the child of Hina and Abram has learned such manners, but then it was always in Ikaika's nature to be polite. This boy is Samuel's age, and yet he speaks like a twelve-year-old. He holds a large book. I crane to see the title but cannot make it out under his sleeve.

Clarice reaches for a bowl of almonds and chews slowly while studying Lee. Another brother she didn't know about. But this is one I doubt she will ever become acquainted with.

"We took a room for the weekend," says Hina. "Abram is gone, and now no one tells me where I need to go." Her speech is more polished sounding, and Lee looks up at her with attention. She has gained a bit of healthy weight. She puts her hands on her son's shoulders. "Lee is the biggest winner at his school. He brings all the awards home."

Will Samuel ever even attend school, I wonder. Like a flash she sees my weakness. "Where is Samuel?" she asks.

"He's with Benjamin Ahsang. We'll have him back on Sunday," Webster answers politely.

Hina's eyes go wide, and I know she is remembering her opium days. She grabs Lee's hand and swings it a little. "Samuel lives with you?" she asks me.

"Yes, his home is primarily with us," I say.

"It's good he's with you," she answers, raising her skirt in nervousness. I remember the day I met her, raising her skirts across her swollen belly. A thirteen-year-old girl Abram turned into my nightmare. Yet here we stand, two mothers trying as best we can to raise young men. Good men. Lee tugs his mother's skirts down, embarrassed, and we say our goodbyes quickly.

"How does that lady know Samuel?" Clarice asks.

I look to Webster for help.

"She knew him when I first met your mother. When I fell in love with her," he says. "A long time ago."

When we return to Nu'uanu on Sunday, we find Ben and Samuel sitting together on the patio. Samuel is very browned and beaming as we come up the steps.

"This child loves the ocean," announces Ben. "Loves it. I think he needs to be taken down daily. I'll have someone fetch him after his lesson each afternoon to take him swimming on the days I can't do it myself."

Clarice runs past us to show her grandfather the soap she collected from the hotel room. She gives her brother a pull on the ear as she passes. He takes it well, letting her run past with a small jab in return. Webster pats Samuel on the head and goes inside with the bags, while I sit in Father's chair.

"If you go swimming every afternoon, you'll have to get your lessons done on time. No straggling or letting your mind wander," I say, smoothing Samuel's hair, which has gone lighter with the weekend's sun.

Sand sprinkles off his scalp as I touch his head. Men never make children wash properly, I think. They probably watched the surfers this morning and then went for a long swim themselves, ducking under the waves until they were out past the reef, looking back at the mountains. And when they'd come in, Samuel had lain himself in the sand to dry off like a little sun lizard, as Ka'iulani and I once loved to do. I can feel the salt on Samuel's skin. But his smile is huge. I continue to prattle on. Ben watches me speak, studying me as if he might try it, too.

"And if you haven't done your work," I say clearly, "and I tell you when you come home you have to finish it, even if you are so tired you want to put your head down the moment you come through the door, if I tell you that I mean it and make you work, what will you say?" I ask, hoping for a nod of yes.

"I will say," he answers slowly, in a voice that learned English late but already has the husky command of Ahsang and the teasing charm of Ben hidden in it, "I will say, it was worth it."

I look down into my lap, waiting for more, trying not to scare him with the tears that come. Ben clutches my hand hard and then lets it go.

I sit on my lanai with my mountains all around me and make a list of the stories I will teach my son so that they are his to tell. He'll need to know about my grandfather, Captain Hezekiah, and the King who sang next door. I want him to know Kaiulani's banyan and Father's newspaper messages, snuck to the Queen. I'll tell him about Mehana's *waipuhia,* the upside down waterfall Mother promised me we could escape safely into if we ever reached it. I think we're there.

AUTHOR'S NOTE

In 1993, Congress issued an apology to the people of Hawai'i for the U.S. government's role in the overthrow of their monarchy and acknowledged that "the native Hawaiian people never directly relinquished to the United States their claims to their inherent sovereignty."

GLOSSARY

ali'i. Royalty, nobility.
'awa. A narcotic drink made of the kava shrub.
'a'ole. No.
haole. White person, American, Englishman, Caucasian.
hāpai. Pregnant.
haupia. Coconut pudding.
holokū. A loose, seamed dress with a yoke and usually a train.
kāhili. A long pole decorated at one end with a cluster of feather plumes and used as a ceremonial emblem.
kauka. Doctor.
kaukau. Food.
kōkua. Help, aid.
kolohe. Naughty.
ku'uipo. Darling.
lolo. Crazy.
luna. Foreman, boss, overseer.
ma'i Pākē. Chinese illness, leprosy.
mu'u mu'u. Loose gown.
pau. Finished, done.
wahine. Woman.

ACKNOWLEDGEMENTS

Thank you, Beth Davey, for your tireless hours championing this story. Thank you also to Kevin Lake, Melvin Spencer, Malena Watrous, Florence Chong, Heather Williams, Janene Williner, and Keala Dickhens for their help and thoughts on various drafts. Thank you to the staff and volunteers of 'Iolani Palace for their thoughtful descriptions of the events which unfolded within those walls. Thank you to the Bishop Museum for providing inspiration through its tremendous collection.

Thank you to my parents, Ian and Judy Mattoch, and my sister, Laura Ludwin, for having endless ideas and support for this project. Thank you to my husband, Jonathan, and children, Jack and Dylan McManus, for being there from the very beginning to the very end.

Further information about this book is available on the author's website: www.maliamattochmcmanus.com.

Made in the USA
Monee, IL
01 May 2021